UNDER THE SUN

WRITTEN BY
MICKY NEILSON

AUROBOROS
COILS OF THE SERPENT

CREDITS

STORY DEVELOPED BY
Chris Metzen

COVER ART
Éva Kárpáti

LAYOUT DESIGN
Mark Bryner, Malea Clark-Nicholson, Rob Dolgaard

GRAPHIC DESIGN
Mark Bryner

PRODUCT DEVELOPMENT
Ryan Collins

BUSINESS OPERATIONS
Lisa Pearce, Mike Gilmartin

PUBLISHING
Anna Wan, Byron Parnell

AUROBOROS: COILS OF THE SERPENT CREATED BY
Chris Metzen, Daniel Moore, Mike Carrillo,
Mike Pirozzi, Sam Moore, William Bligh

★★★★★★★★

ISBN: 9781956916027

WARCHIEF GAMING

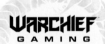

FOREWORD

Growing up, I had a very close-knit group of friends. Though a few of us had been going to the same Catholic school together since the first grade, it was really around 1985/86 when we really came together as a tight crew. It was Sam Moore, Mike Pirozzi, Billy Bligh, and me. We were fairly geeky kids for the time, and we immersed ourselves in all the movies, comics, and transforming robots we could get our hands on back then. It was an amazing era to be imaginative kids—and it seemed like new, exciting franchises were being launched every few months. Transformers, G.I. Joe, Thundercats, He-Man—you get the picture. World after world. Story after story. We just mainlined this stuff. Bonded over it.

But one fateful day—at the fifth grade lunch tables—something unexpected dropped into our geeky lives. Our buddy Bill brought a game for us to play called Dungeons & Dragons. You'd be safe to assume that this was dangerous, rock 'n' roll stuff for good Catholic kids like us.

D&D went off like a bomb in our young minds.

Bill explained the rules as best he could and led us through a quick play session during our lunch break. The specific adventure was the first Dragonlance module, Dragons of Despair—and I got picked to play the barbarian character, Riverwind. All these years later, it's hard to remember the specifics of that exciting, fever-pitched twenty-minute session. But it changed me.

I didn't want to just watch or read stories within the worlds I loved anymore. I wanted to inhabit them.

Over the next few years, Bill ran us through our first D&D campaign as our Dungeon Master. Sam, Mike, and I were joined by Bill's younger siblings, Jennifer and Bobby, as we launched our own characters on a grand, rollicking adventure. Our campaign was a patchwork of one-off encounters and odd bits of dungeon content from published materials of the time. It was a fairly straight-forward campaign.

Until it wasn't.

Somewhere along the way, we started jamming together about where the adventure might lead us— and a distinct world started taking shape in our minds. Drastnia, Bill called it. With him orchestrating the events, our characters uncovered a secret pact between the forces of good and evil who sought to control civilization between them. Our punk-ass characters weren't gonna stand for that kind a shit, so we set out to topple the whole damn system in what would later be known as the "Fall of Old Sularia." Our quirky characters, known as the Five, became real anarchists… Not sure what that says about our collective state of mind at the time, but there ya have it. That irreverence and the desire to push back against authority of any kind would be a hallmark of our roleplaying for years to come.

Playing through those early adventures with my closest friends was an incredibly fun, wildly imaginative and deeply inspiring journey for me. Being part of that creative process and building worlds with them was all I wanted to do with my time. But eventually, we all wound up going off to different high schools, and there just wasn't time to connect and play D&D like we used to.

It was around 1992 or so when Sam, Mike, and I decided to reconvene and launch a new campaign set in our little world of Drastnia. We were joined by our buddy Mike Carrillo and Sam's younger brother, Daniel. We pushed the world forward a few hundred years after the events of "Old Sularia"—and we created a new realm called Lawbrand—a much more grounded setting that featured an authoritarian church that upheld law and order throughout the land. Despite its rigid structures of control, Lawbrand also featured elements that reflected where our heads were at that time in our lives: rowdy rock festivals, hippy druids, talking animals, and smoke-wreathed late nights. Our characters were a band on the run—challenging authority at every turn—testing the world to see if it held any real worth.

Sam and I took turns DMing each week, developing the world and its unfolding mythology together as we went. The Mikes were always hilarious roleplayers and helped keep the story moving along with their usual wit and flair. Daniel was always the wildcard—pushing against the rails and doing truly absurd shit that kept Sam and I on our toes as DMs. Every group has that one player, right?

Our characters made a great team: a brotherhood of jaded outcasts, I guess. I think we worked out a lot of our life-issues through playing that particular campaign together. Our characters were equal parts brazen anarchists and reluctantly heroic knuckleheads. The whole campaignwas just . . . glorious chaos. The story we played through, which we eventually titled "Under the Sun", is contained right here in this very book.

Of course, this book wouldn't have been possible without its author—Micky Nielson.

Micky and I have been friends a long time. We worked at Blizzard Entertainment together for a few decades or so . . . building worlds, telling stories—all that good stuff. Micky was one of the first professional writers I'd ever met—I mean, he'd completed like five great screenplays by the time he was twenty-four! Suffice to say, I've always been blown away by his skill, imagination, and tireless work ethic.

As I thought about the prospect of turning Under the Sun into a novel, I knew the author had to be Micky. Sure, he's an amazing writer with a huge breadth of experience, but he's also someone who grew up with a tight-knit group of friends who played D&D together. He gets this stuff. Not just the "elves and dwarves" bits, but the relationships beneath all the fantasy trappings—the relatable heartbeat beneath all the moving parts.

So, after much begging on my part, Micky agreed to author this monster. And here, almost exactly a year later, I'm in awe of what he's done.

You see, as opposed to conventional novels or film scripts that adhere to the tried and true three-act story structure, "*Under the Sun*" is a bit more… well, let's just say we rolled right into the five-act structure and leave it at that. I really wanted this book to track our actual adventures through the campaign we played and be as authentic to those events as possible. Somehow, Micky deftly wove it all together—and rendered this story's themes and characters with real heart and soul.

I'm so grateful to him for having taken this adventure with me—and for his boundless patience and generosity in the face of all my interminable story notes and suggestions along the way.

Developing *Under the Sun*—through both roleplaying it out thirty years ago and by working with Micky on this novelization—has been a truly amazing experience that I will cherish forever.

A full circle.

Crafting stories and building worlds with friends.

May it never end.

Chris Metzen
Chief Creative Officer,
Warchief Gaming

AUTHOR'S NOTE

Chris Metzen and I go way back, having worked together at Blizzard Entertainment for many years. In 2016 I left the company to contribute to other intellectual properties and to pursue my own projects. A while after Chris departed Blizzard, he told me about a creative endeavor of his own—a Dungeons & Dragons–style RPG game.

Chris is an idea machine. A world builder of the highest degree, so I was ridiculously excited to see what he would cook up. Plus, I had played RPGs at various points throughout my life and loved them. Then . . . I get a phone call from Chris asking if I wanted to write a novelization of the campaign he played with his buddies back in the nineties, to go along with the Kickstarter for his new world. You mean I get to participate? Get in on the ground floor? Sign me up!

I dived into the outline and discovered a story full of heart, built around fun and compelling characters, with a great message at the center of it all. Sure, parts of it were a little offbeat. In one of our early calls, Chris said, "I know this is a little funky, but there's this bit where the characters go and steal a bunch of furniture from some jackass. They screw it all up, giggling and running off into the night. One of them has this big-ass armoire on his back. It makes no sense, it doesn't further the narrative, so I know the instinct might be to cut it. But . . ."

Chris went on to explain why he felt the scene was important. And I agreed. When I read the outline, I actually loved that scene. It was exactly the kind of thing a character in one of my own RPG adventures would have done. It's still one of my favorite sequences in the book, and I hope it ends up being one of yours too. To me, that kind of flavor was important—I wanted to tell an amazing story, but I also wanted to stay true to the spirit of a good ol' freewheeling RPG romp.

In that same vein, I wanted to represent the characters as faithfully as possible, and I believed that most likely, no one would "know" them as intimately as the original players, (I remembered writing out detailed backstories for my own RPG characters.) So I asked Chris if he would share contact info with me for the friends he played with back in the day. He thought it was a good idea, and indeed, when I chatted with the old crew, they provided a ton of great info that found its way into this book.

So . . . for all the roleplayers out there, I hope Under the Sun calls to mind late nights spent around a table with friends, drinking soda (or something stronger), eating chips, and slinging dice. For everyone else, I hope the adventures of Xamus, Oldavei, Wilhelm, Nicholas, Darylonde, and Torin transport you to a world of monsters and magic where danger, excitement, and fun lurk around every corner . . . but also to a place where stealing and trying to run away with an oversized piece of bedroom furniture makes complete and perfect sense.

Micky Neilson

CAST OF PLAYERS

XAMUS FROOD
High Elf, Sorcerer/Fighter

Played by Sam Moore

TORIN BLOODSTONE
Desert Dwarf, Fighter

Played by Mike Pirozzi

OLDAVEI
Ma'ii, Cleric

Played by Mike Carillo

WILHELM WALLAROO
Human, Bard

Played by Daniel Moore

NICHOLAS AMANDREAS
Human, Wraithblade

and

DARYLONDE TALONHAND
Human, Wildkeeper

Played by Chris Metzen

PROLOGUE

It began with screams. Thousands of them.

Scenes then of apocalyptic devastation: Cities consumed by fire. Armies swarming the landscape like ants. Rampaging marauders with eyes of flame and warriors clad in dark, otherworldly armor. Towering monstrosities lumbering behind. Mighty citadels, towering minarets, and steel fortresses exploding to pieces.

Glimpses of carnage and devastation both awesome and terrifying. The sun itself seeming to combust. A blazing form materializing in the bloodred haze, massive wings unfurling, beating—a serpent of flame engulfing the sky. The earth quaking, splitting open. Oceans of fire washing over the world.

The screams silenced.

Troubled by the visions, a tall figure stepped out of a cave system through a rocky opening that resembled the gaping jaws of a bear. Creaks and groans accompanied his every movement. As he gazed up at the bright moon, contemplating, a yellow leaf separated from his upper torso and drifted down past knobby trunk-legs to settle at his root-feet.

He looked to the surrounding hillsides and the scores of trees tinged silver by the moonlight but green nonetheless. The Caretaker felt old. And tired. He wondered if perhaps he was entering the autumn of his life. Either way, there was still much to learn and much to do. The visions confirmed the disquiet he had felt for many long months. Time was short, and he must prepare for who was coming, for *what* was coming: a great and terrible storm—the kind that ended worlds.

PART ONE

NOTHIN' BUT TROUBLE...

CHAPTER ONE

ODD JOBS AND ODDER FOLKS

An excellent day for a wedding.

Shadows had grown long, but it was still comfortably warm outside. Laughter and music drifted on the light wind as a string band played beneath a sturdy pavilion. Here a fire-haired woman in a pale blue full-length chemise stared skyward, arms outstretched, twirling in place. There a red-faced merchant smiled broadly, nodding in time with the melody, mug in one hand while the other rested protectively on the coin purse hanging from his belt. A mangy dog roved about, foraging for dropped food as farmers and tradesfolk and their families milled, mingled, and danced. Revelers from across the country had gathered to fete the young bride and groom, who swayed in a loving embrace in the middle of the wide field, gazing longingly into each other's eyes. A beautiful, uplifting scene . . .

And one that Xamus Frood couldn't give two feks about.

After all, he didn't know them. In fact, he didn't know anyone here. His only aim was to kill time before tomorrow's meeting and guzzle his favorite kind of booze: the free kind.

With one long pull he downed the last of his chilled whiskey and set the clay mug aside. Easing back in the chair, he began rolling a smoke. Lintgreen, first grown by dwarves back in the old world. Or so the story went. Whatever the case, of all the leaf he had sampled—and yes, there had been plenty—Lintgreen was by far his favorite.

Life, Xamus reasoned, was for the living. Not that his people would approve. Stodgy, imperious, narrow in their beliefs, isolated in their refuge, the high elves had turned their backs to the world long, long ago. Contrarily, Xamus was determined to meet it head-on, an attitude reflected in the way he presented himself, from the shirt with the rolled-up sleeves to the fading tattoos along his arms to the wide-bottom dungarees with the oversized belt buckle right down to his travel-worn boots. As often as not, his long, full brown hair served to hide the pointed ears that would otherwise announce his lineage. Though convenient in avoiding long explanations—most folks, after all, believed elves to be extinct—his long hair was not an attempt at disguise, nor was it a symbol of rebellion against the establishment, as some believed. No, he grew the locks simply because he felt no urge to cut them.

Xamus finished rolling, reached inside his vest, and retrieved a pocket lamp. He flicked the lid, thumbed the striker, and lit the smoke. Taking a long drag, he cast his gaze once more at the crowd from beneath the brim of a weathered, wide-brimmed hat.

He blew a plume of blue smoke that swirled, billowed, and dissipated, revealing a late arrival to the party, acknowledged by the others with uncomfortable stares followed by outright avoidance. The newcomer was, after all, considered a savage by clean-living city dwellers. A dwarf, but not of the common iron dwarf variety. No, this short, burly fellow was a desert dwarf, identified as such by his

PART ONE: NOTHIN' BUT TROUBLE...

dark complexion, tawny-blond hair—a long, high strip on top and a braided beard that hung halfway down his leather jerkin—and the tattoos: they adorned either side of his shaved head, his arms, and the portion of his legs exposed beneath the lower edge of his blue kilt.

The stranger waded through the crowd, adjusting a keg balanced on his left shoulder. He stopped to scan his surroundings, then locked eyes on Xamus. He jabbed a stubby finger at the elf. "You!" he yelled, startling the nearest revelers.

Xamus pointed a questioning finger at his chest.

"Yeah, you, ya fekkin' lowlife!" The dwarf directed his attention to a nearby woman. "Don't worry, miss, I'll handle this." With purposeful strides he closed to within a few paces of the elf, fixing him with a flinty glare. The band and the crowd fell silent.

The dwarf stepped over next to Xamus, withdrew the keg from his shoulder, planted it spigot down, then sat atop it. "Us lowlifes shouldn't have to drink alone," he said in a lower voice. "Hand me your mug."

Xamus complied as the band carried on and the guests returned to their conversations, a few of them shaking their heads.

The dwarf bent between his legs to pour what looked and smelled like honey mead. "Torin," he said, turning and shoving the mug into Xamus's hand, spilling half the contents and offering up a smile absent a few teeth.

"Xamus," the elf answered.

As Xamus emptied the cup, Torin leaned in closer, narrowing one eye. "So . . . what brings a stranger all the way to the Guild-Valley of Hearthvale?"

"I'm here for the fishing," Xamus replied.

Torin stared back. A smile crept across his face, followed by a rumbling that began in his belly, bubbled upward, and burst out in one of the loudest guffaws Xamus had ever heard. Nearby partygoers threw nervous looks in their direction, whispering. One woman—a portly farm wife— glanced in the general area of Torin's kilt, gasped, and quickly looked away.

"Horseshit!" Torin blurted, red-faced. "Only thing fishermen catch around these parts is dogfish and crabs! And the crabs come from the brothel!" Xamus kept any response to himself, but he inwardly wondered if there was more to this dwarf than met the eye.

Torin's bluster *did* bely a keen perception. The dwarf had always been good at noticing things. Especially the kinds of things most folks tried to keep hidden. "Here to see the Magistrate too, then," he proclaimed. Xamus didn't answer. That was alright, Torin thought. He didn't have to. The dwarf fell silent, considering . . .

The Hearthvale Magistrate, Raldon Rhelgore, had commissioned outside "help" for some local problem. Dirty work, most likely. Else, why not simply task the local militia? The confederation of Trade-Cities, Lawbrand, of which Hearthvale was a part, were all about their rigid "rules" and high-minded "order" . . . until some nasty bit of business needed tending to; then it was time to call in the uncultured heathens for hire. Lawbrand folks were so two-faced you couldn't tell whether they were coming or going.

But Torin needed the coin and prospects were limited. Life on the road was quite often feast or famine. Lately, it was leaning closer to famine than he took a liking to. The biggest question, now that he knew this "fisherman" was nibbling at the same bait, was whether he would be an ally or a competitor. That, for now, remained to be seen.

"Well," Torin said, bending down and pouring himself a mug. "Come sunrise . . ." he drew up, guzzling the contents, belching gustily, and wiping foam from his mustache. "We may as well go see him together."

★ ★ ★

Everything within Raldon Rhelgore's quarters in the Great Hall was polished, wiped, dusted, or swept. The cushions on the chairs Torin and Xamus sat in, facing the Magistrate's desk, were firm and pristine to the point of being particularly uncomfortable. Torin mused that furniture should be properly worn in, his back already aching as Raldon droned on.

"As I said, this is a local matter." Raldon's skin appeared as though it had never seen sunlight. His meager, partial beard was most certainly greased in an attempt to hide the gray that streaked his chin. Long, slick dark hair lay flat from the widow's peak high on his forehead all the way to just above the base of his skull. His lips tended to remain parted as he spoke, lending him the air of an animal constantly baring its long, yellow teeth.

His high-backed chair rose three-quarters of the way to the ceiling. He fussed at the sleeves of his robes as he continued: "A small number of our youth have gone missing. All of them less than twenty years of age, but none less than thirteen. Some are the progeny of high-ranking Harvest Guild delegates."

"Nabbed for ransom?" Torin asked, picking up a candle and holder from the edge of the desk, fumbling, and pulling the candle from the spike. Raldon stared fixedly as if he wanted to snatch the objects out of the dwarf's hands, but he was seated too far away to do so. Xamus watched quietly, the barest hint of a grin on his lips.

"A logical assumption, but no," Raldon answered. "I believe them to have been taken by cultists. Children of the Sun, they call themselves. An order that has only recently made its presence known in the region. In that time they have sown significant discord and regrettably gained a modicum of favor, especially among the young and . . . impressionable."

Torin attempted to replace the candle on the spike, dislodging the curled handle in the process. It bounced from the arm of his chair onto the floor.

A muscle in Raldon's left cheek twitched as he added in a strained tone, "Rumor has it the cult's aim is to supplant the Sularian faith."

The Sularian Church was the traditional ruling authority of the realm, a blend of government and religion that had existed for centuries. "I've heard of these 'Children,'" Xamus said. "Street corner prophets."

Raldon's eyes flicked to the elf. "And yet, somehow they've gained a small degree of legitimacy despite their rebuke of the church, ridiculous claims that the Sularian faith has failed the masses and their vain, blasphemous assertion that they alone offer a new hope"—he raised his arms theatrically—"salvation for all of Lawbrand."

"Deliverance from sin," Xamus answered.

"Ha!" Torin blurted. "What's the point in that?" He was attempting to reinsert the handle, muttering, "I like my sin just fine, thank you very much. Folks should live however the fek they—" a sudden noise caught everyone's attention.

Xamus and Torin looked over their shoulders to the flung-open chamber door, where a stooped

PART ONE: NOTHIN' BUT TROUBLE...

figure set a black-booted foot over the threshold, clutching the jamb with one hand, the fingers of which bore long, pointed nails. He thrust his upper body forward, sniffing.

"You're late," Raldon exclaimed.

The man bustled in farther, then stopped, raising his half-clenched hands to the level of his chest. His head darted about, nostrils flaring as he continued scenting the room.

"I present to you Oldavei," Raldon said. "He comes to us from the eastern desert."

Torin recognized several characteristics: The newcomer's skin was coated with fine, pale brown hair. He was powdered from head to toe in desert dust. This, along with the topknot and shaved head on either side, the black-and-red vest and breeches, all leather, marked him as ma'ii, a secretive race from the Tanaroch, considered by most in Lawbrand to be no better than feral animals. Dwarves and ma'ii were traditional adversaries. Torin had a history with the fellow desert dwellers that made his own feelings toward them complicated, to say the least. This particular ma'ii struck the dwarf as . . . peculiar. He took note of a tattoo on the visitor's forehead, a circle broken by vertical lines at top and bottom, horizontal on either side.

Oldavei approached, bent, and took several short sniffs of Xamus, followed by one long, indrawn breath. The ma'ii nodded to himself, then whipped his head to Torin, sticking his snout close, sniffing rapidly. Xamus held back laughter. Torin was less amused. "Back up, ya fekkin' mutt!"

Oldavei straightened and took a step back, seemingly satisfied. "Fellow outsiders," he said, revealing a mouthful of pointed teeth. "I'm glad for the company! Thought I might have to do this on my own."

Torin turned to the Magistrate and said, "Anyone else we should know about?"

"Not to my knowledge," Raldon answered, "Three of you won't be a problem, I trust?"

Torin looked to Xamus, who gave a slight shrug.

"I don't give two shits," Torin answered. "Long as the pay's the same."

Oldavei slapped the dwarf on the shoulder, stepped behind Xamus's chair to the wall, then turned and slid down to a seated position, folding his legs. "Please," he said, looking up at Raldon. "Continue."

Raldon's face bore the expression of someone who'd just tasted something disagreeable as he went on. "It has come to my attention that these trespassing cultists have erected a—"

Oldavei giggled, drawing a sharp look from Raldon. "Sorry," the ma'ii said.

Raldon cleared his throat. "They have . . . set up a compound in the northern foothills. You're to go there, and, if the missing persons are present, retrieve them. *Without* undue complications."

"Define complications," Oldavei said.

"Try not to kill anyone," Raldon clarified.

"Understood," Oldavei replied.

Xamus then voiced the very same question Torin had pondered before arriving in Hearthvale: "Why hire us and not use your own militia?"

Raldon smoothed his facial hair. "It is a matter of some delicacy," he said. "The militia is a blunt instrument, likely to spill blood first and ask questions later. Some ruling members of the Harvesters Guild have warmed to the cult's message. That being the case, if I'm mistaken regarding the Children of the Sun having taken the youths and a conflict erupts—"

"Someone else might take that cushy seat," Xamus concluded, nodding at the Magistrate's chair. Raldon's eyes stabbed back. That was part of it, Xamus reasoned, but there was more: having watched and listened carefully throughout the bureaucrat's monologue, he thought it also likely th at Raldon wanted to maintain deniability if the endeavor failed. He would most certainly deny any knowledge of their actions should they be caught. Xamus had been around long enough to learn an unspoken and uncomfortable truth: that in the eyes of stuffed shirts like the distinguished Magistrate here, he and other adventurers of his kind . . . were 100 percent expendable.

PART ONE: NOTHIN' BUT TROUBLE...

CHAPTER TWO

THE WAILING WIDOW

It was nearing midday when the three adventurers met outside the main doors of the Restless Pony, Hearthvale's least expensive—and least populated—inn. Torin had slung his weapon, a well-crafted, single-bladed battle axe, to his back. Xamus wore an exotic, graceful longsword on one hip, dagger on the other. Oldavei, leaning against a hitching post, carried a scimitar on his left side. Travel bags with lashed bedrolls hung from each of their shoulders, save for Torin.

"No travel kit?" Xamus asked the dwarf.

Torin waved him off. "Bah! All that shit just weighs you down. I travel light."

"Right," Xamus said. "Well, I suppose we should look into mounts."

"Mounts?" Torin blurted, squinting one eye.

"Yeah," Xamus answered. "Horses."

"Ah, fek no!" the dwarf replied. "Freakish creatures, horses." He appeared to shake off a chill. "Gimme the damned willies."

Xamus waited to see if his new companion was joking. When it became obvious the answer was no, he turned his gaze to Oldavei. The ma'ii shrugged. "I don't even know how to ride."

The elf nodded. "Right, well I guess that covers mounts." He peered down the narrow backstreet and beyond, to the haze-shrouded Barrier Peaks. "Day to a day and a half on foot, be my guess."

"Let's not dawdle then," Torin said, taking the lead as the three of them struck out. They pushed on through Hearthvale's crowded, cobbled streets, navigating carts and livestock and beggars and laborers until they had put first the city's stone edifices and then the wooden structures of its outer limits behind them. They strode in silence, keeping a light pace as they pressed into the region's historic, sprawling farmlands. Here majestic fields flanked their dirt path; to one side a sweating, hairy-backed hill giant clad in overalls plowed deep furrows along a shallow grade while a kneeling female giant planted seeds. Farther on, where the plains flattened out to either side, human workers tossed grain seeds from burlap sacks behind plows pulled by teams of draft oxen. "Plantin' barley, I'd wager," Torin said. He turned to Xamus with a grin. "Makings of a fine home brew!"

The farming operations were quite extensive, the elf considered. A trade that had been plied exclusively by Old Families until recently. Hill giant presence had increased, a situation capitalized upon by the Harvester's Guild. Seeking to out-produce their Old Family competition, guild farms hired the giants, each capable of doing work in one day that would take ordinary men five. It was the guild's ultimate goal to supplant the old-timers entirely and establish Hearthvale as a unionized Trade-City—one that would no doubt be firmly under their control. Just where and how the Magistrate, Raldon, fit into it all, Xamus was still unsure.

Oldavei quickened his pace and took the lead, tramping ahead with his curious, loping stride. The ma'ii would stop and raise his head intermittently, sniffing the air, taking in all of the varying unique scents the land had to offer. On the road, on an adventure, he was very much in his element. For him the hours and the miles seemed to pass in the blink of an eye, so lost was he in all the environmental splendor.

Finally they passed away from habitation altogether, as the northern foothills drew ever closer, the cloud-topped Barrier Peaks looming just beyond. The sky had turned to tarnished gold when the trio found themselves in a wide, shallow valley.

The low sun was cut off by the basin walls, turning the air cool. To the east, a tributary of the Talisande River trickled down into a gurgling stream that hooked near the road before wending away off to the south.

The trio had ventured to the stream, pausing to drink and refill their waterskins, when a startling cry cut through the silence; a piercing, sorrowful wail that persisted for many long seconds before trailing off.

Torin looked to Xamus questioningly. The elf, gazing out over the tall timber, remained silent. Oldavei, squatting by the brook, waterskin in hand, sighed heavily. Torin turned to the ma'ii, who stood, shaking his head. "What is it?" the dwarf asked.

Oldavei took a moment to answer, as if debating whether it would be prudent to share his opinion. Finally he gazed at the others and declared somberly, "It's the Wailing Widow."

"The what?" Torin demanded.

The ma'ii looked to the forest. "It's said that a newlywed woman and her husband were traveling this road, long ago. They were attacked by a band of brigands, but rather than defend his wife's honor, the husband turned tail and ran. He was felled by arrows while the wife watched, wailing in torment. Showing far more bravery than her husband, she took up a knife and charged the leader, but her dagger was no match for his sword. She was cut down, her corpse and that of her husband left for the buzzards. Legend holds that she haunts these woods, a revenant, tormented by her husband's cowardly betrayal, her ghastly form twisted by rage. One glimpse of her hideous visage, and even the bravest of warriors are said to run in fear, but . . ."

Oldavei tied the waterskin to his belt as the others waited.

"It's rumored that if any male can look upon her and stand his ground, displaying the kind of bravery her husband lacked, the widow's former beauty will be restored and her spirit set free."

Torin stood still, mouth slightly open. Next to him, Xamus said, "Hmm."

Oldavei broke off toward the road. "Just stories, I'm sure. Nothing to 'em. We should keep on."

Torin lifted a brow and gave Xamus a sideways glance. "Sounds like horseshit if you ask me!" he said before setting out. Xamus followed in silence.

Over the next few hours Torin kept a brisk pace, nearly on Oldavei's heels, as he eyed the encroaching shadows warily. The three had not yet reached the valley's far end when full night descended, and they halted to make camp.

Following a light supper of cured meat and bread, they smoked and sat around a crackling fire that cast wavering shadows on the nearby trees. With the smoking done, Xamus had just removed his boots and hat when Torin called "Ho!" and tossed over a flask. The elf caught it and was in the process of drinking when he heard the dwarf exclaim: "I'll be damned!" Xamus lowered the flask to see the dwarf pointing at his exposed ears. "You're an elf!"

PART ONE: NOTHIN' BUT TROUBLE...

Xamus gazed back at the dwarf evenly, then looked to Oldavei, sitting cross-legged, mouth open and full of half-chewed sausage. "That's so," he replied.

Torin was still pointing. "How? Ain't none o' your kind left! Not so far as anyone knows, anyhow."

"We're not all gone," Xamus said. "Some of us still survive, hidden away in secret places."

Torin had lowered his finger but was still staring, incredulous. "But you seemed so damned . . . human. Fooled me sure enough." The dwarf, who prided himself on keen observation skills, especially as they related to others, was slightly unsettled.

"I wasn't trying to fool anyone," Xamus said.

Oldavei regained the power of speech and said, "Yeah, but an elf, walking around with common folk . . . that would cause a real stir. You're smart to hide it!"

"I don't—" Xamus began, but Torin interrupted.

"Magic!" The dwarf said. "I heard the elves know powerful magic!"

"Well I—"

"Why'd you leave?" Oldavei cut in. "With your people hiding . . . why take to the road?"

"Yeah!" Torin added.

Xamus waited before answering. "I just don't see things the way they do," he said.

"Leaving behind friends and family, it's not something that's done lightly," Oldavei said. And the way it was said made it clear he was speaking from experience.

"No, it isn't," Xamus agreed. "But being out here, doing these jobs, learning about the world and drinking with you lowlifes . . . " he threw the flask back to Torin. "This is where I'm meant to be."

"Huh," Torin said, eyeing Xamus somewhat suspiciously as he lay on his back.

The three of them had settled in and begun drowsing when a long, shrieking moan split the night air. Torin bolted upright. Oldavei and Xamus both stirred.

"It's her," Oldavei said. "The Wailing Widow."

"Horseshit!" Torin replied. A log popped on the fire, causing him to jump. This was followed by rustling sounds just beyond the firelight. The dwarf looked over to see two glinting eyes in the dark. "I'll be damned . . ." he muttered, reaching for his axe.

Slowly, the dwarf rose to his feet. "Okay then, Widow, if that is you, come on out! If it's a brave dwarf you seek, you'll find none braver!" Oldavei noted a slight shaking in the dwarf's knees as Torin gripped the axe in both hands and assumed a battle stance.

The burning eyes dropped to the level of the underbrush with a soft thud. Torin tightened his grip and clenched his teeth, eyes widening . . .

A furry creature stepped into the firelight. Roughly the size of an alley cat, four-legged, with a long, slender tail, and large, round eyes set in a rodent-like face. One feature in particular stood out beyond all others: its mouth. Partially open, the maw was lined with small needle-teeth, both ends stretching back nearly to the sides of its neck.

As Torin watched, dumbfounded, the animal planted its feet, raised its snout to the sky, and voiced a long, loud, doleful cry that caused the dwarf to wince and prompted both Xamus and Oldavei to cover their ears.

At last the caterwaul ceased. "You little—" Torin said, taking a step forward. In a flash the animal spun around and was gone. The dwarf stopped, taking in a long, relieved breath as another sound rose above the crackling fire: laughter.

The dwarf turned to see both Xamus and Oldavei trying and failing to restrain their mirth.

"You both knew, didn't ya?" Torin called. "Ah yeah, that's a real fekkin' belly buster!" He pointed his axe at Oldavei. "Speakin' of bustin' bellies," he stomped over toward the seated ma'ii, who thrust out his palms, still chuckling.

"Apologies!" he said. "A thousand pardons. All in fun. A merwin is what the critter's called. Or a yowler. I'd only heard *of* them before now."

"Mm, yowler. A little fun at my expense, eh?" Torin leaned down. "Keep it up, and you'll be the one yowlin'!" Oldavei clamped his mouth shut, hands still up. The dwarf plodded back to his sleeping spot, knelt, and set down his axe. He laid on his back, and over the next few moments the laughter subsided, replaced by the snapping and popping of the fire.

"I can't help but wonder," Xamus mused aloud. "What were you gonna do with the axe? Kill her again?"

With that, Oldavei's chuckling started anew, joined soon by Xamus.

"You can both fek off!" Torin blurted, only serving to bolster the laughter on both sides.

Despite himself, the dwarf chuckled as well.

PART ONE: NOTHIN' BUT TROUBLE...

CHAPTER THREE

CHILDREN OF THE SUN

The trio decamped, set out, and after a few hours emerged from the canyon. They progressed along the path to a fork just short of the wide, low ridges that marked the southernmost boundary of the foothills. East lay the Talisande River Basin, west, more sprawling farmland; the band took a moment to gaze north. Few knew what lay beyond the Barrier Peaks that rose like the curtain wall of some inconceivably colossal fortress. Beyond the mountain range lay the infamous Northwilds, a place where, so far as anyone knew, no living creature had dared to venture for hundreds of years.

Even at this distance, the three of them felt so tiny compared to the mountains as to be almost insignificant as they continued on into the foothills.

By the time they stopped on a grassy ridgetop for their midday meal, the thick wilderness had surrendered to lightly wooded, shallow slopes. They had just finished eating when the wind, which had been blowing from the east, reversed direction.

Oldavei jerked his head up, swiveling in different directions, nostrils flaring as he took several quick, short sniffs. He sprang to his feet, drawing in one long breath as he faced roughly northwest.

He looked over his shoulder, grinning at the others, and said, "I have 'em."

Oldavei led, bounding up and over ridges and slopes until, at a valley between two hills, he turned, put a finger to his lips, then motioned for them to follow. He crouched low and with slow, measured movements crawled to the next crest.

Presently the three lay on their bellies, lined up, peeking through the tall grass onto a wide dale, where they beheld a bustling settlement. Dozens of living quarters, stout in appearance, despite simple wattle-and-daub construction, surrounding a much larger, oblong structure. Here and there robed figures sat around small fires, arms raised, bodies swaying. Oldavei saw that their eyes were closed; he could tell they were chanting, and with the favorable wind, he smelled incense. At the south boundary of the community, supplies were being loaded from what looked to be a storehouse onto uncovered wagons by more robed figures. On the far side, oxen reposed inside a corral.

The simple, soft-hued garments worn by the Children ranged in color from beige to saffron to sage to ochre. This, in addition to the style of dress and lack of any visible weapons, reminded Oldavei of eastern desert nomads—a peaceful and relatively harmless lot. Maybe these Children of the Sun were similar and just poorly understood, he thought.

Xamus motioned to the workers loading the wagons. "They seem fresh-faced enough to be our missing youths," he said. A few of the loaders spoke animatedly as they went about their work.

"What do ya suppose they're jaw-jackin' about?" Torin asked.

"I can—" Oldavei began.

"We could try to get closer," Xamus suggested.

"No need," Oldavei said.

"Mm, not much cover," Torin replied. "Like as not we'll be—"

"I can hear them!" Oldavei said, more loudly. "If you'll shut your traps."

"A thousand pardons, Your Majesty," Torin retorted. "Listen away!" Xamus judged that the distance of the Children made any eavesdropping of their conversation impossible, but he remained silent as Oldavei settled in and concentrated.

"They're excited for an upcoming journey," he relayed a moment later.

Xamus frowned. "Is this genuine, or another jest?" he asked.

"I swear," Oldavei said.

"I wager he's tellin' it straight," Torin confirmed. "I lived with ma'ii for a bit." He pointed to his own ear. "They can hear a fly fart at twenty paces."

Oldavei waited, head pivoted with one ear facing the compound. "They plan to caravan . . . into the desert. There they'll hear . . . teachings of the Great Prophet." Xamus and Torin shared a glance. "It's an honor . . . to leave behind home and family, a necessary sacrifice for the discovery of . . . true self."

"True self? Sounds like a load o' horseshit, you ask me," Torin interjected.

Oldavei raised a hand for silence. After a moment he said, "They wish they could leave now, rather than in the morning." The workers took respite, filling cups with what looked like water from a cask on a nearby wagon.

"Alright then," Torin said, a gleam in his eye as he unlimbered his axe and readied to stand. "Let's break some skulls. On my count—"

"Wait," Xamus said. "They leave tomorrow. That gives us time. Come nightfall we can move closer, watch and wait. Choose our moment and take them tonight. Maybe even do it quietly."

"Quietly?" Torin replied with disgust. "Fek quietly. Time's wasting. What say you?" he asked Oldavei.

"Waiting makes sense," the ma'ii replied.

Torin heaved a deep sigh and rolled onto his back. "Fekkin' ninnies," he muttered, closing his eyes and laying the axe on his chest. "Rouse me when it's time to hurt people."

The day progressed without incident. Xamus and Oldavei took turns watching the settlement, with Torin sleeping soundly all the while. Once sunlight no longer hit the valley, the Children began building larger fires, taking logs from nearby cords. With the coming of night, the faithful gathered in circles about the flames, holding hands and singing.

Xamus woke Torin, and the three made their way down the slope to a predetermined location, where they crouched and waited in thick brush behind a fallen tree, snapped at waist height, the base of the toppled section still attached to the trunk by a few strands of pale wood. To their far left sat the loaded wagons and a few still-empty carts. To their right was the closest hovel, no more than thirty paces distant. Just beyond in the center of an open space was a bonfire, around which the young wagon-loaders formed a ring, swaying and singing, their voices joining with the other Children in an almost mesmeric harmony.

Deeper in the settlement, two robed acolytes flanked the door of the large structure, where smoke had begun pouring from an unseen chimney. The door opened; a man, long-haired and stone-faced in the firelight, emerged. He was tall and, though past middle age, possessed a thickly muscled frame, evident even beneath the robes, which were slightly more fanciful—violet in color, trimmed in shining gold. A sigil adorned his lapel. At his side hung a scimitar of mysterious make and origin.

He stood before the door, arms outspread, and called, "Children!"

All dancing and singing ceased. All eyes turned toward the speaker. "Time now for repast and fellowship. Come!"

The leader turned, spoke something to the guards at the door, and reentered the building. As the Children filed silently into the dining hall, the guards took up firebrands and began, at opposite sides of the compound, a perimeter patrol. Torin, Xamus, and Oldavei hid in the deeper shadows of the foliage as one of the humming acolytes strode past their hiding spot, just out of sword reach, torch held to light his way.

With the patrolman out of earshot, Oldavei bent his keen hearing to the hall. "I can't make out what's being said in there," he admitted in a hushed tone. "But it may be worthwhile to find out."

"Agreed," the elf replied. Information had value, and knowledge of the Children's plans could provide the three with leverage to negotiate a higher price from the Magistrate. "But to get there without a guard raising the alarm—"

"Back up," Oldavei said, removing his travel bag. "I have a way." Torin retreated a step but eyed the ma'ii with a sudden keen interest.

Oldavei grunted, shuddered, and contorted. A strange rippling motion overtook his clothing and scimitar even as they began fading from view. Both Xamus and Torin backed away even farther as the ma'ii's garments and weapon disappeared altogether. Bones and tendons popped and snapped; his skin and muscles undulated as if something stirred beneath. His face and teeth extended even as his body shrunk slightly. His legs reshaped, bending backward as he fell to all fours. A wide, thick tail grew, along with coarse fur. When the transformation was complete, the transfixed elf and dwarf were left staring at a sand-hued coyote.

Torin's voice was low, husky. "Shifters. Not something you see every day, eh?"

Xamus was both shocked and slightly unsettled.

The canine head looked up to regard the two. There was intelligence behind the animal eyes and even . . . mirth? At their astonishment? It seemed so. The beast pulled its lips back in what almost appeared as a smile, then crawled beneath where the fallen tree connected to the trunk. As the next guard came to the south boundary, his sight blocked by a wagon, Oldavei threw a final look to his companions before bounding away.

CHAPTER FOUR

UNINVITED

In coyote form, Oldavei ran behind a cart, crouched, and waited for the guard to move on. Though the first guard was beyond his sight, the ma'ii could smell him as he darted around the closest hovel.

The trickiest part, he knew, would be dashing past the bonfire, which would not only illuminate him but cast a long shadow as well. The window of time in which both guards would likely not be alerted was narrow. Oldavei settled back onto his haunches and scented the air. At just the right moment he sprang, sprinted past the fire, and ran alongside the dining hall opposite the first guard's position. Once at the rear, he huddled at the base of a keg stack. Muffled sounds of revelry drifted from within as he remained still and silent. An interval passed with no alarm. He rose, preparing to jump onto the lowest kegs, when the wind shifted and he detected an odor, one both familiar and yet out of place: the smell of a human, but tied to it, death and decay.

Oldavei crept to the building's rear corner and peered around. At first he saw nothing. Then one of the shadows near the corral moved. A silhouetted human figure, the source of the odors Oldavei sensed, relocated from one patch of darkness to another, not by moving so much as by flowing, like dark water. The ma'ii continued sniffing and determined that while the curious death-scent he detected was not intrinsic to the stranger, it was closely associated. It hung about the interloper like a shroud, suggestive of a being who had passed ample time in death's company.

The shadow-stranger scaled a hovel wall without so much as a sound, even to the ma'ii's keen ears. This newcomer—a man, Oldavei determined; his was a man smell—was clearly making his way deeper into the compound. Surely he could not clear the fire as Oldavei had done; the distance was too great for a human. Surely he would be detected.

As Oldavei watched, rapt, the man crouched atop the roof, launched up and over the fire, body straight but turning like the spoke of a wheel, feet over head, until he landed—again silently—on the next closest hovel roof.

He was working toward the dining hall, Oldavei determined as he leaped onto the lowest keg, then up to the next, and finally onto the roof.

Sinews stretched, grew, enlarged; fur, tail, and muzzle receded. For a brief moment the thing that was part coyote, part man, stood. A wave rippled over his form, and at once clothing and weapon were restored. Oldavei, back in ma'ii form, stepped softly around the smoking chimney. As expected, the intruder flipped up onto the roof's opposite end. He glided forward, drawing from his back an elegant single-edged straight sword. Oldavei stalked to meet him, brandishing his scimitar. Despite the ma'ii's light tread, a creak sounded beneath. He stepped back as the stranger approached within a few paces and stood, tense and alert.

The man radiated a quiet menace. His garb, from sleeveless shirt to soft-soled shoe, was black and otherwise unremarkable save for the fact that the whole of it appeared . . . unused, fresh. The stranger's long dark hair was tied in a tail, and his sharp hazel eyes bore through Oldavei from behind blue-tinged glasses.

A moment passed as each waited for the other to make a move, while sounds of communion emanated from below. Finally Oldavei demanded in a hushed tone, "What's your business here?"

"Death is my business," the husky-voiced stranger answered. "And you'd be wise to stay clear of it."

"An assassin," Oldavei said. "Who have you come to kill?"

"I don't answer to you!" the man replied. "You're obviously not one of them, so make way!"

Despite the stranger's bluster, Oldavei sensed a mild reluctance. The ma'ii thrust up his chin. "I have as much right to be here as you do," he said. "In fact, I'm being well compensated."

"As. Am. I," the newcomer answered through clenched teeth.

"Yes, well, I have backup waiting nearby," Oldavei said. "What say you to—"

"Enough!" the stranger spat, lunging forward with a rapid sword thrust.

The ma'ii's response was reflexive and immediate. He parried, then countered, but his opponent's reactions were fast—almost unnaturally so. Oldavei quickly found himself on the defensive and under threat not just from the blade but from kicks as well, including one that stirred the air over his head as he ducked. The assassin blocked a return swing of the ma'ii's scimitar with his own blade, one-handed, then jabbed two fingers of his free hand into the side of Oldavei's neck, sending a jolt down his right side, deadening his arm and causing him to drop his weapon. The ma'ii was far from defeated, however; he gripped the stranger's sword wrist with his left hand, then lunged in, biting the intruder on the shoulder, eliciting a sharp curse.

Oldavei heard commotion from below even as the assassin wrapped an arm around him, twisted, and threw. The ma'ii flew over his opponent's hip and crashed into—and through—the roof.

From their hiding place, Xamus and Torin had heard the clashing of swords. They had drawn closer to the light and watched two figures quarrel on the rooftop.

"What the fek do ya suppose—" Torin was in the midst of saying when he was interrupted by the cannon crack of timber snapping, followed by the two shadow figures plunging from sight, raising shouts and screams from within the hall.

"Looks like our night just got a lot more interestin'," Torin said, striking out, axe in hand.

On the dwarf's heels, Xamus said, "Try not to kill anyone!"

Oldavei, the assassin, and a fair amount of debris from the roof crashed down onto a thick wooden table. Robed figures—those who weren't already standing—fell off crude benches, crying out in shock and terror. Plates, cups, and food were scattered or spilled. Oldavei's scimitar plummeted from above, its tip splitting a block of cheese as it punched into the tabletop a hair's width from his left ear. The ma'ii swept up his sword and rolled off the table in one motion. As fortune would have it, he now found himself face-to-face with the youths from Hearthvale. Four of them, within arm's reach, stared wide-eyed at Oldavei and over his shoulder at the assassin as well.

"They're here for us," one of the four, a female, cried, backing against the wall. "Come to take us back. We can't go back," she said, on the verge of hysterics. "We want paradise! Help! Help!"

A cultist on Oldavei's right advanced. The ma'ii turned, baring his teeth, growling from deep in his chest, enough to scare the man back. Sensing another advancement, Oldavei spun and grabbed a second cultist by the throat. The young female shouted all the while: "Protect us, brothers! Defend us!"

On the table, the assassin rose, sword in hand, and strode toward the back of the room where the leader stood, just in front of the fireplace, silent and impassive.

"Taron Braun!" the stranger shouted, leveling his sword at the older man. "Your end has come!"

Screams rose anew. Near the leader, one of the Children retreated, tipping a cresset, which in turn sent flames up the wall.

Braun raised a hand and voiced, "The light of the sun burns within me, and I shall fear no evil!" There was a flash, a blinding light from the leader's hand, as a glimmering, amorphous radiance appeared just before the stranger. The assassin cried out, shut his eyes, grasped his head with one hand, and fell to his knees.

Panic ensued as the Children closest the door clumped together in an effort to escape. Oldavei realized that the gasping acolyte he was holding had turned a deep shade of crimson. He let go, and the man collapsed. Near the head of the table, the assassin pitched forward, displacing a bowl of fruit, and was still.

Of the four youths, only the female and one male had stayed put, frozen in fear. Oldavei struck out with the pommel of his scimitar, knocking the male senseless. Sparing a glance to the back of the room, the ma'ii noted that the cult leader was nowhere to be seen.

Outside, Torin and Xamus skidded to a halt several paces from the dining hall as a flood of Children poured forth. The two guards, who had been approaching the hall, as well, caught sight of the duo and charged. "Death to the unbelievers!" one of them proclaimed.

Xamus waved his hands, gesticulating, speaking quietly in the ages-old tongue of his ancestors. Torin watched, somewhat awestruck. He was about to witness magic. *True* magic. And elven at that! His blood surged.

Xamus extended a closed fist, then opened it as he punctuated his chant. The guards screamed, veering off. "Blind!" one yelled. "Gods, I can't see!" the other cried. One of them ran straight into the nearby bonfire, robes catching. The howling, blazing cultist sprinted face-first into the wall of a hut and fell, flailing, as the hovel went up in flames.

Torin was impressed but also confused. "Don't kill anyone, you said!"

"It was meant to be a sleep spell," the elf admitted.

"Wha? Meant to—" Torin stammered. "What good's magic if—" He stopped to crack an onrushing acolyte upside the head with the flat of his axe. The man crumpled. "If it won't do what you want it to do?" he finished.

"Works most of the time," Xamus said as he spotted two of the youths issuing from the smoking structure.

"Most of the time, right," Torin said as the elf charged, tripping one young cultist and wrapping his arms around the waist of the other. Torin came to his side, looking worriedly to the burning hall, where the last of the acolytes had now apparently departed.

"Where's the mutt?" Torin inquired just as Oldavei stumbled out, dragging the male youth he had knocked unconscious, with the protesting female slung over one shoulder. He dropped both, looked to Torin and said, "One more!" then ran back into the billowing smoke.

"Found some rope," Xamus said, kneeling to restrain the young woman.

Torin looked behind to see that the elf had already tied the hands and feet of the other two runaways. "Glad you didn't try to magic that up," the dwarf said. "Mighta conjured snakes instead."

The dining hall was now fully ablaze, illuminating the entire compound and throwing off scorching heat. Torin looked to the doorway. "Come on, mutt, come on . . ."

Roof timbers caved in, causing the dwarf to believe their comrade was lost, when Oldavei suddenly reemerged, a black-clad figure draped over his shoulders, a straight sword in one hand. As he stumbled forth, Torin hurried to assist in lowering the stranger to the ground. Oldavei dropped the sword and put his hands to his knees, coughing heavily.

"What's this?" Torin inquired, gesturing to the prone figure.

"Assassin," the ma'ii said in a hoarse voice. "Came for the leader."

Xamus, having now bound the unconscious cultist, stepped away, scanning the surrounding landscape. "Speaking of, where—" And then the elf spotted him standing atop a low ridge a fair distance away. The man held one hand aloft, and the light that shone above that hand rivaled the luminescence cast by the dining-hall fire. The last stragglers of the faithful rushed to him. An instant later, the light was extinguished.

"Gone," Xamus said, turning to Torin and Oldavei. "Now what?"

The dwarf looked to the south, where floating embers from the burning hovel, borne on the light breeze, had already lit one wagon on fire. "I say we hitch two oxen to one o' them wagons," the dwarf said. "Release the rest, then kick some dust."

The assassin stirred, maneuvered to all fours, and put a hand to the side of his head. "What the hell hit me?" he asked.

"What about him?" Oldavei asked.

Torin and Xamus both answered at once: "He comes with us."

CHAPTER FIVE

AMANDREAS

From his position on the wagon seat, pressed between Torin and Xamus, who held the reins, the black-clad stranger sat grimly silent, rebuffing all inquiries as to his identity or purpose.

In stark contrast to the assassin's silence, a ceaseless clamor persisted in the wagon's bed, where Oldavei sat guarding the Children. There, when passionate invocations of some "Great Prophet" in the desert and lamentations of the youths' exclusion from "Paradise" had stretched the ma'ii's patience to its limit, he opened one of the crates they had left onboard, took the linen from inside, and tore it into strips. One by one he gagged the protesting Children's mouths, then returned to sit atop the crate. With the runaways quieted, Oldavei's attention was once again drawn to the curious odor of their new companion.

"Hey, friend," Oldavei called forward, "why is it you smell as if you've been sleeping in a cemetery?"

The stranger exhaled loudly.

"What are you on about?" Torin asked the ma'ii.

"He carries a smell of death about him," Oldavei said.

"You don't say," Torin replied, leaning in for a quick sniff, from which the stranger recoiled slightly. "I'll take your word for it," the dwarf called to Oldavei. Then to the assassin, "So what's the story? You dabble in necromancy?"

No answer.

"Think you're smart, eh?" the dwarf continued in the stranger's ear. "I have ways to make prisoners talk, you know."

"Is that what you think I am?" the man said, glaring back.

"Oh, did I touch a nerve?" the dwarf replied. "Am I mistaken? You're here 'cause you want to be, that it?"

The stranger bit back a response.

"Something has him on edge," Oldavei called.

"Were any of you to see half the things I've seen, it would do far more than put you on edge . . ." the stranger locked a penetrating gaze on Torin. "It would drain you to white."

Silence hung momentarily, soon broken by Torin and Oldavei's laughter. Xamus chuckled.

Torin looked over his shoulder, wide-eyed. "Drain you to white!" he mimicked, causing Oldavei to laugh all the louder.

The stranger crossed his arms.

"Our new friend has a flair for the dramatic," Torin said. He sighed, leaning back in the seat. "Have it your way, sunshine. the Magistrate will sort you out soon enough."

Hours later, as the sun broke over the eastern peaks, they arrived in Hearthvale.

Following the handover of the youths, Torin, Xamus, and Oldavei found themselves once again inside the Magistrate's chamber, each seated in their previous places while the stranger remained silent at the back of the room, leaning against the wall.

Torin noted disappointedly that the candle and holder on Raldon's desk had been moved to a bookshelf out of reach. He fiddled with one of his beard ties as the Magistrate sat, lips pressed tight, face red. "These . . . strays have spun quite a tale," he began. "Exploits that all but defy belief. Fire. Bedlam. Blindness!" He shot a glance at Xamus, who canted his head and raised his brows in tacit, slightly abashed acknowledgment. "Death!" the Magistrate fumed. "Destruction! Mayhem! Need I continue?"

"We did bring them back," Xamus pointed out.

Oldavei spoke up from his spot on the floor, "And with them a wagon, oxen, some very fine linens . . ."

"Quietly!" Raldon bellowed, eyes ablaze. "It was to be done quietly! Discreetly!"

"Woulda been," Torin said, hiking a thumb toward the stranger. "If not for shithead there."

"Nicholas," the man corrected. He stepped away from the wall to a position behind Xamus and Torin and cleared his throat. "Sir, my name is Nicholas Amandreas. I am a . . . sword for hire."

"Mm. Flourishing occupation it seems," Raldon answered. "What was your purpose at the compound?"

"To kill Taron Braun," Nicholas said. "Leader of the Children of the Sun."

"Who hired you?" Raldon replied.

"Powerful parties, sir. Beyond that, I'm not permitted to say."

"Stop dancing around and answer straight," Raldon shot back. "Else I'll have your tongue removed. Why were you employed?"

Nicholas wrung his hands as he replied, "For what might best be described as business reasons."

The Magistrate leaned in, putting his elbows on the desk. "Elaborate."

"The Children of the Sun are viewed by my employers as a destabilizing force among the Trade-Cities. Disruptive to commerce. Harmful to profit. I've been hired to chop the head off the snake."

Raldon sat back. "Well now, that is interesting," he said. "An outside guild, then, concerned that the Children are a threat to their business interests."

Nicholas did not answer. Raldon tugged at his greased chin hair, appearing to perform some mental calculations.

Torin cleared his throat. "There is the matter of payment . . ."

"You'll receive half," Raldon answered, shifting forward, having apparently reached some conclusion.

"Hey," Torin protested. "We brought the little shits back in one piece."

Raldon raised a stern finger. "And yet it remains that the task was not performed to my satisfaction! You created this mess, you clean it up."

"Clean it up?" Xamus replied.

"Seek out Taron Braun and put an end to him," the Magistrate said, reaching for a quill and small parchment. "Upon completion of your task, I will proffer the balance of our agreed-upon sum."

"What about him?" Xamus asked, indicating Nicholas.

"Work it out among yourselves," Raldon said, handing over a hastily scrawled note. "Take that to the treasurer, and don't show your faces again until the work is done."

★ ★ ★

Midday was fast approaching when the trio collected their weapons from the hall guard and walked out onto the main thoroughfare, their coin purses slightly heavier.

"Half pay, twice the work," Torin said, stepping around a pile of droppings left by a cart horse ahead of them. "I'm liking this situation less and less."

A sudden voice startled them. "Hold!" it said. Pausing to look around, they spotted Nicholas stepping from a darkened shop doorway.

"The fek do you want?" Torin inquired.

"Question," the assassin replied as the three stopped. "I was . . . just wondering if you had some method in mind . . . of finding Braun."

"What if we did?" Torin answered.

"Well, it occurs to me that our goals may align," Nicholas said.

The group advanced as Torin carried on: "And why should we lead *you* to *our* bounty?"

"Children of the Sun could be lurking around any corner. Certainly another set of eyes and ears and a proficient sword arm would only increase everyone's chances of finding Braun. And you've no need to split your coin with me. All I require for my own payment is proof of death."

The dwarf grunted. "Well, sorry to inform you that we have no clue where to—"

"I have a way," Xamus said. Torin sighed. The elf turned aside, facing the town library.

Torin looked to Oldavei, who shrugged.

They entered, found what Xamus sought, and proceeded to a back room. There, with Nicholas preoccupied perusing the bookshelves, they unrolled a large map of Lawbrand on a table in the room's center. "I'll be able to point us in the right direction," Xamus said.

"How?" Oldavei asked.

"Magic," Xamus answered. This drew Nicholas's attention as the elf pulled an object from his dungarees—it was an amulet, a crude, handcrafted metallic sun pendant and black cord. "I took this from one of the runaways when I tied him up," the elf said. "Braun must have gifted it to him; still has his imprint." He held the item over the table and began chanting in his native tongue.

Torin retreated three steps. Xamus stopped, turned. "What are you doing?"

"I've seen your magic at work," the dwarf answered. To Oldavei and Nicholas, he said, "Tried to sleep some o' them fekkers at the compound. Blinded 'em instead!"

Oldavei and Nicholas shared a glance. Xamus shook his head, faced the table, and continued chanting in soft, melodic tones, arm extended. He opened his hand. Rather than falling, the amulet hung in the air, cord suspended like a tail. Then it rose.

Oldavei and Nicholas stepped back, joining Torin.

The object floated to just under the roof beams, where it held momentarily before moving in a spiral, cord sweeping beneath, making small circles at first, then expanding. In the midst of a wide curve, it froze, then fell, amulet first, cord coiling behind.

Xamus opened his eyes. The others stepped up to join him, looking to see what location the amulet had targeted.

"Skarborough!" Torin said.

PART ONE: NOTHIN' BUT TROUBLE...

"If Braun's gone into hiding," Nicholas said, "Skarborough's a perfect place. The Children are sure to have compatriots there."

"Lotta city to search," Oldavei said. Then, indicating Nicholas, "Creepy here may be useful after all."

"Can you narrow the location?" Nicholas asked Xamus.

The elf didn't respond immediately. Finally he said, "No, this is the best I can do."

"It's a rat's-nest shithole of a mining city," Torin protested.

Oldavei spoke: "Filled with the rowdiest, raunchiest, lowest of the low hole-in-the-wall taverns in all the Trade-Cities."

"Good point," Torin said, nodding sagely. "When do we leave?"

Oldavei laughed, then thrust his head near the dwarf, sniffing incessantly.

"Back off, ya crazy fekker!" Torin said, pushing him away. The ma'ii continued chuckling, clearly pleased at his comrade's discomfort.

"Settled then," Xamus proclaimed, snatching up the amulet. "First drink's on me!"

CHAPTER SIX

THE STRIPMINE

They made good time for the remainder of the day and bedded down in a field just off the main highway, ten miles south of Hearthvale's city proper, Centerton, and within earshot of the burbling Talisande River. Throughout the journey, their new companion had kept to himself. Now, as they lounged around the fire, passing the flask and smoking, Nicholas sat just out of the firelight, refusing whiskey, silent but alert while Torin rubbed aching feet and wiggled tired toes. "Shoulda kept the wagon," he said.

Oldavei, huddled with knees to chest, arms wrapped round his legs, looked in the direction of Nicholas. "Something's been bothering me," he said. "Taron Braun, at the dining hall when you went for him, he did something to you. Magic."

Xamus blew smoke and said, "What kind?"

"Weird kind," the ma'ii said. "A flash of light."

Xamus looked to Nicholas and said, "Any idea what it was?"

Torin grumbled, "We didn't even ask if we could keep the wagon."

Nicholas's raspy voice drifted from the dark. "Who's to say? Some parlor trick, blinded me temporarily. It's of no concern." Minor rustling noises and a long exhale indicated that he was bedding down.

"No harm in askin' about the wagon is all I'm sayin'," Torin concluded as he settled in.

Oldavei considered. Back among his people, an interval that seemed now lifetimes away, he had known magic in varying forms. And he felt certain that whatever form the Children's leader had cast, it was no parlor trick. Moments later, as he nestled into his bedroll, he wondered what other surprises the strange cult might have in store for them.

As they continued trekking throughout the next day, Nicholas hung back, remaining reticent while the others chattered idly. Only after they had cut a path along the west-bending Talisande and into Skarborough's borderlands did the assassin begin to warm up. Joining the group, he expounded upon the city's history: after being founded by the prospector Dengun Ironskar 150 years ago, the town thrived on the mining of precious gems, serving as a location of choice for job-seeking miners and the barons who profited from them. Skarborough excelled until greed and rebellion led to the wars with the neighboring Trade-City, Talis. In the aftermath, the so-called "Jeweled City" never quite regained its luster. Later, an earthquake sank much of Skarborough's most well-to-do district into a quarry, resulting in an exodus of the population that further reduced the once-mighty industrial stronghold to a mere specter of its former self.

For all of its trials and tribulations, however, one constant remained: alcohol.

"They even have a Brewers Guild," Nicholas informed them.

"Now you're speakin' my language," Torin replied.

By midday, as they closed on the city, the air took on a heavy quality. A thickening pall obscured distant objects and landmarks and diffused the light, making the hour seem later. Several odors hung in the stagnant atmosphere, the most prominent of which bore a mineral essence, a kind of tang that lingered in the airways. The smells were accompanied by a rising din of chinking pickaxes, clattering ore cars, the splitting of stone, and the chorus of work songs. The peculiar acoustics of their surroundings created the aural illusion of sound emanating from every direction at once. The ubiquitous noise and pungent smells proved especially off-putting to Oldavei's heightened senses, causing the ma'ii, who normally ventured well ahead of the others, to remain close, eyes ranging, head darting side to side.

They rounded a stony ridge whose eastern face was punched through by an adit. Songs and pick strikes emanated from the timber-framed tunnel mouth as they crossed a set of rail tracks and followed a dirt path, transitioning from an expanse dotted with rickety shacks, tents, and fires to a dizzying maze of narrow streets that wound through ramshackle, tumbledown structures, increasing in height and number of levels the deeper the party plunged. Music of all forms assailed them as they progressed, accompanied by whoops and laughs and shouts and songs, drifting from rooftops and doorways and open windows.

The meandering streets increased and decreased in grade, adding in some cases to a trick of the eye that made the dilapidated structures appear to crowd and lean precariously as if they might topple onto the rough-paved stones at any instant. The volume and abundance of sound increased as they reached a district where citizens ambled or stumbled to and fro, most garbed in filthy work attire, skin coated in grime, eyes bleary and blank as they muttered or hollered and made their way from one tavern to the next, singly or in pairs or groups, often in the company of scantily clad females whose unkempt, beleaguered appearance rivaled that of their companions.

A retching noise caused Oldavei to gaze up and behind. The others looked back in time to witness a stream of vomit splash down onto the street behind them. Torin laughed heartily. The group had scarcely resumed walking, hugging the right side of the thoroughfare, when they spotted a peculiar creature standing in a doorway directly across. It was short, green-skinned, clad in bib overalls, with a wide mouth and reptilian features. It stood statue-still, arms hanging limply at its sides, gawking at them with round, unblinking eyes.

"Salamar," Nicholas announced, his voice tinged with slight fascination. "Master botanists."

A long tendril of tongue slipped out of the lizard-thing's mouth, extended upward, licked its left eyeball, then slithered back out of sight.

"Creepy fekkers, more like," Torin replied, looking as if he had just sucked on a lemon.

"Well," Xamus said as they continued on round a bend, "now that we're here, might as well get to work."

Not far ahead, a booming voice called from the boardwalk, "Open Lute Night! Open Lute Night here!" The caller was a ruddy, leather-faced, scruffy-bearded man, bedecked in extravagant yet tattered finery that might have once belonged to some member of the Skarborough elite. "Look no farther! Beer half price! The finest bards in all the land! Not to be missed! The show starts now!" Above the old man, a wooden sign hung from a drooping cantilever. It read The World Famous Stripmine in faded letters.

"Time enough for work tomorrow!" Torin said, beelining for the doorman. Oldavei followed, grinning widely. Xamus looked to Nicholas, who shrugged and fell in behind.

"Right this way, good sirs," the doorman croaked as Torin stepped through. "Unparalleled entertainment awaits! The hobgoblin shimmy dancers have the night off, and for that you should be grateful!" he announced with a smile and wink as the others filed in.

The smoke-filled Stripmine was far more spacious on the inside than its exterior indicated. Chairs and tables crowded the main floor, where spectators sat facing a small, currently empty stage at the back of the room. A bar, stocked with kegs representing every manner of drink imaginable, ran the length of the wall on the right side. To the left, a rickety wooden staircase ascended to a second floor, packed with patrons of all gender, size, and type: an iron dwarf raised a mug and shouted next to a gnoll pumping its fist. A minotaur, towering over both, let loose a thunderous roar and poured a stream of ale down its gullet. A few humans whooped and gyrated. On the first floor, to either side, ogre bouncers clad in tight-fitting tunics stood with arms folded over barrel chests, scanning the crowd.

A handful of besotted miners vacated a table near the foot of the stage, which the party immediately filled. Torin had barely unlimbered his axe and taken a seat with the others when a plump, blonde-haired serving woman in a too-tight corset demanded their choice of drink.

Moments later the barmaid delivered a flagon of ale and four cups. "Let's get hammered!" Torin declared, pouring the first round.

A frumpy minstrel in a coif cap ascended to the stage, announced himself as Beauregard Goodchurch, and, with theatrical flair, began reciting poetry. Xamus, who sat with his back to the stage, prepared to turn his chair around, then thought better of it. At the table to his left, a group of three loud burly miners paused long enough to laugh and point before returning to their ale.

When the barmaid returned and swapped out their empty flagon for a full one, Xamus asked if she had heard of or seen men in robes calling themselves Children of the Sun. Looking mildly put off, the woman said, "Don't know nothin' 'bout it," and left.

Torin, puffing on a pipe, stared with one squinty eye at Xamus across the table. "What?" the elf said.

"How do we know," Torin answered, "that your 'magic pendant' hit the right spot on the map?"

Xamus lit a smoke of his own before answering. He drew in, exhaled, and said, "The spell didn't go wrong."

"How do you know?" Torin pressed.

"Because I can feel when it goes wrong," Xamus said.

Oldavei, who sat to Xamus's left with his feet on the seat, knees splayed, cup cradled in his hands, asked, "Why does your magic go wrong sometimes?" Xamus glanced over, somewhat surprised to find that the ma'ii seemed genuinely intrigued.

The elf downed his cup and waited, debating his next words. Finally he said, "Because it's wild magic."

"What the fek is wild magic?" Torin asked.

A new performer, wearing fool's clothing, including a three-point hat, took the stage. "The Great Gambolo" produced balls from his pockets, then juggled as he crooned about lovely maidens and lost loves in a warbling, singsong voice. From the nearby miners' table, a bearded man shouted for the fool to piss off. Next to him, a long-haired miner yelled for him to play with his balls somewhere else.

"I learned a little about wild magic back with my tribe," Oldavei said. "Shunned by most, isn't it, for being unstable?"

"Yeah," Xamus answered.

"So why fekkin' use it?" Torin said, seeking the whereabouts of the barmaid. He spotted her on the steps and waved the empty flagon.

"*Because* it's unstable," Xamus answered. "Because it's wild."

Nicholas, who sat slightly apart, spoke. "Taking the long path instead of the short makes you stronger. I read that once."

Oldavei's eyes had drifted a bit. "Some magic's better left alone," he said.

Nicholas scooted his chair up, put his elbows and cup on the table. "You asked before about the magic cast by Taron Braun," he said. "I said it was of no concern, but I lied . . ." he cast his eyes down. "In fact it felt . . . for just an instant it felt as though my soul had caught fire."

The table was silent for a moment.

"Agh, enough pissin' and moanin'!" Torin declared, slamming his cup. "Woman!" he shouted, "where's our—" he turned to see the barmaid, standing not a hand's width away, holding a full flagon. She thumped the new container down, gave the dwarf a stare that could melt stone, and snatched up the empty.

"Sneaky, that one," Torin said, setting aside his pipe and taking up the new flagon. Nicholas slid his cup for a refill but was snubbed when Torin tilted the vessel to his own lips and began guzzling.

Just then a new entertainer took to the stage, pushing up blue spectacles that had slid down his nose. The tall man was laden with an excess of gear, including a worn-out kick drum and stylized mandolin. He bore a horseshoe mustache and a strip of chin hair that extended beyond his jawline, and his thick, curly black mane rivaled Xamus's in length. He wore a leather jerkin and leather pants, both black, and atop his head was an overly tall sky-blue-and-white-striped floppy hat, the stripes of which spiraled from bottom to top like a coiling snake. Before proceeding, he stopped to wrangle the various encumbrances, endeavoring to offload pieces one at a time, getting straps tangled or hung up, fiddling with one, then giving up and proceeding to another, creating discordant notes when he accidentally struck mandolin strings. At last he succeeded in liberating a travel pack and belt with longsword and dagger, which he placed upstage. The lack of these accoutrements revealed that his jerkin was fully opened to expose his chest as the bard took center stage. He set the kick drum at his feet, picked at the mandolin experimentally, and when satisfied, planted his boots wide and gazed out over the crowd.

"Listen close, you tight-ass heathens!" he called out. "I'm Wilhelm Wallaroo, and I'm here to blow your breeches off!"

He commenced to playing, fingers dancing over the strings at lightning speed, striking chords in dizzying succession as the drum pounded its beat. From his lips gushed a song that matched the music's rapid pace:

Call it fate, call it luck, call it anything you like
Gonna make my mark this time
Fortune only smiles for those who stand tall
And push through to the end of the line

"Damn, this kid's good," Xamus said, turning his chair around.

"Gets the blood pumpin', that's sure!" Torin said as the bard continued:

Travel on, dusty miles, made my way across this land
Y'know I've seen a thing or two
But fortune sings, she beckons me on
Gonna find me a muse that's true

Nicholas found himself bobbing his head to the quick-fire riffs. The crowd, however, did not share the adventurers' appreciation. Many sat with hands over their ears to muffle the thumping of the drum. Several of the patrons on the second floor had stopped dancing and drinking, leaning down to stare over the handrail. The nearby miners' faces were twisted in revulsion. "What the fek is this shit?" the bearded man shouted.

"Enough already!" yelled the long-haired man next to him. The third took aim at the stage and flung an empty cup.

Wilhelm dodged the projectile deftly, then modified the words of his song, looking the bearded man squarely in the eye:

Speaking of muses, saw your momma today
She was hot and bothered for this bard

The man pointed, tilting his head as if to say, "Don't do it." Wilhelm smiled:

So I pulled that sweet thing to my loving embrace
She whispered 'I can't believe it's so—

The bearded man sprang from his seat and rushed the stage, taking a swipe at Wilhelm's left leg, but the bard was too quick. He slipped the leg back, cocked his foot, then kicked the attacker square in the forehead. The miner fell back into his long-haired companion. The third miner skirted his mates, passing near Oldavei's chair. The ma'ii lowered his legs from the seat and thrust out his foot. The miner tripped, smacking his face on the edge of the stage. He crumpled, wailing, hands pressed to his bloodied, broken nose.

Torin, laughing uproariously, stopped when Xamus looked back at the tavern proper, eyes flicking from one side to the other. The wooden floor shuddered. Torin turned to see the two ogres swiping patrons out of their way, smashing chairs aside as they surged forth. He once again regarded the stage, noting that Wilhelm was now in a tussling match with the long-haired miner.

"I don't like these odds," Torin said, assessing Wilhelm's chances.

"Agreed," Oldavei said. "This is no way to treat a gifted musician."

Torin lifted his axe and broke into a gap-toothed grin, eyes gleaming. "Let's crack some skulls!"

CHAPTER SEVEN

GREENLIGHT

Chaos broke out.

In the wake of the ogres' reckless charge, patrons throughout the Stripmine traded blows. Cups and flagons flew; tables overturned. A cacophony of shattering crockery, splintering wood, shouts, curses, and cries of pain rent the air.

At the stage, the broken-nosed miner grabbed his bearded friend under the armpits and dragged him away. Oldavei launched from his seat at the first onrushing ogre, mouth open wide, clawed fingers flexed, a fearsome battle cry erupting from his throat.

The bouncer reached up, seized him by neck and groin, turned, and heaved. The ma'ii flew over the heads of drunken brawlers, spinning like a discus until he crashed onto the bar and bounced off, smashing into one of the small kegs lining the wall behind.

The ogre stomped onward, stopping just short of the stage as Xamus leaped onto his back and wrapped his arms tightly around the guard's thick neck.

At the same time, Torin spun, swinging the flat edge of his axe into the side of the second bouncer's right knee. The brute roared in pain, stumbling headlong into Nicholas before the assassin could mount an attack of his own, driving them both to the floor. The ogre landed atop the assassin, blasting the air from his lungs, while Wilhelm tossed the long-haired miner from the stage onto the table, breaking it in half.

Torin delivered a swift kick between the prone bouncer's legs, sparking a bellow of pain and prompting the massive weight to roll off Nicholas. As the ogre sat up, Torin reached their fallen flagon and tossed it to Nicholas, who deftly caught the vessel and smashed it over the bouncer's head, knocking him senseless.

The ogre being choked by Xamus spun in circles, flinging wild blows over his shoulders in an attempt to dislodge the elf, his face turning deep shades of red, eyes bulging. His revolutions and swats slowed, and his steps faltered until finally he fell face-first onto the stage, unconscious.

Wilhelm, poised to bash his mandolin over the bouncer's head, looked down and said, "Hey, thanks for the assist!" Xamus unmounted the ogre, looked up, and tipped his hat.

Oldavei stumbled past the barmaid, who gripped a limp, kneeling miner by the collar, punched him repeatedly in the face, and made his way back to the stage just as a booming voice shouted, "You!"

The group turned to see a burly, wild-eyed man in an apron approaching. "This is your doing!" he cried, pointing at Wilhelm.

"Fek, the owner," Wilhelm said.

"Militia's on the way!" the owner yelled.

"Time to leave," Nicholas said, groaning as he gained his feet. Wilhelm swept up his pack and belt, slung both over his shoulder, took a slight pause to lament his kick drum, now smashed to pieces, then hustled along with the others toward the door.

"You're finished in this town, Wallaroo!" the tavern owner's voice followed them onto the street. "You hear me? Finished!"

The group ran deeper into the night-shrouded city, stopping when a rhythmic stomping of booted feet carried to them from ahead. "Here!" Wilhelm said, indicating a narrow alley.

Odors of urine and feces were pungent as half the party hid behind a pile of wooden planks on one side and the second half crouched behind a stack of barrels on the other. They shrank back as a squad of twelve lightly armored Skarborough Militia filed past.

When the soldiers had gone, Xamus, Torin, Oldavei, and Wilhelm emerged from hiding and breathed a collective sigh of relief.

"That's Skarborough for you," Oldavei said, "never a dull moment."

"Off to one hell of a start," Nicholas said, issuing from deeper shadows and taking Wilhelm by surprise. "No bother, though. We'll find an inn, get some sleep, resume our search tomorrow."

"Search?" Wilhelm asked.

"We seek the leader of a cult," Xamus said, "Children of the Sun."

"Oh," Wilhelm said. "Yeah. I've been in town a while, heard talk of some strange sun worshippers." He headed back the way they had come and said, "This way!"

"He doesn't like to sit still, does he?" Torin said to Xamus as they followed.

The group eyed every shadowed nook and light-flooded tavern door as they progressed, bombarded by sounds of music and festivity as they passed the occasional, stumbling reveler. Wilhelm adjusted the mandolin on his shoulder. "I heard the cultists frequent a warehouse in the Greenlight District."

"Mm," Nicholas said. "Arboretums and greenhouses. Tended by the Salamar, no doubt."

"Wonderful," Torin said.

"This leader you're after," Wilhelm continued, "is there a reward?"

"There is!" Oldavei piped up. "A bounty. If you help us find him, we'll cut you in."

"Oh, yeah," Torin replied. "Great idea. Let's just keep addin' to the party. Anyone else we should recruit? Hey, you!" He grabbed the arm of a passing drunk. "Wanna join our secret quest?"

"I'm afraid of bees," the old man said.

"Fair enough," Torin answered, releasing him.

"Hmm?" Wilhelm said, seeming distracted. "Oh hey, man, no problem. It's your show. But you helped me back there, so, you know, taking you to the warehouse is the least I can do. It's up this way."

They traveled on until the lights and sounds faded and they found themselves navigating twining, darkened streets that widened and leveled out as the oppressive air lifted. Tightly packed structures gave way to squat, more expansive constructions, some made of glass, separated by lush gardens and groves and walkways. Here, the mineral smells had been replaced by a cornucopia of botanical fragrances, with an undercurrent of manure. Occasionally from within pockets of the dense foliage, curious, unblinking round eyes peeked out.

Moments later, Wilhelm looked around, said, "Follow me!" and swung onto a narrow dirt path between tall shrubs. They carried on until a wooden toolshed came into view on their right. Wilhelm climbed onto a cart at the building's side. He removed his travel bag and mandolin, put them in the cart, then clambered onto the pitched roof and crawled to the far side. As the others joined him, lying on their bellies and peeking over the roof's ridge, he pointed across a field of parsel weed, over a wide lane, to a warehouse, imposing for its sheer size, looming in the light of the newly risen moon.

Two guards stood at the entrance. The color and style of their robes were similar to that of the cultists in Hearthvale but slightly more elaborate in design, made of finer cloth, with a blazing sun on the chest.

"They appear . . . capable," Xamus observed. These guards were big, sturdy of build, erect in posture, with booted feet and curved swords on their hips.

"True," Torin said. "Not like those milksops in the foothills."

"Well," Wilhelm said, "now that you know where to find 'em, I guess it's time for me to—hey, where's your friend?"

Oldavei, at the opposite end, looked to see that Nicholas was not next to him. He craned his neck, took several sniffs at the air, and set his eyes on the warehouse roof. "There," he said.

The others followed his gaze, seeing nothing at first, then just the slightest movement atop the structure, a shifting shade, there and gone. Soon after, a flitting shape crossed the lane, like the shadow of a bird in flight.

An instant later, as quietly as he had left, Nicholas returned.

"Trying to collect the bounty for yourself?" Oldavei asked.

"Not at all," Nicholas said. "Especially with nine armed guards inside."

"Nine?" Torin said.

"That I could see through the skylight," Nicholas replied. "There may be more."

"Any sign of Braun?" Xamus asked.

"No, but there were areas I could not see," Nicholas answered.

Oldavei looked to Torin and Xamus. "Having an extra sword arm tonight could come in handy," he said. "We know he can fight."

Wilhelm looked over, surprised. "Tonight? You want to do this now?"

"I vote we do," Oldavei answered. "We've no idea if Braun's there or not, but if he is, we can't risk him leaving." He looked to Torin. "You drank more than the rest of us, what say you?"

Torin released a rumbling belch and said, "I say we get to it. I fight better when I'm drunk anyhow."

"Tonight it is," Xamus said. Then to Wilhlelm, "How about you, bard? You in?"

"Well . . . yeah, I could use the extra coin," Wilhelm replied. "Trying to save up for the Bard-In Festival entry fee."

"Ooh," Oldavei said, "Bard-In! The biggest, loudest, most rollicking festival in all of Lawbrand! At least I think it was. I drank enough to drown a bison."

"Sounds like someplace I need to visit," Torin said.

"First things first," Xamus said. "Right now we need to come up with a plan to kill Taron Braun."

CHAPTER EIGHT
BRAINS VERSUS BRAUN

The large pane of the skylight was levered into a raised position midway along the warehouse's shallow-pitched roof. Xamus and Nicholas crouched low, peering in. The periphery of the voluminous space was packed with stacked crates and boxes of varying shape and size.

Along the center of the space ran a wide, long table, lit by rows of candelabra. One cultist on each side removed items from crates at the table's end—what appeared to be woven and studded leather armor. The cultists passed the pieces to companions next to them, who inspected the items, then handed them to the next in line, who wrote on a parchment and transferred to a fourth, who placed the item in any one of a number of open crates. The eight men at the table appeared unarmed.

Maneuvering silently, Xamus changed position to afford him a better view of the warehouse's back end, where a set of wooden steps led to an enclosed room atop timber supports.

Two men walked down the wooden stairs, talking. One of them, tall and thin, wore an ornate amber robe, scimitar on his hip. Next to him, similarly armed, was Taron Braun. Xamus pointed; Nicholas nodded in acknowledgment. The robed men conversed at the bottom of the stairs for a moment. Braun then reascended the steps while the tall man went to supervise the workers at the table.

Without a sound, Nicholas lowered himself onto a thick tie beam and crawled out to make room for Xamus, whose added weight caused the timber to creak. The men below, absorbed in their work, took no notice. From their new position, Xamus and Nicholas noted that the back room was accessed by a door at the top of the stairs, with a paneless window looking out over the warehouse floor.

For the moment, the two men crouched and waited.

Outside, between the warehouse and the wide lane, near the structure's back end, Wilhelm stood. He began plucking his mandolin, drawing the attention of the two guards at the front, who appeared, shouting, "You there! Stop that!" and "What's your business?"

Wilhelm sang, turning and walking to the rear:

A virtuous young maid named Anne . . .

He quickened the tempo as he skirted a pile of broken crates.

Thought she loved her man
But when he reached in, to his chagrin . . .

The bard moved to stand near a locked back door.

She knocked him senseless with a pan!

As the guards came round the crate pile, Torin and Oldavei sprang, coldcocking both men with the pommels of their weapons, rendering them unconscious. Wilhelm took from one of the guards' belts a set of keys, then gagged them and bound them with rope taken from the garden toolshed.

Torin, now in possession of Oldavei's travel bag, tossed the men's weapons across the lane into the parsel weed, while Oldavei undertook his change from ma'ii to coyote, to the obvious astonishment of Wilhelm, who stood with his arms at his sides, mouth open.

As Torin returned and Oldavei completed his transformation, Wilhelm said, "I, uh, I thought you were just fekkin' with me when you said he could do that."

"Understandable, but no," Torin said, waiting. Oldavei looked up at Wilhelm expectantly, tongue lolling, tail wagging. Torin pointed at Wilhelm's left hand. "Keys," he said.

"Oh!" Wilhelm replied. "Yeah." He inserted the keys one by one until the backdoor lock clicked. He then opened the door wide enough for Oldavei to dart in.

Atop their spot on the beam, Xamus and Nicholas witnessed the arrival of Oldavei, who ran about near the legs of the men at the table, attracting their attention, along with that of the armed supervisor.

"There's our distraction," Nicholas said. The assassin then leaped nimbly from one beam to the next, making his way rearward. Xamus watched, impressed. The elf's own dexterity was not inconsiderable, but the acrobatics of the assassin far outstripped his own abilities, so he resignedly lowered himself onto a crate stack and set about dashing across their tops toward the back room.

Oldavei led the cultists on a merry chase, running in between crates and back and forth under the long table. The supervisor stomped his way to the back door. "Who the hell let this—" a hefty punch from just outside by Wilhelm rocked the tall man onto his heels, and the follow-up blow laid him out flat.

A cry arose from one of the distracted cultists. "Unbelievers!"

"Heathens!" another declared.

Xamus launched from the crates to the foot of the stairs and surged upward, taking steps two at a time. Nicholas dropped from above and raced after, sword drawn.

Taron Braun had risen from a desk in the corner of the room and stepped around when Xamus kicked in the door. As Braun raised his hand and opened his mouth, the elf spoke a rapid incantation. Braun reared his head back, screaming at the top of his lungs, his eyes wide in disbelief. He threw both hands over his gaping mouth in an attempt to stifle the outcry.

Nicholas pushed his way in. "What's this?" he said to Xamus.

"I meant to silence him," the elf replied. "Seems to have had the opposite effect."

On the warehouse floor near the crates Xamus had jumped from, Torin brained one cultist with the flat of his axe and dropped another with a leaping headbutt to the jaw as the acolyte rushed in. The wailing of Taron Braun temporarily distracted a third, who then shouted at Torin, "A great and terrible power rises in the east! You will be purged!" He drew a curved blade from within his robes and charged. Torin slashed, connecting axe blade to dagger blade, knocking the knife from the cultist's grasp, then spun and swung low, smashing the butt of the axe on the attacker's shin, sending him screaming face-first into the floorboards.

Wilhelm, gushing blood from a battered nose, his glasses trampled beneath him, had already felled one acolyte and now traded vicious blows with two others on the opposite side of the table. The heftiest of the two spat a tooth and proclaimed, "The Great Prophet will remake civilization!" just before Wilhelm feigned a left punch and caught him in the temple with a crushing right.

Oldavei, still in coyote form, chewed on the wrist of a screaming cultist, the two of them spinning in circles at the end of the table closest to the front door, while a second cultist tried to grab the ma'ii by the tail.

In the corner room, Nicholas stood poised to decapitate the doubled-over, still-screaming leader. "What are you waiting for?" Xamus asked, drawing his own blade.

"I don't—I don't think I can," Nicholas said as Braun's cries began to fade.

"Remember you," Braun said in a choked voice, "foul creature." Xamus raised his own blade. Braun straightened. "Light consume you!" He clenched his right fist, around which appeared a dazzling light that temporarily blinded Xamus while a similar, pure-white luminescence flashed just in front of Nicholas, causing him to drop his sword and clutch his head. Braun bolted, tucking and rolling even as Xamus swung for where his neck had been an instant before. The leader sprang up onto the windowsill and jumped from there down onto the floor, where he rolled once again and bolted upright, drawing his scimitar.

Wilhelm, who had just downed his final opponent, spun and bared his blade. Scimitar and longsword clashed as Braun sped forward. The leader's blow knocked Wilhelm's sword aside; a backswing with the pommel caught the bard behind the ear as Braun raced for the door. Wilhelm stumbled into the table, caught himself, turned, and felt a breeze on his left cheek as a whirling object flew past. The spinning axe buried itself high in Braun's back just to the left of the spine. The leader arched, stumbling to a halt, reaching feebly upward with his left hand. Crimson spewed from his mouth, his hand fell limp, and he pitched forward and was still. For a moment there was silence as Torin strode past Wilhelm to reclaim his weapon.

The acolyte who had been grabbing for Oldavei's tail backed toward the front door, tears streaming down his cheeks. "The b-blood of the unbelievers will flow!" he said, before turning and rushing out.

Oldavei had let go of the other cultist's hand. That man stood in mute shock, staring at the body of Taron as the ma'ii shifted behind him. While Torin wrenched the axe from the leader's body, the cultist turned, too late; Oldavei, now back to normal form, lashed out with the pommel of his scimitar, striking the acolyte on the point of the chin, buckling his legs beneath him.

Torin rolled the leader over, then held out his hand toward Wilhelm. "Dagger!" he said.

The bard handed over his small blade, watching curiously as the dwarf began cutting the sigil from Taron's lapel. "What are you—"

"Proof of death," Torin said.

Xamus reached the bottom of the steps, Nicholas's arm slung over his shoulder. Torin finished his cutting, stood, handed the dagger back to Wilhelm, and deposited the sigil in a kilt pocket. He looked over the assassin as Xamus drew near. Nicholas's eyes were unfocused, appearing to see something or someone that wasn't present. "I'll never submit!" he blurted. "You won't have my soul!" He fell to muttering too low to hear.

Just then a militia captain filled the doorway, sword in hand. He stepped in, followed by two soldiers, one of whom turned and shouted, "Here! We have them here!"

Speaking just below his breath, Xamus raised his left hand. The features of the three militiamen went slack, their eyes closed, and they collapsed, fast asleep.

"I'll be damned," Torin said, acknowledging the elf with a nod. "Finally worked."

Wilhelm threw Nicholas's free arm over his shoulder, and the group made haste, stepping around the just-awakening supervisor on their way out the back door. As the remaining militia arrived at the warehouse's front, the adventurers hurried across an open lot, through a passage between two smaller structures, and on, beyond the tree line at the district border.

Beneath the leaf canopy they paused. Torin eyed Nicholas. "My life is my own," the assassin murmured. "Mine, do you hear?"

"Braun fired off a spell," Xamus said. He looked to Oldavei, "Like what you described from the foothills. Blinding light. I recovered quickly, but he"—the elf's eyes flicked to Nicholas—"didn't fare so well."

"Maybe the same spell," Oldavei said, taking his travel bag back from Torin, "but the babbling is new."

"He's out of it," Torin said. "We'll not make Hearthvale soon, and we can't lay low here. Militia knows our faces."

"We could head west along the river," Wilhelm offered, "make for Talis."

"They'll be watching the river," Torin said. "Talis might do, though, if we take back roads."

"I'm sure we could 'borrow' a small cart to carry him in if we need to," Oldavei said, motioning to Nicholas.

Torin considered, then looked to Xamus, who nodded.

Nicholas's eyes grew heavy and were now half closed. As they set off through the brush, he mumbled, "Not the end. Death is not the end," before falling silent.

CHAPTER NINE
WANTED

The Trade-City of Talis was known far and wide not only as the trade hub of Lawbrand but also as a city of free-thinking exploration and technological marvel; an awe-inspiring wonder of the age, demonstrating unparalleled feats of engineering; a place where ingenious minds had dreamed bold new methods of harnessing the mighty Talisande River. Unlike Skarborough, Talis was not simply a riverside community, and in fact, the more fanciful among tale-tellers might be forgiven for proclaiming that in Talis, the river and the City of Bridges were one, for here a complex series of interlocking canals, levees, and dikes channeled and redirected the river's waters. As the Talisande coursed its way through and around the city, so too did the vessels borne upon it, often packed in together, bow to stern, transported not just by the river's natural, slow current, but lent a human hand via a masterfully constructed system of central locks, created as a control system to regulate the flow of ships and goods. Two lanes of central locks existed, one designed for transporting ships upriver, the other down. These locks, through the raising and lowering of water levels and opening and closing of gates, elevated ships, carried them from one end of the city to the next, and deposited the vessels once again into the river on the other side. Above the city's canals, shipyards, plazas, and waterways, interconnected arches, bridges, and skywalks soared in a complex, majestic web of polished stone.

While Talis's progressive flavor served as a beacon to the greatest minds across the land, the sheer spectacle of the City of Bridges presented an irresistible lure to people from all other walks of life as well. So it was that erudite scholars and starry-eyed mystics might walk the same cobbled paths as unwashed vagrants.

In an old bathhouse in Middentown, Xamus, Torin, Wilhelm, Nicholas, and Oldavei had taken up occupancy. The room was small and musty, the wood soft, with black mold growing in the cracks and corners and nooks and crannies. Stacked beds occupied two of the walls. Oldavei, when he had slept, slept on the floor. Nicholas presently lay in one of the lowermost beds, gripped in a fitful slumber, while Torin sat at a table in the center of the room, sharpening his axe. Oldavei sat on the table's other end, one leg dangling, the other bent to his shoulder as he watched Xamus, whose chair was pulled away, facing the open window and the last fading light of the day.

Xamus spoke the words of his ancestors, gesticulating. A pinprick of flame appeared between his hands, expanding, slowly at first to the size of a human fist, then condensing rapidly before sputtering and dissipating entirely. Xamus heaved a sigh. Oldavei cleared his throat.

"My teacher once told me," He said, "the key to wild magic is in understanding that nature is chaos."

"Hmm," Xamus replied. He flexed his fingers and began the familiar motions once again, reciting words of power, contemplating the inherent instability of the ball of fire he was attempting to conjure and control. The spark of heat and fire ignited, guttered, then held, burning intensely. Xamus smiled as the flame roiled and spun between his hands, heating his palms, its light glinting in his eyes. But his grin slackened as the ball grew rapidly, flaring outward, causing him to jerk his head backward as the flames singed the brim of his hat.

"Not the hat, not the hat!" he protested, dispelling the fire.

The elf removed his hat, examining the toasted brim. He narrowed his gaze at Oldavei. "Your teacher didn't really tell you that, did he?"

The ma'ii drew up, hopped off the table, and placed a hand on Xamus's shoulder.

"Actually, what my teacher said was: 'If you have half a brain, stay away from wild magic; it's dangerous.'" As Xamus brushed Oldavei's hand off his shoulder, the ma'ii continued: "Perhaps there's a lesson to be learned here: play with fire and we might all get burned!"

"Can't believe a fekkin' thing he says!" Torin grumbled in the midst of his sharpening.

Nicholas's voice then sounded from behind the dwarf. "What's happened?" The assassin sat up, rubbing at his temples.

"Braun's attack took quite a toll," Xamus said, coming to stand in front of him. "After that light spell he cast, you became dazed." He looked to the dwarf, who had stopped sharpening and was turned in his seat. "Torin finished him, though, and we brought you here."

"To Talis," Oldavei said, standing now beside Xamus.

"Three days!" Torin blurted. "Been stuck here for three bloody days!"

Nicholas looked about the room. Sounding mildly alarmed, he said, "Where's Wilhelm, is he—"

"He's fine," Oldavei said, holding up a placating hand. "Just figured maybe he'd try his luck with the mandolin tonight, make some extra coin."

Nicholas was visibly relieved. He licked dry lips, then shook his head and said, "You could have left me. You *should* have left me."

"Yeah, well, us lowlifes gotta stick together," Xamus answered. He looked to Torin, who grunted, a sound the elf took for begrudging approval.

"Anyway, you would have done the same, right?" Oldavei said, offering a wide, pointy-toothed grin.

When Nicholas didn't answer, Xamus said, "You talked a bit. While you were . . ." he searched for the right word and settled on "afflicted."

The elf couldn't tell whether Nicholas paled slightly or if it was a trick from the candle Torin lit at the table. "What did I say?" the assassin asked.

"Talked about your life, your soul," Xamus said. "You said death wasn't the end."

Now Xamus was sure of it, Nicholas *had* paled.

Oldavei said, "It was like you were talking to someone who wasn't there. Rest of the night, when we brought you here, you kept on, but most of it was too low to hear."

"Any of this related to your hesitation in killing Braun?" Xamus asked.

"Taking a life is no easy thing," Nicholas said. "Still, I'm not sure why I faltered."

"Anything more you want to tell us?" Oldavei asked.

An internal struggle was evidenced in Nicholas, in the wringing of his hands, the lowering of his gaze, and the tight pressing of his lips. Finally he said, "Clearly I was rattled by the spell. Talking nonsense. I'm thankful for your aid. Did you take proof of death?"

"Yep," Torin answered. "Have it right—"

The dwarf was interrupted by Wilhelm bursting into the room. The bard stomped in, dropping his mandolin on the small table on his way to Xamus and Oldavei. He waved a parchment in his hand. "Found this shit outside a tavern," he said, thrusting the item at Xamus.

The elf looked down to see a wanted poster, with all of their faces crudely rendered on the upper half. The lower half read FUGITIVES WANTED FOR THE MURDER OF INNOCENTS IN SKARBOROUGH AND HEARTHVALE. SUBSTANTIAL REWARD OFFERED BY THE SULARIAN ORDER-MILITANT. A blocky scripted signature at the bottom read "KNIGHT-PALADIN, IRONSIDE."

"Just look at this shit!" Wilhelm said. "Look at my face!"

Xamus glanced at the bard. "No," Wilhelm said, "on the poster!"

The elf looked down at the poster as Wilhelm continued, "Does *that* man look ruggedly handsome to you? They couldn't even get my face right!"

"I'd say we have bigger problems," Xamus said.

"That's a glaring understatement," Nicholas said, standing. "This isn't just militia. This is a Knight-Paladin of the Order-Militant, sanctioned by the Sularian Church to stamp out evil in whatever form it's deemed to reside by any means necessary. Unlike militia and their local jurisdictions, the Knight-Paladins enjoy a broad-reaching mandate, allowing them to operate freely across the entirety of Lawbrand." He came around to Xamus. "And Ironside . . . I've heard of him," he said in a low voice, taking the poster. "He and his band of Enforcers are feared and hated in equal measure. Ironside is said to be tireless in pursuit of his quarry and merciless in his disbursement of justice." He handed the poster back to Xamus. "This is disastrous."

"I don't understand the charges," Xamus said. "We only killed Braun."

"Mm, there was that cultist in the foothills you set on fire," Torin pointed out.

"I only blinded him," Xamus corrected. "He set *himself* on fire when he ran into the nearest blaze. Still, for this 'Ironside' to take such action seems . . . excessive."

"We just need to get to Raldon," Oldavei said. "Show him the job's done so we can be paid, and he can set things right with the Knight-Paladin."

"And what if it's Raldon who's levied the charges?" Nicholas asked.

After a moment of considered silence, Xamus asked, "To what purpose? To not pay our second half? It's not his coin. He's little more than an administrator. The Trade-Guilds wield the true power."

"The guilds and the church," Torin put in.

"Yeah. So if this does come from higher up," Xamus said, "then I think Oldavei's right, we should go back to Hearthvale, speak to Raldon."

The elf cast his eyes about the room. One by one, the others nodded. When he looked to Wilhelm, the bard said, "I know someone. Name's Trevon. We worked for a stretch as deckhands on a galleon a few years ago. Last I heard, he has his own little merchant boat now. And . . . I heard he's not against a little smuggling."

"You want him to smuggle *us*," Oldavei said.

"Might not be easy to go upriver, but once we're past the city gates, we could grab an oar and help out, probably get there a lot quicker and stay off the roads," Wilhelm replied.

"Would you trust him?" Xamus asked. "Even with a reward in the offing?"

"Yeah, man, I trust him," Wilhelm answered, making for the door. "I saved his life once."

PART ONE: NOTHIN' BUT TROUBLE...

★ ★ ★

Come first light they were on the move. A short trek along the southernmost canal saw them to a stair tower. Up the spiral steps and onto a span they walked, stopping midway to where the bridge ended at the next tower.

Southward stood a mountain of stone, what was at one time a fort—now the headquarters of the local constabulary, the Bridge-Keepers—the flags mounted atop its turrets hanging lifeless in the still air. A bustling plaza lay at the foot of the structure, stretching beneath the span, giving way to a dock and slips with various small vessels—cogs with sails furled, barges stacked with massive, lashed crates. A narrow waterway led from the marina to one of Talis's southernmost canals, where ships of all sizes queued up, waiting to merge with other vessels bound upriver. Behind the canal, a steep levee rose; just beyond the wall, the upper reaches of large trade vessels inside the locks creaked, clusters of towering masts straining from their decks to the cloudless sky.

As each member of the party laid hands on the waist-high bridge wall, looking out, their attention was drawn by a piercing shriek from directly above. All eyes rose to see a falcon circling in the brightening sky. Not thinking much of it, the observers returned their gaze to the northern vista of ships and waterways and towers and spans before looking to a single vessel moored in the slip just below, a two-masted schooner where a long-haired lean man in a light shirt and breeches fidgeted with a small hatchet, casting his eyes about the marina.

"That's Trevon," Wilhelm said, pointing.

"*This* was the only slip available?" Nicholas asked, casting a wary glance over his shoulder. "Across from the Bridge-Keepers?"

"I told you, I trust him," Wilhelm said. "Besides, this is where craft bound upriver moor."

Torin, pointing over the wall, turned to Xamus. "He look nervous to you?"

Indeed the man did appear anxious, fidgeting with a hatchet, continuing to scan his surroundings, casting his gaze all about, finally looking up to notice Wilhelm and the others. His eyes widened slightly. He reached up, scratching the right side of his head.

"That's not good," Wilhelm said. "He's signaling us."

"Signaling what?" Oldavei asked.

"Danger," Wilhelm replied.

CHAPTER TEN

IRONSIDE

The falcon cried once more and flew for the fort, over a crenellated parapet and into the recesses of a darkened archway.

The group, who had crossed the bridge to watch the falcon, reacted to a noise on their right. There, a behemoth ducked and turned sideways to fit through the stair-tower door. It was an ogre, or it appeared to be; the layers of plate mail the giant wore made it difficult to discern, and its features were hidden behind a visored helm. A long, thin tunic hung over the warrior's armor, black, trimmed in silver. The plated brute carried an iron-headed maul that he casually laid over one shoulder as he advanced two steps and held fast.

To the left, a strongly muscled figure emerged from the stair tower. His facial features were primal yet elegant: a flattened nose, prominent brow, and gently curving horns sweeping back from high on the forehead on either side. He was a satyr, cloven-hooved, with digitigrade legs coated in beige fur exposed below the thigh. The rest of his body was clad entirely in dark brown leather, including a three-finger shooting glove on his right hand. He wore a tunic identical to that of his colleague. Morning sunlight reflected off the facets of a green gem amulet resting upon his chest. A quiver of expertly crafted arrows slung on his back complemented the polished-wood longbow in his left hand. As with the warrior, the archer proceeded only a few strides before halting.

At the fort, a tall, thin woman issued from the arches, dressed in cloth and the now familiar black tunic, a short sword on her hip. Her sleek black hair was tied in a tail. She wore a long-cuffed leather glove on her left hand and held that hand up and away from her body, for perched on the glove was the previously glimpsed falcon, its long talons dug in. With a swagger like royalty, chin held high, and the hint of a smile on her face, the falconer strode to the parapet.

Oldavei looked left, right, then to the fort and called out, "Is there a problem, officers?"

A deep voice, its origin undetermined, boomed in response, "Hand your weapons to the ogre."

Nicholas stepped forward. "There's been a misunderstanding," he said. "We're operating lawfully under the aegis of Hearthvale Magistrate Raldon Rhelgore."

"You mean this fool?" the voice piped. Raldon stumbled out of the arches as if pushed. He was gagged, greased hair in disarray, blood running from a broken nose onto his robes, his hands manacled before him.

The speaker strode forth next, crystal blue eyes piercing the distance between them from within a wide, fur-lined hood. He stepped slowly, deliberately, the steadfastness and self-assurance of his gait reflected in his chiseled features—high cheek bones, angular jaw, and short beard, gray on the sides. Over a black chain-mail tunic he wore a silver breastplate polished to such brightness that it gleamed in the rising sun. Emblazoned upon its face was the Sularian Cross, or the Lawbrand, a cross bearing a small circle at the intersection, with short segments of a larger broken circle at the extremities of the arms and stem. It was the symbol of both the church and the land. Completing the commander's attire was the fur-fringed cape, draped over one shoulder. In his left hand he carried a stout great-headed flanged mace.

"Ironside," Nicholas said for the others to hear.

"Bears little resemblance to the old, glorified paladins I've heard tales of," Xamus said.

"Times change," Nicholas answered.

The commander shoved Raldon to the parapet and stopped just behind. "I'll say it once more and once more only," Ironside called in a stentorian bass: "Give your weapons to Gundr."

"Raldon's the one who hired us!" Oldavei shouted back. "If you just remove the gag, he can—"

Ironside switched the mace to his right hand, raised it cross-body, and swung down in a crushing arc, burying the blade flanges into the left side of the Magistrate's neck. Blood gushed from both the grisly wound and from Raldon's mouth, soaking the gag. Ironside ripped the mace away and kicked Raldon in the back, knocking him to the wall, where he collapsed onto a crenel, eyes glazed, before sliding down and out of sight.

"I'm sorry, were you speaking?" Ironside replied.

"Fek's sake," Oldavei breathed.

"Raldon's sins were among the most grievous," Ironside called. "Obstruction of justice. Taking the law into his own hands. He damned himself and, in so doing, he damned you."

A light breeze lifted, stirring the commander's cape and the flags atop the turrets; the wind blew, Nicholas noted, from west to east.

"You have been judged." He raised the mace, pointing it at them. "And found guilty!"

Xamus evaluated the greatest threat. Gundr, the ogre, would have to close the distance, while the archer suffered no such restriction. The elf began whispering a sleep spell beneath his breath. Casting a sideways glance, he caught the slightest glimmer off the amulet dangling from the archer's neck—not sunlight this time. The satyr glared back at Xamus and gave a knowing smirk. *That amulet,* Xamus thought, *was enchanted to guard against magical attack.*

"Daromis!" Ironside bellowed. The archer drew an arrow, nocked . . .

At that instant it was Nicholas who reversed their immediate fortune; the assassin had dug into a pouch on his belt, retrieved two items, and now cast them to the limestone at their feet. A gush of air accompanied an erupting cloud of smoke that quickly engulfed them. "On me!" Nicholas barked, rushing to the wall behind, feeling his way along the coping as the smoke bank drifted toward the archer. Thunderous, clanking footfalls vibrated the span, signaling the charge of Gundr, as Nicholas reached his desired spot, whispered huskily, "This way," and vaulted over the low wall, dropping onto the uppermost crate on the barge moored beside the schooner. From there Nicholas leaped over the narrow finger dock onto the deck of the next vessel in line, a cog. Xamus trailed just behind, reaching the cog while Wilhelm fell to the crate and stepped toward the schooner.

"I didn't give you up, I swear," Trevon called.

As Oldavei dropped next to him, Wilhelm simply nodded and said, "Hatchet!" pointing to the implement in the sailor's hand.

Oldavei made for the cog as Torin dropped next. Trevon threw the hatchet and said, "Good fortune to you!"

At the cog, Oldavei assisted Torin, who had barely made the leap, onto the deck. Wilhelm jumped beside them, crossed the deck, hopped onto the opposite gunwale, and sprang onto the paving stones of the plaza walkway. Xamus and the others paused as the bard rushed to the tower from which Gundr and Daromis would no doubt soon emerge. Indeed he heard footfalls from the steps within as he tossed down the hatchet, blade facing out, and kicked, wedging it beneath the closed door.

Screams drew all eyes to the fort, where Ironside thundered onto the plaza, shoving panicking denizens aside and shouting in an effort to disburse the crowd.

The tower door shuddered from a push, then rocked from repeated blows.

Xamus looked for an escape path along the plaza walk, but there just in front of the market stalls, members of the crowd parted, revealing another of Ironside's Enforcers.

It was a stooped, squatting old crone, humpbacked, with stringy white hair that hung to the stones. Her right arm, withered and unnaturally bent, was held close to her body. She wore little more than a rag-dress and no shoes or stockings; as with the others, she was draped in a black tunic.

"That's no good," Xamus muttered. On the waterway to his left, he spotted a cutter close to the walkway wall. The vessel was manned by a sailor at the aft with a setting pole, pushing to join the queue of upriver-bound craft. "Here!" Xamus shouted to the others, bounding from the walkway onto the surprised sailor's boat, then leaping off the opposite side, keeping his head above water as he swam for the canal dividing wall.

Ironside had cleared half the distance between them, charging like an enraged bull as Oldavei, Nicholas, Torin, and Wilhelm followed Xamus. Wilhelm leaped to the cutter and dove into the water on the other side, while not far away, the tower door exploded outward. Gundr stormed forth with Daromis close behind.

Wilhelm proved a strong swimmer and reached the dividing wall just as Xamus hoisted himself up. The elf immediately leaped from the wall onto the deck of a slender yawl, with the bard on his heels. One of the surprised sailors took a swipe at Xamus, provoking a shove from Wilhelm that sent the man overboard. Oldavei gained the deck next, twisting to shake off the water in the manner of a dog. He then held up his hands to the incredulous sailor. "Sorry to intrude!" he said, smiling.

Xamus rushed to the bow of the boat and jumped from there onto the stern of the next boat in line, another cutter, taking just enough time to glance upward in response to a falcon cry from above. In that instant, sunlight glinted off a metal object—small, starlike in shape, that flew like an arrow, ripping through one of the raptor's wings. The bird floundered, then dove awkwardly.

"Bolo!" a female voice called out.

Xamus looked to see the falconer, stepping onto the deck of a skiff two boats ahead on the canal. Her winged companion hurtled down, striking the woman's outheld glove with force. The falconer drew her short sword, murder in her eyes as she stalked toward the bow of the skiff.

"Good shot!" Torin remarked to Nicholas as the assassin pulled him onto the dividing wall. As they stood, a danger sense alerted the assassin; his hand shot out, snatching one of Daromis's arrows in midflight, its razor tip a thumb's width from Torin's head. The wide-eyed dwarf gave the assassin a hasty nod before jumping to the yawl.

Nicholas was in midleap when he felt a sharp impact and a searing pain in his back, between the ribs on his left side. He landed on the yawl deck, wincing, and turned to look at the plaza where a cluster of the startled crowd rushed, blocking Daromis's next shot. Nicholas reached back, ignoring the angry shouts of the yawl sailor and snapped the arrow in half, close to where the shaft pierced his skin. He then spotted Xamus. The elf and the ma'ii were climbing a ladder just ahead, anchored to the levee that separated the canal from the locks. One last backward glance showed a loaded barge on the waterway now crossing in front of Daromis's position, providing a narrow window of safety while the archer relocated to line up his next shot.

At the plaza market, the shouts and cries of the patrons rang out; Ironside raced through, shoving men, women, and children out of his path, knocking some into the water. Torin, looking over his shoulder, muttered, "Crazy fekker!" and climbed the levee ladder.

Gundr, unseen by Xamus and the others, came to stand near the crone, who clambered up the left side of his armor and onto his back. With the hag thus mounted, the ogre sought out the nearest stair tower.

The top of the levee wall was wide enough to accommodate four people abreast. There, dockworkers toiled among crates, barrels, and coiled ropes, operating the machinery that opened and closed the lock gates and the great wheels that regulated the raising and lowering of the water levels. Currently, laborers gripped and strained at multiple thick ropes, the opposite ends held fast to capstans aboard a massive frigate. The men braced, checking the ship's forward progress as it was moved into position for lowering and proceeding to the next lock. The fugitives, having gained the wall top, ran headlong, behind the workmen, eastward toward the gatekeeper and the stairs that led down to the next lock level.

As the group rushed along the wall, Nicholas, at the back, kept an eye south on the canal and plaza market. They ran far enough to the lock side that below, Daromis could not venture a shot. However, movement on a bridge high above the market and nearly at their same level caught his eye.

"The bridge!" Nicholas shouted, pointing.

The others slowed long enough to see the crone, her good arm wrapped around Gundr's shoulder, feet set on his hips, her white hair waving in the wind, at the halfway point of the bridge. Though he could not hear the words, Xamus knew she was chanting. As they watched, one by one, sparks flared to life in a high arch above her head. Each expanded to the size of a quarry giant's fist. The spheres were wreathed in green fire and held a black essence at their core that unsettled the elf. "Run! Run! Run!" he shouted.

The strange fireballs streaked across the sky as the group ran full tilt past a cluster of massive casks on their right side. The projectiles impacted, igniting the wooden barrels. Black stains along the rim and head hoops of the casks provided indication of the contents within: oil.

"Hurry, for fek's sake!" Torin shouted, pumping his shorter legs faster than ever before, his heart feeling as though it would rupture in his chest. The fugitives sprinted headlong past the gatekeeper to the stone steps leading to the lower lock, having just initiated their frantic descent when the casks blew.

The resultant explosion was cataclysmic.

The blast propelled the gatekeeper down into the next lock. The wide staircase shook as though the earth itself was set to crack open. Of the five fugitives, only Nicholas and Xamus kept their footing.

Flaming bodies of dockworkers atop the levee were blown in all directions. The frigate's entire starboard side was largely demolished, the ship set afire. A jagged seam split the wall beneath where the casks had sat. At the midway point of the levee, workers from the accompanying lock had rushed in, feverishly spinning wheels to drain the lock's water, but too late; a fissure ran down the wall from the explosion site, water streaming through the breach. The canal boats drew alongside the market walkway, and all crew, including the falconer, abandoned ship.

Farther ahead in the canal, a strange craft, unlike any Xamus had previously seen, made for the open gate. The vessel, its deck laden with animals of every description, was close enough for Xamus and the others to attain in a desperate leap. From the staircase they flew, one by one, Wilhelm landing on the deck just as the levee wall farther behind failed. Goliath chunks of masonry broke loose, the entire section of levee wall giving way, collapsing amid a deafening clamor, smashing the canal ships to pieces.

The market-goers scattered like leaves in a whirlwind. Ironside slid to a halt and took evasive action as the frigate in the gushing lock listed and swung about, sailors jumping free; the flaming ship nosed out over the canal, then rode the behemoth wave of emptying lock water down, the bowsprit snapping like kindling as the vessel's upper half sheared off at the heap of levee debris and skidded out and onto the market walk. The three towering masts held vertical for a breathless instant before teetering to the west and crashing down, the foremast tumbling onto the market walk, the mainmast and mizzenmast shivering and splintering on the jagged chunks of fallen levee. Fires that had diminished as the disaster unfolded now flared anew amid the tangled wreckage.

Riding the tidal upsurge, the curious craft bearing Xamus and the others raced on toward the gate, while from the afterdeck, surrounded by panicked wildlife, the fugitives looked back to see Ironside. He was standing just this side of the ship's ruin, backlit by flame, hood lowered to reveal long hair with streaks of gray, his eyes glittering with hatred and determination . . . but most of all with single-minded purpose.

PART ONE: NOTHIN' BUT TROUBLE...

PART TWO

OUTLAWS

CHAPTER ELEVEN
FLIGHT

"We are right and squarely fekked," Torin said, staring back at the diminishing visage of Ironside and the wreckage, where black smoke funneled skyward from growing fires and the tidal surge of the collapse still wreaked havoc, capsizing craft both farther along the canal and in the marina. "Might be better off," the dwarf continued, "if not for your so-called friend," he added, throwing Wilhelm a hard look.

"He warned us!" the bard protested.

"After he set us up!" Torin argued. "Damn near got us killed!"

"He said he didn't give us up, and I believe him," Wilhelm replied, stepping closer, looking down at the dwarf. "It was likely the falcon spotted us on our way to the marina."

Before Torin could reply, Xamus cut in: "Doesn't matter," he said. "Stay sharp, the main gates are ahead."

The craft pushed on, past the remaining structures on the outskirts of Talis, toward what was called the main gates—in fact, four massive barriers that currently lay submerged beneath the water, each capable of being raised to a forty-five degree angle to either aid in regulating the river flow or to block off incoming or outgoing ships.

"Think they'll stop us?" Oldavei asked. All eyes stared ahead. The lookouts on the bridge above the lowered gates were in a state of frantic activity, shouting, running, some pointing to the collapsed levee.

"I'd say they're a bit distracted just now," Xamus said.

A raspy voice carried to them from midships: "I can't be harborin' fugitives!" A short, white-bearded, hunched old captain stepped from behind an ostrich pen.

Torin stormed forward, axe drawn, scattering chickens and smaller fowl. He thrust the short spike that jutted from the eye of his axe under the old man's chin. "You keep quiet and hold her steady, or I'll carve you like one o' them turkeys," Torin said, canting his head toward the fowl.

"Them's roosters," the captain replied. Torin pressed upward, lifting the man's chin. "Yeah, o' course, call 'em what you like! On we go!" he said, offering a feeble smile.

Xamus took the opportunity to more closely inspect the vessel. There was not a mast in sight. Stepping around a goat to the port side, he leaned over the gunwale to get a closer look at a feature he had glimpsed earlier: at the midpoint of the hull, a large paddle wheel propelled the craft forward. For the life of him, however, he could not determine what force was powering the wheel. At his shoulder, Oldavei said, "There's one on the other side too."

Xamus turned to look across the deck but was distracted at the sight of Nicholas, faced outward, leaning against the taffrail, head drooping. A small amount of blood stained the deck at his feet. The elf rushed over, eyes widening at the jagged bit of shaft jutting from the muscle on the left side of his back. Wilhelm, who had been fixated on the barrier-gate bridge, noticed and said, "Oh fek!"

Torin had turned from where he stood. Next to him the captain spoke urgently, "Come! Come!" and beckoned, motioning toward the portside cargo hatch.

Nicholas insisted he could walk on his own as the others led him to the hatch, with Xamus taking one last look at the main gate bridge just before the vessel passed beneath. So caught up were the guards in the disaster at the levee, none appeared to even notice the ship's transit.

Down in the hold, amid the myriad animal odors and noises, Xamus's confusion regarding the paddles was addressed—for there, individual oxen yoked to capstan bars moved in slow circles, turning the upright cylinder, which, Xamus had no doubt, in turn produced the revolution of the outside paddle wheels. The oxen and capstans were positioned midships, to both port and starboard.

"I've bandages back here," the captain called, waiting for one of the oxen to pass through the center of the hold before continuing aft into the darkened recesses. The others followed, proceeding just as carefully, attempting to avoid not only the oxen but the droppings left by the other animals: pigs, hares, sheep, numerous fowl, and yet more goats.

At the far end the captain opened a battered chest. Inside were cloth wrappings beneath a wooden bowl of salve. The old man stepped away, stopping near Nicholas, glancing down. His reaction mirrored what the others already knew: the injury was a grievous one. "I'd best see to steerin' the ship," he said, heading for the hatch.

Nicholas moved unsteadily, and a light sheen coated his skin. He displaced a protesting lamb, leaned against a stack of crates, and said, "Go ahead and . . . pull it out."

Each member of the group looked to the other, silently dissenting . . . though Oldavei especially looked as if he wished to intervene yet thought better of it. Subsequent rounds of nonverbal evasion continued until Torin finally sighed in defeat. Xamus handed his flask to Nicholas, who took a hefty pull, nodded his thanks, and handed it back.

Torin put his right hand to Nicholas's shoulder, his left hovering near the broken shaft. "Might do more damage on the way out than it did goin' in," the dwarf warned.

"Just do it," Nicholas growled.

Torin gripped tightly with thumb and forefinger, losing purchase on the first attempt due to the blood. He wiped his fingers on his kilt, tried again, and felt the shaft give a finger's width. Nicholas snarled. Torin steeled himself, squeezed tight, and pulled with all his force. Nicholas gave one last prolonged grunt of pain as the arrow pulled free. With the obstruction removed, a steady flow of blood pumped from the open wound. "Bandages!" Torin ordered, pressing hard against the arrow hole.

"Wait!" Oldavei blurted, pushing the dwarf out of the way. "Bandages won't stop it, but I might." He closed his eyes and whispered a series of words below his breath, pushing his palm against the wound. The others watched and felt a slight, inexplicable draft of cool air. After a moment, Oldavei opened his eyes and removed his hand. The blood had stopped.

Torin stepped in, pulling up the back of Nicholas's shirt to see that the wound had scabbed over. "A healer!" the dwarf proclaimed, making it sound like an accusation. "You!" He waved his hands like a conjurer. "Mister Holy Man all of a sudden!"

Oldavei backed up a step, looking mildly sick. "No no no, look, you don't understand. I haven't done this in—I don't like to do it, okay? I'm not even good at it! That's why I turned my back on it a long time ago, but I couldn't just let creepy here die, so I did it . . ." His shoulders slumped. "What I couldn't heal, though, is the damage that's been done *inside*."

Xamus considered briefly why Oldavei had taken such an interest in the nature of wild magic . . . what the ma'ii did was a completely different kind of magic, and yet—the elf understood, or at least thought he did: maybe Oldavei had difficulty controlling his magic. Was that why he said he didn't like to do it? Xamus stowed the information away for the time being.

All eyes were staring at the ma'ii as Nicholas turned, pulling his shirt down. "I'll mend," he said. "It'll be fine." He gave Oldavei a pointed look, as if seeing him for the first time. "Thank you." Then to the others he said, "We should discuss what to do next."

When he didn't receive an answer, Nicholas cleared his throat.

"Yeah," Wilhelm said, still gazing at Oldavei. "Yeah we oughta debark soon, before hitting any ports or checkpoints."

"But where to?" Xamus asked. "Hearthvale's out."

"As are all the Trade-Cities," Torin said. "Or any place else, for that matter. We're fugitives, for fek's sake! Do you honestly think there's any place we can go that Ironside and his lapdogs can't find us?"

"I may know a place," Oldavei said. "I've heard tales—do you know of Kannibus Hills?"

"*What* hills?" Wilhelm replied, brightening.

"Kannibus Hills," Xamus broke in. "I know of it. A druid commune that's said to offer sanctuary to outcasts and wanderers."

"And fugitives?" Torin said.

"Maybe," Xamus replied.

"Do you know where to find it?" Wilhelm asked.

Xamus shook his head.

"I know the general area," Oldavei said. "Maybe five days' journey after we debark."

"Five days . . ." Torin said.

"And . . ." Oldavei continued.

"And what?" Torin demanded.

"And from what I've heard, this isn't a place that you necessarily find. More like *it* finds *you*."

"Ah, perfect then!" Torin said. "Five days' journey to some mythical fantasy land in the hopes that it finds us before Ironside does."

"Yeah, this is crazy," Nicholas spoke up. "We're better off going our separate ways. Easier to hide individually than as a group."

"Until they sniff you out," Wilhelm replied. "If they do, and you don't have a small army at your back—"

"And you're in no condition to be going *anywhere* on your own," Oldavei added.

Wilhelm said, "We could make it if we stay off the highways, avoid anyone and everyone . . . travel both day and night for the first leg, then mostly at night 'til we get there."

"It won't be easy," Xamus said. "But I think Oldavei's right. There's no other place for us to go."

After a moment of silence, Torin said, "Right, fek it then. Are we agreed?"

One by one, they answered in the affirmative, save for Nicholas, who remained silent, giving only a slight nod.

★ ★ ★

Within an hour, the captain swung his vessel as close to the bank as possible. The outlaws made no mention to the old man as to their intended destination.

PART TWO: OUTLAWS

"Whatever the bastard asks when he catches up to you," Torin said to the old man, referring to Ironside, "tell him true. You didn't harbor no fugitives, 'cause we didn't give you no choice, savvy?"

The old man nodded.

"Oh, and . . . here," Torin said, handing over a palm full of coins. "For your trouble. I can't spend it right away anyhow."

The old man's eyebrows lifted. "Thank you," he said. "Fair winds! And a following sea."

One by one the group tossed their belongings onto dry land and jumped overboard, swimming to shore. The sun sunk low to the horizon as they pressed eastward, through brush and timber and tall grass. Oldavei scented the air for any indications of pursuit or of nearby hunters or camps, his keen ears listening intently while the others maintained a steady watch on the skies, alert to any sign of the dreaded falcon.

Xamus's attention, however, was divided. He monitored the skies, but he observed Nicholas also. His initial worry—that the assassin's fever might worsen, that he might experience difficulty breathing or that loss of blood *inside* his body would cause him to decline—proved unfounded. In fact, as day turned to night and their trek continued, now to the north, Nicholas took and held the lead position, guiding them unerringly over the shifting terrain, on and on until dawn broke once again in the east. The strange thing wasn't simply that the assassin's health didn't falter; it was that with each passing hour, Nicholas's health seemed to *strengthen*, even as his skin appeared—at least to the elf—to turn a lighter shade of pale.

They rested only after long stretches and for brief periods of time. By the end of the second day they sighted a small cave in the face of a stony outcropping, and there they paused at last, laying bedrolls to dry by the fire and succumbing to an exhausted sleep.

Xamus awoke hours later. In the midst of adding more wood to the fire, he noted that Nicholas was nowhere to be seen among the sleeping bodies.

So, the elf thought with a fair bit of disappointment, *he decided to chance it on his own after all.*

A figure then stepped from the cave opening into the firelight. It was Nicholas, and he had with him three dead hares. His features were stark in the flames' glow, his eyes gleaming. He gave Xamus a nod, then sat and set to work skinning one of the rabbits. Xamus began on a second hare as the others stirred. In short order the rabbits' organs were removed, their carcasses roasting on a spit. As the whiskey flask made its rounds, Wilhelm strummed his mandolin strings, humming a low melody. After a few moments, he set aside the instrument and accepted a hunk of rabbit meat.

"Where did you learn to play?" Oldavei asked.

"Believe it or not, I began with the classics," Wilhelm replied. "Chaubin. Krosky. Ballard."

"Really?" Oldavei replied with genuine interest.

"Oh yeah! In a previous life I came from a very well-to-do family. Highly regarded!" Wilhelm straightened, lifting his chin in exaggerated self-importance. "Wallaroos weren't just the talk of the town, we *were* the town!"

Oldavei chuckled. Wilhelm went on: "Had an entire community named for us, I'll have you know. Whatever's above upper class, we were it! No expense was ever spared." Wilhelm rose on one knee, thrusting out his chest. "Silver spoons? Laughable! I ate with a golden fekking shovel!"

Oldavei burst out in a cackle.

"So what happened?" Torin asked, seated across, munching on a rabbit leg.

Wilhelm sat, deflated. "Ah, I don't know. That shit just wasn't me. Always seemed like some big put-on. Never felt right. So when I got old enough, I left . . . drifted from place to place, losin' myself in the music, in the life. Tryin' to find myself, I guess."

"Did you?" Oldavei asked. "Find yourself?"

Wilhelm smiled. "The search goes on, man, the search goes on. But hey, maybe there's truth in the words of the great philosopher Rasmusen: 'When the journey to find oneself has begun, start not with how far you have to go—'"

"But look at how far you've come," Nicholas finished.

In response to the surprised reactions around him, the assassin said, "I was a schoolteacher." He looked to Wilhelm. "Also in another life." It was a significant admission by their traveling companion, who had mentioned almost nothing of himself or his personal history thus far. He reached across his chest and to his back, brushing his fingers across the wound that was now fully healed, along with the internal injuries he had sustained. "All too eager to teach," Nicholas said, his eyes and voice distant. "Yet somehow still unable to learn."

He came out of whatever reverie had claimed him, sighed, and rose. "We should keep on the move," he said, "now that we're rested and fed." Without waiting for a response, he gathered his travel kit and made for the mouth of the cave.

The sun broke once again over the far mountain ridges, though it offered scant warmth as the adventurers' journey resumed. The farther north they pressed, the more the terrain changed from expansive flatlands to gently sloping hills. Through the day and night and on they traveled, four days gone when they ventured into the midland foothills. Here shrubs and groves and tall grasses were replaced by increasingly thick forestation, with pines and alders substituted for towering oaks and cedars and fir. Here the lush, sprawling woodland became a world all its own, a place where direction became more difficult to discern, where sunlight surrendered to canopy-leaf, where hard earth turned to soft loam, where strange animal noises and the creaking and groaning of timber abounded, accompanied by the occasional cannon crack of a falling limb.

The ambient light faded and surrounding shadows darkened. Torin, who had fallen to the back of the pack, tripped on a root, cursing up a storm. Oldavei had begun to tire from maintaining his constant state of high alert, and he came to walk next to the dwarf. He remained quiet at first, though Torin discerned that he was engrossed in some deep, troubling thought.

Finally the ma'ii spoke up: "Why do you suppose he did it?"

Torin waited for Oldavei to clarify. Somewhere nearby, wood snapped. The ma'ii slowed, sniffing, then relaxed, looking at the dwarf and continuing. "Ironside, why do you think he killed Raldon?"

It was a matter to which the dwarf had in fact given a fair amount of thought. "A few reasons," he answered. "First off, I suspect the church has been conductin' its own investigations into the Children of the Sun. Raldon overstepped when he hired us. That's what Ironside was on about—'obstruction of justice' and 'takin' the law into his own hands.'" Here the dwarf hesitated. "But I think the most important reason was to teach anyone who might think about steppin' outta line a very specific and very public lesson, usin' first the poor bastard Raldon—and then us—as an example: That it's them and them alone who enforce the law. And that defyin' authority won't be—"

A host of sounds arose just then, causing the entire group to stop and draw blades. The noises seemed to come from everywhere at once, closing in, and though they undoubtedly originated from nearby, their sources could not be immediately discerned.

Suddenly the shadows around them shifted and began to take form as the entire forest appeared to come alive.

PART TWO: OUTLAWS

CHAPTER TWELVE
GOSHAEDAS

The figures appeared from apparent nothingness or perhaps from the forest itself; it was hard to tell. Oldavei stood dumbfounded, for he hadn't known that anyone or anything was there until the strangers were nearly on top of them.

Two, one on either side, appeared bestial and short in stature, and now that they had fully materialized, Oldavei detected from them a canine scent, though they possessed a humanoid form. Yet another at their rear bore a familiar odor, similar to his own—a fellow ma'ii, Oldavei surmised. To his right appeared what he judged to be a satyr, resembling Ironside's archer Daromis in appearance, though with larger, curling horns and wearing garments apparently composed of leaves. He held a small dagger.

Ahead of them a powerful voice challenged, "Friend or foe?" Oldavei squinted but saw no one. Even Xamus, with his heightened elven sight, could make out no figure in the darkness. Whoever it was, they *sounded* human.

Xamus hesitated slightly before answering: "Friends. We're . . . on the run. Unjustly accused of crimes by the Knight-Paladin Ironside. We heard rumors of a sanctuary in these hills."

For a moment there was silence, and Xamus felt as though he and his companions were being assessed. Finally the challenger answered in a softer tone, "If you come in peace, and it's refuge you seek . . ." and then a figure materialized from the foliage as it stepped forward. Even then, the only details any of them could make out were softly glowing eyes and a raised bow, the nocked arrow aimed in their direction. "Then you'll have no need of weapons," the challenger finished. Two other figures appeared from the brush, also archers, hooded and cloaked.

Xamus waited, still holding his longsword in the ready position. He glanced back to Oldavei, who nodded. "Of course," the elf answered, sheathing his sword. The others followed suit.

Seemingly satisfied, the speaker and the archers lowered their weapons. "Follow me," the challenger said and proceeded noiselessly through the timber. The gait of the leader, Xamus noted as they went, was like a jungle cat, stalking, tensed, seeming ready to pounce in an instant.

From somewhere ahead, a soft glow arose. As they advanced, the light increased in brightness and intensity, as though a multitude of candles flared to life one by one. And indeed, as the outlaws neared the origin of the luminescence, Xamus identified small, individual sources, not candles, but wisps, flitting and wheeling and tracing looping patterns in the air.

They stepped free of the thicker forest into an open space, dotted with hut-like shelters, composed of boughs sprouting from the earth, twining and interlacing, with smaller leaf and needle-bearing limbs forming canopy roofs.

In the increased light, Xamus spared a closer look at the group leader. He was a man of average height with long, curly brown hair, tied in the back. He wore a green headband and a sleeveless pullover, also green. The garment was tattered and patched from many years in the field. Black leather breeches and high boots completed his garb, and various trinkets and fetishes jangled and clinked as he walked. Upon his back was an arrow-filled quiver, and there also he had now placed a bow made of bone. From his right hip, a longsword hung. He turned to Xamus and said, "I'm Darylonde Talonhand," locking eyes on him. Those eyes were silvery, gleaming, like moonlight, and over the left, a ragged scar ranged from brow to cheek. The gaze peered not at him but *through* him, it seemed.

"I'm Xamus," the elf replied, and one by one the other party members followed suit.

"Mm," the man acknowledged. "This way." He motioned with his right hand, and Xamus noted two things: one, the hand—and only the right hand—was covered in a thick black glove. Two, the hand possessed only four digits, including the thumb. Darylonde saw Xamus studying the hand and quickly lowered it as he led them on.

They soon emerged in a wider, brighter glade, an open space dominated by what appeared to be an amphitheater, the half circle of tiered seats sunk into the earth, the stage composed of a mammoth gently curved stone, sheltered by a canopy dome formed in much the same fashion as the previously viewed huts: through the trunks and boughs of interwoven trees. The seating pit gave no indication of being dug; rather, it rendered the impression of being shaped by the earth itself. In fact, insofar as Xamus or the others could tell, no axe or shovel had played any part in the construction—or maybe creation was a more fitting word—of the amphitheater or any other facet of the refuge. At the center of the theater's earthen floor, between the lowest seats and the stage, stood a serene pool, roughly twenty feet in diameter.

The entirety of their surroundings was lit near to the point of daylight, an effect achieved through the presence of wisps as well as larger, more complex and more glaringly bright life-forms. One of these spiraled down to hover within reach of Torin, who gazed back in open-mouthed wonder. The creature was a human-looking female, no larger than his own hand, wearing a simple, robe-like garment and thick, heavy boots. "I've heard tell of fairies," Torin said in awe. "Never saw one up close. She wears boots!" Behind the dwarf, Wilhelm beheld another that had flown close.

"They all wear boots, looks like," he said. "No one's gonna believe this!" The fairy near Torin, with brightly glowing insectile wings and spiked white hair, winked at the dwarf before darting up and away to join a hundred others among the thicket of trees that surrounded the open area.

"Welcome to the Grove of Lights," Darylonde said, standing at the edge of the pit, gazing upward. The group members who had walked with them, the ma'ii, the dog-men that Oldavei now realized were gnolls, the satyr, and the two hooded figures had all dispersed, but they returned now, weapons put away, bearing fruits and cups of water instead, which they distributed to the visitors. One of the cloaked hosts, hood now lowered, held Xamus's eyes as she presented the offering. She was another satyr, with slightly animalistic—but attractive—features and thick, short horns that swept close to her temples. She offered a brief smile before breaking away.

The fruit was both sweet and filling. And the water . . . the water's consumption proffered a benefit beyond simple refreshment or fulfillment, a quality that the elf could only identify as *cleansing*. He moved to a near tree, leaning against it as he finished eating and drinking. Darylonde strode to the far edge of the pit and turned, hands extended to the surroundings. "You're welcome to rest, eat, and drink," he said. "Whether you're allowed to stay, however, is not up to me. There's another you must speak to."

"Who'd that be?" Xamus asked.

"You're leaning on him," Darylonde answered.

A deep, roughly textured voice emanated from behind the elf, vibrating the whole of the tree, causing him to push away and turn. "Greetings, travelers." Xamus retreated a step and turned as, incredibly, the tree strode forward. Its leaves were varied in color, from green to autumn shades of yellow and brown. It was roughly three heads taller than the elf and bore the rudiments of a face: smooth, round, bare spots in the bark indicated eyes, set above a small, bulbous stump of a nose. A shifting cavity, surrounded by leaves and hanging moss that suggested a beard, served for its mouth, and from it the rasping, rumbling voice issued. "I am Goshaedas," it said. "Caretaker of this refuge."

Stunned silence followed. Xamus stared back, speechless. As with Torin and the fairies, Xamus had heard stories from his elders of tree-folk, but he had never laid eyes on one, much less heard one speak.

Goshaedas cast his gaze over the gathering. "I ask you this," he continued, two large branches on either side moving in gesticulation, creaking with their motion. "Are you believers? In destiny? Purpose?"

Members of the group looked from one to the other. Darylonde shook his head slightly and appeared to bite back a response. Finally, one by one the group nodded. Xamus answered, "Yes."

"That is well," Goshaedas said. "For your journey to this sacred place was no accident. Your arrival was foreseen and indeed destined. All is as it was meant to be. So yes, not only are you welcome here, but you are *meant* to be here. I ask only that you follow one simple rule," and here the right branch bent upward, three twigs curling down, one standing up, as a raised finger. "There is to be no fighting within my sanctuary. Here, apart from perhaps any other place in the known world, here you will find peace so long as you help to maintain it. Never"—he paused for emphasis—"never take that peace for granted, for it is hard-won."

As the hosts collected from the party their empty cups, Goshaedas said, "Now rest. Sleep wherever the mood takes you. And awaken rejuvenated." Xamus noted that Goshaedas's trunk split at the halfway mark, forming two boles, that he now realized served for legs, as the towering giant turned and plodded into the forest depths. Xamus looked about to find that all of the strangers had departed.

Of their hosts, only Darylonde remained, standing now at the point where they had entered the Grove of Lights. "Rest," he said, "and we'll talk more tomorrow." With that he wheeled and disappeared into the night.

Torin looked back and forth between Oldavei and Xamus, red-eyed and sleepy. "Sanctuary, you said. Nothin' about walkin', talkin' trees and fekkin' faeries! You might warn a fella!"

"I didn't know . . . details," Oldavei replied, yawning.

"Thought I'd seen everything," Wilhelm said, sitting on the lip of the pit, the soles of his boots resting on the uppermost seat. "Maybe it's all a dream." He leaned back, folded his hands over his stomach, and closed his eyes.

"Dream or not, I'm fekkin' wiped," Torin said. He sat heavily, then lay on his side, Oldavei already lying down and stretching out next to him. Xamus, feeling his eyelids begin to droop, lowered himself in place, lay on his back, and watched through increasingly blurred vision as the fairies and wisps hurried out of sight. In the clear patch above, distant stars shone through as his eyes began to close.

Nicholas held on to the last, seated with legs crossed, holding vigil until his chin dipped, and he too drifted into a mercifully dreamless slumber.

CHAPTER THIRTEEN

ORDER AND CHAOS

They woke with the dawn, each of them feeling more rested than they had ever felt before. Despite the severity of their predicament, the food and drink from the night before, along with the uninterrupted slumber provided, as Goshaedas had foretold, a sense of rejuvenation. For the time being, at least, the menace of Ironside and his Enforcers was set aside.

Birdcalls carried from the dense woods, each twitter, chirp, and coo unique, together forming a soothing, melodic, natural symphony. Xamus, Torin, Wilhelm, Oldavei, and Nicholas all rose in place. With the exception of Torin, who carried no travel bag, they realized that so great had been their exhaustion the night before, they had not even laid out their bedrolls. Fortunately, there had been no need; the grass beneath them was soft, and the temperature remained perfectly comfortable throughout their slumber.

"Good morn." All eyes turned to Darylonde, standing where the main path opened to the glade. He wore his weapon belt and sword as well as his bow and quiver. "I've been instructed to familiarize you with the refuge." He extended his gloved hand to the amphitheater. "This is Woodsong. The water there"—he indicated the pool in the earthen pit—"is the Silver Spring. Don't drink from it," he cautioned. "Now, take up your belongings and follow me." The party members could not help but note the curtness of his manner; they were forced to quickly gather their belongings, as their new guide had already spun and was heading into the woods.

Moments later they trekked along a narrow, winding trail, terminating at a small glade where they beheld five small shelters of the same make—interwoven boughs—as those the group had witnessed upon their arrival. "Your new dwellings," Darylonde informed.

Torin squinted one eye. "Who'd you kick out?"

"No one," Darylonde answered. "Where there is need, nature provides."

Xamus nodded, impressed. The refuge itself had formed the shelters for them, it seemed. Perhaps in response to a command from Goshaedas? Or simply because it knew to do so? The elf had questions, many questions, as he was sure the others did. For now, he chose to wait and not bombard their host with queries. Besides, oddly, the elf felt no true sense of urgency.

Each of them chose a shelter, stored their kits and weapons, and accompanied Darylonde, who led them to a deep place within the timber. Here the birdcalls ceased, and the forest cover seemed to block more sunlight than anywhere else in the refuge, as if a great bank of clouds had obscured the sun. Colors dimmed; bark had fallen in patches from tilting trees whose branches drooped. Over all, a listless gloom pervaded.

"Farther to the east," Darylonde said, lifting his head in the direction of the dark wood, "is a place best avoided. There, dark spirits dwell." He threw them a hard look, and one by one they nodded their understanding.

Next their guide took them through a patch of forest just north of Woodsong—or so Oldavei believed. The refuge caused the ma'ii to sometimes question his normally unerring sense of direction. Sound, also, and to a lesser extent smell, Oldavei believed, behaved differently in this place. Assorted noises—a smattering of overlapping voices—associated with their first destination only reached their ears when they had nearly come upon it. Oldavei initiated a burst of nostril-flaring and sniffing as he followed Darylonde out onto an expansive,
grassy field.

There, rows of tents and stalls stood bright in the morning sun, with vendors hawking everything from food and wine to textiles, garments, and trinkets. The atmosphere, unlike the hectic clamor and bustle of the overcrowded Trade-City bazaars, was subdued and relaxed. Rather than shouting at the top of their lungs, vendors waited patiently for browsers to approach, engaging prospective buyers with low, warm greetings and sincere smiles. The crowd, such as it was, consisted of a few satyrs, a gnoll, a human couple who appeared to be travelers, a strolling old man playing a lyre, and a human-size tree-folk perusing various pipes. There were also the ma'ii from the night before, who set their sights on Oldavei. Mild confusion showed briefly on their features before they walked away, whispering. Oldavei brushed his fingers over the tattoo on his forehead and stepped behind Nicholas.

The style of dress among all of the patrons was fairly common: loose-fitting garments in colors of indigo, purple, violet, and lilac; wide-bottom dungarees similar to those Xamus wore, sandals, simple beads, stones, hemp, and bone accoutrements.

"Oh, fek yeah!" Wilhelm exclaimed, rushing to one stall that offered a host of eyeglasses. Torin strolled to another nearby tent; the others waited while a female satyr vendor handed Wilhelm various glasses to try on. Nicholas stood, arms folded, seemingly paying little heed to anything that was transpiring around him.

Oldavei looked to Darylonde. "So, are you a druid?"

"Of a sort," Darylonde answered. "More of a soldier, you'd say."

The ma'ii continued, "Aside from faeries and wisps and such, is most everyone here a druid or soldier?"

"Mostly. There are the enchanted beings of the wild as well and the occasional visitors."

Oldavei nodded. Wilhelm handed over a few coins, said, "Many thanks!" to the vendor, and turned around, showing off a new pair of glasses that resembled the pair he had lost at the warehouse in Skarborough.

"Nice," Xamus said.

"This place is fine by me!" Torin remarked, looking very pleased, approaching with a horn full of mead.

"Let's keep moving," Darylonde said.

The tour continued on through sun-dappled woods. Xamus noted that their guide seemed always tense, always on guard, scanning not just his surroundings but keeping an eye on them, as well, for any sign of threat.

Soon they passed a curious creature curled up and dozing at the base of an old cedar. Wilhelm nudged Oldavei, pointing toward the beast. "Fekkin' manticore!" Wilhelm was correct, the ma'ii noted. The animal's fur-covered body was leonine, with a thick, dark brown mane about the neck. The tranquil, softly snoring visage within that mane was both bestial and human in appearance. The long tail, resembling that of a scorpion, flicked upward, perhaps in response to some dream, then fell lazily to the grass.

They arrived soon at a quiet valley. Here Darylonde paused, placing his gloved hand over his heart, head bowed, eyes closed. A zephyr blew through, and everyone gathered felt as though they detected the slightest whisper on the breeze, though each of them questioned whether the voice was real or a figment of their imagination. In the center of the glen, a thick, towering, mighty oak stood, branches raised to the sky.

"We come now to Oram's Rest," Darylonde said. "Named for the founder of our sacred refuge, Oram Moonsong. A tree-folk. He expired here, peacefully, in times long past."

The group nodded sagely and held a reverent silence. "There . . ." Darylonde said, pointing above and to the north; they lifted their eyes and saw for the first time the silhouette of the massive mountain peak shaped in the visage of a colossal bear's head, in profile, roaring toward the east. "*That* is why you're here. In due course, you will enter the Bear Mound, and there your true path will be revealed."

Xamus, Wilhelm, and Torin all felt a stirring within their breast, a subtle but undeniable force reaching from somewhere in the direction of that mammoth peak, an ancient and primal calling. Nicholas seemed acutely uncomfortable, standing with arms close to his body, staring skyward, stone-faced. Oldavei also was visibly stricken, his features betraying a terrible sense of dread. "What—what's going to happen there?" he asked, but Darylonde had already begun to depart.

"I trust you can find your own way back," he said, moving quickly into the dense brush and out of sight.

"When's the appointed time?" Oldavei called after him, but no answer came.

"I don't think he cares for us very much," Wilhelm observed.

"Ya blame him?" Torin replied. "We're wanted for sedition and murder. I wouldn't want us here either."

The remainder of the day was spent quietly strolling the market, sating hunger, slaking thirst. Later in the night, several of the refuge residents gathered at Woodsong for a show. The performance, given musical accompaniment by the same lyrist who played at the market, depicted one of many battles between druids and an unrelenting host of nightmare creatures collectively dubbed "the Howling." Howling performers wore bits and pieces of various animals and creatures—some of which the group recognized, and some they did not—to represent the malevolent forest-kin.

The Howling forces battled a smaller force called Wildkeepers—elite soldiers created by the local reigning druid order, the Oram Hai. Seated at the lowest earthen tier, in the center, Oldavei leaned to Darylonde and asked, in what he no doubt thought to be a quiet voice, "When was this?"

"Different times throughout the centuries," Darylonde replied.

On the stage, several Howling creatures fell to wooden swords. Torin, who had been uncharacteristically relaxed for several hours, whooped, coughing smoke. "Put that in your pipe and smoke it, ya fekkers!" He then returned to his own pipe and took a long pull.

"When was the last time?" Oldavei asked Darylonde.

The soldier kept his eyes on the stage as he answered. "Not long. They slaughtered their way across the Barrier Peaks for years until . . . recently. Until they were driven back. But they remain a constant threat."

"Mm," Oldavei said, nodding, seeming satisfied as the stage battle continued. A moment later he asked excitedly: "Are *you* a Wildkeeper?"

Darylonde sighed. "Yes," he said. "Now pay attention."

Oldavei remained silent, deducing that talk of former exploits made Darylonde uncomfortable, while onstage the battle entered its final phase. Moments later the Wildkeeper performers routed the Howling to thunderous applause.

Music and dancing and drinking carried on into the night. Much later, with the wisps and faeries departed and the sanctuary inhabitants drifting into a contented slumber—save for Nicholas, who had taken a solitary walk—Xamus sought out a private location in which to continue his practice of wild magic.

He sat on a stump beneath the moonlight and removed his hat. The moon, the forest, the solitude . . . all reminded him of home and of his people, who so loved nature and landscapes such as this. Deep within his chest arose a sensation he had not experienced in many a long year: a heavy pang of loneliness and, with it, a longing for his own home, his own people. He took a long, deep breath and pushed the thoughts away, choosing to focus instead on the task at hand. He whispered the appropriate incantation and gesticulated. Though it took a bit longer than usual, in time a spark ignited. Fire danced . . . then expanded, flared, and vanished. The elf fetched a long, heavy sigh.

"I didn't know elves practiced wild magic." The voice was female. Xamus turned to see the satyr from the night before, walking out from the trees, lowering her hood.

"Most don't," Xamus replied.

"Hope I didn't startle you," she said, approaching. "I like to roam at night."

"No harm done."

The satyr came to stand next to him, gazing at his ears with a warm fascination, the full moon casting a soft glow on her crystal blue eyes, fine blonde hair, and keratin horns. "Granted, my knowledge of elves"—here she reached out and lightly touched his right ear—"is sorely lacking."

The contact sent a shudder through Xamus's core. "They are, uh . . . notoriously secretive," he said.

"They?"

"What?"

"You said 'they.'" She lowered her hand, fixing her eyes on his.

"Oh." Xamus smiled, gave a subtle shrug. "Habit, I guess. I haven't been . . . among them for a long time."

The female nodded and said, "I'm Amberlyn."

"Xamus," the elf replied.

Amberlyn smiled. "Well met, Xamus."

A moment of awkward silence followed, broken by Amberlyn. "So, how long have you been practicing wild magic?"

"Not long enough to be as good as I would like," Xamus answered. "Learning it has been quite a challenge."

"And you like a challenge, I wager," Amberlyn said with a smile.

"Admittedly," Xamus replied.

"Consider this," Amberlyn said. "Magic flows through all of the world, all of creation. Twining and coiling like a river . . . or a serpent. At their core, magical disciplines—arcane, druidic, shamanic, wild—aren't all that different, for they all flow from a common source."

Xamus was taken aback. His own people, wise as they were, never spoke of magic this way. *Small wonder*, he thought. Far be it for the staid, egocentric elves to recognize or entertain differing viewpoints. Yet another reminder of why he left them in the first place. If one never ventured beyond their doorstep, one could never learn.

"So," Xamus answered, "if wild magic isn't so different, at its core, from say, druidic magic, how do you control it? A friend told me not so long ago that nature is chaos."

"Your friend was right," Amberlyn said, beaming. "Nature *is* chaos. But perhaps this is where you've faltered, for nature is also order. Consider a hurricane: storm and eye. The eye is a calm stillness. Peace. Order. Close your eyes."

Xamus did as Amberlyn asked. "This place is very much like that eye," she continued. "The calm stillness is all around you. Be patient. Draw on it. Quiet your mind and find your center."

The elf tried to do as she asked, attempting to find an inner calm to match that which he felt surrounding him. He released all thoughts, concerns, distractions, focusing on this precise moment in time, in this place. Stillness.

"Good," Amberlyn said, her voice soft, coaxing. "Now summon."

Xamus nodded, whispered his incantation, worked his hands. He felt heat in the space between them.

"Now hold steady," Amberlyn said. "If fire is the storm, *you* must be the eye."

Xamus held tight to the stillness he embraced, maintaining a calm control.

"Now look," Amberlyn said.

Xamus obeyed, and to his astonishment, beheld a roiling sphere of fire rotating slowly but holding steady. Stable. He laughed. "I'll be damned," he said, staring into the hypnotic flame. He shook his head, chuckling. He had done it, not only summoned the flame but harnessed it, exerted his will upon it. One last test now . . . he whispered a final incantation and watched with both joy and relief as the fiery globe shrank and disappeared.

"I can't thank you enou—" he began, turning, but Amberlyn had already gone, departing as quietly as she had come.

PART TWO: OUTLAWS

CHAPTER FOURTEEN

THE SLOW AND STEADY ECLIPSE

Over the course of the next day, excited talk circulated of an impending arrival, a legendary figure called Palonsus—an ancient centaur metalsmith, respected and admired and revered among many for his acts of heroism during the Breakwar.

Roughly 250 years ago, the legend-steeped lands of the far north had been embroiled in a conflict that resulted in the fall of Old Sularia, an overthrow accomplished by an alliance of humanoid races. Nevertheless, the high-minded ideals, tenets, and religion of Old Sularia had managed to survive long enough in the hearts and minds of survivors to experience a resurgence with the founding of the Trade-Cities.

All of the outlaws were fascinated at the prospect of meeting someone who had not only lived through such history but perhaps helped shape it. Palonsus, they were told, rarely traveled—the last time he had been to the refuge was nearly sixty years ago, so the timing of the group's stay and the centaur's arrival was fortuitous, to say the least.

While awaiting the eagerly anticipated meeting, Oldavei made the most of his time, conversing at length with Darylonde. It was the ma'ii's goal to glean information from the Wildkeeper—he broached all manner of topics, from the nature and lure of the wild to the recurring Howling threat and the history of Kannibus Hills. These queries Darylonde addressed, but always tersely, maintaining a gruff standoffishness. It was shortly after midday, as they sat near the market at the base of two trees, munching on dried fish, that Oldavei decided to press further and take a stab at the questions that were truly on his mind. "So . . ." he asked offhandedly, "I thought I might ask again what you meant about that 'true path' bit you said at the mountain." A light breeze drifted through their sitting place, stirring the leaves above them, something not lost on Darylonde.

The grizzled soldier, still chewing on his fish, locked his silver eyes on Oldavei with such a fixity that the ma'ii fairly squirmed beneath his gaze. "I wager you have a way of getting through to people," Darylonde said, his voice a low growl. "Maybe even getting your way at times, hmm?"

"I don't, I'm not—I mean, I'm not sure what you—" the ma'ii stammered.

"Relax," Darylonde said, leaning back against the tree. "You'll get your answers in time."

Oldavei held his silence, then responded hotly: "I have a suspicion that by 'true path,' you meant destiny. I'll let you in on a secret." Standing, he looked down on the veteran soldier. "I've seen my destiny already. And I've no wish to see it again." He spun and loped away.

Later in the day, word came to the Grove of Lights that Palonsus would soon be there. Xamus had spent the morning enquiring as to the whereabouts of Amberlyn, learning from one of her fellow druids that she had struck out that morning on some undisclosed mission.

He sat on the rim of the pit at Woodsong, contemplating the words of Goshaedas, who had said that their coming was "foreseen." What, exactly, had the old tree-folk meant? Foreseen by whom? But most especially, why? The elf was musing that somewhere, someone must have made a mistake when a hand clapped him on the shoulder. He looked up to see Torin grinning. "I hear good things about this Palonsus fella," the dwarf said. Wilhelm stood next to him, strumming lightly on his mandolin. Other inhabitants had begun to gather in the Grove, chatting idly. The same booted, spiky-haired fairy Torin had seen upon his arrival flew down, tapped him lightly on the nose, giggled, and flew away.

"I think she likes you," Wilhelm said. Torin grunted.

Xamus looked back to the Silver Spring, sheltered by the interwoven limb canopy, where Nicholas had descended and was now cautiously drawing up to the water. It was something the others had all done; gone to the glittering spring and looked down to see what many of them had not seen in quite a long time: their reflection. Nicholas, however, had not joined them on any of those occasions.

The assassin stood now at the edge, not looking down. Finally he inclined his head, remained breathlessly still, his features stonelike. He backed up two steps, whirled, quickly ascended the steps on the other side, and hurried to the forest edge.

"What's with him?" Torin said.

"Hmm," Xamus said. "I'll be back in a bit." He traveled down the steps, across and up, and then followed Nicholas into the shadowy woods.

"You're gonna' miss the—bah!" Torin waved a dismissive hand, looking to Wilhelm, who simply shrugged and continued plucking. The Grove became more crowded, and soon Darylonde arrived, standing a few paces away. He offered a brief nod, then directed his attention to where the main path met the clearing.

There, two cloaked druids arrived and stood to either side. They raised horns to their lips and blew. A figure emerged, using an upside-down spear as a walking stick. The lead half was human; there was long, black, curly hair atop the man's head, a thick, unkempt beard on his chin, and bushy brows over his glittering eyes. From his burly, hairy torso a black leather apron hung, both the apron and the bronzed skin stained with soot. Upon his hands the newcomer wore thick ironworking gloves. He stepped farther into the open, revealing his back half, that of a great black horse with feathering over the lower legs and hooves and a thick, curling tail.

"Greetings all!" Palonsus declared in a hearty, deep voice. He walked slowly, exchanging salutations with several members of the community, until Darylonde approached the centaur and spoke in a low voice. The two looked over to Torin and Wilhelm. Palonsus's twinkling eyes appraised them briefly before he returned his attention to Darylonde. The centaur responded to the Wildkeeper, then strode to the dwarf and bard.

"Hail!" Palonsus said in a loud yet warm greeting. "Fugitives, I'm told! Upstarts, eh? Scoundrels, perhaps!"

Wilhelm hesitated, Torin grinned.

Palonsus bent down, thrusting his chin forward. "Well, that's just my style. You boys drink?"

"Does an owlbear shit where he pleases?" Torin answered.

The centaur straightened, threw his head back, boomed laughter, and then said, "I like you already! Follow me!"

While Palonsus led Torin and Wilhelm away from the Grove, Xamus continued his foray into the woods in pursuit of Nicholas. He found the assassin at last seated with his back against a giant boulder at the edge of the cursed stretch of forest Darylonde had told them to avoid.

Xamus joined him, and for a moment the two sat in the eerie silence.

"Who's Katrina?" the elf asked.

Nicholas looked to him, eyes narrowed above his glasses.

"It was a name you spoke," Xamus continued, "after the warehouse, while you were incapacitated."

"No one of consequence," Nicholas answered, staring once again into the darkened wood. "A former lover back in the capital of Sargrad. We didn't end on good terms."

"I see," Xamus said. "And is she the reason for your condition?"

"What condition?" Nicholas asked quietly.

"Oldavei healed your wound on the outside but not the inside. And yet you've fully recovered," Xamus said. "Your night vision seems better than mine, and you're no elf. Your physical abilities border on inhuman, and the night you brought us rabbits . . . you didn't eat. But I suspect you had already eaten one. *Before* it was cooked."

Nicholas's shoulders and head slumped.

"And then, just now, when you looked in the spring—"

"Fading," Nicholas answered, barely above a whisper. "My reflection is fading. I'm losing myself, bit by bit, day by day. And this place, this place where Goshaedas spoke of peace, I have known only turmoil. Deep within, a slow and steady eclipse of the soul."

"And was it Katrina who made you this way?" Xamus asked.

"Yeah," Nicholas replied. "Yeah, she made me as I am."

"But you've not fully turned," Xamus said.

Nicholas answered slowly, clearly taken aback, surprised by Xamus's understanding. "Not fully, no. I'll come to the very edge of the precipice, but only *after* my body dies will I come back as . . ."

"A vampire," Xamus said.

Nicholas huffed. "How do you know of such things?"

"I was told of vampires in my studies. Creatures of the old world. Night Devils . . ."

A sullen expression overcame the assassin.

"Sorry," Xamus said quickly. "But look . . . there's time. Time for us to figure something out."

"And if I die before then?" Nicholas asked.

"No sense in fearing death," Xamus replied. "We're all gonna die, eventually." He reached into a pocket, pulled out a packet of Lintgreen, and began rolling a smoke. "My people," he said, "they live these long lives and yet . . . they stay in the same place, doing the same things, practicing the same magic, keeping to themselves. Already since leaving their refuge I've seen and experienced things that they will never know in a thousand years." Finished rolling, Xamus put the smoke to his lips, flicked the lid of his pocket lamp, and lit the end as he drew in. "All I'm saying is it's not a matter of how much time you have left" he offered the smoke to Nicholas—"it's a matter of what you do with that time."

Nicholas looked over. "Hmm," he said, accepting the smoke. "And what is it you think I should do?"

"Live," Xamus said, staring into the forbidden forest. "Live every minute as if it's your last."

Far from where Xamus and Nicholas held their conversation, on the other side of the sanctuary, Wilhelm, Torin, and Palonsus were already well into their cups.

They sat in an area the outlaws had not yet visited; it was Palonsus's workspace, his smithy, the dominant part of which was a great hearth, built not of brick and mortar but of stone with all features, including the cooling tank, shaped as if by hand rather than chisel. The only elements crafted by man appeared to be the apparatus and tools of the smith's trade—a massive anvil, bellows, workbench, grinding wheel, hammers, tongs, stakes, and punches.

The black mead they imbibed—sweet, earthy, and spicy—was the finest Torin or Wilhelm had ever tasted. The dwarf sat atop a massive swage block, tilting back his horn. The fairy who had seemed to take a liking to Torin, whose name he had come to learn was Wittabit, lounged on the giant anvil. Wilhelm leaned against the unlit hearth, partaking from a huge clay mug. All had been enrapt by Palonsus, holding center court, flagon in hand, recounting in a thunderous voice tales of adventure and wonder and battles in the mystical lands of the north in forgotten times.

Now he described the aftermath of one of the Breakwar's grisliest melees. "The smoke was so thick you couldn't see your hand in front of your face!" he declared. "You couldn't take a single step without tripping over a corpse . . . and if you opened your mouth even the slightest, you could *taste* the blood on the air!"

Wilhelm bolted up, holding his mug aloft. "I will recount your exploits! Your deeds! The sacrifices of those who fought and bled with you!" He hoisted his mandolin with his free hand. "I will sing of your bravery and honor and—"

A realization settled on him, and he suddenly fell back against the hearth, arms dropped to his sides.

"What happened?" Torin asked, clearly confused.

"Sorry," Wilhelm said. "It's—it just hit me—I won't perform at Bard-In. With Ironside and his goons after us, there's just no way . . ." The bard shook his head, staring blankly. "What if I never perform in front of a large crowd again? That can't be my path . . . that'd be worse than death."

Wittabit flew from her spot on the anvil, landed on Wilhelm's shoulder, and patted him reassuringly before darting away.

"Well, young bard, I'll tell you this . . ." Palonsus said in a rumbling voice. "You never know what surprises lie in store." The centaur then looked over his shoulder at the surrounding wood. "What say you, Goshaedas?"

The tree-folk stepped out from the timber, plodding forward on bole-legs. He stopped and cast his wooden gaze over Torin and Wilhelm.

"What say I?" he began. "Tomorrow, say I! Tomorrow when the sun reaches its peak, you"—he leveled a branch arm and twig finger at the dwarf and bard—"you will enter the holy Bear Mound, and there, you will unravel what mysteries the future holds!"

PART TWO: OUTLAWS

CHAPTER FIFTEEN
VISION QUEST

At sunrise, Xamus leaned into Torin's shelter and asked, "Where's Oldavei?"

"How the fek should I know?" the dwarf replied, wiping tired eyes.

Wilhelm, Torin, Xamus, and Nicholas spent the early part of the day searching all the places they had come to know, with no luck finding the ma'ii. They came back to the market, scanning the light crowd. Xamus spotted and prepared to approach Darylonde in the center thoroughfare when Torin spied a shadow in the sky. "Falcon!" he said, "Falcon!"

Nicholas pulled from a pouch on his waist a four-pointed star and threw, but before the projectile could impact the approaching bird, an arrow sliced the air and drove the star off its course.

Darylonde had already drawn and nocked a second arrow, leveling it at the assassin, when the bird came to rest on his shoulder. Torin and Xamus both stepped forward, hands raised. "One of the Enforcers who hunts us uses a falcon," Xamus quickly explained.

"Apologies," Nicholas said, turning and walking to the far end of the tents.

Darylonde relaxed, inserted the arrow in his quiver and slung the bow. The falcon hopped down onto his extended, gloved hand. The Wildkeeper removed a small, rolled parchment from its leg and read as Xamus, Wilhelm, and Torin approached.

"It's from . . . one of our spies," Darylonde said. "In Lietsin. She says the Knight-Paladin Ironside is there . . ."

"Lookin' for us?" Torin asked.

"No," Darylonde, replied, still reading. "Preparing some operation against the Children of the Sun."

"They're the ones we were hired to go after," Xamus said.

"Hmm," Darylonde replied.

Sudden realization dawned on Wilhelm. "If Ironside's in Lietsin, then maybe I could go to Bard-In after all."

"Just because Ironside's not there doesn't mean you wouldn't get recognized," Torin said. "There's posters with our faces on 'em everywhere."

The excitement in Wilhelm's eyes dimmed. "Yeah," he replied, "Yeah I guess that's true."

"Have you seen Oldavei?" Xamus asked Darylonde.

"No," the Wildkeeper answered. He whispered to the falcon on his shoulder, lifted his arm, and watched the raptor take flight. "The sun will be at its peak soon," he said. "Ready your things. I'll find the ma'ii."

The three hesitated. "Relax," Darylonde said. "I know what I'm doing. Like your friend, I'm also very good at not being found when I don't want to be."

Xamus considered, nodded, and led the others away.

Not long after, Darylonde discovered Oldavei sitting opposite the dozing, lightly snoring manticore at the old cedar. He came and sat cross-legged in front of the ma'ii, who eyed him warily.

"It's not a matter of courage," Darylonde said. "You have that. I know it. I can sense it. It's not a matter of whether or not you have what it takes to face what you might see up there." He canted his head toward the mountain. "It's something else. You said you've seen your destiny once already . . ."

"Yeah," Oldavei said.

"And what happened after?"

Oldavei started to answer, then reconsidered. The manticore's snoring grew louder.

"I spoke with some of our local ma'ii," Darylonde continued. "They told me the meaning of that symbol on your forehead. That mark. It means 'outcast.' I sense that you're running."

Oldavei stared hard at the Wildkeeper and said carefully, "What I saw . . . is the reason I'm no longer with my people. The reason I abandoned my calling to be a shaman."

The manticore finally snored loud enough to wake itself up. It grunted, repositioned, then quickly fell back to sleep.

"Look," Darylonde continued, "when I was younger, I was . . . lost, trying to figure out who and what I was. I chose to undergo a druid ritual to bond with my spirit animal. Part of what I did was a test of faith. I believed that my totem would be the eagle." Darylonde's eyes became distant. "So I went to the edge of a high cliff, steeled myself, and I jumped. That day, the spirits saved me. My totem saved me and I *was* bonded. And yes, it was the spirit of the eagle that I was bonded to. I want to show you something . . ."

With his left hand, Darylonde reached for the glove and removed it. What was revealed was not another hand, but a large, four-digited talon, similar to that of a large bird of prey.

"Oh," Oldavei said. "Oh, wow."

"What happened that day left its own mark. And what I went through on the other side of it all, in the war against the Howling, nearly broke me. But in the end it gave me strength to do the things that needed to be done. Hard things, things that left the marks that you *can't* see. Invisible, but no less permanent. But I'll tell you this: if I could go back and choose a different path"—he regarded the talon—"I wouldn't change a thing." Slowly he stood, turned, and faced the mountain. "You've already seen your destiny once," he said. "And by your own admission, you fled your calling. But it's not often that any of us get a second chance. I guess the question, when all is said and done and you've glimpsed your path once again"—he looked to Oldavei—"is will you finally stop running?"

Oldavei sat quietly, considering. "Now come," Darylonde said. He stepped over and extended his gloved hand. "It's time."

Darylonde and Oldavei met the others at Oram's Rest, where the soft breeze once again seemed to carry voices, but other sounds reached their ears as well. A ringing, perhaps of hammer on steel.

Their guide said nothing but led them to the oak in the center of the dale, where each observed a moment of silence, laying a hand on the great tree before proceeding on. Followed by the clang of hammer falls they climbed a narrow, winding trail that led steadily up through the timber, taxing their lungs so that all save Darylonde were heaving long, deep breaths when they at last reached the summit.

The bear's likeness in the stony outcropping before them was unmistakable but crude—as though a great sculptor had begun the work, achieving the rough shape but abandoning the project before refining the details. Darylonde guided them through the gaping mouth, above which two large, slightly curved stone projections loomed, calling to mind massive fangs.

They stepped into a chamber intersected by many tunnels. Darylonde led them down one, where some unknown fungus on the walls emitted a soft blue glow.

The humidity was thick, and at various points between the echoing footfalls the sound of dripping water reached their ears. Among some of the wider sections of tunnel, they passed bubbling pools that Darylonde claimed possessed healing properties.

As the humidity increased, so too did the heat. The tunnel twisted, then climbed until they at last came to a larger central cavern, where their walkway swept down along the wall and to the floor. A hole in the center of the ceiling admitted a shaft of radiant light that revealed scores of stone-engraved, druidic sigils along the walls. In a pit directly beneath the light beam, a pile of stones hissed clouds of steam.

"Sit around the stones," Darylonde instructed.

The party complied, with Oldavei remaining until last. He took quick, deep sniffs of the air, then regarded the Wildkeeper, glancing also at the black glove. Darylonde nodded. Oldavei gave the surroundings a last tentative look and sat. The stifling heat prompted each of them to remove clothing from their upper bodies, as sweat began to bead and run down their skin. Darylonde took a seat nearby.

"So . . ." Oldavei began, but was quickly hushed by the Wildkeeper, who sat erect, legs folded, hands resting lightly on his thighs.

They waited quietly so that the other sounds in the cave—dripping water, hushing steam, and their own steady breaths—became more prominent. Over what felt like a long expanse of time, their heartbeats seemed to merge with the fall of the water droplets. Darylonde finally rose, stepping between Oldavei and Wilhelm to the edge of the stones, where he tossed what looked like dried herbs. There was a sizzle and flash and a sudden burst of blue flame—there and gone in an instant. A mist, however, violet in color, lingered.

The participants reacted to the mist with apprehension. "Don't be afraid," Darylonde advised. "Just relax. Breathe. Slowly, in and out . . ."

Pushing away their reluctance, they did as instructed. As the mist entered their bodies, their muscles immediately began to relax. Their eyelids started to droop. A strange sensation overcame them, a feeling of drifting, of disconnection from time and place.

Darylonde initiated a low, soft chant. The party, with their eyes now fully closed, swayed softly. Distantly, Wilhelm smiled at the strange, rhythmic vocalizations. The speech was unfamiliar even to Xamus, whose people had given voice and ear to some of the first languages ever spoken . . . or so he had always been told. The words and melody were at once haunting and stirring. Soon, the chant, the steam, the water drops, and their heartbeats all merged into what each of them felt must be music of not just their innermost spirits but of the world around them and perhaps even the music of nature itself.

The world began to tilt, the cave drew in around them, myriad colors exploded before their closed eyes, and in a mad rush, images followed . . .

Some parts of the vision were seen only by each individual and only in very quick snippets: Nicholas glimpsed Katrina, eyes at first warm and inviting, then hardened into jealous possession; Wilhelm saw himself running, carrying a large, curious piece of furniture, giddy in the act, as if all the world were bound up within its frame; Torin exulted in the deafening, rage-filled roar of a goliath prehistoric creature; Xamus spied the visage of Ironside, illuminated by firelight; and Oldavei beheld a pack of his ma'ii kin in animal form, running beneath a pale moon with *him* at the lead . . .

Other flashes of the vision were shared among all of them: speeding chariots, a desert caravan, a robed man silhouetted in dazzling light, a towering, multitiered ziggurat, then light again, growing to blinding

brilliance . . .

And then, as quickly as they had come, the visions were gone.

One by one, the participants opened their eyes and looked from one to the other, judging by the expressions on their faces that all of them had seen . . . something. Darylonde was no longer present. Nicholas put on his shirt and stood. The rest followed suit, eager to withdraw from the oppressive heat.

Outside they traveled quietly back down the trail, grateful for the slight, cool breeze. They paused and touched the great oak at Oram's rest, pounding noises once again reaching their ears from somewhere to the west. As they worked their way back to the refuge proper, Wilhelm spoke. "So are we . . . supposed to talk about what we saw?"

"I don't know," Xamus admitted.

They walked around the limb canopy of the Woodsong amphitheater and joined Darylonde, who stood waiting just beyond the seating area. A small number of druids and guests had gathered, and the pixies and wisps had just begun to emerge from their forest dwellings.

"So, now you have seen," the Wildkeeper said as the outlaws approached.

"Yeah," Torin responded. "But what I saw was a jumble. Don't know what it had to do with a 'true path,' if anything."

The group voiced general agreement. Even Oldavei, who had anticipated the event with dread based on what he had previously seen, had come away feeling uncertain of the visions' meaning.

"I suppose only time will tell," Darylonde answered.

Wilhelm, who had been quietly musing, suddenly spoke. "My mind's made up. I'm goin' to Bard-In."

The others looked at him curiously.

"Music, performing," Wilhelm said, "it's the only thing I've ever felt called to do. I didn't see anything in my vision about getting arrested at Bard-In. There was some really weird shit about a . . . cupboard? Wardrobe? I don't know furniture. But anyway, I'm going." He looked to Darylonde, "How far to Innis?"

"Three to four days," the Wildkeeper responded. "Depending on how fast you travel."

"It'll be tight," Wilhelm said, "but I can make it if I leave now."

"Well, then," a voice boomed, followed by a sound of clomping footsteps. Palonsus strode in from a side trail, his torso covered in a sheen of sweat. He carried a bundled, metallic object in his right hand. "If you're to be singing my praises," he declared, advancing to Wilhelm and holding out the item, "you damn well better look good doin' it!"

Wilhelm held the object with both hands, hanging in front of him. "Whoa!" he exclaimed, "are you fekkin' serious?"

It was a finely crafted chain-mail shirt, blue with a red cruciform symbol on the chest.

"'Tis the symbol of the Breakwar," Palonsus said. "A rebel symbol. A symbol of courage for the peoples' movement. It guided me through many a dark time. It reminded me that my destiny was my

PART TWO: OUTLAWS

own. And . . . you may even find that it brings you a bit of good fortune."

Wilhelm immediately slipped the shirt over his own, running his fingers down the intricately woven metal links. "That was the sound we heard. The hammering. This is . . . it's epic," he said. "I don't know how to thank you."

"No need," Palonsus said. "You can thank me by having the kind of adventures that others will sing about one fine day." He put a hand to Wilhelm's shoulder. "Fare thee well, bard."

Oldavei stepped up, saying, "I don't think it'd be right to let you go and hog up all the excitement in Bard-In on your own." He gave Darylonde a pointed look, then glanced questioningly at Torin, who sighed, grunted, and stepped forward as well.

Palonsus walked back as Xamus joined the circle. "Count me in."

"You sure?" Wilhelm said, looking to each of them as they nodded in reply.

"I suppose we can't just hide out here forever," Nicholas said, coming forward.

Wittabit flew down, landed, and lay on Torin's shoulder. "We'd best say our farewells, then," he said, giving the fairy a warm look. "And gather our things."

CHAPTER SIXTEEN
BARD-IN

Innis, located in the fertile Deano Valley north of the midlands of Lawbrand, was called the City of Melodies.

What had once been nothing more than a quiet, peaceful, and relatively isolated valley grew over time into one of the most vibrant, well-known, and economically influential societies in the land. It all began with a small rural community built on textiles and livestock operating under the protection of Bohen Dur monks sequestered in their windswept monastery high atop the nearby Korosoth Peak.

The fledgling city gained early success in the unlikely field of fashion. In the hands of trailblazing, visionary creators, Innis's textiles were incorporated into designs that blended comfort, utility, and imagination. As the local Garmenters Guild rose to preeminence within the confederation of Trade-Cities, many renowned clothing designers made Innis their permanent residence, and the city in turn became a magnet for free-thinking philosophers, dreamers, and artists of nearly every stripe, including painters, poets, and bards. Over time, musical expression gained more and more of a presence. Embraced by the local populace, a cornucopia of music styles and genres permeated the alleys and taverns and inns, taking root to the point that over the last several decades, Innis and music had become synonymous. By far the most popular style to emerge was dubbed "windsong," a captivating, almost *trance-inducing* blend of chimes and wind instruments that not only enjoyed early success but continued to grow and evolve until it had taken root throughout the land's farthest reaches.

Innis held no reputation for being wild or debauched. Far from it. The overwhelming majority of creatives who called the city home were relaxed and good-natured—albeit eccentric—law-abiding citizens. Once every year, however, Innis's veneer of serenity was stripped away. In the earliest years, the festival of Bard-In was fairly low-key. But over time, as word spread of the sights and sounds and vendors and acts, people from all corners of the realm and all walks of life—critics, aficionados, curiosity-seekers, vagabonds, devotees, and powerbrokers—began making Bard-In their annual pilgrimage. And with this surge of crowds came also a surge of general mayhem.

Their overall distaste for unruliness notwithstanding, local officials understood that the spectacle Bard-In had become was very good for the economy. Warts and all.

At festival time, event planners put the largest nearby open pasture to good use; Cornell's Field, just east of the city's Shepherd's Gate, was chock-full of revelers representing just about every race in the land, with the exception of enchanted creatures, such as those the outlaws had become acquainted with in Kannibus Hills. The crowded field had just come within sight of the travel-weary outlaws as they crested a rise and paused to take in the glory that awaited them.

"There she is," Wilhelm said reverently, hands aloft. "There's my baby. This, my friends, *this* is our destiny . . . to get hamro!" He chuckled and set off. "It's gonna be wild! Come on!"

Their journey had transpired without incident. The vision quest, and the specific images each of them had seen, had been discussed, though any meaning behind their premonitions—if such they were—remained mysterious. As to Nicholas's vampiric "condition," the assassin had convinced Xamus to keep the matter private, at least in the short term. It was clearly something Nicholas was intensely self-conscious and embarrassed about, though the why of it was something that Xamus suspected went much deeper than just the dread of becoming some monstrous Night Devil. The elf had resolved to learn more, knowing full well that it was a delicate subject and that additional answers might take time.

The group had once again traveled mostly at night, resting for only a portion of each day. The sun was just setting now in the west, the air had begun to cool, and the soft grass was a welcome comfort to their tired feet as they beelined for the mass gathering.

The timing of their arrival could not have been more perfect. On the field stages, musicians had performed throughout the day, but the most highly anticipated shows were reserved for nightfall, and many of them were getting ready to perform as various warm-up acts completed their final numbers. Bright, striking, multicolored flags and banners abounded; acrobats, fire-eaters, contortionists, ventriloquists, and puppet masters whose acts would normally be seen on street corners had taken up various spots on the pasture or roved among the crowd. Many of the attendees held red cups brimming with alcohol of every type: whiskey, wine, ale, mead, and beer. Vendors sold all manner of foodstuffs as well—snacks and pastries ranging from turkey legs and corn on the cob to cakes, custards, and fritters. Oldavei's head swiveled and swept, attempting to take in each and every tantalizing aroma. Among those scents were various pipe-weeds, herbs, and tobaccos. Braziers and cressets of every size and description had been lit, in addition to log piles and wooden constructions, some built in crude animal or human representations. Towering above the heads of those gathered, at the fringes of the field, quarry giant security guards wearing thin yellow jackets with the words Event Staff emblazoned across their backs stood watch.

A shirtless minotaur in knee-length leather breeches with a large keg strapped to his back, drinking from an oversized flagon, came close and paused long enough to vent a roar that caused the ground directly beneath the outlaws' feet to tremble. They continued on.

"Watch it!" an irritable gnome with skull face paint blurted when Wilhelm nearly tripped over him.

A few steps later they were forced to take quick, evasive moves in order to avoid being crushed by a teetering, drunk ogre. Once that danger had passed, they came near a stage where an old, red-haired, bearded minstrel with a crimson headband voiced a warbling tune about heartache and the open road.

"That's Wild Willy!" Wilhelm said. "Hey, Willy!" he called, waving. The old man lifted his head in response and continued his serenade.

They passed another stage where a sweaty, bare-chested, long-haired man in purple leather breeches thrust his hips while blowing a chalumeau and crooning of belief. They kept on, stopping before yet another, larger stage. Here they witnessed a tall female satyr, pale, with striking blue eyes and calf-length silver hair. She wore a white gossamer gown and held a long, rune-inscribed ivory flute to her lips.

"Ooh," Wilhelm said. "This is the Loudest Flautist. She's insane!" Even as Wilhelm spoke, the runes along the instrument began to glow. From the end of the flute, something emerged that all save Wilhelm assumed to be smoke. The substance, however, was best described as a spectral mist that expanded, lengthened, and assumed a vaguely human, phantasmal form. The apparition lent a voice of its own as the musical tempo increased. A second tendril of energy emerged from the flute, slinking down and around the flautist's back, assuming another similar shape opposite the first phantom. This vapor gave voice as well, the two specters vocalizing a wailing chant that rose in concert with the flute's stirring melodies in volume and intensity, until the entire piece reached an impassioned crescendo.

Shouts at a nearby stage drew Torin's attention. He and the others shouldered their way to get a better view. A halfling, called a xu'keen, wriggled and writhed in the middle of the stage. He was wrapped in chains, snarling and kicking, wearing nothing more than a loincloth. As with most others of his race, this xu'keen was slender and pale, with intricate scarification and crude piercings marking his bare torso. Blue eyes blazed as he set his pointed teeth to work on chewing through the gag in his mouth.

"Oh, this one's an animal!" Wilhelm enthused. "The Screaming Hawbutt!"

At the edges of the stage, large, shirtless men coated in red clay pounded a slow and steady beat on massive drums. Two more men, thinner, also shirtless, and caked in clay, approached with syringes. A glowing, green, toxic-looking substance filled the syringe barrels, which the men injected into each bound arm of the xu'keen, who suddenly began convulsing. One of the men produced a key and opened locks on the small performer while the other removed chains. They then backed away and watched. The xu'keen rolled, arched, flailed, squealed, and mewled. His wriggling slowed, then ceased altogether as he fell silent and still. The drums ceased. The crowd remained hushed, watching.

Suddenly the xu'keen shot to his feet, rearing back, veins bulging on his neck as he curled his fists and screamed at the sky. The drums resumed at a furious pace as the performer arched back and bent forward, tossing his head up and down in time with the drumbeats, howling all the while. Many of the spectators leaned forward and tossed their heads as well, including Wilhelm, whose striped hat flopped wildly.

The xu'keen, still wailing, broke into a kind of hopping run around the stage, thrashing his arms and slamming his head. He then cut loose with an ear-pounding roar, charged to the edge of the stage and leaped off, over the heads of Wilhelm and the others, quickly clearing a circle where he landed, screaming, head-bashing, and running wild. Some members of the crowd ran in terror, and others followed him, bashing their heads as well. The revelers at the stage yelled and stomped and slammed together.

The outlaws were caught up in churning tide, a cauldron of roiling, jostling, colliding bodies, laughing all the while.

"Don't know what I expected," Oldavei said, leaping and body-slamming Wilhelm, "but this is glorious!"

"Hell," Torin said, head pounding to the drums, "this might be worth gettin' caught for!"

"Yeah, it's—" Wilhelm began, but stopped as he glanced at the darkened sky. "Oh shit, man, I gotta get to my show! Follow me!" He led the way as they forced themselves through the packed field to the edges and beyond, toward the massive stone wall that enclosed the city and the towering Shepherd's Gate, its formidable doors open to facilitate crowd flow to and from the field. Just beyond the gate they finally slowed once more to a walk, out of breath, wiping at sweat-soaked foreheads.

The streets were filled with revelers of every size and type, a crowd not altogether dissimilar from that which they navigated in Skarborough, absent the unnerving Salamar lizard-folk. The architecture evinced a similar style to that of the Jeweled City as well, though the structures here were far better maintained and aesthetically pleasing. Even in the midst of a raucous celebration, the community set forth an image that mixed style, whimsy, and sophistication.

They kept on along the cobbled thoroughfare, passing on their left the King Keg, a three-story affair with a gargantuan keg atop the roof. Along either side of the street, banners announcing BARD-IN in bold letters hung over the boardwalks from horizontal, spear-tipped flagpoles.

"It's up here," Wilhelm said.

When they arrived at the inn, Wilhelm looked to the rooftop, where a behemoth yellow sun could be partially seen, as if cresting the horizon. Above the main doors, just below a second-story balcony, were words painted in flowing white script across a wooden facade: House of the Rising Son Inn—and written smaller, just below—And Microbrewery.

"I'm gonna have the manager announce me with a different name," Wilhelm said. "Just in case, you know, since we're bein' stealthy."

"Mm, smart," Oldavei said.

The interior was expansive, with twin bars that wrapped from the flanks of the entrance to either side, halfway to the back of the massive space, which was dominated in its entirety by a large and relatively upscale stage. Rows of ornate sconces cast light on the mass of milling bodies. So far as any of the group could tell, all of the audience was standing; any chairs and tables, if they did exist, must have been removed to create more space. Near the back was also a staircase leading to the inn's upper levels. "I'd better get to the manager," Wilhelm said, breaking off and pushing through the crowd.

As the rest of them made their way toward the stage, Torin's axe brushed against a massive figure—the minotaur they had seen earlier out on the field, red-eyed, stinking of alcohol, keg still strapped to his back, flagon in hand. A thick coat of dark brown, coarse hair coated the upper portion of his chest, shoulders, back, and much of his head. His horns, roughly a forearm span in length, extended upward, curving to sharp points.

"Mind your toothpick, desert-trash!" the beast growled.

Torin jutted out his chin. "And you mind your fekkin' business," he retorted.

The minotaur pressed closer, glaring down, voice dropping even lower. "And what if I make *you* my business?"

"Ya might wanna fill up on more liquid courage first," Torin said, pointing to the flagon.

"Liquid death is more like it. One ounce of this brew would put you on your ass," the beast replied.

"Challenge accepted," Torin said with a grin.

Xamus, Nicholas, and Oldavei, who had been watching the interaction with mounting tension, waited, poised to intervene if necessary. Now they relaxed as the minotaur broke into a wide smile, revealing a set of thick, yellow teeth. "Grab a flagon!" he said.

A moment later, the outlaws had reached the foot of the stage, their path cleared by none other than the minotaur himself, whose name, they learned, was Molt Thunderhoof—a gladiator of some renown at the Grand Coliseum in distant Lietsin. During the off-season, Molt had become a regular at all of the realm's various festivals, though Bard-In was, not surprisingly, his favorite. And his brew, Torin acknowledged, was indeed potent. The dwarf had nearly finished his flagon, while the others had opted for separate mugs of various house ales.

Presently the manager, a paunchy, red-faced man wearing a frilly shirt and beret, announced from stage right, "And now, a hearty welcome for our next act! From parts unknown, the one, the only . . . Wallham Willaroo!"

Oldavei looked to Nicholas and Xamus and shrugged. Wilhelm came on and took a wide stance at center stage, mandolin at the ready. "Innis! If you don't get drunk enough tonight to forget your own mothers, then you did something wrong! Let's get hamro!"

Torin looked to Xamus. "What did he say?"

"I think he said 'hamro,'" the elf answered. "He said it earlier too."

"The fek is that?" Torin asked.

Xamus shrugged. The crowd's energy quickened with the anticipation of an explosive performance. Wilhelm surprised both the audience and the outlaws, however, when he initiated a series of melodic chords, joined by a set of smooth and soulful lyrics:

It gets heavy, life on the road
All paths lead to where you are
Through ups and downs you're lookin' back
To see you've come so far

The formerly boisterous drunks moved back and forth in a slow rhythm to the tune, drinks raised high.

The road ain't meant to be walked alone
Always better with a crew
When good times come just like the bad
It's good friends who see you through

The crowd cheered, clapped, and pounded on the tables. Molt cut loose with a roar of approval, pouring more "special brew" down his throat. Not to be outdone, Torin downed his entire flagon in one long pull. Oldavei looked around to see that Nicholas was missing. "Back in a bit," he told Xamus, and began working his way through the throng, scenting the air, tracing the assassin's particular odor to one of the side bars near the entrance.

Nicholas stood at the bar, awaiting a drink refill, looking to the stage. He was surrounded by a small group of men garbed in amethyst cloth, apprentices of Lietsin's Arcanimus Academy. Oldavei didn't like the demeanor of these drunken apprentices, and he liked the appearance of his companion even less: Nicholas's eyes appeared sunken, and his skin had become more startlingly pale than it had been over the last several days.

"Why can't they just once get some real fekking talent in this place?" a thin, scruffy-haired apprentice next to Nicholas said. He yelled toward the stage, "Go home, you oversized shit!"

As Oldavei worked his way to the bar, Nicholas engaged the heckler. "Why don't you show some respect?"

"Oh apologies, princess," the man replied, "Didn't realize that was your sweetheart."

"Continue speaking at your own peril," Nicholas warned.

"Ten of us," the man retorted. "And one of you—"

"Two," Oldavei said, stepping to them. "Still, no reason to bloody those fine garments of yours. If you don't like the music, do what you should do anyway: just keep drinking!" He offered a grin as he took Nicholas by the shoulder. "Off we go!" The man and his colleagues stared hard as Oldavei attempted to pull Nicholas away. The assassin shrugged Oldavei off, brought his face to that of the heckler, and said, "Outside. Now."

Nicholas's unnaturally penetrating glare caused the apprentice to back up a step.

"What, Brandyn, you lose your nerve?" a nearby apprentice mocked.

"Not likely," Brandyn replied, though the statement lacked conviction.

Oldavei considered leaving to retrieve their companions but knew that if the situation broke bad, they may not reach their friend in time. Nicholas and the heckler moved into the street, followed by Oldavei and the gang of mage apprentices.

A throng of revelers already on the cobblestones outside sensed the impending confrontation and cleared space. Nicholas stepped into the void, facing the array of students on the opposite side. Oldavei stood just a few paces away, weighing their odds. Arcanimus Academy was a college that taught mostly magical theory and history, so it was unlikely that many of these "fraternity brothers" were true magic casters. Still, the odds were not at all in their favor, and the murderous glint in the assassin's eye informed Oldavei that his friend was blind to that fact.

Nicholas assumed a fighting stance, glared at the men, and said, "Which one of you gutless pups is first?"

CHAPTER SEVENTEEN

ALL HELL BREAKS LOOSE

Brandyn was huffing, flexing his fists, clenching his jaw—working up his nerve.

"Any day now," Nicholas said.

"Don't worry," a fat apprentice on one side of Brandyn said, "you're covered." The others taunted Nicholas or encouraged their comrade. Brandyn moved forward, and Oldavei made ready to step between them when a voice cut in:

"Don't you see?" A bronze-skinned, dark-haired youth in saffron robes sauntered from the boardwalk opposite the House of the Rising Son, oozing smugness and arrogance from every pore.

One of *them*, Oldavei thought. *One of the Children.*

"This is where your depredations lead," the man declared. "To violence. And from there . . . what?" He strode to a spot between Brandyn and Nicholas, holding out his hands palms up as if catching rain. "The Sun-scriptures teach that a violent life ends in violent death. The pursuit of sex, material wealth, fame . . . these sins have blinded you, tainted your everlasting souls." He stuck out his index finger and turned in a slow circle. "Each one of you has fallen so low that only through holy fire may you be raised anew!"

He lowered his hand. "But only . . . if you join us. For some, maybe, it's not too late to become a Child of the Sun."

Nicholas took a step but was checked by Oldavei's clawed hand. The ma'ii walked in front of him, sniffing. "I smell a rat!" he said. The cultist glared back. Someone outside the ring of apprentices chuckled.

"No surprise," the man replied, "seeing that I'm surrounded by vermin."

Oldavei advanced, slowly, just as a light breeze blew through the street. "And what makes *you* fit to judge *us*?"

Nicholas understood, or thought he did, at first—the ma'ii had been trying to defuse the situation with the apprentices. Now, however, it seemed that a change had come over him. It was a curious shift, from peacemaker to . . . aggressor? Suddenly all the assassin's thoughts of tearing the mage-apprentices limb from limb evaporated as Nicholas considered the normally cheerful ma'ii's odd behavior.

The Child acolyte was set to answer when someone on the boardwalk called out "Yeah!" The cultist's look of smug confidence fell slightly.

"But you don't just judge, do you?" Oldavei asked, continuing forward.

Nicholas drew up to Oldavei, touching his arm. "Hey," he said, "let's just go. There's no value in arguing with fanatics."

Oldavei carried on as if he had not heard a word Nicholas said. "You're no better than all the other stuffed shirts and officials and hypocrite bureaucrats who think you're above everyone else. What's next? Maybe tell us what to eat? Or drink?" His voice was low but intense.

"Moderation is, ahem, key," the cultist replied. "The body is a temple of the Sun." Stirred by the ma'ii's words—many of them unsure as to why, only knowing that his speech stoked within them a sudden an undeniable assent—the street spectators closed in, crowding out the apprentices and surrounding the cultist, who backed up a step. Even Nicholas felt a rising hatred for the acolyte that he couldn't immediately account for. For a moment the assassin was confused. Did this animosity come from within him, or were these new and sudden feelings sparked by Oldavei? He fought to tamp down the rancor.

Oldavei continued fanning the flame he had sparked: "And where do you go from there? Maybe tell us how to talk, what to say?" Voices of accord rose from the crowd, including, now, one of the apprentices. Brandyn stood in place, looking hopelessly confused.

"The Sun scripture commands that—" A man in a leather jerkin spat at the robed man's feet as he continued to backpedal. The breeze strengthened, undulating the long banners hanging from the flagpoles.

Oldavei's eyes burned intensely. "Maybe tell us what to do, and how to do it?" Calls of agreement rose in volume. A tall woman with spiky hair pushed the robed man, whose head swiveled now in every direction, his eyes wide.

"Tell us who to love? Or why to love one over another, or tell us how many kids to have, or not to have any at all?" Oldavei stalked forward.

Nicholas attempted to pull him away. "Hey, enough. Don't you see what's happening?" But the ma'ii took no notice. Nearby, the fat apprentice threw his cup at the cultist, who quickly turned and forced his way through the throng that had doubled now in size.

Oldavei's voice rose. "Who are you to tell us what to think and what to be?"

"Who are you?" members of the crowd repeated, faces twisted in anger. "Who the fek are you?"

"Who are you?" Oldavei called out. "Who are you to tell us anything?"

"Fek 'em all! Tear it down!" the tall woman bellowed. And just like that, in an instant, all hell broke loose.

With Wilhelm's set completed, the bard had rejoined Xamus, Torin, and Molt at the base of the stage. The performance had been met with a wild, enthusiastic response, and several admirers—all of them female—had pressed the stage simply to meet the bard. He was conversing freely when all heard what sounded like absolute pandemonium outside. Patrons swarmed the inn's doors to catch a glimpse of the mayhem. Torin moved to join them, but Xamus tapped him on the shoulder, pointing to the ascending staircase.

They had reached the second floor when Xamus looked back to see that the minotaur had not followed them. Torin led on through a wide passage that opened onto the balcony. There, the trio looked down onto a screaming, rampaging mob. Windows were being smashed, small fires were being set, and shop fronts were being ripped away amid outcries of "Fek Lawbrand!" and "Fek the Children of the Sun!"

"Ho-ly shit!" Wilhelm exclaimed.

A thunder peal of booted feet drew their attention to the opposite end of the street, where light-armored city militia stormed forth, bludgeons at the ready.

Down in front of the inn, while Oldavei continued ranting, Nicholas glanced at the oncoming militia and took the ma'ii once again by the arm. He yanked Oldavei back toward the inn, shoving through the crowd, only to come face-to-face with Brandyn.

"You—!" Brandyn began just as the assassin launched a palm-heel strike into the underside of the apprentice's chin. His head rocked back, then forward, as he emitted a whimpering groan and spit out pieces of broken teeth.

In the middle of the street, the riotous mob met the advancing militia in an earsplitting tumult of crunching metal and breaking bone. The numbers were not on the militia's side, and the tide of raucous bodies quickly swelled over them.

High above, where Xamus, Wilhelm, and Torin watched, the balcony floor vibrated beneath their feet. They glanced to the far end of the street, where one of the yellow-jacketed quarry giants appeared. He reached up to the rooftop of the King Keg and ripped the massive decorative barrel free of its supports.

Xamus ran to the far end of the balcony, knowing what he must do even as he considered the chaos around him—the storm of riot and rage. He remembered the words of Amberlyn: *Quiet your mind and find your center.*

He controlled his breathing, thinking of that quiet clearing in Kannibus Hills. The stillness, the peace. He heard Amberlyn's soothing voice:

You must be the eye.

The crowd fled in a blind panic, away from the giant and toward the near end of the street, only to be faced with a second, yellow-jacketed, partially bearded colossus at the intersection. The giant squatted down and swept a hand from right to left, smashing several festivalgoers into the closest storefront.

Xamus focused his intent, whispered his incantation, and gestured with both hands held before him. A spark ignited into a flaming sphere. He looked to where the first giant at the end of the street was holding the giant keg aloft in one hand, preparing to throw it onto the crowd. He exerted his will on the fireball and sent it streaking from between his palms, out over the street, and into the massive barrel.

The flaming sphere immediately engulfed the keg, the flames bursting, searing the startled giant's palm. The behemoth bellowed, turned, dropped the barrel, and grasped the wrist of his badly burned hand, fire now igniting on the sleeve of his jacket. The giant ran, attempting to remove the blazing garment as he did so, around the street corner and out of sight.

The balcony rumbled again, a tremor too severe to be caused by either the fleeing giant or the bearded behemoth, who was still on his haunches and swiping at the crowd. Wilhelm looked to Torin, and as one, the two peered behind them. Xamus joined in as they ran back through the passage to the gallery overlooking the main floor of the inn, at first seeing nothing amiss. Then the entire back wall exploded inward, and the stage blew apart as a third giant broke through.

"Fekking hell!" Torin swore. The remaining spectators below, most of whom had thronged the inn's entrance, now stampeded out into the street as the giant barreled forward straight for the gallery where the trio stood.

"Go go go!" Wilhelm said, rushing back to the balcony.

Outside, the bearded giant had now plodded to a spot in front of the inn. Wilhelm leaped over the balcony rail, onto the brute's shoulder. He moved quickly to make room for Torin, who jumped next,

PART TWO: OUTLAWS

succeeding only by scant inches, grasping the thick, yellow jacket material for dear life. The giant backed away, reached up to grasp Torin, but Wilhelm slashed out with his sword, slicing one plump finger and causing the massive hand to recoil.

The balcony was shaking so violently Xamus could barely keep his feet. There was no more room on the giant's shoulder, so he went to the opposite end from where he'd sent the fireball. He put one foot onto the side rail, raised up, and shoved off into thin air, wrapping his arms around a dangling Bard-In banner just as an immense fist blasted the balcony to pieces.

On the street, a wild stampede of festivalgoers sought escape, trampling anyone in their way. Nicholas was grasping Oldavei's wrist and had been pulling him away now from the inn and its falling debris, away from the bearded giant toward the boardwalk on the opposite side of the street. The newly arrived giant swung their way, raising one gargantuan booted foot. Oldavei looked up wide-eyed . . .

Nicholas yanked him clear just as the boot came crashing down, turning cobblestones to dust. The giant stepped and lifted the foot for another stomp. A roar sounded from the alley next to the half-ruined inn; Molt charged from the darkness, head lowered, and impacted the giant's planted leg full-force, striking the knee and eliciting a startlingly loud, echoing pop! The leg buckled; the collapsing giant caught himself with one outstretched arm, and without hesitation the crowd turned on him, swarming, venting their terror and frustration and rage with multiple blows, piling on and over their gargantuan victim until a heap so great had collected that the giant could no longer be seen beneath.

On the other side of the devastated inn, Xamus slid down the banner and onto the top of a food vendor cart. Just a few paces away, the bearded giant spun in circles, grabbing at Torin and Wilhelm, who held on desperately and stabbed at the monstrous hands whenever they came near.

Though not much else remained of the House of the Rising Son Inn, the uppermost story had stayed mostly intact. Now, with very little left to support it, a cacophony of creaking, groaning, and snapping wood heralded the imminent collapse of the top floor. The bearded giant, who was situated just in front, looked up in time to see the massive sun decoration dislodge from the tumbling roof; the giant's realization came too late, and his reflexes proved too slow to prevent disaster. Whatever material the frame beneath the sun's yellow skin might have been, the outer layer must have been metal, for it set off a resounding *bong* when it struck the bearded giant's forehead. The globe bounced off and pulverized the nearby vendor cart as Xamus dove away from it.

The entirety of the giant went limp, and his eyes rolled upward into his sockets as he stumbled backward two steps, Wilhelm and Torin scrambled to clamber down the jacket as the behemoth fell back, an action that seemed to occur almost in slow motion. While the remainder of the inn's roof caved, the giant toppled as well, obliterating the storefront behind him and throwing up a voluminous cloud of dust. Wilhelm and Torin had just reached the giant's lower extremities when he struck earth, and as a result the jolt they suffered was minor. They crawled over the massive splayed legs, out into the street, where Xamus greeted them in front of what had once been the food vendor cart, now a pile of kindling with a jumbo-size sun on top. Nicholas and Oldavei made their way to join the three, and together they cast their eyes about, taking in the clearing dust, spreading flame, billowing smoke, and broken bodies. Down the street, a mound of rioters were still pummeling what was left of the giant Molt had charged. The minotaur was nowhere in sight.

CHAPTER EIGHTEEN
DISBANDED

Following the previous night's carnage, the outlaws had snuck away to the cheapest inn they could find on the opposite side of the city. Unlike their lodgings in Talis, this third-floor room, while not luxurious by any stretch, was at least clean and mold-free. The sheets of the four stacked beds were clean, the walls were painted, and the floor, which Oldavei claimed as his bed, was carpeted. Shortly after entering and doffing their equipment, each of them fell quickly into a long, deep slumber.

Nicholas was one of the first to awaken, well after sunrise. He moved to the window, pulled the curtain shut, and took a spot at an empty round table situated in the center of the room. Xamus soon came and sat across from him.

"So," he said. "One hell of a night, huh?"

"Mm," Nicholas replied.

"The way I understand it," Xamus went on, "you picking a fight with those students lit the fuse on the whole thing."

Nicholas glanced to Oldavei, just waking up on the floor a few paces away, looking concerned.

"Seriously, when I said, 'live every minute as if it's your last,' that wasn't exactly what I had in mind," Xamus said. "We gotta know that you can maintain control."

"Because I might draw unwanted attention?" Nicholas shot back. "What do you call coming to a festival with half of Lawbrand in attendance?"

"That's valid," Xamus answered, leaning in, "but it was a risk we all agreed on. The point I'm making is that we have to know we can rely on you. Our lives depend on it."

Nicholas frowned, the purple veins in his face standing out against his pale skin. "Me? Oldavei incited the mob," he said.

"That's true," Oldavei said.

"That's a separate matter," Xamus replied. Wilhelm and Torin had now sat up in their beds, listening. "He got drawn in because he was trying to wrangle you. Because of—"

Nicholas's eyes flashed. He bolted out of his chair. Xamus rose to meet him.

"What?" Nicholas said. "Go on, speak your mind. I was more than ready to bleed those fools, and if you don't watch your mouth—"

Nicholas moved to get closer to Xamus, but Oldavei was at his side, hand to the assassin's chest.

"Hey," Oldavei said, looking to Xamus, "he's right, you know. I was the one who—"

"This isn't about you, not right now," Xamus said to Oldavei. Then, returning his gaze to Nicholas, he said, "*You know* what this is about."

For a brief instant the rage in Nicholas's eyes flared. Then, like a passing storm, it dissipated. His frown relaxed. His eyes cast about, he retook his seat, and he sighed heavily. "I suppose I do," he said. "Still, you have to admit"—he smiled faintly—"it was glorious chaos."

"I think it's time to share your truth," Xamus said.

"What truth?" Torin called, standing up.

Nicholas gazed at Xamus. "Seems you're leaving me little choice," he said. The assassin looked around to the others, who gazed back, waiting expectantly.

The assassin swallowed, nodding. "Very well. Not so long ago I was involved with someone. A woman named Katrina. I love—loved her. And—"

"Ah, a woman," Wilhelm said as if he understood fully. "I shoulda known, it's always—"

"Pipe down and let him tell it!" Torin snapped.

Nicholas clenched his jaw, then continued. "I suppose she loved me, in her way. I never fully understood—always wondered what it was she saw in me. One day I finally just asked. She said that she detected something within me. Rage, strength, power, she said . . . lurking just below the surface. I responded to her words . . . because a part of me yearned to be something more than I was. Braver, tougher, better, more important, more confident. I could go on, but what it comes down to is that Katrina said she knew my deepest desires and could grant them." Nicholas stood, walked to the wall next to the window, and leaned against it. "She bit me," he said. Xamus sat quietly. The others looked to each other.

"A Night Devil," Torin said in a voice tinged with disbelief. "Well now, that explains quite a bit."

"Vampire, Night Devil, yeah," Nicholas replied. The others remained silent. "But I'm not fully turned. Yet. Katrina's people said they could teach me how to control what I'll become. Not just a vampire but a true assassin as well. They trained me to be what they call a Wraithblade. When I came across all of you in Hearthvale, Taron Braun was to be my first assignment. A way to prove myself."

Nicholas waited while the others processed what he had told them. "Anyway," he said, "maybe now you can understand why I haven't been so eager to share."

After a moment Oldavei spoke up: "What happened to Katrina?"

"She's still out there," Nicholas said. "Somewhere. Waiting for me to report back. When everything went to hell in Skarborough and then Talis, I figured I'd failed so miserably—"

"But you didn't," Torin said. "You didn't fail. At least not so far's your old flame knows. Your job was to kill Braun. Braun's dead."

"That's true enough," Nicholas said. "The crux of it is . . . I don't wish to go back. After that bite I just—I didn't feel like I belonged. Whatever it was she said she saw in me, whatever she was supposed to bring out in me, it didn't work. In fact I started to feel as though the best parts of me were slipping away, little by little. And recent months have borne that out." Nicholas's voice dropped. "I'm scared, if you want to know the truth. I'm scared because if I die"—he paused—"if I die, I *will* come back. But anything that was good in me will be gone forever."

Torin came to the chair that Nicholas had abandoned. "Well, that is quite a tangled knot." He dropped to the seat. "Maybe there's something we—"

"I've asked too much of you already," Nicholas interrupted. "You welcomed me, but the truth . . . the truth that you finally now know, is that Katrina and her associates *will* come looking for me. I'm destined for a bad end, and anyone who stays by my side is not likely to fare much better. And so"—he pushed off from the wall—"I'm taking my leave."

"No," Xamus said. "That wasn't why I—"

Nicholas held up a hand. "No. Me leaving is the right thing. I never should have put you in this position in the first place." He walked to the bunk he had slept in and gathered up his things.

Before Xamus could rise to stop him, Oldavei said, "He's right." Xamus glanced at the ma'ii in disbelief. "He's right 'cause I put all of you in danger too. All that . . . filth the cult freak was spouting, I just couldn't listen anymore." Oldavei's voice took on an edge. "I am so sick of people trying to control others. These so-called faiths and systems that . . . rob people of who they are. That kind of thing just makes me so mad . . ." He looked to the floor. "I used things that I learned when I was training to be a shaman. Magic, the kind that moves hearts, influences people. I didn't think, I just did it. I just wanted to shut his mouth, and I didn't think about anything else. We're supposed to be avoiding the law, and I did the very thing I hate . . . basically *controlled* that crowd. Started a riot. That's pretty much the opposite of helping." Oldavei went and collected his belongings as well.

"You don't have to do this," Xamus said.

Nicholas looked to Oldavei and nodded understanding. "Yeah," he said. "We do."

"Do this much, at least," Xamus said. "Stay local, for now. Give it some time. Meet back here in a fortnight, at sunset. If you still feel the same, we can all go our separate ways. In the meantime, if Ironside picks up our scent, maybe we stand a better chance if we face him together."

Nicholas considered, said, "Fair enough," and walked out the door to the hallway.

"Sure," Oldavei agreed. "Two weeks. See you then." He paused, as if he wished to say more, but ultimately he kept his own council and left as well.

Xamus sighed heavily and looked to Wilhelm and Torin. Wilhelm shrugged and said, "I can maybe find a gig for a couple weeks."

Torin sat, contemplating. After much deliberation he said, "I reckon I can occupy myself for a while." He looked around the room. "Might as well stay here, meantime, split the cost."

Wilhelm sat on his bunk. "Yeah, good plan."

Xamus stood, crossed to the window, and pulled the curtain. He gazed out over the city, thinking back to the visions inside the Bear Mound. What had any of it meant? Was there truly some destiny that awaited them, and if so, had they taken a wrong turn by coming here? He felt strange, unmoored, a sensation he was not used to.

As he looked above the rooftops to a bank of dark and foreboding thunderclouds, he sighed heavily, for in that moment, the future seemed more uncertain than ever.

PART TWO: OUTLAWS

CHAPTER NINETEEN

RECONSTRUCTION

Though Xamus had heard once that one should never return to the scene of a crime, later on that first day, while Wilhelm and Torin sought out their own distractions, the elf walked beneath a rumbling sky to the street where all of the previous night's mayhem had occurred. A small army of dedicated townspeople and local shop owners had set about the task of cleaning up. A tall ladder was brought and leaned against the King Keg. There a man with long gray hair climbed and pulled from a flagpole the tattered remains of an enormous yellow jacket.

Carts were brought in to haul away debris. Amid a thick downpour, Xamus observed the process quietly until sunset, at which time he returned to the inn, where he dried off and passed the night mostly alone, Wilhelm and Torin only returning shortly before first light.

Xamus spent the next day in much the same way and the next, while storefronts along the street of the riot were repaired. During the nights, he traveled the music-filled streets, seeking out wanted posters bearing their names and likenesses, ripping them down when he was certain no one watched.

After four days, Wilhelm secured another booking at a relatively upscale club called Smooth Moves. Xamus and Torin attended opening night, where the bard completed his set to a half-packed room and scattered applause. Later, as they smoked and drank, Torin spoke of a local sport he thought of taking up called skins, in which teams fought over possession of a leather ball; control of the ball, he said, was no privilege, as whosoever attained it suffered a brutal beating at the hands of other players. "Right up my alley," Torin said with a grin. "Got too many damned teeth as it is. They get in the way o' drinkin'!"

On the sixth day, reconstruction on the Inn of the Rising Son began, as well as the tenement the bearded giant had fallen into. At first, Xamus only did as he had been doing, and watched. At the outset of the next morning, he set to work with hammer and nail, assisting in reconstructing the frame of the Rising Son. Day after day he toiled, and night after night he and Torin attended Wilhelm's performances. Sadly the bard's irreverent songs and searing mandolin riffs proved an unfitting substitute for the trendy horn music the well-heeled clientele was accustomed to. After only five performances, Wilhelm was politely asked by the manager to leave and not return. "I'll find something new," the bard promised his comrades.

Steadily, the rebuilding of the inn continued, floors and stairs were completed, and work began on a new balcony. The labor not only passed the days but instilled in Xamus some small sense of accomplishment, and even, perhaps to the slightest degree, restitution.

At last the day of their meeting with Oldavei and Nicholas came. Wilhelm, who had slunk in during the hours just before dawn, had suffered a black eye since Xamus had last seen him, and he groaned as he sat up in bed, holding a hand to bruised ribs. "Don't wanna talk about it," he said when Xamus inquired as to his injuries. Torin, who sported bruises of his own from his ongoing participation in the game of skins, only chuckled.

Oldavei arrived shortly just before sunset, with Nicholas just moments behind. The assassin's skin was stark white with small, blue veins even more evident than before, and his sunken eyes had taken on a kind of reddish tinge.

After agreeing to talk over drinks, the outlaws walked out into the night, to a nearby establishment Torin had been meaning to visit, a sea-themed tavern called the Salty Dog. There, in a far corner, a three-piece band in pirate attire performed sea shanties on a stage made to resemble the deck of a boat. Ship's wheels, sails, and netting adorned the walls. Small knots of patrons lounged at the round tables or on stools at the bar along the wall. The group took up a spot not far from the entrance and ordered drinks from a plump, blue-eyed, black-haired beauty whose appreciative gaze lingered on Nicholas.

Torin held up his hands as if to say, "What the hell?" then looked to the others to see if they had noticed. Oldavei shrugged. Nicholas didn't seem to notice. Torin shook his head and said to Wilhelm, "Okay, you spill first. What's with the eye?"

Wilhelm hemmed and hawed as their drinks arrived, the barmaid offering Nicholas a smile before leaving. Wilhelm finally confessed, "I was askin' around about, you know, work opportunities . . . I mighta been slightly inebriated at the time. Anyway some joker says, 'You should try street fighting.' So I did; man, I figure I'm okay with my fists, so I went up against this freakish brute who musta been half ogre, but uh . . . yeah, I got in a few shots, you know, stick and jab"—Wilhelm mimed punches—"light on my feet, layin' a hurt, and then *pow*! Next thing you know I got hit outta nowhere, didn't see it comin'—they say it's the one you don't see that gets you, and that was no horseshit, 'cause it felt like gettin' rammed by a runaway bull, and that was it, man, snuffed me out like a candle."

Torin huffed. "Ah, just do what I do, drink the pain away."

"Yeah," Wilhelm said, smiling. "Get hamro."

"That's what you said up on stage," Xamus interjected. "What's it mean?"

"You know, man," Wilhelm replied. "Get hamro! Get drunk!"

"Call it what you like," Torin said, "long as the result's the same." The dwarf downed his drink, then recounted his daily battles on the skins field. "Lotta fun to be sure," he said. "Don't pay worth a damn though." He looked to Oldavei. "So what about you? Chewin' bones, chasin' your tail . . . ?"

"Pssh!" Oldavei scoffed. "For your information I gained perfectly respectable employment . . . at the Central Zoo."

"They let you out, or you escape?" Torin replied. The others laughed.

"Cleaning cages!" Oldavei said loudly, overenunciating. "I love animals. Love 'em a little too much I guess." He took a drink.

"What does *that* mean?" Wilhelm asked, eyebrows raised.

"I . . ." Oldavei cleared his throat. "I mighta had a few drinks one night and set a few of 'em free." The table burst out in laughter. Oldavei snickered along. "Turns out the zookeepers frown on that."

When the laughter died down, Oldavei and Torin both looked to Xamus, who was leaned back in his chair, boots on the table. He said, "I didn't do much of anything, really. I helped out rebuilding the Rising Son a little bit. It's comin' along. Should be good as new in a while, I imagine."

Nicholas and Oldavei both looked uncomfortable. "Well," Oldavei said, filling the silence, looking to Nicholas, "that leaves you." The others looked to the assassin and waited.

"I drank," Nicholas answered, avoiding their eyes. "A lot. Got a room at the Frosty Saddle and I drank. And when I wasn't drinking, I was sleeping. Didn't feel like doing anything else." He left it at that, and the table fell silent as everyone finished off the flagon and called for another.

"So . . ." Xamus said, pouring a new drink. "Where does all this put us?"

"I did a lot of thinking," Oldavei said, "while I was cleaning cages. What I think is . . . we'll never be able to stop running if we don't do something about clearing our names."

"Like what?" Torin asked.

"Find out more about the Children of the Sun," Oldavei said. "I've been thinking on this a while. The thing that gave me pause, though, was the worry that the Knight-Paladin is already moving to destroy the Children. But one night while I was out drinking, I overheard a conversation; a man who had come in from Lietsin said the Knight-Paladin and his Enforcers raided a warehouse there, but it was empty. They didn't find whatever it was they were looking for, he said, and that got me thinking: maybe they need information. Or proof of whatever it is they think the Children are doing. If we can get that, then we can use it . . . as leverage. Give that proof to the Knight-Paladin in exchange for a pardon."

"That's one of the reasons they killed Rhelgore, remember?" Torin pointed out. "Interferin' with their law."

"We wouldn't be interfering," Oldavei replied. "We'd be helping. Rhelgore was operating in secret, for his own ends. Ironside's sure to keep after us either way, if we find out something worthwhile and we play it right, maybe we stand a chance."

More silence, broken this time by Xamus. "Hell," he said, "I agree. Don't know if going after the Children is supposed to be our fate or destiny or whatever, but I think it makes sense. It's better than . . . whatever it is we've all been doing for the last two weeks. I think Oldavei's right. Ironside will find us eventually no matter what we do."

Around the table, heads nodded. Xamus looked to Nicholas. "And I wonder . . . with the Children's light magic, with the effect it has on you, maybe we can use that, find a way to solve your problem."

Nicholas exhaled. "What you all should do is get as far away from me as you—"

"Yeah, yeah, we've heard that before," Torin said. "And yet here we are. So quit your whinin'!"

Nicholas appeared ready to continue protesting, but he looked at each of their faces and saw only solidarity and something else as well, a kind of unconditional acceptance. With all that he had told them, they were still somehow willing to remain at his side. A rare emotion, one Nicholas had not experienced in a great while and feared he might never experience again, rose from deep within.

"Besides," Wilhelm said, grinning, "who else would bring us down when we all got too happy?"

Xamus took his feet off the table, leaned over it, and stretched his arm out, palm up. "We'll find the Children of the Sun," he said. "We'll find proof that they're a threat to Lawbrand, and we'll use that to clear our names." He looked to Nicholas. "And we'll figure out how to make things right for you again. We'll do it together." He looked to the others. "Are you in?"

Oldavei was the first to lean in and add his hand to the elf's. "I'm in," he said.

Wilhelm was next. "Hell yeah."

"Is a bullywug's ass watertight?" Torin said, forced to lean farther than the others.

Looking somewhat pained, Nicholas reached out and clasped his hand over those of his comrades. "In," he said.

"It's settled then," Xamus said. "We start tomorrow."

The knot of hands separated. "Another flagon!" Torin yelled out.

When the next pitcher arrived and the drinks were poured, Oldavei held up his mug and said, "Let's get hamro!"

The others held up their cups as well. "Hamro!" they replied in unison. The newest flagon was emptied in record time and led to more of the same, until all agreed that the time had come to settle the bill.

Xamus dug in his pouch and looked at the sparse coins in his hand. "Mm," he said. "Still have to pay for the room . . ."

Torin grunted. "Right. I'm runnin' a little low myself."

Oldavei slunk in his seat. "I was already tapped. Then the zoo withheld my pay."

"I hear that, man," Wilhelm said. "I got mugged while I was knocked out."

"No fear, gentlemen," Nicholas said, "I have the matter well in hand." He began pulling at a ring on the third finger of his left hand, a thick, lustrous loop with a black stone.

"Whoa," Xamus said, "we can—"

Nicholas waved him off. "Katrina gifted it to me," he said. "I have no more need of it."

When the barmaid returned and was asked to accept the ring as partial payment, she appeared skeptical at first. But the knowledge that it had been a possession of the assassin's, along with a pledge—disingenuous thought it was—from Nicholas that he would return the next night, succeeded in swaying her.

Wilhelm, Torin, and Oldavei rose and made for the door.

Before exiting, Torin looked back to see that Nicholas had stopped Xamus. The two spoke in whispers. Xamus's eyes widened slightly, and he shook his head. Nicholas grew insistent, and after a moment, the elf lowered his head and appeared to relent. As the two approached, Xamus in the lead, Torin asked if all was well.

Xamus pulled the brim of his hat over his eyes and said, "Yeah," in passing.

Torin grabbed his elbow. "'Cause it don't seem that way," the dwarf said.

"It's between us, and that's all I'll say about it," Xamus answered as he made his way out into the cool air.

They joined the others on the cobblestones and began retracing their earlier steps. A field of stars shone brightly above, while a thin veil of fog hovered at their feet. Clopping sounds echoing off the storefronts alerted them to a carriage, black in its entirety—drawn by two ebon stallions harnessed in black and silver with gently swaying black plumes, driven by a figure draped in midnight robes, face hidden within a darkened hood.

Halfway to the intersection, the outlaws passed the carriage. Torin watched, noting the sturdy construction, the absence of windows. It was a peculiar conveyance, he thought.

Oldavei's eyes were not on the coach; he was scanning their surroundings—the storefronts, a few inns with music and laughter pouring out. The ma'ii's ears pricked up, and he suddenly turned his attention to the rooftops. There he saw forms darting. Shadow figures leaped from one roof to another through . . . mist? The fog was on the ground, not the roofs, but the dark shapes appeared to shift from tangible to intangible, something that must assuredly be a trick of the light, the ma'ii thought. He stopped, as did Nicholas, peering up, a crestfallen look overtaking his pale features. "Damn," the assassin rasped, "she found me."

CHAPTER TWENTY
BLADES IN THE MIST

Oldavei stepped forward between Wilhelm and Xamus, as incredibly, mist poured down from the roofs to the cobblestones just ahead. Two clusters of the strange haze mingled with the fog, then morphed and lifted, much like figures rising from a crouched position. The swirling masses quickly assumed forms that were—however impossibly—human, as they solidified before the startled outlaws' eyes.

The assassins stood just a few paces away and were, like Nicholas, deathly pale. They wore garb similar to the group's companion as well—black sleeveless tops, black cloth breeches, and soft-soled cloth shoes, with straight swords strapped to their backs. Black, cold-weather-style masks obscured all but their eyes. They smelled, to Oldavei's enhanced senses, like death. It was a similar odor to that which he had detected on Nicholas upon their first encounter but, in the case of the newcomers, far more pungent. They didn't smell as if they courted death; they smelled as though they were, in fact, dead. Perhaps most off-putting of all were their eyes, the irises of which glowed a striking red.

"Night Devils," Oldavei said, his voice tinged with awe.

Behind Xamus, Wilhelm, and Oldavei, Nicholas spun. Torin, who stood relatively close, looked behind as well. A figure dropped from the roof above, impacting the stones in a low crouch not far from the black carriage. The female, dressed like the others but in finer cloth and with no mask, drew up. Two swords extended from behind her back, angling out to either side. She stepped forward, revealing stunningly beautiful features set against alabaster skin, framed by long, platinum-white hair. Her eyes burned like small, crimson rings.

"Katrina," Nicholas whispered, while at the coach the hooded figure stepped off and onto the cobblestones, looming silent and grim, wrapped within cloak and hood.

"*That's* your lady friend?" Wilhelm called to Nicholas, then followed up with, "Nice!"

"Shut it!" Torin barked.

Katrina addressed Nicholas in a smooth, deep voice. "You were given a task to perform." She took a step forward. "Perform the task, report back. Simple. And yet, you force me to track you down. How long did you honestly think you could hide?" When Nicholas didn't answer, she said, "It seems to me that you've lost your focus. No more games. Say farewell to these"—she looked to his companions—"distractions. Return with us to where you truly belong. It is time to rejoin your family, Nicholas."

Nicholas shook his head. "You are not my family."

"What are we then?" Katrina said. She tipped her head toward the others. "What are they? You will come to see them for what they are: worthless wanderers. Street trash. Not worthy to be in the company of one such as you. Have you told them . . . who you are? What you are?"

"Yes," Nicholas answered.

"Who and what *we* are?"

Nicholas understood the import of the question. The wrong answer would most assuredly result in yet another target on the group's heads. "They don't know anything that should cause you concern," he answered. "Leave them be."

Xamus had made a three-quarter turn to see Katrina but also keep the assassins before him in his peripheral vision. He said, "We stand with Nicholas. And he's not going anywhere he doesn't want to go."

"Mm," Katrina said, glaring at Nicholas. "Somewhat impressive, I'll admit"—she reached up, arms crossed, and drew both straight swords from her back—"that these friends of yours are so ready and willing to die for you."

A blur of movement: Katrina lunged for Torin but met with Nicholas's blade. The two whirled away in a frenzied flash of clanging steel. Torin drew his axe to assist, but the robed assassin threw back his cape and pulled from his belt a sickle. He was thickly muscled, with a scar beginning just under his left eye and disappearing beneath his mask. Determined to strike first, Torin charged.

Several paces away, the two masked Wraithblades in front of Xamus, Oldavei, and Wilhelm bared steel. Following his comment to Katrina, Xamus had already begun whispering, concentrating on a somewhat obscure spell, but one he hoped would be affective. The ma'ii and the bard rushed to engage the vampire who faced them as tendrils of fog rose up and clung to the enemy just in front of Xamus. Amazingly, the wispy haze gained increasing substance while its surface texture took on a cloying, gummy quality. The vampire looked down, briefly distracted and confused by the webbing that had silently, craftily ensnared him. Xamus, blade drawn, rushed in, burying his sword to the hilt in the assassin's chest.

Just down the street from the carriage, a tavern door opened. A couple, arm in arm, staggered out, took one look at the battle raging before them, and rushed back indoors.

Near the coach, Torin swung with all of his might and speed at his scarred adversary. Wherever the dwarf struck, aiming for some vital piece of anatomy, he was stymied, for the assassin was there one instant and gone the next, his movements almost too rapid for the eye to follow. Nearby, Nicholas and Katrina battled no less ferociously. For every strike, it seemed, there was a parry and counter. Katrina used the left-handed blade deftly for defense, the right-hand weapon for attack.

"You've grown more skillful," Katrina said in between strikes. She smiled. "Good."

Nicholas had, thus far, held his own, yet while his opponent's energy seemed inexhaustible, his own vitality was rapidly dwindling.

Though Oldavei and Wilhelm fought expertly and held the advantage of two against one, their foe managed to somehow always outmaneuver them. Of the two outlaws, the ma'ii acquitted himself best, nearly matching their adversary's speed, and even landing some superficial slashes with his scimitar, though the wounds seemed of small concern to the devil—and why not? Oldavei reminded himself that if these Wraithblades were indeed truly dead—as both evidence and myth suggested—then cutting them would surely yield little result.

A short distance away, this theory was being put to a very definitive test by Xamus. The sword thrust that certainly would have ended the life of any mortal being had failed to snuff out the existence of his foe. The man simply stared with his fire-ring eyes. Xamus, boots caught up in his own webbing, recoiled. The assassin reached with his free hand to yank down the black mask. A slow smile crept across his pallid face; his mouth opened, revealing pointed canine teeth as a hiss escaped the devil's throat. Suppressing the shudder that rippled down his spine, Xamus ripped free of the web, yanking his sword out of the nightmare-thing's chest and taking several backward steps. The devil, still smiling, began slashing at his bonds with his straight-edged sword.

At the coach, Torin missed an axe swing, leaving himself overextended, a mistake that he immediately moved to correct, jerking his head backward, evading the counterslash aimed at his neck by a hair's breadth. He did not, however, escape the swift, savage kick that followed, catching him midchest and catapulting him hard enough into the side of the carriage to knock him immediately senseless.

At the same instant, a small throng of patrons exited a door not far from where Oldavei and Wilhelm battled their enemy. The band of merrymakers disgorged in a loud, aimless torrent, laughing uproariously and nearly tripping over one another, their momentum alone carrying them over halfway across the street, sweeping up both Wilhelm and Oldavei in their surge and cutting Xamus off from his freshly disentangled adversary.

The action diverted Nicholas's attention for only a second, but such was all Katrina needed; she delivered a vicious spinning kick that caught her opponent on the chin just as he turned to face her. As Nicholas crumpled, Katrina shouted a command in what sound like a foreign language.

The sight of drawn swords awoke the confused tavern crowd to the danger of the situation, prompting them to scatter in all directions. Wilhelm, Oldavei, and Xamus drew into a tight formation, scanning for any sign of their vampire foes, but the two had suddenly vanished.

Xamus spun, ready to rush to Nicholas's aid, but he, Torin, and Katrina had all disappeared. The elf's eyes flicked to the closed, secured doors of the carriage. "Yah!" a voice blurted from the coach's seat, and the stallions immediately bolted. The three outlaws gave chase as fast as their legs would allow, but to no avail—one half block later they could only watch helplessly as the grim conveyance gained the far intersection and wheeled round the corner and out of sight.

CHAPTER TWENTY-ONE
THE OSSUARY

They had spent the rest of the night, until sunup, searching all of Innis for the black carriage, asking those they passed on the street if they had seen where the coach went after it had escaped the outlaws' sight. Their efforts had been in vain, but as they slouched back along the cobblestones toward Xamus's inn, a thought struck the elf. He snapped his fingers. "Frosty Saddle," he said. "That's where Nicholas told us he was staying." Xamus set off at a rapid pace, Wilhelm and Oldavei following on tired legs.

"I'm pretty sure they didn't take him back to his room," Wilhelm said.

"No, but he might have left something behind," Xamus replied. "A possession. Something, anything, that I could use . . ."

"Ahh . . ." Oldavei said, loping faster.

"I'm lost," Wilhelm replied.

"There's a trick he can do," Oldavei said, indicating Xamus. "You missed it first time around. But he can use a personal item to help locate someone."

"No shit," Wilhelm replied, flabbergasted.

"How'll we get into his room?" Oldavei asked.

"I've picked a few locks in my time," Xamus answered.

"Of course you have, lowlife!" the ma'ii replied.

They continued on to where Xamus had remembered seeing the inn. There they stormed inside and found the innkeeper, a man with a sunken eyes and thinning hair, behind his desk.

"Morning," the elf began. "We're seeking a friend. Black cloth from head to toe, blue glasses, carries a straight sword." Xamus was unsure if Nicholas would have provided his name. "Could you tell us what room he stays in?"

"Stayed," the innkeeper corrected. "Didn't come in last night, and he was already two days behind on payment."

"I . . . see," Xamus replied. "But his travel kit—"

"Sold to a local merchant," the innkeeper said with a wide grin, revealing stained teeth. "To pay for the aforementioned room."

"The merchant's name?" Wilhelm asked.

"Farley," the innkeeper replied.

Xamus was already on his way out the door as the innkeeper called out, "Why such an interest in his travel kit?"

On the street, Wilhelm and Oldavei struggled to keep up.

"To the market, I'm guessing," Oldavei said.

"To the market," Xamus confirmed. "And quickly. 'Cause for all we know . . . we might already be too late."

★ ★ ★

Torin awoke, blinking rapidly to clear his blurred vision, waiting for his eyes to adjust. Flickering ambient light from a curving tunnel illuminated the square earthen chamber he found himself in. How long had he been here? Where was "here"? Despite not knowing precisely how long the carriage ride had taken, for he had been unconscious all the while, the dwarf couldn't shake the sense that a significant amount of time had passed. Maybe a day, maybe more.

He was aware that his wrists were shackled high above his head; a quick upward glance revealed chains extending to a ring set into the cracked stone ceiling. Blood had dried on his tattooed arms, from cuts in his wrists. His shoulders, thankfully, were numb, and his boots dangled roughly two feet off the ground. Smells of damp earth and decay were pungent. Small, whitish chunks and bits littered the floor, increasing in size and quantity to where they formed small mounds along the periphery of the space—bones of every description, including skulls and pieces of skulls. Torin felt gooseflesh raise along his skin.

To his left, Nicholas hung, wrists manacled above him as well, feet hanging nearly to the floor. The assassin's head lolled, chin to his chest, but he was both alive and awake, breathing roughly, blank eyes gazing down. His blade was nowhere to be seen. Torin craned his neck, behind, then to his waist, to find that his own weapons were missing. A faint shuffling noise drew his attention to a plump gray rat, roughly the size of his fist, rearing up on hind legs, whiskers twitching as it sniffed at his feet.

"Fek off!" Torin barked, kicking empty air. The rat squeaked and ran for the tunnel, dragging its long tail behind.

Torin looked to Nicholas. "Where the fek are we?"

"Sargrad," Nicholas answered without looking, his voice hoarse. "Under the streets. Place called the Ossuary."

"Huh," Torin said. "Somebody oughta tell 'em they have a rat problem."

Footsteps alerted them to someone approaching. A shadow bounced and fluttered on the tunnel wall outside the chamber, followed by the arrival of Katrina. The vampiress swept in to stand a short span from Nicholas, fixing him with a crimson stare. "I took you in," she said. "I trained you. Brought out the best in you. I made you one of us." Her features twisted. "And not only do you try to flee, but I couldn't help noticing when I bound your wrists . . . there was no ring." Her voice was low, menacing. "The symbol of our love. And you . . . what? Gave it away? Sold it? Did it truly mean so little?"

Nicholas licked dry lips. "You should have told me . . . should have told me what you were from the beginning. Should have warned me that courting you meant forfeiting my soul."

"And if I had?" Katrina asked.

"I would have told you to take a long walk off a short pier."

The hand that struck out was little more than a pale blur. Nicholas's head whipped to the side, bleeding from a slash on the left cheek.

"Hey!" Torin exclaimed. "Hurt feelins' aside, he did what you wanted. He killed Braun." Katrina turned her lustrous eyes to Torin, and the dwarf became briefly lost in her gaze. "I, uh, I have proof," he said, recovering. "In this pouch, just here." He dipped his chin to his kilt.

UNDER THE SUN

Katrina was next to him without his registering that she had even moved. She pulled from the pouch a snatch of cloth that bore Braun's sigil. "See?" Torin said, "He did it; Braun's dead. But after that, the Knight-Paladin Ironside put a bounty on us, forced us into hiding."

"Hiding?" Katrina responded, holding the cloth in one hand. "In a tavern, for all to see? Seems an extraordinarily foolish way to evade capture." She stepped back over to Nicholas. "And if *you* killed Braun," she said to him, "why does the dwarf carry his token?"

She wadded up the fragment in a clenched fist. "We do not work with outsiders. You know the rules. And you chose to break them." Behind her, the firelight in the passageway guttered, its faltering light crossed by a great shadow. Katrina looked over her shoulder, turned, and put her back to the side wall.

A slightly hunched figure glided through the tunnel, tall enough that his head nearly scraped the roof. He issued into the chamber, moving with both grace and lethal intent, and as he rose to his full height in the larger space, everyone, including Katrina, seemed to shrink in his presence.

"Master Dargonnas," Katrina said, bowing her head.

Dargonnas's hair, swept back from a widow's peak, gleamed darkly in the scant light. Blue veins traced the contours of his starkly pale skin. He wore a black frock coat, gray formal shirt and ascot tie, and brocade vest, formal pants, and lace-up boots, all in black. The man's unblinking, penetrating eyes captivated Torin, while at the same time seeming to draw all warmth from the room. As the newcomer's stare fell on Nicholas, the assassin felt nearly powerless, like a rabbit cornered by a wolf. "Loyalty," the master said, in a voice deep as a bottomless pit that reverberated inside Nicholas's and Torin's chests.

"Loyalty is what I demand, above all." He whisked forward to Nicholas. "And it is precisely your loyalty that has been called into question. You were Katrina's pet, and she, ever the idealist, believes you might still be redeemed, that you only momentarily lost your way."

The vampire reached out with long, skeletal fingers that terminated in shining, pointed nails. He gripped Nicholas's chin and raised it to meet his gaze. His hand was as cold as the grave, and when he spoke, no air seemed to leave his lungs. "I do not share her optimism." Dargonnas wheeled to Katrina. "I wish to know all that transpired, in detail and without doubt."

Katrina inclined her head. "Of course."

Nicholas blinked, and in the hair's breadth of time that his eyelids were shut, Dargonnas had left the room, guttering the tunnel flame once more with his departure. Katrina turned to Nicholas. "This is a misery of your own making." Leaning close, she whispered, "I would have given you the world." With that, she turned and wafted from the chamber.

Nicholas looked to Torin, his face slack. "They're going to torture us," he said. "I'm sorry. I'm so sorry that I got you involved in this."

"Don't be," Torin replied. "Xamus, Oldavei, and the bard . . . you mighta gotten us into this, but they'll get us out. Just you wait and see."

CHAPTER TWENTY-TWO
THE PROMISE

In the process of making their way to the market, the outlaws passed the House of the Rising Son Inn, where a massive replacement yellow orb had been constructed atop the roof and was being hoisted by workers onto new supports to the applause and shouts of spectators in the street.

Once at the market, a brief search led Xamus and the others to a canvas-covered stall between two textile vendors, where Farley stood at the ready, miscellaneous items and tools neatly arrayed on the table before him. When asked, the swarthy, suntanned merchant recalled purchasing the travel kit. "Mm, yep that was me," he advised.

The trio waited. "And?" Xamus pressed.

"Sold," Farley answered. "First thing. To an old prospector."

"Local?" Xamus asked, already dreading the answer.

"Nope," Farley replied. "Traveler. Already set to leave, just needed the kit. Took it and hit the road."

Xamus's jaw clenched.

"He say where he was going?" Oldavei asked.

The merchant shook his head. "And I didn't ask."

"Now then, my good friends," Farley said, grinning widely and sweeping his hand above the table, "pick an item or make way for paying customers."

* * *

Torin had at least two broken ribs. Every breath felt like shards of glass being ground into his side. He was missing yet another tooth, somewhere toward the back of his mouth on the upper right. His boots had been removed, and a small vein in his right ankle had been nicked. After torturing him, vampires, including the scarred one he had fought, bled him, but not too deeply, enough to fill a goblet before they had stanched the flow.

Despite all of this, the dwarf felt that Nicholas had been dealt the more rotten hand. The interrogators had asked him questions: "Have you told anyone who you work for?" "Are you a spy?" "Do you know of anyone plotting against us?" and they had commanded him to recount all of his actions since leaving on the task to kill Braun. After Nicholas had complied, they burned his shirtless torso repeatedly with branding irons. They would desist for a short interval, then return and repeat the entire routine from the start. This had gone on for hours.

The assassin, who had fallen unconscious, now came to and regarded Torin through bleary eyes.

"You still think they'll come?" he asked.

"I do," Torin answered. Nicholas huffed.

"Been meanin' to ask you," the dwarf said, squinting one eye at Nicholas. "At the Salty Dog, before we left, you cornered the elf and had words. What about?"

Nicholas didn't reply.

"Don't you think there've been enough secrets?" Torin asked. "Come on, spill! It's just us."

More silence. Finally Nicholas said, "I made him promise me . . . that if I died, he wouldn't let me come back. As one of them."

"I thought as much," Torin said, his voice tinged with . . . something. Nicholas thought it to be anger. "Let me tell you somethin'. When I was little, my people had just started to settle Red Bluff. Basically, back then, it was just a big refugee camp. Rough goin'. Hardly no water or supplies, whole families separated, and orphans like me scattered all over the place. I had to scrounge or fight for every crumb I ate. It was a miserable fekking existence, and there was no reason to think it would ever get any better. There was a saying among all us orphans, one that for a long time I thought was stupid. They used to say, 'Keep the faith.' You know what that means?"

"I can guess," Nicholas said.

"It took me a long time to understand, to think about it in a way that made sense. You know what it means to me? Got nothin' to do with what gods you answer to or what you believe in. It's a way of saying, 'Fek you,' to everyone who's trying to grind you under their heel. It means that shit gets bad. We get tested to our limits. But so what? What the fek are you supposed to do, give up? Horseshit! Sometimes all you can do is keep the faith. They can beat my body to shit, but there's somethin' else, somethin' deep down they can't lay a finger on. I said the others'll come for us. Maybe they will, maybe they won't. Maybe we'll find our own way out. Either way, what do you do?"

Nicholas clucked his tongue.

"Say it," Torin said.

The assassin hung silent.

Torin persisted, louder: "Say it, fekker!"

"Keep the faith," Nicholas said. "Happy? I'll keep the faith."

Torin smiled. "Damn right you will."

And Nicholas realized that what he had detected in the dwarf's voice a moment before was not anger but grim determination.

★ ★ ★

As the sun set, Xamus, Wilhelm, and Oldavei sat at the table in the elf's room. He stared across at the bunk where Torin had slept, wishing that rather than "traveling light," the dwarf would have left behind a travel bag or some other personal items.

They had spent the rest of the day wandering, looking for any sign of the carriage. In the waning hours they returned to Xamus's room, sat, and argued about what to do next, without resolution. As much as Xamus hated to admit it, they had hit a brick wall.

"I do a much better job of thinkin' when I'm drunk," Wilhelm said.

"You and me both," Oldavei replied. "Not like we can afford it though."

"That's it!" Xamus, whose mind had been drifting, snapped to attention. "Idiots," he said. "We're all idiots. Let's go!" He stood, grabbed his sword, and rushed for the door.

PART TWO: OUTLAWS

"Where?" Wilhem asked.

"The Salty Dog," Xamus replied.

Wilhelm frowned, as did Oldavei. Then, like a bolt out of the blue, it hit them, and they said in unison, "The ring!"

CHAPTER TWENTY-THREE
BOHEN DUR

Torin's right eye was nearly swollen shut. The draining of blood had caused him to grow light-headed and slightly confused. His breathing had become a constant struggle for every shallow, agonized intake of air. He had lost all ability to measure the passage of time and, denied sunlight, had no sense of day or night. Sleep was impossible, so his only respites from the waking agony were the short periods of time that he fell unconscious.

Nicholas had resorted to breathing through his mouth due to his nose being repeatedly broken. His chin hung to his chest, his body a limp mass of dead weight.

Katrina came, practically appearing out of nowhere, and held Nicholas's cheeks in her hands, lifting his head. "I have Dargonnas nearly convinced to relent, but in order for this to pass, you must swear fealty. Only through a pledge of your undying loyalty will he permit your continued existence."

"Horseshit," Torin said through swollen lips.

"Listen to me," Katrina said, ignoring the dwarf, her forehead to Nicholas's. The assassin shut his eyes as Katrina continued. "For generations, I have suffered under the rule of small-minded masters who are mired in the ways of old, incapable of envisioning a future where we emerge from the shadowed alleys and gutters. Far too long have we hidden among rats and crumbling bones. I recruited you for a reason. It has always been your loyalty I desired, not for Dargonnas, but for myself alone. To bolster me. Be my right hand. Support me in forcing change. Do you understand what I'm saying? A change in leadership. Together there is no limit to what we might accomplish. This has always been my plan, to conduct our business in the open, to wield power rivaling that of the mightiest guilds. But I needed to trust you before I might share it. I implore you, play the part: appease the master's ego; swear fealty to him, kiss his feet for three days, long enough for him to carry out the plans that *I* set in motion. The contract that I negotiated, that he takes credit for. When the time is right, I will give the word, and together—together!—we will supplant him, destroy the old and ring in the new."

Nicholas shook his head. "Even if you were to take over as leader and do all that you say, you would still be nothing more than a slave." He opened his eyes, gazing deeply. "A slave to what you've become. And you'd have me be a slave as well. My answer is no. When I die, I wish to die free. I want no part in your schemes."

Katrina lowered her hands. She locked eyes on Torin and approached him, close enough that he could feel the coolness radiating from her skin. "And how fare you, dwarf?" she asked.

"It's the . . . absence o' alcohol that's got me downright agitated," Torin answered, spittle dripping to his chest. Nicholas, who had seen Torin shivering, thought the comment might possess a kernel of truth. It pained him to think of withdrawal piled on top of all the other tortures the dwarf had stoically endured.

Katrina returned to Nicholas. "I like your friend," she said. "I like his spirit. Keep in mind, you can heal, he cannot. I give you one hour to make your choice. Swear yourself to Dargonnas. Pledge your sword to him; pledge your heart to me. Do this, and I'll convince the master to spare your friend. We'll make him one of us. An eternal warrior. Refuse me, and he dies. Slowly, painfully, and permanently." Katrina turned and breezed from the chamber.

★ ★ ★

Because the barmaid had been enamored with Nicholas, she had kept the ring. Also because she had taken a liking and because she had become attached to the ring—which she wore on the pointer finger of her right hand—she was loath to part with it.

It had taken almost an hour of convincing, along with a number of items—a fetish trinket from Oldavei, a ring from Xamus, and Wilhelm's glasses—to finally persuade the barmaid to relinquish Nicholas's ring. From there, the trio raced to the library, waking the owner, who stayed in a lodging just above, pleading for just a moment with a map, convincing the wiry, white-haired man that it was a matter of life and death.

They stood now in an open area on the main floor, surrounded by tome-stuffed shelves. On a low table before them, a large map of Lawbrand lay unrolled, the ends held from curling by candleholders.

Wilhelm and Oldavei watched, transfixed, as Xamus held the ring in his open palm, over the map's center. He closed his eyes, chanting softly. As the ring lifted, rising toward the ceiling, Xamus withdrew his hand. The ring flew in a wide circle while the quiet incantation continued. The loop tightened; the ring slowed, until at last it came to a stop, hovering, then fell, not bouncing but speeding and adhering to the map and table as if pulled by a magnet. All three looked to see where it had landed.

"Sargrad," Oldavei said.

"Nicholas mentioned he'd met his lover there," Xamus said. He put his finger on the map, on Innis. "How long?" Wilhelm asked.

Xamus traced his finger from Innis to Sargrad as Oldavei spoke: "Two days by carriage. By foot . . . maybe twice that."

Xamus's heart sank.

★ ★ ★

Nicholas tried to gauge how long Katrina had been gone. Though he could not say with any certainty, he felt sure that their time had nearly come to an end.

"I'm going to do what she wants," Nicholas said.

"Like hell you will," Torin replied, speaking in between wheezing breaths.

"At the very least, it might buy you time," Nicholas reasoned.

"Even if your . . . lady friend's bein' straight with you," Torin said, "you think her master would spare me just . . . on her say-so? These don't seem like the kind to leave . . . loose ends."

Nicholas, who had still not divulged all he knew of their captors, didn't answer.

Torin continued, "They aim to kill me in any case . . . so don't go makin' rash decisions based on my welfare . . . we'll find another way."

"I have to try," Nicholas argued.

"Just do what I said," Torin replied.

"Keep the faith, yeah," Nicholas said. "Look, that's not—" Just then, noises reached their ears, sounds of struggle. A pained grunt, a gasp, a shout silenced midway through.

Hushed voices, then, from just around the tunnel bend, where Torin knew their guards to be, a scuffle, a flicker of the torchlight, and a sound like a long exhalation.

"Ha!" Torin chuffed. "What'd I tell ya?" Torin said, "I knew they'd—" He and Nicholas both felt a presence then before any presence made itself visible, a strong, undeniable sensation. Neither the assassin nor the dwarf detected any of the cold menace emanated by the vampires. Nonetheless, the unseen presence unsettled them.

A few small particles that appeared to be ash blew into the bone-filled chamber. A shadow approached. Nicholas looked to Torin, who would have shrugged if he could.

A figure crossed the threshold then, a medium-size male garbed in travel-worn cloth and leather with a wide orange scarf around his neck, trailing over one shoulder. In his hands, two fighting sticks, sharpened to points. He stood and gazed at them placidly through slate-gray eyes.

The captives stared back, mouths open. Torin broke the silence: "Who the fek are you?"

CHAPTER TWENTY-FOUR

ESCAPE

The newcomer looked from Nicholas to Torin, then back again, appearing as if he wanted to ask questions, maybe who they were and why they were there; instead, he placed the two sticks into sheathes on his thick, pouch-laden belt. He bowed his head, closed his eyes, and raised his hands. At once, the shackles on both Nicholas and Torin's wrists snapped open and dropped heavily to the floor.

"How . . . the fek—" Torin groaned.

The stranger picked up Nicholas's shirt, discarded in a corner, and tossed it to the assassin. He spoke in a quiet, controlled voice. "We must hurry. Can you walk?"

Nicholas, grunting, donned his shirt, gained his feet, and stumbled to assist Torin, whose legs would not yet hold his weight. Once Nicholas had Torin's arm around his waist, he nodded to the stranger.

Their liberator led the way, through a short, curving hall, past a flickering sconce to a larger intersecting passageway. He looked both ways, then set off to the right. When Nicholas and Torin gained the passage, they observed a wide, arch-roofed, sconce-lined brick tunnel. Small piles of what looked like ash lay in spots along the corridor in one direction. Nicholas faced the opposite way, his arm around Torin's waist, pulling the hefty dwarf along, his own legs barely able to withstand the effort.

For his part, the dwarf cursed at the sight of what filled the corridor—more bones. Heaped to either side along the floor, smaller pieces crunching beneath their feet. More disturbing, however, were the full skeletons that lay in repose, inside shadowed recesses—three high—in the walls, cadaverous hands folded over collapsed ribs, some with shreds of cloth still clinging, some clad in bits of armor or, in some cases, full suits. At the trio's approach, rats scurried and skittered among the remains, making the corpses sound as if they had begun to stir and might crawl out from the darkened alcoves at any instant.

Their guide moved past a side chamber and halted; Nicholas and Torin drew to the space and looked in to see a room filled with weapons—shields, helms, pikes, swords, some stacked or leaning against walls, others haphazardly tossed to the floor. Nicholas's short sword and Torin's axe both lay near the far wall.

"Go," Torin said. Nicholas slipped the dwarf's arm away, leaving him leaning against the stony edge of the entry. The stranger glanced back, drew his sticks, then took two steps forward to where a passage intersected theirs, from the same side as the weapon chamber.

Torin stumbled forward, barely capable of standing but not wanting to place his hands near the corpses, as the man glanced down the adjoining tunnel and thrust one stake toward the opposite wall. The dwarf heard rattling and clinking from an alcove there; his jaw dropped as the stranger flung his arm across his chest, and a skeleton clad in a helm and chest plate flew out from its hideaway, tilting upright and smashing into a dark blur—what the dwarf realized was an oncoming and now very surprised vampire. Torin took another step.

A dark streak sped toward them from the tunnel ahead. The man pointed his stake forward and slightly to the left, then swiped across; fragments of another skeleton launched from a recess, jagged pieces perforating the onrushing devil, who stopped, perplexed.

Nicholas issued from the weapons room carrying his straight sword and Torin's axe, which he handed to the dwarf, stopping to watch as the stranger ducked under a sword swipe from the first vampire, who closed distance after discarding the armored skeleton. Timing his counter perfectly, the man struck out with the stake in his left hand, impaling the Wraithblade before he could deliver a follow-up strike. The vampire's entire body, clothing and all, turned gray, cracked, and crumbled into a fine dust—a process that transpired in less than an instant.

No sooner had the stranger dealt this blow than he threw the stake in his right hand, which flew at remarkable speed, end over end, striking the second, onrushing devil in the center of the chest. That assailant also turned to ash.

Even as the remains settled to the dusty floor, a mist raced from behind, flowing over the fallen stake, condensing as it approached the trio. The stranger shoved out his empty right hand, palm forward, and he seemed, to Torin and Nicholas's surprise, to emit some kind of aura, though each assumed their eyes might be playing tricks on them. The mist ceased its forward motion as if meeting with an invisible wall. It then flowed backward, its movement seeming chaotic, uncontrolled—smoke caught in a turbulent wind. It passed the stake, roiling, collecting, taking form finally as a stumbling Wraithblade. The would-be attacker turned as the stranger threw the stake in his left hand. The new foe however, a female, was either faster or more aware than her less fortunate counterparts. She caught the projectile with both hands, its deadly tip a finger span from her sternum. A smile spread across her face but quickly fell as the stranger pointed his fingers to the stake on the floor and flicked upward, launching the second missile into the woman's chest. She fragmented and turned to falling powder as the two stakes hit the floor.

Nicholas and Torin remained transfixed, staring in silent awe, only regaining presence of mind as the newcomer advanced farther down the corpse-flanked tunnel.

By the time the two caught up, the man was standing at another side passage, gazing to the far end. There, Nicholas and Torin beheld, barely, an iron door with a barred window, scantly lit by distant sconces.

The stranger made as if to move forward but caught himself, screwing his head slightly to his left. "What—" Torin began but was quickly shushed.

"More approach," the man said in a placid tone. He glanced their way, narrowing his eyes slightly. "Too many for me to fight alone. Come!"

He moved quickly, assuredly, as Nicholas and Torin struggled to keep up. Katrina, Nicholas knew, was on her way. He could feel it.

Their new companion felt it too. "Hurry, hurry!" he urged, leading them beyond the chamber where they had been held captive, pushing on along ghostly corridors, past occasional ash piles, through twists and turns at last to a short passage, from which they ascended winding stone steps. Up and up they climbed. At times when Torin would stumble and pull them both down, Nicholas hoisted them both back up. Their battered and weakened legs had neared failure when a voice—Katrina's voice—echoed loudly through the halls.

"Nicholas!"

The stairs ended at an egress, where they stepped onto a stone floor. The stranger sheathed his sticks, slammed a trapdoor closed, and shut the bolt, sealing the stairwell. It would not be enough, though, Nicholas knew. And once again the stranger seemed to be of the same mind. He stepped back, perspiration now beading on his forehead.

The trapdoor shuddered violently.

Nicholas and Torin risked a look at their surroundings: casks, massive casks, some sitting upright, most lying crossways, stacked to the brick-vaulted ceilings. A wine cellar. The stranger reached out, and it was one of the giant upright casks that he was endeavoring to move through whatever mystical power he wielded; the barrel obeyed, rasping slowly across the floor. The glow that Torin and Nicholas thought they witnessed enveloping the man earlier was now undeniable.

The trapdoor heaved once again, wood groaning and cracking. Torin and Nicholas both struggled to reach the barrel, which stood a head taller than the assassin. They leaned their weight behind, hastening its progress. The door, Nicholas knew, would not withstand another charge. One more shove, and the cask came finally to a stop, its bulk covering the trapdoor entirely. A muffled impact vibrated the staves, followed by a muted howl of rage.

The stranger, looking only slightly fatigued, stepped around and dipped his chin to them, the strange aura now gone. "Well done," he said. "That will hold them for now. I am Piotr."

"Nicholas," the assassin said. Torin followed with his own name.

Piotr nodded. "Follow me," he said. "I will take you someplace safe."

CHAPTER TWENTY-FIVE

STRAND

The trio cut through several alleys, making their way slowly out of the Meatpacking District, stopping for rest as needed. Visibility was poor, with moon and brazier light being constantly filtered through a murky haze, not fog but smoke. It tickled the back of Torin's throat, further complicating his already labored breathing. Their guide, who had wrapped the orange scarf around the lower half of his face, turned back every once and again to ensure the two were still following.

They encountered no one up until the first main thoroughfare, where a band of what looked to be drunk dockworkers approached, eyeing first Torin and then Nicholas as if the two were freaks in some carnival show. A wary look at Piotr, however, compelled them to focus their attention elsewhere and pass in silence.

They approached a boulevard corner, where a hoary old Sularian street preacher appeared out of the smog, arms thrust wide as he sermonized: "'Tis faith that braces the strongest bastions! Faith that girds the cathedral spires!" As they drew nearer, the robed man fixed them with his wild-eyed gaze, jabbing a knobby finger. "Nay, you say, 'twas steel! And yet I say unto you that faith and steel are one!"

Faith and steel, thought Torin as they pulled away from the rambling preacher. Two words that summed up everything he knew or had ever heard about Sargrad. Many considered it the capital of all Lawbrand. Its population eclipsed that of any other Trade-City, its preeminence built on a marriage of religion and industry. And of the indomitable, fortresslike structures that squatted or soared among the various districts, none exemplified the power of the church and commerce more than the Cathedral of Saint Varina.

Even as Torin considered this, the edifice itself appeared, looming through a pocket in the smoke like some majestic marble and steel mountain. Its myriad spear-like towers stabbed skyward; soft-glowing lights bathed its varied levels, faces, and facades. Twinkling pinpricks of luminescence glittered from a thousand-thousand windows. It was an awe-inspiring sight, one meant to impose, to subjugate. And indeed, Torin felt miniscule in its presence. He had only heard tales of the cathedral, had never seen it, but now those tales, bombastic as they had been, did not do justice to the spectacle that greeted him.

"Yeah," Nicholas said at his side, gazing upward. "Stopped me in my tracks first time I saw it too."

The dwarf only then realized that he had halted, stopping the assassin in the process. A few paces ahead, Piotr was waiting. "Just a little farther," he said.

"Where is it you're taking us?" Nicholas asked.

"To an ally of mine," Piotr said, voice muffled through the scarf. "No friend to the devils." He faced forward, and once again they were on the move.

A clamor soon met their ears: sounds of activity, raised voices. They came to a wide boulevard lined with stalls and tents—an open-air market. Few customers at this hour, packed instead with supply carts delivering fresh foods for the coming morning. Near the corner where they stood, a wiry man tossed some of the biggest salmon Torin had ever seen from the rear of his wagon to a bearded fishmonger.

Piotr pointed across the street to a single structure that occupied the end of the block, appearing to be a cross between a keep and an inn. A wide tower took up one corner of the Gothic-style, four-story building. At the ground floor, Torin noted three separate entrances, one at either end and another in the middle. All across the face of the strange dwelling and up the tower, windows of every size and description from tall to square to arched looked out onto the street, some dark, others lit from deep within, or showing flickering candles on interior sills.

"That is my ally's home," Piotr said, having pulled down his scarf but speaking loudly still, as a now-empty delivery cart rattled by.

"Which part?" Nicholas asked.

"All of it," Piotr answered.

Nicholas glanced over his shoulder, first to the dark avenue behind, then the rooftops above. So far as he could tell, they had not been followed. He and Torin trailed their guide through the market to the center door. Piotr opened it with a key, then quickly ushered the two inside before closing the door behind them. The space they entered was one long, relatively narrow hallway leading to a dead end. Only one other door existed in the middle of the wall to their left. Nicholas approached, his hand stopping just shy of the knob, when Piotr said, "Don't open that door."

He shouldered past the two of them and strode to the end of the hall, where he motioned for them to approach. As they complied, the man leaned his full weight into the end wall on one side. The section rotated around a central, vertical pivot with a grinding sound. Piotr passed through the right side followed by the puzzled assassin and dwarf, who found themselves in a similar dead-end hallway, this one with no doors, only a lit sconce on one side. Piotr rotated the wall shut, then moved to the sconce. He told Nicholas and Torin to make room as he grabbed the sconce base, turned it a quarter of the way and back. The assassin and dwarf retreated slightly as a section of ceiling swung down, and a three-tiered ladder telescoped downward, feet striking the floor.

"Come," Piotr said, and climbed up.

Nicholas assisted Torin as they ascended to the second floor, down a hall to a staircase, and up, beyond the third floor. "I've about had my fill of stairs," Torin commented as they at last reached the top floor and proceeded through an open entryway into a large, circular room—evidently within the tower—where a man in a sharp gray suit stood, gazing out of the arched windows.

A desk took up space near the far wall, with a fancy leather chair behind, not far from a small oak bar stocked with spirits. Sconces elsewhere bathed the room in warm light. A large rug occupied the center of the floor.

Piotr stepped around this as he entered, pointing to it and saying, "Don't step there."

The man turned to regard his new guests. The eyes that surveyed them were a light green; the face presented high cheek bones, thin lips, and a hawk nose. Short, thin hair that appeared to be a mixture of brown, gray, and white topped his head. He stood with a peculiar posture, straight but leaned back and slightly to his left side. In his right hand he held a delicate glass, half filled with a pinkish drink. His left arm hung at his side, the hand—

Torin, squinting his unswollen eye to see in the firelight, noted that the hand appeared to be held in a closed fist. But something about it struck him as . . . off.

The man was looking questioningly to Piotr. "They were being held," Piotr said. "Tortured. This is Torin," he indicated the dwarf.

"And I'm—" Nicholas began.

"I know who you are, Amandreas," the man spoke in a tenor textured with age. "My agents have tracked you, off and on, over many weeks. You"—he raised the glass, pointing with one uncurled finger—"were one of the very few to escape the devils. Almost anyway."

"And who the hell are you?" Nicholas replied.

"This . . ." Piotr said, holding out his hand toward the older man, "is Archemus Strand, vampire hunter."

The older man turned slightly, affording Torin a better look at his left hand. Or what had been made to *look* like a hand. It was wooden.

"Hunter, huh?" Torin spoke in a still-weakened voice. "Must not be easy to hunt, given your, eh . . . condition."

Without a word, Strand raised his fake arm, pointing the fist in Torin's direction. Four holes existed where knuckles on a real hand would be. Something akin to an arrow launched from one of these, impacting the wooden entry frame just a short distance from Torin's shoulder.

The dwarf turned to see a polished wooden stake jutting from the frame. "Well, that's handy," he quipped.

"Archemus has killed more vampires than any living human," Piotr informed.

"What of the others?" Strand asked Piotr.

"I couldn't reach them," Piotr answered.

"And now the element of surprise is lost," Strand said. "That's unfortunate."

Torin spoke up. "Anyone care to clue us in?"

Piotr looked enquiringly to Strand, who returned a slight nod.

"We speak of my brethren," Piotr said. "Bohen Dur monks. Sworn to protect the people of Lawbrand for as long as any can remember and destined to oppose the vampires."

Nicholas had heard of the monks, practitioners of something they called the Eminence, a psychic projection of will. "However, I thought you were peacemakers, not warriors," he said.

"The world sees us as we wish to be seen," Piotr replied. "In truth we wage a shadow war against evil."

"Piotr and I met hunting the devils," Strand said, advancing assuredly despite the slightest limp on his left side. "Lately Dargonnas and his scum have been killing or scooping up the monks, locking them away down in the Ossuary." He stepped around the rug to a spot between Torin and Nicholas and yanked the stake-arrow from the wall. "It's one of the ways we knew they were readying for something. Something significant." The old man rotated the stick in his hand, narrowing his eyes as if contemplating shoving the stake into Nicholas's chest. "You'll tell us all you know of their plans," he said.

"We know little," Nicholas admitted. "Just that one of their . . . top agents, Katrina, negotiated a contract, one that Dargonnas took credit for . . . and a mention of 'three days.'"

Strand and Piotr shared a look. The old man glared at Nicholas. "Three days, you're sure?"

"Yes," Nicholas answered.

PART TWO: OUTLAWS

"Mm!" Strand said. Crossing to the desk, he sat down his drink, deposited the thin stake into the empty hole in his fake limb, then pressed the wooden fist down onto the desktop, locking the arrow in with a click.

"This number means something to you?" Nicholas asked.

"Together," Strand replied, reaching his drink once again, "Piotr and I have formulated a list of possible operations the devils might carry out. Over time, with the help of my many spies, we've narrowed that list to a handful of scenarios. But three days . . . that number only aligns with one event on our list."

"*A Sunset in Torune*," Piotr said, and Torin and Nicholas both felt waves of raw energy flow from him.

"Sunset?" Torin asked, clearly confused.

"It's a play," Strand replied. "One of the city's most beloved. Three nights from now will be its final performance, at the Grande Theatre. Rumors have it all of Sargrad's high society will be in attendance. Fabricator's Guild, Sularian Cardinals, upper clergy . . ."

"All of the church elders in one place at one time," Piotr said, and Nicholas and Torin detected again from him the powerful, invisible ebb and flow. "The vampires intend a purge."

"Katrina did say that she intended for the Night Devils to emerge from the shadows," Nicholas said.

"You also mentioned a contract," Piotr replied.

"I've long harbored suspicions that certain Cardinals within the hierarchy wish to ascend beyond their station," Strand said, looking mildly apologetic. "They might have paid handsomely to have their competition removed."

"*Or* this may be a plot to overthrow the city leadership," Piotr offered.

"Whatever the intentions," Piotr said, "we will see them undone."

"Agreed," Strand replied. He looked to Nicholas. "*If* your information is good."

"It's all I have," Nicholas answered.

Strand nodded and walked to the windows. "We'll formulate a strategy." He looked over his shoulder to the assassin and dwarf. "And while you convalesce, you'll remain here."

His tone made it clear there was no room for debate.

CHAPTER TWENTY-SIX

ARRIVAL

"Hooo!" the wagon driver called over his shoulder, announcing that the caravan had neared Sargrad's outer walls.

Two days after setting out from Innis, Xamus, Oldavei, and Wilhelm's journey had been shortened by a day, owing to the good fortune of taking up with a lumber caravan from Orinfell bearing fuel for the city's great steel forges.

There had been no room on the driver's seats of the six-wagon caravan, so the trio had ridden atop one of the massive piles of two-foot-thick timber on the last wagon in line, sitting or lying on the rough bark, aware of every subtle shift beneath them whenever a wheel—each one roughly Xamus's height—struck either rock or rut.

Oldavei had given his dagger in exchange for the transport, happy to do so in the interest of saving precious time in the search for Nicholas and Torin. The driver's only caveat: that they may not ride atop the lumber through the gatehouse at Sargrad's outer wall. Such would certainly draw the attention of the guards and delay their delivery. The arrangement, of course, sat well with the outlaws also, who wished to go unnoticed.

And so, when the creaking wagon slowed and the driver gave the previously agreed-on shout, the trio disembarked and stood, watching the massive carts rumble toward the Iron City's monumental gatehouse and outer walls. Factory peaks rose from behind the wall, surrounded by smokestacks belching thick plumes, carried away by an easterly breeze, and above all, the Cathedral of Saint Varina prevailed, its spires seeming to rake the sky.

A smattering of raggedy peasants and hooded pilgrims ambled along the highway, making for the city as well. The outlaws hugged the side of the road close behind a stooped man with a walking stick. Wilhelm removed his hat, eyeing their destination wearily.

"Guards are bound to be on the lookout," the bard noted.

"Something I've been thinking about," Oldavei said.

"Thought we agreed that 'thinking' was a bad idea," Wilhelm said.

The ma'ii ignored him and continued: "Knight-Paladins like Ironside are run by the church, right?"

"Yeah," Wilhelm answered, a question in his voice.

"Sargrad is the base of the church in Lawbrand. See where I'm going with this?"

"You mean that we're entering the heart of the lion's den?" Wilhelm replied.

"Something like that, yeah. I mean it's not just militia here, it's the Order-Militant. So-called Peacekeepers. The exact same people who want our heads."

"Like I said," Wilhelm answered. "Thinking's a bad idea."

Xamus regarded the massive entry, the guards on the wall walk, and those posted outside. He watched as the sentries briefly inspected the lumber wagons one by one, then let them through. A clatter arose behind them, directing Xamus's attention to a covered merchant wagon pulled by two draft oxen with a single driver.

"Pick up your pace," Xamus said, and the three passed the hunched man. Up ahead, the last of the lumber wagons passed through the gate while the merchant wagon drew alongside. Xamus whispered an incantation, gave a slight gesture with his left hand, and watched the driver's head slump to his chest.

Wilhelm and Oldavei, who had both been watching the elf, realized what he had done and grinned widely. They quickened their pace as the wagon pulled ahead, the oxen's reins now hanging limply from the driver's slack hands.

"Ho there!" one of the lightly armored guards called, raising a hand as the transport approached. "Ho, I said! Stop!" The guard, who had placed himself in front of the oxen, jumped to one side as the wagon continued on and through the gate. The sentry, along with two other guards, rushed after it, and those stationed on the wall walk turned to watch the runaway wagon as well.

"Hurry!" Xamus said, and within an instant, the three were through the gate, watching the wagon rumble down one of the outskirts' cobbled streets followed by a handful of shouting guards.

They sped on, casting occasional backward glances. All around them stood—or in most cases leaned—dilapidated structures shabbily constructed from scrap materials. To the side of a doorway covered in ragged cloth, a dog-faced gnoll sat on his haunches, gnawing on a bone.

"Still think we should split up," Wilhelm said, donning his hat. The gnoll watched them warily as they passed, while at a street corner ahead, a dark-haired man of medium height clad in a leather jerkin and breeches kept eyes on them as well.

Xamus ignored the bard's comment, having already expressed his opinion during the journey that the vampires were far too dangerous for any of them to potentially confront alone. The elf cleared his throat, aggravated by the city's thick air.

"So what now?" Oldavei asked. "Maybe if we start with taverns around the perimeter and work our way in . . ."

"You three!" the man called, approaching. He fixed them with dark eyes beneath thin, arched brows. In a lowered, nasally rasp, he said, "Your friends, I can take you to them."

Wilhelm, Oldavei, and Xamus all exchanged incredulous looks.

"What friends?" Wilhelm replied.

"Don't play stupid," the man said. "Do I look like Order-Militant? I'm just here to help."

"You're serious?" Oldavei asked.

"Yeah," the man said, looking around to see that they weren't drawing attention.

"How could it possibly be that easy?" Wilhelm asked.

"Your descriptions were provided," the man said. "By your friends. Who are waiting."

"And who are you?" Xamus asked.

"Slayde," the man huffed, eying each of them expectantly.

"Uh . . ." Wilhelm looked to the others, at a loss. Oldavei shrugged.

"Do you want to see them or not?" Slayde demanded.

Xamus considered that the man might be operating in service of the Knight-Paladins, but surely if the order knew they were there, they would just arrest them. Same with Ironside and his Enforcers.

Or, perhaps more likely, Ironside would kill them outright. Of course the stranger might work for the devils as well, luring them to a trap. But if so, he might also lead them to Torin and Nicholas.

"Okay." Xamus nodded to Slayde. "Take us."

Slayde led them around the corner where he had stood. There, a horse-drawn coach was waiting. This conveyance was fully enclosed, but unlike the one that had swept Torin and Nicholas away, this coach was smaller, with curtained windows and comfortable seating for four. The driver was a jovial-looking fellow in a floppy hat. Once inside, Slayde banged on the roof, and the carriage set off.

They ambled through busy streets. Occasionally, on the side where Xamus and Wilhelm sat, they looked out to see the cathedral through the hazy morning air, forced to squint against sunlight reflecting off the spotless glass and polished steel. Moments later and a few blocks away from Saint Varina's, they passed another massive, ornate structure that Slayde identified as the Grande Theatre. It sat alongside the Talisande, which bisected the city's east side. The structure was more ostentatious than almost any that the outlaws had seen up close. Oldavei leaned over to see past Wilhelm, transfixed by the theater's powerful yet graceful flying buttresses and the elegant lines of its glass-and-steel construction. Marquee banners announcing a coming play—*A Sunset in Torune*—swayed in the breeze.

The coach proceeded over a great stone bridge that spanned the river and came to a stop. As the outlaws exited, they were bombarded by a riot of raised voices. Slayde walked them to a corner, where they looked onto a spectacle which made all other Trade-City bazaars seem half-hearted affairs; here, all along the wide thoroughfare, crowds of patrons thronged shoulder to shoulder amid the clustered tents and shouting vendors. "Welcome to the Sweep Markets," Slayde announced.

As they waded into the thick of the herd, Oldavei put a hand to Xamus' shoulder, who in turn laid his hand on Wilhelm's shoulder so that the three of them would not be separated. It was only Wilhelm's height that allowed him to keep eyes on their guide as they jostled their way to a corner door at the base of some castle-like structure just behind an apothecary tent.

Slayde unlocked the door, which opened onto a wide, empty hallway. He locked the door behind them, walked to a wall sconce, twisted it, and pushed, swinging a short section of wall into a shorter hallway, where he stood and motioned them in.

"Uh, no," Wilhelm said, shaking his head. "No, no, this does not look right . . ."

"Stop bein' a baby!" a voice called, and in that same instant, Torin stepped from the small hallway, his face bruised, right eye slightly swollen, smiling his increasingly toothless smile. "What are you fekkers afraid of?" he said, then laughed heartily.

"You're alive!" Oldavei said, rushing past Slayde, wrapping his arms around the dwarf and sniffing furiously at his neck and shoulders.

"Ah!" Torin blurted. "Get off me, ya spastic shit! Of course I'm alive." The dwarf looked to Wilhelm and Xamus as Oldavei stepped back. "Now that you're here, quit fiddle-fartin' around and come downstairs."

Torin descended a set of stone steps at the end of the small hallway. Oldavei, Wilhelm, and Xamus followed as Slayde swung the wall door shut.

They emerged into a spacious subbasement. At one end, beyond square, floor-to-ceiling pillars, two long tables and a handful of chairs, Nicholas waited. "Took you long enough," he called out, throaty voice echoing. He appeared far less battered than Torin, who, Xamus noted, was moving a bit slower than usual.

The assassin motioned to a man standing nearby, with short salt-and-pepper hair, wearing cloth and leather and an orange scarf around his neck. "This is Piotr," Nicholas said. "A Bohen Dur monk. And this gentleman . . . " the assassin extended his hand to where a gray-haired man sat at the end of one table, dressed in an expensive-looking smoky-colored suit. "Is Archemus Strand. They're both experts at exterminating vampires."

Torin joined Nicholas as Wilhelm, Oldavei, and Xamus stepped up and nodded at the monk and vampire hunter. Xamus's eyes wandered then to the wall behind Nicholas and Torin, where all manner of items were hung or displayed: some whose purposes were easily determined, such as crossbows and wooden practice swords, while others—vials, medicine-style bottles on shelves, and what looked to be garlic cloves—hinted at more curious functions. Added to the array were wooden stakes. A multitude of them varying in size and length. A thought struck Xamus then, a claim he had heard long ago, that a wooden stake through the heart would dispatch a Night Devil.

He shifted his attention to Nicholas and Torin. "It's good to see you two alive," he said. "We were worried."

"We have them to thank," Nicholas said, using both hands to indicate Piotr and Strand. "And I'll tell you all about how we survived, but there are other things to be said first. I want to thank *you* as well. You came to Sargrad for me. For us—" Nicholas looked to Torin.

"Just like I said they would," the dwarf interjected with a nod and wink to the others.

"You've stayed by my side through the worst of things," Nicholas said. "Your loyalty has been tested and proven again and again, and it is appreciated beyond what I could ever express. But if you stay with me this time, you *have* to be aware of what you're up against. There's an explanation you need to hear, and one that's long overdue. Have a seat."

Wilhelm, Oldavei, and Xamus complied, sitting at the table's near side.

"It's time I told you," Nicholas said, "about the Draconis Malisath."

It was something else Xamus had heard whisperings of late at night in tavern corners; tales spilled from drunken lips, no two ever the same, though all of them revolved around some powerful, shadowy criminal empire.

"The Malisath are a vampire cabal," Nicholas said. "They operate in complete secrecy, yet they guide the operations of organized crime across the entirety of Lawbrand. They run everything from gambling to smuggling to extortion to theft. And through various means they directly control some of the Trade-Cities' most influential figures in both politics and the church."

Nicholas paused, allowing this to sink in. It was a tremendous statement: one faceless organization manipulating all criminal activities across the land.

Torin scanned the faces of his comrades. "First I'm hearin' of this too," he said. Then to Nicholas, "At some point you mighta casually mentioned, 'Hey, by the way, I'm mixed up with the scariest, most powerful, bloodsucking criminal-mastermind fekkers who ever existed!'"

"I should have," Nicholas admitted. "And I apologize deeply for not doing so. There were many occasions that I wanted to, but I always knew that such knowledge could easily get all of you killed."

Torin waved a dismissive hand. "Ah, everybody's tryin' to kill us anyway."

"As I said," Nicholas continued, "I should have told you before, but this knowledge is more important now than ever. Because it will inform what you choose to do next." He walked over, grabbed one of the empty chairs, and placed it in the open space before them, taking a seat, leaning forward, looking to each of them in turn as he continued.

"We believe that the Malisath is going to make some kind of power play, possibly by executing several high-ranking members of the Sularian Church at a performance tomorrow night at the Grande Theatre. I've pledged my sword to both Strand and Piotr, who are dedicated to seeing the Malisath purged from our world. I'll be there tomorrow night, along with the monk and the vampire hunter, to face down both my former lover and whatever scheme the Malisath may set in motion. We'll be heavily armed with weapons that are known to be lethal to them. Strand," Nicholas said, nodding to the older man, "he has a small army of spies . . ."

"They are not, however," Strand spoke up, "trained killers." He gazed hard-eyed at the elf, ma'ii, and bard. "And Piotr's Bohen Dur comrades, who would be valuable allies in a fight, have been taken captive by the devils. All of this is to say that we could use your help. And I'm willing to pay handsomely for it."

For a moment, silence hung.

"I for one don't take kindly to bein' tortured," Torin said. "Which means the devils have some payback comin' due."

Nicholas marveled at the dwarf's resilience. To have gone through so much at the hands of the vampires, to be fully aware of their capabilities and yet be willing to confront them once again.

Strand nodded. Xamus, Wilhelm, and Oldavei all considered. "This may be the only way that you'll truly be free of them," Xamus said to Nicholas. "Because of *that*, I'm in."

Though Nicholas didn't respond, his expression and his gaze conveyed the gratitude that he felt.

"It's a good point," Wilhelm replied. "Plus, if we save some high and mighty church officials, who knows? Knight-Paladins might be less inclined to kill us on sight."

"I doubt it," Torin said.

"Either way, I'm for it," the bard said.

All eyes turned to Oldavei. He grinned, and in the back of his mind, he thought about his conversation with Talonhand, about running from fate, whatever that fate may be. "Sounds like fun," he said. "Count me in."

"Excellent!" Strand said, groaning as he rose to his feet. "I suppose the next order of business then . . . will be getting all of you fitted for tuxedos."

CHAPTER TWENTY-SEVEN

A NIGHT AT THE THEATER

Masterful, ornately framed paintings depicting various scenes from throughout Lawbrand history lined the walls of the immense foyer, hanging above bars serving only the finest drinks and vendors selling everything from gelatin to cakes to wild boar. Newly emerging stars peeked through the high glass-and-steel ceiling. In one corner, a trio of violinists provided soothing mood music. Arched entryways barred by velvet ropes attached to gilded stanchions bounded the reception area on one side. Marble statues of mythological heroes stood atop plinths at various places among the growing crowd, many of whom were openly staring at the clustered outlaws.

Almost every one of the adventurers had either provided specific directions in the tailoring of their tuxedos or made modifications of their own—Nicholas's shirt was open, exposing his chest beneath the jacket; Torin had refused to wear breeches and was garbed instead in a tuxedo shirt and jacket on top and a tailor-made kilt on bottom, feet shod in fine leather boots. Xamus had insisted on wearing his hat, as had Wilhelm, who wore the traditional shirt and bow tie but ripped the sleeves off both jacket and shirt immediately upon donning them.

Oldavei, despite wearing the most "normal" formal evening attire in some ways seemed the most out of place. He tugged constantly at his jacket and collar, looking acutely uncomfortable as he tramped around, scenting the air for any telltale vampiric death smells. He strolled next to one impeccably dressed, bejeweled older lady with hair piled atop her head and leaned in, sniffing her neck. The woman shrank back in revulsion. A tall, mustached man next to her stared open-mouthed. "Sorry," Oldavei said, offering a toothy smile. "You look lovely this evening."

Some attendees—local journalists—deigned to approach the group, one female asking Wilhelm and Nicholas if they would be playing in the orchestra, pointing to the cello cases each carried over one shoulder.

"Ah, dumpling," Wilhelm answered. "My sweet serenades would straighten your hair and curl your toes." The woman shrank back, looking mildly horrified. "Alas, I can give nothing away at this time."

"I . . . see," the female scribe said, offering a forced smile before departing. Wilhelm downed his third glass of pricey merlot, purchased with a portion of the generous advance paid by Strand.

Seemingly satisfied for the time being, the remaining journalists hastened away to harass actual celebrities, who numbered heavily among the crowd, their arrivals accompanied without fail by the screaming fans who had gathered just outside, held back by the theater's security force.

"Well, at least we're not attracting attention," Torin cracked, taking a pull from his flask and handing it to Xamus. All of them maintained a watch on the ten robed individuals gathered in the center of the massive space—the church officials they had been tasked with monitoring. The men and women, Cardinals and elders of the Sularian faith, looked resplendent in their robed, formal regalia as they engaged in polite conversation with members of Sargrad's upper crust.

Slayde approached, black hair meticulously gelled, cutting a slick figure in his formal attire despite the cello case on his own back. "No vampires yet, so far as I can tell," he reported. Strand soon joined the group as well, his flawless tuxedo fitting him like a second skin.

"If any of the theater officials are aware of Dargonnas or Katrina, they're not admitting it," Strand said. "Of course, they may very well use different names."

Wilhelm, able to see over most of the guests, spotted Piotr, who kept watch on the church hierarchy from a different angle, near a bank of food vendors. The monk had chosen a rougher cloth for his suit and a jacket that was loose-fitting to hide the weapons he carried. He met Wilhelm's eyes and nodded to indicate that nothing was amiss.

"Hey now, who's this?" Torin spoke up, tipping his flask toward an extravagantly attired female iron dwarf.

"Lyanna Ironbraid," Strand answered. "Executive-Director of the Fabricators Guild."

Even as Strand spoke, the iron dwarf looked over in their direction. Torin smiled and waggled his eyebrows, causing Lyanna to scrunch her face, looking at Torin and his expensive clothing as if trying to reconcile the two. She positioned herself with her back to him and returned to her conversation. It was a reminder of the enmity between iron and desert dwarves, and a reinforcement of the discomfort Torin already felt here among the upper crust. He shook his head, chastised himself for being so sensitive, and took a pull from his flask.

"Who's that she's talking to?" Xamus asked, indicating a stern though beautiful woman speaking to Lyanna, wearing dark, more intricately designed robes than the other church leaders.

"Laravess Kelwynde," Strand said. "Grand-Justiarch of the Sularian Church."

"Ah, the top banana, huh?" Torin said. "Tonight's show really did bring all the muckety-mucks."

Just then, a voice called from just outside the central theater entrance. "Ladies and gentleman, the performance will begin shortly. Please take your seats!" The man pulled the velvet rope to one side, as did his counterparts at the adjoining entries, who then positioned themselves to check tickets.

"Here we go," Strand replied.

The group waited for the church leaders to begin making their way. As they did, Strand, Slayde, and Piotr maneuvered in front of them. With their tickets and the tickets of the Sularian party taken, the outlaws fell in directly behind.

Strand had tapped his contacts to learn the clergy's assigned seating and had worked with the adventurers to plan accordingly, using those same contacts to secure the desired seats for himself and the team. Torin, Nicholas, and Oldavei broke off, guided by an usher up a set of stairs toward their private balcony while the others continued on down a massive corridor and through another arched entry. Wilhelm let out a low whistle as he and Xamus followed the church officials into the largest auditorium either of them had ever seen.

The two took a moment to drink it all in: a cavernous space with seating for thousands on the main floor and mezzanine. Two wide aisles sliced through the tiers, with additional seating extending along the flanks, and two more perimeter aisles. The building was rounded at one end, where they entered, and squared off at the opposite end, occupied by the proscenium, the enormous stage, and its towering black house curtain, now drawn. The entirety of what would have been wall space was occupied by arch-framed balconies, stacked one atop the other seven floors high. And above all, a domed ceiling where a dazzling, multisegmented crystal chandelier hung, its countless facets reflecting the flames of a hundred candles.

"Hohohohoooo," Wilhelm remarked. "Someday, man, I'm gonna play here. For a crowd of thousands! Mark my words, I'll be the brightest star you've ever seen!"

"I believe it," Xamus replied. Piotr, Strand, and Slayde proceeded forward, taking their seats, Strand and Piotr on either side of the aisle, ten rows from the stage, with Slayde going around the front to his seat on the opposite aisle, same row. The clergy continued to their reserved seating all along the front row just in front of the orchestra pit.

Xamus and Wilhelm were shown to their seats toward the back of the house near the mezzanine, Wilhelm on one side of the aisle and Xamus on the other. The bard placed the cello case between his legs and glanced to the forward balcony on the far right side, looking for the others.

After the seventh flight of stairs, Torin, Nicholas, and Oldavei were led down a narrow, lavishly carpeted corridor and shown to their private balcony, the usher handing the dwarf a set of opera glasses before departing.

Torin stepped around the cushioned seats to the balcony rail and looked out, astounded. Their booth was just a few rows back from the stage. The Sularian hierarchy were visible, though from this height, they appeared to be a mile below, along the front of the central seating section. In the orchestra pit not far ahead of them, musicians began taking their seats. Several rows behind the clergy, Torin glimpsed Piotr and Strand, then Slayde, situated closer.

Torin looked up and directly across, where he spotted empty balconies, while those beneath and extending back toward the mezzanine began filling up. He then raised the opera glasses and scanned the audience for Xamus and Wilhelm, finding them near the mezzanine section. Wilhelm, looking back at the dwarf, offered a lopsided grin and two-fingered wave.

Torin lowered the glasses, shifting his attention to what was by far the most astounding sight—the colossal chandelier. He leaned forward and gazed up at the luminous display, each section of polished, flowing arms, scrollwork, prisms, and festooned beads suspended via cables, the massive center column hung on a thick, shimmering silver chain. The dwarf marveled at the craftsmanship, wondering just how one might go about dousing the flames when he spotted the snuffers next to each candlestick. Then, as if on command, unseen hands from somewhere in the ceiling pulled on thin wires, rotating the snuffer arms on tiny pivots to cover and extinguish the candle flames.

In that same instant, the orchestra struck up, the curtains parted, and the show began.

CHAPTER TWENTY-EIGHT
HOUSE OF PAIN

By the midway point of act two, nothing noteworthy had happened. Torin, bored at first and dismissive of the show's overwrought theatrics, had slowly found himself taking a slight interest. By the end of act one, he was increasingly invested in the storyline, which concerned a well-intentioned though shortsighted emperor, Saldred Oth'Sular, and his relentless drive to unite the world under the Sularian faith, all at the expense of his own family. The undisputed star of the show was a female gnome whose name, Torin had earlier overheard, was Tovi. She served as a kind of narrator, muse, and at times, the voice of Saldred's tortured conscience. Torin, though he would be loath to admit it aloud, found her vocal performances captivating, particularly as she sang the aria for Saldred's wife, who died alone, giving birth to the emperor's only heir, Ravic.

Now, as the play's timeline skipped forward several years, tracing Saldred's conquest abroad, with battle sequences featuring a cast that filled the entire stage, Torin had to force himself to look away, sweeping his gaze from the clergy—who had been relatively sedate throughout the production—to Piotr, Strand, Slayde, and finally Wilhelm and Xamus. For the latter two he was forced to allow time for his eyes to adjust to the darkened house before spying them through the opera glasses, slumped in their assigned seats and appearing wholly disinterested.

Torin returned his attention to the performance as Oldavei popped his head in from a curtain at the back of the booth. "Anything?" he asked.

"Hmm? No, nothin'," Torin replied with an offhanded wave.

Oldavei kept watch on the corridor while Nicholas maintained a roving patrol, moving among the stairs and corridors of the other levels. The assassin had slung a crossbow over his back and a belt of wooden stakes beneath his coat. He had brought along his sword as well, all weapons that had been hidden inside the cello case that leaned now against the wall of the booth that Torin occupied.

At the end of the epic stage battle, props were switched out, and the story returned once again to the home of the emperor, where his only son lay dying from a fever caused by wasting sickness. Tovi once again came to the foot of the stage dressed in mourning attire complete with veil and began a solemn dirge. Torin was hoping the poor lad might battle through his ailment, but, alas, if the wailing lament was any indication, that wasn't to be the case. It was all so tragic! The dwarf wiped at the corner of his eye, tearing himself away to check the house once again. Below, all seemed well. He looked up and across at the balcony, which had remained empty along with the others on the uppermost floor. He squinted, as it appeared that something shifted in the booth's shadows. Raising the opera glasses for a closer look, he peered across, seeing at first only a black void. Then twin points of light appeared as something took shape and came sliding forward from the dark—Katrina, her face pale as the moon, ruby-red lips raised in a smile. Her crimson-ringed eyes stared back, boring into the dwarf, whose blood chilled.

On the stage, the gnome's song was reaching its crescendo as poor Ravic took his final breaths. Torin shouted down to Slayde, but his cries went unheard, the man's attention currently focused on the stage. The dwarf looked then to Piotr, who glanced over as if alerted to Torin's distress. The dwarf pointed to the opposite balcony. Behind him, Oldavei whipped the curtain aside.

"Company!" he informed.

Oldavei wheeled, fired his crossbow, and disappeared down the corridor as Torin threw a belt of wooden stakes over one shoulder and a wreath of garlic cloves around his neck before whipping up his preloaded crossbow from where he had set it on the seat cushion.

Oldavei tumbled back, falling just outside the booth. A black-clad Wraithblade appeared, sword raised. Torin fired, hurtling a bolt between the devil's ribs and straight to its heart. As the vampire became ash, Torin shot a glance out to the auditorium, where, from the empty balconies all along the top level, unnatural mist streams cascaded, winding their way to the house floor.

The dwarf joined Oldavei in the hall. The ma'ii was still wincing, recovering from a kick to the ribs as the two faced the rear of the passage, where a thick mist churned forth from the stairs. Torin held his crossbow in one hand, wooden stake in the other. Oldavei did likewise. The corridor provided just enough room for the two of them to stand shoulder to shoulder.

"Be ready to stick 'em soon as they turn solid," Torin said, as screams erupted from the auditorium.

On the house floor, Xamus and Wilhelm had both loaded up on weapons taken from the bard's cello case. Wraithblades materialized from the darkness clad in all black, eyes glowing. Terrified audience members screamed and collided in their blind haste to escape, finally spilling over the seats toward the rear exits, several of the older women being assisted by male counterparts. At the opposing end the actors had ceased their performances. Tovi stood at the foot of the stage, squinting to see what transpired beyond. Orchestra musicians rose and began emerging hesitantly from the pit.

In the front row, the clergy stood. Piotr and Strand took up defensive positions while Slayde did the same in the opposite aisle, weapons raised. Strand called to the church leaders "Stay here for now, we'll protect you!"

"Forget this!" A bald-headed cardinal exclaimed, stepping toward the stairs at the side of the stage. A wafting mist crossed in front of him, however, causing him to retreat.

"Stay calm and let security handle it!" Grand-Justiarch Kelwynde commanded.

The mist drifted across the stage, swirling at its center, driving away Tovi and the boy playing Ravic. It coalesced and took the form of Katrina, luminescent eyes drilling into the church leaders. "Look at you," she said, drawing her twin swords. "Like lambs to the slaughter. If you think security will come to the rescue, you're sadly mistaken."

"They have additional help as well." A gruff voice broke in as Nicholas stepped out from the wings on stage left.

Katrina's head whipped over, eyes blazing. "What does that mean?" she snarled. "You're here to defend them?" She pointed a sword toward the leaders.

"Yes," Nicholas answered. "With my life, if necessary."

Katrina remained quiet for an instant, then swung the blade in his direction. "So be it! You have disappointed me for the last time." She strode toward Nicholas while he stalked to meet her. The two collided, and steel rang on steel.

At the rear of the theater on both sides, a handful of security personnel fought through the stampeding crowd, batons held ready.

Night Devils, standing or crouched on seats or slinking along the aisles, drew their swords as one and attacked.

In the seventh-floor corridor, the roiling mist solidified into a figure Torin instantly recognized—the muscular, sickle-wielding, scarred vampire that had overcome him on the streets of Innis.

He fired the crossbow, but the devil was a fraction quicker, batting the weapon aside, the stake-bolt bounding off the wall and down the corridor. The next actions happened instantaneously, Torin thrusting a stake with his right hand, his enemy swinging the sickle, slicing the meat of his palm, forcing him to let go; Torin discarding the crossbow and grasping the sickle handle, Oldavei stabbing for the devil's chest, impaling instead the forearm, suddenly barring its path as the vampire relinquished the hold on his own weapon. The foe then lunged headfirst, smashing Oldavei's forehead with his own and following up with a kick that sent the ma'ii flying. The devil and dwarf tussled; Torin buried the commandeered sickle into the side of his enemy's neck but soon found his legs swept from beneath him. In the ensuing scramble, the vampire moved to the dwarf's back, grasping his head and shoulder, mask now down, fanged mouth open wide and poised over the jugular. Torin snapped a foot up to the wall and kicked outward, sending both of them into the empty balcony.

The Wraithblade's grip loosened as it struck the couch. Torin spun but found himself snatched up and hoisted into the air. The vampire kicked the seat aside, dashed to the railing, held the dwarf by belt and collar over his head . . . and threw.

In the instant of being held aloft by his enemy, and unknown to same, Torin had grasped either end of the wooden stake that skewered the devil's forearm. The vampire emitted a surprised grunt as the weight of the falling dwarf carried them both over the balcony rail. Torin's revenge was short-lived, however, for as they fell, the vampire turned to mist, leaving the plummeting dwarf holding only the stake. Torin felt sure his life was at its end when somehow he slowed, as if some giant, invisible hand were arresting his descent. He came to a stop, hovering just inches above the floor before dropping the remaining distance without injury. At once he bolted to a stand and jabbed just as the mist before him formed into the scarred enemy, whose crimson eyes widened in disbelief as the stake tip pierced his heart.

Through the collapsing ash, Torin spotted Piotr far across the central seating section, hand still extended in the dwarf's direction. A glowing aura, brighter than what Torin had witnessed before in the Ossuary, surrounded the monk. Grateful for the assist, Torin nodded his thanks, then wheeled to greet an onrushing vampire. The devil's charge was thwarted by a liquid flung from just behind the dwarf—contents from one of the vials the defenders carried, a concentrated form of garlic. The devil hissed, the drops of garlic steaming on its skin, just before a wooden crossbow bolt found its heart.

Torin turned to see Slayde, who handed him a backup crossbow.

Across the massive seating section, where the vampires had made short work of the theater's unfortunate security forces, Xamus and Wilhelm were engaged in the fight of their lives.

Advantageously, the elf and bard both experienced a clarity of thought and response such as they had never before known; each felt as though they knew where to strike and at what precise time, as though they anticipated their enemy's movements. It was this distinct benefit that allowed the outlaws to hold their own against their faster and more powerful foes, and Xamus believed he knew the source of their extraordinary assistance: Piotr. Somehow, the elf believed, the monk was predicting the vampires' attacks and using that information to guide his and his comrade's responses.

In support of that assumption, the mysterious aid was briefly interrupted when Piotr shifted his focus to saving Torin from a certain and gruesome death. Though the pause was slight, it allowed one vampire to land a vicious head kick that knocked Xamus clean off his feet, while another closed and grappled with Wilhelm, and one more broke through, rushing farther up the aisle; the latter, overly ambitious attacker met her end via a missile from Strand's wooden fist.

Meanwhile, the sense of clarity and prescience returned to both Wilhelm and Xamus, and the bard's stake succeeded in finding his opponent's heart.

Xamus landed in a more dire situation. He had flown into one of the rows several seats deep, his crossbow flung from his grasp, scuttling backward on elbows and heels as his opponent stalked closer. He considered throwing a stake but knew he could not hurl it fast or hard enough to defeat his foe's superior reflexes. His enhanced presence of mind, however, offered another solution: as he continued retreating, the elf closed his eyes, found his center, whispered words of power, then sat up and held his hands before him. A spark fired from between his palms. Rather than a fireball, however, lightning arced in a jagged stream, lighting up the theater, striking the Night Devil midchest, sending the surprised foe flying back to the row entrance. Xamus witnessed a stake tip emerge from roughly where the lightning had struck. As the cremated remains of the Wraithblade fell, Wilhelm stood just behind, grinning, stake in hand.

"Neat trick!" he said.

On the seventh level, Oldavei itched to join the fight. He retrieved Torin's fallen crossbow, slung it along with his own, and leaped from the balcony nearest the stage, sinking his claws into the gathered curtain and allowing his body weight to pull him down, shredding the thick fabric in the process.

On the stage not far away, the hurricane battle between Katrina and Nicholas raged. For every strike there came a counter; for every opportunity a baffle. The difference, however—as before on the streets of Innis—was that Nicholas began to tire while his adversary did not. Their fight moved backstage amid a menagerie of hastily abandoned props. "Dargonnas is the past," Katrina declared. "There is a cult in the east, the Children. The future. I've seen it! *They* are willing to make bold moves. To overthrow the establishment."

Between lightning-fast sword blows, Katrina loosed a front kick that launched Nicholas into and through a fake castle wall. The assassin's head spun, not just from the impact, but from Katrina's words: had it been the Children who contracted the Draconis Malisath to exterminate the clergy?

Further thoughts were prevented by a vicious cycle, of Nicholas regaining his feet just as Katrina surged forth with a kick that would catapult him again; this repeated from one set piece to another, leaving Nicholas battered, bruised, and utterly exhausted.

At the stage-left curtain, where Oldavei landed and prepared to rush to Nicholas's aid, he was distracted by a call from Slayde, who stood in the aisle several rows distant surrounded by ash piles as Torin scanned the balconies for additional assassins. "Get the clergy to—" Slayde began, his statement cut short by the violent impact of a projectile that penetrated him, back to front, bloody tip emerging at a downward angle from just below his sternum. Slayde crumpled to his knees and fell to one side, dead, revealing the object's other end, a silver cane head.

"Enough!" a voice boomed, loud enough to force half of those gathered to cover their ears. All eyes lifted to see Dargonnas, dressed as he had been when Torin and Nicholas had last seen him, though with the addition of a bell top hat and dress gloves. He hovered a few feet below the chandelier finial, his strident voice carried to maximum effect via the auditorium's pitch-perfect acoustics.

"I grow weary of these distractions," he proclaimed as a fresh wave of Wraithblades rushed into the theater. "Time for this pathetic drama to reach its tragic end!"

CHAPTER TWENTY-NINE

FINAL CURTAIN

The defenders had not yet lost any of the vampires' intended targets when the second onslaught came. The church leaders huddled now in the orchestra pit, clinging to one another for support as the Grand-Justiarch led prayers for their safety and that of their protectors.

And though the guardians were fatigued and seemingly outmatched, they noted almost immediately that their adversaries were fewer in number than the first wave and that their assault was uncoordinated, rushed, sloppier than what came before. Xamus got the sense, though he possessed no proof of his assumption, that these devils were lower ranking, less powerful, and less confident. If so, it was something the defenders could take advantage of.

Wilhelm and Xamus fell back as Piotr and Strand advanced, the two parties converging at the aisle's halfway point, while across the center section, Torin and Oldavei advanced also—Torin armed with the both a stake and the crossbow the ma'ii brought for him and Oldavei carrying his own crossbow as well as Slayde's.

Piotr, surrounded by a luminous halo, gestured toward the ceiling, exerting the mysterious projection of his will, his Eminence, to restrict Dargonnas's movements as Xamus, Wilhelm, and Strand all took aim at their advancing attackers. Strand fired three of his fist projectiles, missing twice but striking one vampire dead center.

Wilhelm caught a blur of speed as one of the more experienced adversaries bypassed the defenses and came rushing at Strand's back, sword poised for a decapitating blow. The bard spun and fired from the hip, piercing the devil's heart, the forward momentum of the dispatched assassin coating the old man's back in ash. At the same time Xamus loosed a shadowy arcane missile that stunned one opponent long enough for the elf to stake him. The vampires paused and, one by one, slunk into the shadows.

Piotr reached high with his right hand in the direction of Dargonnas and held it, trembling slightly. The aura around him brightened briefly as he closed his fist and swung down, a motion mirrored by the master vampire, who dove to the floor as if he had been blasted from a cannon, his impact accompanied by a shockwave that radiated outward, shearing the seats from their bolts and obliterating everything within a twelve-foot radius.

As with their counterparts, the vampire assassins who faced off against Oldavei and Torin paused their attack, retreated, and became one with the surrounding darkness.

Dargonnas, laid out facedown, prone, slammed one palm to the floor, then another, pushing himself up, struggling as if against an unseen weight. He pulled in his knees, posted one foot to the floor and then the next.

"A valiant . . . effort," the master vampire intoned. "Though sadly doomed . . . to fail."

Piotr stood with hand outstretched, beads of sweat breaking on his forehead, teeth clenched, the halo around him fading slightly. Everyone else looked on, save for Katrina and Nicholas, their struggles continuing to echo from backstage.

"Your . . . will, monk . . . " Dargonnas continued, still pushing upward, "is no greater . . . than mine." He rose to full height as Piotr's head began to tremble, veins protruding at his temples.

The master then shot like a streaking comet, striking Piotr full force, launching him past Strand into the wall beneath the lowest level of balconies, shattering priceless mosaic tiles.

Piotr pushed off and hurtled across the floor, slamming Dargonnas with enough power to send him sliding backward, scattering debris, though the vampire remained upright. The flat end of one of Piotr's sharpened fighting sticks protruded from Dargonnas's chest, but it was high and to the right, missing the heart, for the master vampire had shunted the strike at the last instant.

Strand, who had quietly loaded more stake arrows, fired two simultaneously, which the master effortlessly batted away with one hand, even as he removed and snapped in half Piotr's fighting stick. He then answered Strand by snatching up the back of a chair and slinging it with blinding speed, striking the old man midchest and knocking him off his feet.

Piotr moved to retaliate, and the two clashed at the center of the cleared space, trading titanic blows that shook the auditorium.

Backstage, Katrina opened a gash in Nicholas's wrist that caused him to drop his sword. She swung again, missed, then kicked him to a far wall, where he landed beneath a mounted contraption—a row of horizontal spindles, six to each side, wound with taut, spooled cable that extended from the ceiling's shadows. In the center, the chandelier's thick silver chain, drawn tight from hidden mechanisms above, fed through a set of gears and a massive windlass, to dangle and finally coil on the floor.

"I would have given you everything on a silver fekking platter," Katrina called.

"Why send me to kill Braun?" Nicholas replied through bloodied lips. "If the Children hired you—"

"They wanted him gone!" Katrina snarled, approaching quickly. "All you had to do was trust me. Follow instructions. Now the only boon I can offer is the mercy of true death." She rushed and slashed for Nicholas's neck. As the outlaw ducked, his attacker sliced one side of the cables all the way to the center chain. The cables whipped upward as the rafters creaked, and the apparatus in its entirety shuddered.

With a grunt of effort, Katrina lunged, thrusting her left-hand blade; Nicholas slipped to one side, the sword tip slicing the bottom of his earlobe before driving through the hole of one chain link, lodging in the wood behind him. Nicholas flicked the safety catch, then kicked the brake. With another loud groan and several snaps, the remaining cables broke free; the windlass and gears spun furiously as the rapidly ascending chain broke the sword blade, surprising Katrina, a distraction that Nicholas capitalized on by drawing her in for a kiss, catching her completely off guard, while he pulled a stake from his belt and drove it up beneath her sternum and into her unbeating heart.

Nicholas squeezed his eyes shut as the lips that touched his turned to ash, and behind him, the entire contraption broke free from the wall, racing toward the rafters.

At the center of the now-empty space in the house, Dargonnas grabbed Piotr and lifted, choking him with both hands.

Xamus, Strand, Wilhelm, Torin, and Oldavei, all ready to rush in from both sides, paused and glanced upward at a sudden cacophony of cracking, whining, and a strange sound—one that the elf likened to a heavy gale disturbing a great tree filled with hundreds of wind chimes.

From the orchestra pit, several members among the clergy screamed.

Piotr pried Dargonnas's thumbs with such force that he broke the bones in each. Lifting and pressing his boot soles to the master vampire's chest, he thrust, launching himself back to the base of the mezzanine. Above, the clinking, tinkling, rushing sound grew to a roar. Dargonnas looked up just as the massive chandelier crashed into him.

Everyone present ducked and covered as crystal shards flew, a million-million tiny projectiles streaking, embedding in skin and clothing and resounding with a clamorous, discordant peal.

All eyes looked to the glassy rubble where the chandelier's central column leaned to one side, silver chain and cables—the last to fall—coiling atop the ruin. Dust wafted and settled. An instant later, the piled debris near the column shifted, rose, and sloughed off Dargonnas's rising body. The master vampire's suit was fairly shredded, his hat missing, his skin gouged and perforated in several places, shards of crystal still jutting out.

The outlaws moved to the edges of the chandelier's main debris field. Nicholas, his sword retrieved, stumbled to the foot of the stage and looked out at the carnage. As one, the defenders raised their myriad weapons at Dargonnas and fired. Rather than deflect, the master vampire simply tucked his chin to one shoulder, crossed his arms over his chest, and turned away.

All of the missiles found their mark, and wooden arrow stake ends now joined the crystal pieces that bristled from Dargonnas's form. As the defenders reloaded their crossbows and Piotr prepared to rush forth with his remaining fighting stick, the Wraithblades emerged from the shadows, speeding into the wreckage and forming a wall around their leader.

Swords raised, the vampire assassins moved as one slowly toward the mezzanine exit on one side.

"We can't just let them get away," a hoarse voice next to Wilhelm spoke. The bard turned to see Nicholas.

"Agreed," he said.

Xamus moved to where Strand lay against the wall, left hand pressed to his ribs. "You okay?" the elf asked, glancing over to see the vampires disappear through the exit in a blur of motion, leaving no sign of Dargonnas.

"I'll live," Strand said. He nodded toward the rear door. "You know where they're headed. Go and finish the bastard if you can. Go!"

CHAPTER THIRTY

DESCENT

The outlaws, joined by Piotr, raced to a street-corner hackney coach, ordering the driver to transport them to the Meatpacking District in all haste, speeding away just as the Order-Militant's Peacekeepers marched in from all sides.

From their seats at the right-side coach windows, ducking down and casting their eyes skyward, Wilhelm and Xamus watched shadowy figures dash across rooftops, turning to streams of mist that cleared the spaces between buildings and became shadow once again.

Moments later horse hooves and coach wheels skidded to a stop outside the winery where Piotr had led Torin and Nicholas in their escape from the vampires in the days previous.

With the coach driver paid, Piotr broke through a winery side door and led the others down narrow stairs to the cask-filled basement, grateful to see that the massive keg the fleeing trio had placed over the trapdoor had been returned to its former place.

Through the trapdoor and down they sped, intent on seizing upon Dargonnas's weakened condition, determined to end the Malisath's clandestine reign.

They reached the Ossuary, traveling along rat-infested, corpse- and bone-lined corridors, past where Nicholas and Torin had been tortured, arriving once again at the passageway where the monk had spied the iron-banded door.

"I must see to my brethren," Piotr said.

Wilhelm and Oldavei kept watch while Piotr and the others rushed to the hallway end, the monk using his powers to break the lock and push through the door into a larger space where a barred cell occupied one side.

Four men and six women, gaunt, dressed in little more than rags, approached but did not touch the prison bars, which Xamus noted were etched with strange sigils.

Piotr, glowing, extended one hand toward the cell door, an action that prompted the bar sigils to glow crimson. "It won't work," warned one hollow-cheeked female monk.

"Dampening sigils," Nicholas said, moving to the door. "This problem calls for a more ordinary solution." He retrieved from one suit pocket a lock-picking kit, kneeled, and set to work. "Ironic, I suppose, that it's the Malisath who taught me how to do this."

The task was accomplished in less than a minute. "Thank you," Piotr said to Nicholas as the other monks filed out.

Nicholas nodded back. "I can take us to where Dargonnas is likely hiding."

"It may take a little time for us to regain our strength," said the same female monk who had spoken before. "But we're with you."

"Thank you, Marlena," Piotr said, then motioned for Nicholas to lead on.

Those who possessed additional stakes provided them to the monks. They proceeded then as one to a dark, winding staircase, which after several turns admitted light from somewhere below. At the base of the steps they issued into a brightly lit, voluminous space that stood as a stark contrast to the filthy, corpse-ridden Ossuary: clean, opulent, and stately with high, vaulted ceilings, ornate floor tiles, tapestries, and paintings of expensively clothed, stern-faced men and women on the walls between intricately fashioned candelabra sconces. Several lush divans and settees occupied floor space, and it was at a cluster of these near the center of the primary chamber that the vampires had gathered to discuss the night's developments and await further instructions.

Clearly surprised to find intruders in their den, half of the devils hesitated long enough for a few well-aimed crossbow stakes to find their marks. Piotr froze two more of the assassins, allowing for Torin and Nicholas to stake them, while the remaining monks, even in their beleaguered condition, raced ahead of Oldavei, Wilhelm, and Xamus, exhibiting dazzling speed, grace, and martial ability in outfighting and staking the final Wraithblades.

Wilhelm looked to Xamus, eyebrows raised. "These monks are some bad fekkers."

"What of Dargonnas?" Piotr asked, but Nicholas was already on the move to the end of the main area and through an arched access. The others followed into another equally decadent chamber to a short, wide hall with an ornately decorated door at the end.

"The Forbidden Door," Nicholas said, standing before it and turning to face the others. "None but Dargonnas have ever been allowed to enter."

"Can you pick it?" Xamus asked.

Nicholas, looking down to the handle, replied, "I may not have to." He reached out, turned the gilded handle, and swung the door open.

"Gods, what's that smell?" Oldavei remarked. The others smelled it too, a thick, pungent, oppressively musty odor that immediately engulfed them.

Through a short hall they entered another vast space, similar in architectural style to that which they had just left, but this one crumbling, worn, the brickwork and pillars cracked, pieces missing from the arched passages. No paintings or tapestries graced the drab walls, only rusted sconces bearing torches that provided dim light. Half-filled gutters ran along the stone walkways, and water dripped in various places, echoing in the stillness. The weak torchlight played on the gutter water, casting strange reflections on the walls and lofty, vaulted ceiling.

From that ceiling, scores upon scores of bats hung, remaining still for the most part, though some wriggled and shifted.

The floor squelched beneath their feet, coated in some slick substance. Torin stepped forward and looked down, lifting his boot, face twisting in disgust. "Shit!" he said. "Bat shit! This'd be the source o' that smell."

To their left, the sanctum stretched into darkness. To the right, it reached a dead end, a simple brick wall, before which sat an eerily glowing artifact on a weathered stone pedestal—a perfectly round orb roughly the size of an ogre's head appearing to be made of glass. Within it, an odd, crimson mist swirled.

Before the relic, Dargonnas kneeled, head bowed. "You think you've won," he said, his voice reverberating in an unsettling fashion as the outlaws and their monk comrades cautiously approached. "You think I'm beaten, and you've come to see the task complete." He chuckled. "How arrogant. How stupid. And yet, for me . . . " He screwed his head toward them, revealing misshapen facial features: a deformed brow, leathery skin, and in the place of a nose, malformed nostrils. He smiled, open-mouthed, his two front teeth extending into thick, sharp fangs. "How absolutely delightful."

He turned and rose. What remained of his clothes ripped away as his physical form shifted, popped, and cracked. He increased in overall size, his ears extending upward and outward, mimicking the ears of a bat; projections extended from his back, lengthening into twin limbs that transformed into massive fully jointed and articulated membranous wings. The master vampire's already long digits grew longer, the nails turning to daggerlike claws. His red eyes blazed as his clothing fell away entirely, revealing a fur-covered body.

"*That's* gonna give me nightmares," Torin said. In that same instant, all those who possessed crossbows fired them; Piotr at the same time flung his fighting stick. In an eyeblink, the missiles raced to their target—but their adversary was faster. The beast's back wings folded in front, providing barrier enough to prevent the stakes from reaching their intended target. Those same wings then snapped wide, flinging the wooden projectiles in all directions, and began beating, lifting the thing that had once been Dargonnas several feet off the floor, whereupon it let out a deafening screech.

Piotr, enveloped in a soft glow, moved to control Dargonnas once again but found himself instead on the defensive—as all of the newcomers were forced to—against the swarming bats that now descended from the ceiling in a chaotic flurry, scratching, biting, and harrying the suddenly overwhelmed party.

Piotr effected around him an invisible barrier through which the bats could not pass. With his mental focus thus engaged, however, the monk was unable to mount an effective offense against the master vampire, who even now swooped down through the bat storm, snatching the stake from the hand of Marlena, the female monk, seizing her, and ascending. Grasping her by shoulder and head, the bat-thing bit deep enough to remove half of the woman's neck. He then dropped her bloodied corpse to the guano-coated floor.

Piotr searched for the other Bohen Dur, gathering them one by one inside his protective barrier. Dargonnas flew just above the floor, speeding toward Torin, who dove at the last instant; the bat-thing narrowly missed grasping Torin's leg, but one razor-sharp claw opened a sizable gash in the dwarf's left calf.

Not far away, Xamus, arms raised, chin tucked, hands draped over his pulled-down hat, conducted a mental tally of every spell he knew, seeking one that might turn the tide. Dargonnas, it seemed, was a far more formidable foe than they had calculated. Were they able to even see their opponent, they might stand some chance. As it was, the creature was sure to pick them off one by one.

Unless . . . In his hasty review of magical options, the elf thought of one, dismissed it, then returned to it again. It was insane, even for wild magic, an act that his kind would never consider in a hundred lifetimes and something he himself had never entertained, though he had never outright dismissed it. He had merely pushed it aside, as on some level it offended even his deeply buried elven sensibilities.

The spell was conjuration. A method of calling upon a powerful entity from beyond. A way to summon *something* to even the odds. The risks, however, were profound: he might draw forth some entity with powers beyond his control, a being that may simply kill them outright . . .

Which was exactly what Dargonnas was about to do, Xamus reasoned. It was a roll of the dice but, given the circumstances, a risk he was willing to take.

The spell, however, would require energy beyond what he was able to channel. He needed a focal point.

The artifact.

He shut out the chaos around him, finding the quiet stillness necessary to do the magical working. He cast his mind's eye to the crimson orb, bending all his will to it, drawing upon its immense power. The response to his invocation was immediate and nearly overwhelming in its sheer malevolence. The elf immediately feared that he had made a dreadful mistake, but he knew with equal certainty that it was too late.

A sense of foreboding, a powerful sickness, twisted his gut. What had he done? He had opened a door that he could not be shut. And now something was coming through it. But what?

Dargonnas didn't seem to be attacking anymore. Xamus risked an upward glance and spied the man-beast through the raging bat-storm, hovering but turned, looking toward the back wall.

The elf walked quickly along the nearest gutter to get a better view of what the master vampire was reacting to. He spotted, through the maelstrom of leather wings, the crimson orb; it had left its pedestal and hung in the air. As he watched, incredibly, the globe began to increase in size, the blood-hued miasma within churning with greater force until at last the sphere shattered.

The force of the blast killed many of the bat swarm instantly and drove the rest into the depths of the vaulted corridors. The energy that had been held within the artifact, and the force of its release, shook the walls violently and sent wide cracks along the ceiling. That same luminous energy then flattened to a single pane that extended to the peripheries of the space, inclined at a slight angle, swirling like a gyre. Dargonnas, illuminated in the crimson light, remained aloft, wings buffeting the air. The look on his misshapen face was unmistakable: fear.

Xamus, who had begun to sweat, held a hand over the gutter to the wall to steady himself. Something then emerged from what the elf now understood was a portal—the head of some massive beast. It was a creature that most believed only a myth, though all elves knew that they had existed at one point in time. Nonetheless, to actually behold one was an occurrence Xamus never would have dreamed possible, and now, confronted with its visage, his mind nearly retreated within itself. How could it be, his rational mind asked, that such a thing might exist?

A dragon.

Or what had once been a dragon. No scales remained on its emaciated countenance. And though its red eyes burned with fierce vitality, the majority of the beast's anatomy was desiccated, rotten—fleshless muscles stretched over creaking tendon. Its teeth, however—each the size of an average human—appeared perfectly, terrifyingly capable.

Oldavei shrank to his knees and stared up in abject horror, shaking uncontrollably, every hair on his body standing erect. Torin, from where he still lay on the floor, emitted a vocalization pitched far higher than his normal speaking voice. Wilhelm stood frozen, incapable of movement or speech as warm urine ran down his leg.

Piotr, along with the other Bohen Dur, recognized and inwardly acknowledged the shock, terror, and disbelief that threatened to unhinge them. With their fears and misgivings thus recognized, they suppressed them, for fear held no place in the quiet mind.

Nicholas, though his heart thundered in his chest and his knees nearly gave out, was slightly more equipped than his fellow outlaws to retain a semblance of composure, for he had heard whisperings among the Malisath, of just how the vampires had received their unholy "gifts." A dragon, it was said, from some shadow dimension. A dragon that had died and somehow cheated death, enduring as an undead abomination, a dracolich that reached across worlds to impart some portion of its unnatural essence to mortal thralls, binding them forever to its will in exchange for powers beyond mortal ken. It was also rumored that the vampire cabal took its name from this benefactor: Draconis for dragon and Malisath after the name of the dragon, Malis.

Gazing now at the impossible creature, Nicholas reeled from the knowledge that the legends were indeed true.

Xamus, for his part, unaware of any myth, experienced not only the threat of mental breakdown but the added guilt of knowing that the sudden presence of this abomination in the world was *his* doing.

Though no lips existed on the dragon to move in the way of a human's, the beast spoke, its voice the roar of an avalanche, shaking the surroundings, spreading cracks along the walls, dislodging dust and chunks of stone from the ceiling. "Am I to be summoned now," it thundered, "like some lapdog?"

The Dargonnas-bat croaked. "I . . . I did n-not—"

"No matter," Malis answered, its eyes roving the chamber. "I see that you have admitted the enemy to your very doorstep. How are you to serve me if you are incapable of defending yourself?"

"I . . . I—" Dargonnas stammered.

"You reek of failure," Malis decreed. "And you, above anyone, should well know: failure is death."

Before the master vampire could attempt a response, the dracolich lunged, thrusting from the portal all the way to its bony shoulders, its great jaws opening above and below Dargonnas and snapping shut, muffling his cries, the tips of each bat wing extending from either side of the dragon's maw.

The emergence of the forward portion of the colossal beast's body proved the final straw for the lair's structural integrity. Debris rained down as Piotr called everyone to join him inside the barrier he had established. The outlaws, most of them still in a state of shock at the sight of Malis, remained transfixed until each of them experienced an instant of mental clarity, a kind of wake-up call provided by the elder monk.

Once again in possession of their senses, they united with Piotr, noting that the Bohen Dur had all now joined hands, their bodies enveloped in glowing auras similar to that which surrounded Piotr, only weaker. Above them, the enormous, cadaverous neck and head of the dragon retreated, the portal vanishing after. The disappearance of the anomaly caused a deafening shockwave that reverberated far and wide, at first pushing debris outward, then opening a vacuum that drew it in.

Boulders the size of carriages plummeted, rebounding off the shield maintained by the monks, and were followed by yet larger pieces of earth and stone until it seemed as though an entire portion of the Meatpacking District itself must be crashing down around them. The collapse was deafening, forcing the outlaws to cover their ears, seeming to last an eternity, though in truth it transpired over the course of less than half a minute before, at last, the rumbling and quaking ceased.

The adventurers were distressed at first, believing themselves trapped, as the barrier ceiling and three sides were buried under an unguessable amount of debris. They looked then in the direction of the vaulted chambers, relieved beyond words to see that the Bohen Dur had cleverly manipulated the barrier to form a tunnel that led several paces through the rubble to the very edge, where it opened to unobstructed though dust-clouded spaces and perhaps, to freedom.

CHAPTER THIRTY-ONE
ONE FINE DAY

They emerged from the depths, Torin's leg now bandaged, through old access shafts into a shipping warehouse near the docks. Alarms were ringing throughout the Meatpacking District. From an upper story of the building, they gazed out to see fire, rubble, and open pits the size of buildings, all half concealed in rolling banks of smoke and hanging dust.

If all had gone well, the outlaws, Piotr, and Strand would have reconvened at the old man's Sweep Markets Mansion following the events of the theater.

All had most certainly *not* gone well.

"Strand knows what district we're in," Piotr said. "He and I have a meeting place here. He'll get there if he can, but we must go now." The outlaws agreed. Piotr's fellow monks, having the option to simply return to their monastery and take some much-needed rest, insisted on departing to aid in the disaster response.

They made their way along the periphery of the devastation, the group moving slower than usual to accommodate Torin's compromised pace. At length they came to the base of the tallest smokestack in the district within sight of the docks, and there they waited for over an hour. Sounds of a coach then drew their attention, and Strand arrived in a carriage similar to that which the travelers had taken with Slayde upon their arrival. The driver even appeared the same.

"How badly are you hurt?" Piotr asked, assisting the old man out of the coach.

"Just a rib," he said. "It'll heal. Not important now. What's important is getting you lot"—he waved the fingers of his good hand at the outlaws—"the hell out of the city."

"Why should we go anywhere?" Torin protested. "We're fekkin' heroes. Saved the clergy! Wasn't our fault half the district collapsed, you should have seen the damned—"

"It doesn't matter!" Strand snapped. "What matters is half the district *is* destroyed. Casualties are still being assessed. Peacekeepers are rounding up outsiders and anyone else who seems out of place. They'll shackle everyone first, then get to sorting out the truth. Even then, in matters of politics, the truth holds little sway. And talk of secret cabals and vampires is likely to do you more harm than good. Safest bet for now is to be scarce."

"How?" Wilhelm asked.

The old man gestured to the coach. "You'll find all your belongings inside," he said. "From here it's a short walk to the docks. Go to slip ninety-nine. There you'll find a vessel, the *One Fine Day*. Her captain is a close associate. Best I could do on short notice is get you to Orinfell. From there you can trek inland into the wilds and lay low. Give time for the dust to settle at least and reevaluate from there."

The outlaws agreed that it made sense. Once they had retrieved their bags and weapons, Piotr addressed them.

"The devastation that took place tonight," he said, "rests squarely on the shoulders of the Draconis Malisath, a blight on the face of the world that has suffered a critical blow, thanks in large part to your actions. Thank you. All of you. The world owes you a debt of gratitude, whether they know it or not. The Bohen Dur, for one, will never forget your service and selflessness. And I vow that our order will continue to do our part, by maintaining a close vigil, ever watchful for signs of the Malisath's return."

The outlaws issued their own thanks and bid farewell to Piotr and Strand before cutting a path to the docks. There, in short order, they located a single-masted cog called the *One Fine Day* and were urged aboard by her captain, a curly-haired, wiry, middle-aged man who insisted on being called Chopper. "Lawbrand Navy's not deployed yet," he said, "But we can't take any chances. Gotta get underway."

Soon after, the ship set sail. The bone-tired outlaws crawled into net hammocks belowdecks among crates of textiles bound for Orinfell and quickly dozed off to the lapping of waves and creaking of the hull.

Come dawn, Chopper notified his passengers that the voyage to Orinfell would take a full day. It was welcome news for the adventurers to have some respite after all they had endured.

Torin peeled away his bandage to reveal a gruesome gash caked in dried blood. Oldavei came and had a look.

"I know you don't like to—" the dwarf began.

"I'll do whatever I can," the ma'ii said. He put his hands to Torin's leg, closed his eyes, and spoke under his breath. The dwarf felt a warmth on the wound even as a cool breeze stirred his hair.

When Oldavei finished, Torin stood on the leg. "It's better," he said, smiling, gripping the ma'ii's shoulder and shaking him in thanks.

The outlaws changed out of their suits and once again donned their accustomed clothing. They began the day with drinking, partaking heavily of a potent grog that Chopper kept on board in ample supply. The captain imbibed with them intermittently, joining Wilhelm in the singing of shanties and sharing jokes that would make a bordello madam blush. As more alcohol worked its way into their systems, and smokes and pipes were lit, the passengers shared with Chopper tales of the attack at the theater and the subsequent chase and battle inside the Ossuary. Chopper, in hearing the recount, often only shook his head, nodded, or sat with his mouth open in awe. When their telling arrived at the appearance of the dragon, the captain, who had heard many a sailor's tall tales, took the revelation in stride and with more than a few grains of salt.

Nicholas then relayed the history of the dragon Malis—what it was and how it factored into the origins of the vampire cabal. It was information that his fellow outlaws found particularly intriguing, especially Xamus, who considered telling them that it was he who summoned the dracolich, that all of the events surrounding its arrival were his fault. He grappled with the notion but then convinced himself that, as Piotr had said, the blame rested with the Malisath. The dragon was *their* patron, after all; ultimately he saw no upside to delving into his particular role in the creature's appearance and the subsequent catastrophe, and therefore he remained silent.

"Damn," Torin said, reacting to Nicholas's words. "I can tell you this much, when that thing stuck its head out of that swirly whatever-the-hell-it-was, I damn near pissed myself!"

At that point, Wilhelm, looking suddenly uncomfortable, cleared his throat and changed the subject.

Much of the remaining afternoon was spent trolling for fish off the stern. It was an endeavor that paid off for Nicholas, who got a bite early on and hastily enlisted Chopper's aid. The captain guided Nicholas in slowly reeling in and letting out, battling the fish and tiring it, a process that took a full ten minutes before a sore-armed Nicholas drew the forty-pound, thrashing kingfish close enough to the ship for the captain to fetch it with a gaff and end its struggles on deck with a blow from his club.

Their generous host then gutted, filleted, and grilled the catch. Nicholas especially savored every bite, a fact not lost on Chopper. "They say the tastiest is the one you catch yourself," he remarked, before downing the remainder of his grog and returning to the helm.

Later, Xamus, who had stayed mostly silent throughout the day, departed the hold to stretch his legs topside. He found Nicholas standing at the portside bow, gazing out over the calm sea at a dazzlingly vibrant sunset.

"Meant to tell you," Nicholas said. "Katrina said the Children hired the Draconis Malisath for the attack at the theater. She also said that for some reason, they wanted Braun dead. I honestly think she felt like she was doing me a favor giving me that assignment. Like it should have been some honor."

"I'm sorry," Xamus said, "About how things ended with her . . ."

"Time and again," Nicholas replied, "she declared that she and the devils were my family. But all she ever really wanted was an accomplice. A tool to help her reach her own ends. She damned me in the process, without a second thought, and still I loved her. Truly, with all of my heart. Stupid, right? I've spent most of my life running toward the wrong things. Looking for connection, safety, in places where I could never find them. But you, you and the others, all you've ever done is try to help me, even when I couldn't—or wouldn't—help myself. You, Torin, Oldavei, Wilhelm . . . you are my family. A family I never wanted but one that I desperately needed."

He fixed his hazel eyes on the elf's. "You've risked your lives for me without asking anything in return. When the opportunity comes, mark me," he said, raising a finger, "I will repay that debt. I *will* balance those scales."

"There's no repayment needed," Xamus said.

Nicholas grasped Xamus's shoulder before turning back to the sea. Then, looking once again to the sunset, he did something Xamus had only seen him do on a few occasions since the two had first met: he smiled. "That sunset," he said. "Just beautiful." As the sun dipped below the watery horizon, he propped his foot on the gunwale. "*One Fine Day*," he continued, "a good name for a ship. And that's just what this day has been. Drinking—excuse me, getting hamro . . ."

Xamus chuckled. Nicholas continued: "Singing, lounging, catching that fish!" He shook his head, still grinning, as if in disbelief that he had succeeded in reeling it in. "More than just a fine day. A perfect day."

Nicholas then frowned slightly, facing Xamus. "And what of you?"

"Hmm?"

"I've been standing here babbling about myself, but I couldn't help noticing that you've been even more quiet than usual. You okay?"

Once again Xamus thought of confessing that he had summoned the dragon, of admitting to a deep, lingering unrest . . . but the last thing he wanted to do was spoil Nicholas's rare good mood.

"Yeah," the elf answered. "Yeah, I'm okay."

Nicholas's eyes traveled to midships, where Chopper was hastily adjusting the sails. "Everything alright?" the assassin called.

"Just gonna pick up speed," Chopper yelled back. "I spotted the Lawbrand Navy."

As the light of day faded, Chopper kept a steady watch from the stern, peering at intervals through a spyglass at the pursuing navy vessel. After an hour of contending with the uncertain wind, the relieved captain announced that they were creating distance between the lighter *One Fine Day* and the navy ship.

CHAPTER THIRTY-TWO

THE GREY CITY

In the small hours before dawn, every lamp aboard the *One Fine Day* was lit as she approached Orinfell's harbor. Such was the necessity, given the thick fog that had reduced visibility to nil. The captain's only visual reference were soft orbs of light, barely detectable, evidence of the lighthouses that dotted the bay's breakwater.

Chopper, who had navigated the port more times than he could count, expertly guided them into the harbor and finally to an open slip. With the ship tied off, the captain shared meat, cheese, and waterskins from his own provisions. "I can restock at the mercantile easily enough," he said. More importantly, he gave them three bottles of his addictive grog.

A rugged, bearded man came then and addressed the captain, whispering close while keeping an eye on the outlaws. When the stranger departed, Chopper said, "Order-Militant Peacekeepers are scouring the city. They must suspect you left Sargrad. You'll need to move quickly!" Pointing inland, he said: "Head straight through there, eight, maybe ten blocks, and you'll hit the forest. No deviations! It's possible to go unnoticed in these parts, but elsewhere—" He looked around as if worried he might be overheard. He spoke lower. "The citizens here, they're not normal. And they're highly distrustful of strangers. They'll be especially watchful with the Order-Militant about."

"Vacation's over," Torin said. The outlaws quickly pitched in to pay for their passage. Farewells were exchanged, and they set off. Though Torin's leg was in better condition than it would have otherwise been, thanks to Oldavei's ministrations, it was not fully healed, and he moved with a pronounced limp that slowed their pace.

As with Sargrad, Orinfell was a city with deep religious roots. Whereas Sargrad was considered the home of the Sularian Church, Orinfell served as its intellectual and educational center. It was here through the seminary that the holy doctrines were taught. And it was here that the most ardently devoted followers in all of the land might be found; here also where more fanatical offshoots had taken root.

It was termed the Gray City, and with good reason. Every building the party passed was some variation of gray, from the roofs to the foundations. As well, a coating of gray ash was evident in several places: on roofs, dusted on glass, collected in the corner panes of windows, on sills and doorsteps, and forming a chalky layer on the street.

"What's with all the ash?" Torin asked.

"I heard the religious weirdos here have some annual ritual," Wilhelm said, "where they burn effigies and never clean up the 'sacred' ashes. They got a real thing for bonfires, too."

But the city's appellation encompassed more than just the color. Everything about the place seemed muted, suppressed, or bleak. Even the sound of their footsteps on the cobblestones rang flat in the damp fog. The few lights from windows they passed glowed weak and dim. A conversation between two wandering sailors didn't reach their ears until the men were almost upon them, passing thereafter like ghosts without a comment or even a glance.

As they came to the third block, one sound that did manage to cut through the cloying mist was the lonely, seemingly distant tolling of a church bell. It was at the next intersection that Oldavei darted ahead, motioning for them to stop, a finger pressed to his lips. Having heard something the others did not, he pointed to their right, and sure enough, a noise reached them of dully clopping hooves accompanied by a feeble light, a lamp held out no doubt by the horseman. The hoofbeats, however, were not just one set but multiple. And though the others could not detect it, Oldavei could just barely hear the clinking of armor. "Patrol," he whispered.

They hurried on, Torin managing as best he could, with Oldavei in the lead. The ma'ii stopped them again at the next intersection, where once more a dim light was sighted and hoofbeats drifted through the haze, this time in front of them. With the horse patrols closing in, they changed course, fleeing parallel to the city's border.

Two blocks on, they attempted to press inland once again but were met with a dead end. They backtracked, paused.

"Which way?" Torin asked.

Oldavei sniffed about only to find that smells, as with everything else in the bleak city, were muted and ineffectual.

"We gotta keep moving," Wilhelm warned.

Oldavei chose a path, though by now the clinging fog had all but sabotaged his sense of direction. Which way to the forest? Even as he contemplated, sharp, repetitive sounds issued from the gloom. As the group proceeded cautiously along a wide thoroughfare, they were soon greeted by a wraithlike figure in the now-thinning fog, a bald, gaunt man in simple robes, the upper portion of cloth pulled down to his waist, revealing a cadaverous torso. He shuffled slowly forth in the middle of the avenue, cracking a cat-o'-nine-tails over first one shoulder, then the other. Seeming at first to be in a trance, the man caught sight of the outlaws, stopped, and stared intensely.

He declared in a haggard voice, "Awful early to be out for a stroll."

"Same to you," Torin said, provoking a deep scowl from the penitent, whose eyes traveled to the weapons they carried.

"Where you bound for?" the man challenged.

"The local tavern," Torin answered.

"No taverns in these parts!" the man replied with disgust. "Nothin' here in fact for the likes o' you. What are your names?"

"No harm," Oldavei said, pulling on Torin's shoulder as he shuffled back. "We'll just be on our way."

The group retreated and hastened down a side alley. With the dispensing of the fog, sounds once again carried through the air. "Your names, I said!" the man yelled after them. "Come back here!"

The party found themselves at the side door of what appeared to be an abandoned building. Hearing more hoofbeats approaching, Oldavei worked the handle, and the door swung wide. What greeted them was a nearly vacated warehouse: mostly empty crates, a few tools amid a large, dusty, open space. To the immediate left, a set of worn, wooden steps ascended. Oldavei took to these, followed by the others. The second floor revealed more of the same, as did the third, which was bordered on all sides by large multipaned windows that composed the walls' upper half.

Oldavei rushed to the windows nearest the stairs, gazing down on the alley. Dawn's first blush had just begun to manifest, and the fog had cleared enough now that the ma'ii saw a patrol consisting of three approaching Peacekeepers roughly a block away. "Three inbound on this side!" he called out.

From his spot at the wall to Oldavei's left, Wilhelm added, "Damn it, three more comin' this way!"

Xamus, midway along the wall across from Oldavei, spied just beneath him a mounted soldier who appeared to be a Marshall-Captain alongside a single, massive, barded ox, and astride it, Gundr, the plate-armored ogre from the confrontation at Talis. Behind him sat the rag-clothed crone from that same encounter.

"Ironside's Enforcers," Xamus called. "They're here!"

"What? How?" Wilhelm replied. "Were they waiting for us? Did they know we were coming?"

"Got that falcon-woman here and some others," Torin informed from his spot at the fourth wall.

With a nervous moan Oldavei rushed to the corner of the room overlooking the intersection where they had been a moment ago. There the robed penitent spoke to the Peacekeeper patrol. The ma'ii noted two of the armored soldiers dismount and force their way into the buildings to either side in the block adjacent to theirs. "Uh . . . they're going door to door," he said, voice breaking slightly. "And I hear more coming."

"They're gonna surround us," Wilhelm called. "We shoulda gone straight to the woods!"

"I tried to get us to the woods!" Oldavei countered.

"We might have to fight our way out," Torin warned.

A powerful baritone voice called out below Xamus' position: "Report!" a powerful baritone demanded. Gundr paused, looking over one shoulder. The Marshall-Captain reined his horse, turned, and said, "We believe they're near." A new figure approached from Xamus's right side, mounted atop a mighty armored warhorse, the imposing, hooded rider eyeing his surroundings carefully, an enormous flanged mace strapped to his back.

"Ironside!" Xamus informed.

"Fek!" Torin barked.

"This could be it . . ." Oldavei said. "End of the road."

"Trapped like fekking rats," Wilhelm said, pacing in tight circles, fists balled. "Fek it, if we go out, we go out swingin'!"

Through it all Nicholas had remained quiet, observing, contemplating. Deciding. Or, more accurately, cementing the decision he had already come to. He stepped to Xamus's shoulder and said, "All will be well, my friend. As you told me once, make every minute count." The elf felt cold hands, one at the base of his neck and the other on his shoulder, and a voice close to his ear. "*Live.*" The hands lifted. Before the elf could respond, Ironside's voice drew his attention.

"Find them!" the Knight-Paladin thundered.

Oldavei looked to see the Peacekeepers cornerwise from their position reemerge from the two buildings they had searched, leading their horses on foot into the street.

Xamus turned to look for a roof access and realized that Nicholas was no longer next to him. He stepped away from the window. "Where's Nicholas?" he asked, looking but not seeing the assassin anywhere. A cold dread washed over him. "Where's Nicholas?" he repeated.

Oldavei moved from the corner back along the wall to just above alley door. There he saw a shadowy blur, barely perceptible in the weak light, issue into the alley, away to the left and out of sight.

"I—I think he left," Oldavei said.

"What?" Xamus asked, rushing over.

"I think I just saw him," Oldavei said. Xamus's head spun. What was the assassin up to?

An instant later the Order-Militant patrol Oldavei had been watching came into the alley and paused just below. One of the soldiers made for a locked door across from them, while the other reached for the alley door.

"Peacekeepers!" a voice yelled out, barely audible with the windows closed but loud enough to draw everyone's attention. "Enforcers!" It came from the opposite direction of where Oldavei and Xamus now stood. Oldavei looked down to see the Peacekeeper at the alley door glancing questioningly at his comrade, who held up a hand in a sign to wait. Xamus raced across the floor and cranked a lever to open the window slightly, looking for the source of the voice.

"Bloodhounds!" the speaker continued. "Manhunters!" Ironside, Gundr and the crone, and the Marshall-Captain all rode to the intersection, where the Knight-Paladin gazed down along the avenue.

Xamus spotted a figure two buildings down on the opposite side of the street atop the roof, two stories up.

Nicholas stood with one foot on the corner of the roof's parapet, sword drawn. "I couldn't stand to watch you chase your tails any longer," he declared, arms outstretched. "I'm here! I'm right here, you sorry rat bastards. So come and take me!"

CHAPTER THIRTY-THREE
BALANCING THE SCALES

"What the hell's he doing?" Wilhelm asked, standing at Xamus's side. Across the room, Oldavei looked down at the Peacekeepers, mounted now, walking their horses to the intersection. The ma'ii came to them and said, "The door's clear."

"He told me he'd balance the scales," Xamus said.

Torin approached now as well. "What?"

"For the times we risked our lives for him, he said he'd balance the scales," Xamus replied.

Order-Militant soldiers, including those who had been searching the buildings, filled the avenue around Ironside, who rode forward and shouted to Nicholas, "Don't tell me you're playing the 'noble sacrifice' card!" He wheeled his horse in a slow circle, yelling not directly at Nicholas but at the surrounding structures, an overt warning to the outlaws: "Half the Meatpacking District destroyed, over a hundred dead at last count! Not to mention your escapades at Talis, and, yes, thanks to witness testimony, we now know Innis as well. Seems everywhere you go, you leave a trail of destruction. And for that, all of you will pay, not just one!"

He stopped, once again addressing Nicholas. "Your ploy will only delay the inevitable. And the more you inconvenience me, the slower your death will be!"

"I know what drives you," Nicholas said, pointing his sword at the Knight-Paladin. "You thrive on the fear of those you hunt. You rant and rail and expect all who hear to quake in terror. Do you see me quaking? You're an impotent, ignorant piece of shit. You know nothing of fear. But I'll be happy to teach you!"

"Save your riddles!" Ironside piped back. "You'll plead for mercy soon enough!"

Armored Peacekeepers flooded the roof, and Nicholas turned to meet them. He fought fiercely, outmatching their speed, exploiting the weak points in their armor, in the pit of the arm or the seams between plates. In short order he had dispensed with the first wave of five soldiers. He paused near the edge of the roof, preparing to call down to Ironside once more, but stopped and executed a lightning-quick response, a contortion of the upper body and a deflection by his sword of an arrow that missed his chest by scant inches. The missile was fired from another roof directly across the street.

All eyes in the warehouse spotted the shooter at the same time: the master archer and Enforcer, the satyr Daromis.

In answer, Nicholas reached to a belt pouch and in an eyeblink retrieved and flung three throwing-stars. Two of the projectiles embedded in the leather sleeve of Daromis' left arm—raised just quickly enough to prevent a punctured eye and throat—and a third struck him low on the left side, though his jerkin and tunic blunted the sting.

As a second surge of Peacekeepers stormed the roof, Nicholas snatched another item from his belt and smashed it at his feet. The resulting smoke cloud engulfed the roof nearly in its entirety.

At the warehouse, the outlaws watched breathlessly. Oldavei ran to the opposite side, looking down on the alley. "It's clear," he said heavily, as more Peacekeepers rode to Ironside's position.

Xamus wrung his hands, shaking his head. "We need to help him! Do something! We can't just—"

"There's nothing to be done," Torin answered, his voice breaking. "There's a hundred o' them and four of us."

"We have to try!" Xamus protested.

"Try what? You'd only give up your own damn life! He did this to give us a way out!" Torin stared out at the street. "What he's doing . . . don't let it be for nothing."

Xamus eyed the smoke, remembering the last thing Nicholas had said to him to "make every minute count," to live. Anguish roiled within the elf; dread sat like an anvil on his chest. He stifled an agonized groan.

"I hate it too, but Torin's right," Wilhelm said, a hand on Xamus's shoulder. The elf looked to Torin, who gazed back pleadingly, then across to Oldavei. Eyes watering, the ma'ii gave a slight nod.

Xamus glanced once more outside, then in a kind of daze moved with the rest of the team to the stairs, down and out. The rooftop smoke, which had obscured all but the sounds of battle and the cries of the wounded and dying for several long seconds, began to clear as the outlaws hastened toward the edge of town.

Nicholas, as silent as death itself, launched from the roof, both arms raised high, sword blade pointed down.

A hastily fired arrow from Daromis impacted the assassin on his left flank, even as Nicholas crashed onto the mounted Marshall-Captain, who had looked up just as the blade came driving in, behind his chest plate, shattering the collarbone, goring the chest, and skewering the heart.

Nicholas yanked the blade free and flipped backward off the horse, which trotted away with the dead Marshall-Captain slumped in the saddle. The assassin took another arrow hit from Daromis high to the right side of his back as he began cutting a swath through the dismounted Order-Militant, slashing, stabbing, hacking, carving a path of bloody ruin toward Ironside, who turned his horse sideways and waited, appearing wholly unconcerned.

On the roof not far away, Daromis grew increasingly frustrated. Every time he lined up a kill shot, either a soldier moved into his path—one arrow had already struck and rebounded off a Peacekeeper's pauldron—or the assassin, constantly in motion at speeds that seemed at the edge of human capability, would shift just enough to prevent the satyr's arrow from striking his heart.

Nicholas slew all of those within his immediate vicinity and, with a clear but single-minded focus, surged for Ironside. A third arrow struck him in the back, piercing his left lung. He was three paces away from the Knight-Paladin, sword raised for a killing blow, when he felt his speed and movement forcibly decreased.

Not far away, on the back of the ox, the crone held one hand high, that hand surrounded by an orb of stygian power.

Nicholas, so intent on killing Ironside, had not heard the stomping of armor boots until it was too late, having been slowed just enough by the crone's dark magic, he took the full brunt of Gundr's maul swing, turning his guts to pudding and catapulting him back over the corpses he had made, landing and rolling, smashing arrow shafts protruding from his body and shoving arrowheads farther in. He gained his feet, breathing open-mouthed now, wheezing; he rushed to meet the ogre, rolled under the armored behemoth's maul swing, and slashed just behind the right knee.

Gundr cried out and leaned to one side, using the maul as a crutch to arrest his fall. A fresh wave of Peacekeepers closed in as Nicholas circled around the ogre and stabbed for the open spot under the helm. Gundr grasped the blade with his gauntleted free hand and snapped it in half. A final arrow from Daromis struck the assassin, piercing his heart at last, in the very same instant that Nicholas plunged his broken blade to the hilt in the ogre's left eye slit.

Gundr fell back, stone dead, as Peacekeepers rushed in, taking no chances, thrusting their broadswords into Nicholas's crumpling, lifeless body from all sides.

PART TWO: OUTLAWS

CHAPTER THIRTY-FOUR
PENITENTS SQUARE

In the woods just outside the city, the outlaws hid, waiting and watching. Xamus stood with one hand on a thick cypress, eyes on the outermost buildings as he asked Oldavei, "What do you hear?"

The ma'ii, standing at the tree line, ear cocked, said, "They're on the move, all of them." He pointed to where a steeple rose above the structures around it. "That way!"

"I can't leave yet," Xamus said, breaking from the woods into an open field toward the city.

"Wait, it's still too—" Torin blurted, but the elf was already on the move. Oldavei looked to the dwarf, shrugged slightly, and set off in pursuit.

"Can't let him go on his own," Wilhelm said, following.

"Yeah, I get it," Torin said, limping to catch up.

They returned to the city, climbing a fire escape on the tallest perimeter building they could find, up to the roof, huddling between the supports of a massive water barrel near its edge, where they beheld a commanding view of the city square. There, in the wan predawn light, armored Peacekeepers hemmed the plaza where a multitude of robed citizens gathered, waving hands to the sky, chanting, many of them shouting for the "subversive" to be brought forward.

The shouts heightened as the Enforcers and a slew of Order-Militant Peacekeepers emerged from a narrow street and made their way into the square, parting the crowd. Ironside led, atop his warhorse, the female falconer walking on the right flank, Daromis on the left. The crone came next, draped over the back of Gundr's ox. The beast had been fitted with a plow harness, but rather than a plow, it was Nicholas's body that was dragged along the ash-coated stones, his body bruised, battered, and bloodied in its entirety.

Beneath the water tower, upon seeing the gruesome display, Xamus removed his hat and knelt with his head down, one hand resting atop his head.

Wilhelm and Oldavei wept silently. Torin, fighting back tears, grimacing, whispered, "Fekking savages."

In the center of the square stood a massive statue, several times the height of an average human, of Saint Jehnra, the city's founder, in sculpted robes and hood, arms held out as if to embrace. It was here that the small procession halted. A ladder was brought. Ropes were tied to Nicholas's wrists as he was brought by two soldiers to the statue's base. The opposite ends of the ropes were taken up the ladder and tossed over the statue's outstretched arms. With the ladder removed, the rope ends were pulled from each side, hoisting Nicholas into the air until his shoeless feet dangled inches above the paving stones. The soldiers held fast, wrapping the rope ends around their forearms.

The circle of fanatics closed in. Stones, rotten fruit, and dung were all hurled at the body, along with shouts of "Sinner!" "Trespasser!" "Subversive!" and "Unbeliever!"

Ironside dismounted and came to stand before the hoisted corpse, dispersing the zealots, waiting until all was quiet. "Each year," he bellowed, "the Harrowing is observed. Effigies of our beloved Saints are burned, and our sins are borne on the wind. This day . . ." he declared, projecting even more loudly, "you will witness a different ceremony. You will witness the futility of rebellion. This day, it is the wicked intentions of an unbeliever that will be swept away, as the sacred ashes carry not atonement but judgment!"

The crowd roared. Ironside stepped aside as scores of fanatics brought wood and stacked it at Nicholas's feet.

A soldier came and handed Ironside a flaming torch. The Knight-Paladin came to within a few paces of the corpse, turned to the crowd, and spread his arms theatrically. "This," he proclaimed, "is justice! This is the fate of all subversives!"

The mob responded with rapturous approval. Ironside turned, torch in hand, took a single step and froze. Something happened, something that shook the Knight-Paladin to his core. The dead, mutilated body . . . *opened its eyes.* The red-ringed glare was not that of any human. Nor was the face twisted in rage that of any normal man. Nicholas opened his mouth, a ghastly hiss escaping his throat as he began straining against the ropes.

Ironside dropped the firebrand and stumbled back, eyes wide, mouth opening and closing, forming no words at first, until he managed, in a tremulous whisper: "Night Devil."

The gathered fanatics gasped in shock and revulsion. "Demon!" they shouted. "Devil!" "Unholy!" They made signs of protection and crossed arms in front of them, some stumbling back, others tearing at their hair or averting their eyes.

Beneath the water barrel, no one save for Xamus moved. The elf crawled to the edge of the roof and sat back, feet folded beneath him. Knowing what he must do, he began working his hands, whispering the proper
words . . .

Nicholas opened his mouth. Spittle ran from his extending canine teeth. He looked to Ironside and said, "*Now* you know fear."

Xamus set his will to the creation of a fireball unlike any he had summoned thus far: a much more concentrated projectile, capable of not just burning, but of completely incinerating its target. The flaming orb took form between his hands.

Wilhelm, Oldavei, and Torin came next to the elf. "What are you doing?" the bard asked.

"Keeping a promise," Xamus said. He sent the projectile streaking forth over the intervening roofs above the heads of the zealots as it grew in size and sped to the center of Nicholas's chest. It struck with tremendous force, consuming his torso in its entirety and exploding outward in a burst of devastating flame. Furiously burning pieces flew out, demolishing the left half of Ironside's face and searing wherever they struck, their intense heat radiating through his armor even where it did not touch skin. The Knight-Paladin collapsed, writhing in agony, screaming his rage to the impassive sky as a cheerless dawn broke in the east.

PART TWO: OUTLAWS

PART THREE

WASTELAND

CHAPTER THIRTY-FIVE

THE KEEP

Their journey was long and silent. For the first two days they traveled headlong, nonstop, pushing their bodies to the absolute limit. On the third day they rested, taking turns on watch, with no sign of pursuit from Ironside. While they felt certain that the Knight-Paladin and his Enforcers were putting their best efforts into the chase, the dense forests of Lawbrand provided near-infinite routes of evasion, and as before, the thick canopy shielded them from sharp avian eyes.

Once again they traveled mostly at night and slept during the day. Xamus's slumber, however, when it did come, came only in snippets, during which he was beset by dreams alternating between the gaping maw of Malis set to consume him and the image of Nicholas's disintegration. The latter dreams always unfolded the same, with Xamus standing just a few paces away from the assassin, Nicholas's red eyes fixed on him as the fire ate away more slowly than had actually happened and without any explosiveness, just a slow burn beginning with his chest and traveling the entire course of his body before reaching the head and very last—those gleaming eyes.

From then on, the skies opened up in perpetual rain, a nonstop deluge that soaked them to the bone, muddied the earth, and made every step a burden. They stopped only in short intervals, huddling together beneath the canopy, silent and miserable, unable to sleep, resting their muscles long enough to begin the slog again.

By the fourth night they came at last to the outer reaches of the Hearthvale Foothills. It was by a sudden flash of lightning that they saw it as they crossed an open glade—a lonesome stone edifice set high atop a craggy peak. No lights shone from its glassless windows, and portions of the structure appeared to have toppled and spilled down the face of the peak onto the earth below.

"What's that?" Torin said, pointing.

"I heard stories," Oldavei replied, talking loudly to be heard over the pounding rain. "Hundreds of years ago, refugees from the north built keeps in places throughout the foothills. Some are said to be abandoned."

"Let's get to it," Torin said. "And get out of this gods-damned rain!"

At length the adventurers found themselves atop the peak, moving quickly on the gravel approach, sighting the main entrance and the remains of what had once been a stout wooden door—one piece hanging from a hinge, another leaning against the stone frame, with smaller bits strewn about. To the far right lay a heap of what had once been one of four corner towers.

The structure was three stories high and, though long neglected and in a decrepit state, still communicated a sense of privilege, steadfast strength, and dominance.

Torin was the first to cross the threshold, soon followed by the others. A quick tour revealed a largely empty ground level, wide crumbling stairs leading to the desolate halls and rooms of a second story, and a waterlogged third level entirely without a roof, much of the upper portions of walls collapsed, floors covered in rubble.

The question on all of their minds, though none spoke it, was whether time had exacted such a toll or if the stronghold had come under an attack that it could not withstand.

They ventured once again to the bottom level, the wind whistling eerily through deserted corridors, thunder rumbling as they progressed. In a rear corner of the main floor, they came upon a descending stone staircase, which brought them to a spacious storeroom where discarded items still remained piled along the walls and in the corners, partially covered by dust-coated linen.

"We could build a fire here," Torin said, standing in an empty spot at the center of the room. "One that won't be seen outside."

Furniture was broken into kindling, and a fire was made. Some garments and headgear were removed and hung or held near the heat to dry. Torin lit his pipe and drank from one of the grog bottles provided by Chopper. No songs were sung. Oldavei and Wilhelm sat staring at the lethargic flames while Xamus idly surveyed the abandoned items, lifting sheets to find mostly broken furniture, old sconces, and ragged tapestries. For long moments they did not speak or even look at each other, so heavy was their guilt and shame. Rain battered the stones above like a thousand hammering hooves.

Torin felt the tension build within until he could no longer constrain it. "Fek, this is ridiculous, this silence and tiptoein'. Elf!" he called. Xamus looked over to see the dwarf holding out his bottle. "Have a pull?"

Xamus waved the offer away. Silence resumed while the deluge continued outside and the occasional thunder boomed. The overall mood was dour, the air thick with the weight of the loss they all still felt.

"I miss him too, you know," Torin said.

"Then by all means, we should drink and pretend he didn't give up his life for us," Xamus replied. "Just try to forget."

Torin bolted to his feet and stormed over to the elf. "Don't you think it kills me?" he said, voice trembling slightly, face red. "After everything . . . after all we went through in the Ossuary at the hands of those fekking devils! I told him to keep the faith . . ." The dwarf raised a trembling fist. "I told him things would work out! And now he's gone, and it does, it kills me! It also makes me more determined than ever to make his sacrifice mean something." He uncurled one finger. "So don't fekking tell me I'm trying to forget!"

Xamus sighed and put a hand to the dwarf's shoulder.

"You're hurt," Oldavei said, arms hugged tight to his body, sitting cross-legged by the fire, still not meeting any of their eyes. "We all are." Wilhelm nodded somberly. Torin took a deep breath and returned to where he had been sitting.

Xamus lifted a sheet and spied behind a chair an object beneath yet another sheet, one corner of an ornate frame peeking out. He moved the chair and pulled free a painting on a thirty-by-forty canvas. He wiped away a layer of dust to reveal a depiction of a daytime scene looking over the shoulder of a young man on a horse, gazing at a suit of armor hanging on a wooden frame outside a tent—the plate armor of an old Sularian Knight-Paladin, the chest plate emblazoned with the Lawbrand.

Something about it captivated Xamus, though he couldn't put a finger on it. He brought the art out and leaned it against the remains of an old loom.

"What piece is that?" Oldavei asked, looking to Wilhelm. "Is it famous?"

The bard shrugged. "It's old, I can tell you that. I'm not as knowledgeable about history as—" Wilhelm caught himself.

"As Nicholas was," Torin said.

The act of saying his name out loud appeared to ease the tension in some of them—Oldavei unfolded his arms. Wilhelm took a deep breath and exhaled heavily, then said, "He could have told us the name of the piece, the story it represented, who painted it, and probably what brushes they used."

"And what they ate for lunch during," Oldavei added.

Torin chuckled. "True enough! When we first met him, he wouldn't say shit, and later on there were times you couldn't shut him up."

Oldavei and Wilhelm snickered and nodded. After another quiet moment, Torin held out his bottle, said, "To Nicholas!" He drank and passed the vessel to Wilhelm. "To Nicholas!" the bard said and drank. Oldavei repeated the process, preparing to hand the drink to Xamus, when the elf stood up suddenly and took to the stairs without a word. Oldavei held on to the bottle for a moment as if unsure what to do with it.

Xamus's hasty departure dampened the mood once more. Torin retrieved the grog from Oldavei and corked it, saying, "No reason we shouldn't stay here for now. We can see for miles around, we can hunt our food, and there's a stream less than a mile to the east . . ." He looked to the others questioningly. Each of them agreed, and soon after, while Xamus stood watch in one of the towers, the three outlaws fell to a restless slumber.

The following day, with the storm having passed, Torin kept watch in one of the keep's towers while Oldavei, in his coyote form, caught rabbits. Xamus, who had remained reticent, gathered wood and scouted the forest while Wilhelm filled everyone's waterskins at the stream.

After sundown, Oldavei and Wilhelm ate and passed another bottle of grog back and forth while Xamus sat apart, eating only a few bites, refusing alcohol. Wilhelm went to relieve Torin from his watch, and the dwarf came and heartily devoured rabbit as Xamus found himself staring once again at the painting.

Questions. That was what he found fascinating about the piece. It sparked questions. Who was the young man? Why was he mounted? Was he preparing to depart, turning his back on the armor, on the life it represented? Or had he come there to don the armor? The elf asked himself why he cared and had no ready answer. Torin finished eating and said to him and Oldavei, "Come to the tower with me, somethin' I want to show you."

They complied, joining Wilhelm in a relatively small room at the top of the southwest tower. "See anything interestin'?" Torin asked the bard.

"Matter of fact, yeah," Wilhelm said. The others joined him at the arched aperture, looking to another rocky hilltop a few miles away. There, a second keep stood silhouetted against the full moon, lights twinkling from its windows.

"I saw it before," Torin said. "Wondered if it was abandoned like this one. Now I got my answer."

"They shouldn't pose any threat," Oldavei said.

"Maybe, maybe not," Torin replied. "Right now we don't who they are. Me, I got two guesses: they're either vagabonds like us . . . or high and mighty well-to-do. In which case . . . we got an opportunity to have us a little fun."

"Fun doing what?" Xamus asked.

PART THREE: WASTELAND

"Inventory," the dwarf said with a mischievous smile.

"You wanna rob 'em," Wilhelm said.

"How much did you drink while you were on watch?" Oldavei asked.

"I did find that up here," Wilhelm said, motioning to an empty grog bottle on the floor.

"That's beside the point!" Torin walked to the window and peered out. "If they are what I think, they're just like those uppity fekkers in Sargrad," he said. "Thumbin' their noses at people like us, makin' their coin off the backs of those less fortunate. I say we knock 'em down a peg or two." He turned and added, "Besides, we're almost outta booze!"

Wilhelm tilted his head to one side, deliberating. Oldavei scratched at his beard. "Well?" Torin said, "what do you think?"

"I think it's stupid," Xamus said. "Reckless. I don't want any part in it." He turned and descended the stairs.

"We can't all just sit here mopin' for the rest of our lives!" Torin called after him. He eyed the ma'ii and bard sternly. "Fek it, we'll do it without him!"

CHAPTER THIRTY-SIX

FURNITURE RUN

The journey to the keep took just under an hour. As they drew near, they left the path and crept through the trees, maneuvering into a position where they could observe from cover. This second stronghold was much like the one they inhabited, though in far better condition. Despite its age, the structure appeared undamaged and was certainly well kept.

The lights they had seen earlier were now extinguished. A bored-looking guard in leather armor and a steel skull cap stood a fair distance away from the large double-door entrance, staring up and pointing at the night sky, moving his finger as if attempting to identify constellations.

"This'll be a piece o' cake," Torin whispered. He led them behind stables around an empty cart to a place where they could observe the side entrance. There, just outside the door, sat another guard, this one overweight, slumped in a chair, snoring intermittently.

Torin whacked Wilhelm on the shoulder and whispered, "Look at that! Won't even need the elf's sleep spell!"

They snuck up to the unlocked door, watching the guard for any signs of waking, and quietly pushed their way through.

A short hall led them to a great chamber, the interior only dimly illuminated by ambient moonlight from the windows. "Right," Torin said, "grab what you want and meet back here."

With that, the party split up. Torin located a cellar filled with kegs of various sizes. He hoisted one onto his shoulder and returned to the chamber to find Oldavei already waiting, wrapped in a blue, luxurious, fur-lined silk blanket.

"What do you think?" the ma'ii asked quietly.

"Uh . . . yeah. Whatever tickles your pickle," the dwarf replied. "Where's the fekkin' bard?" They heard odd noises, then grunting, struggling sounds from beyond the chamber, a thump like a table being struck, a stifled curse, then a groan as Wilhelm finally stumbled into the room drenched in sweat, carrying a massive piece of furniture on his back. He bent his knees, eased the monstrosity to the floor, and stepped away, wiping sweat from his brow, admiring his choice. It was built of dark teak wood, with two large doors polished to perfection, ornately carved with foliage and various geometric motifs.

Torin looked aghast. "What the fek is that?"

"It's a . . . I don't know," Wilhelm admitted. "Wardrobe? Cabinet?"

"I think it's an armoire," Oldavei said.

"Yeah," Wilhelm said. "It's an armoire." He turned and rubbed the wood, gazing at the piece in wonderment. "Just look at it, man. I'm pretty sure it holds some kind of magic. The most gorgeous thing I've ever seen!" After seeming entranced for a moment, he turned to them. "This is what I saw in my vision in the cave."

The more Oldavei stared at the giant cabinet, the more a low chuckle built in his throat, until his eyes were watering and he was forced to cover his mouth.

"You can't take that with us!" Torin warned.

"Oh, I'm definitely takin' it," Wilhelm replied. "It'll class up the place."

"You won't make it more than twenty feet!" the dwarf argued.

"I'll do whatever I gotta do!" Wilhelm shot back, eyes flaring. "I'm takin' this . . . thing, and you fekkers can't stop me!"

Torin threw up his hands, exasperated. "Alright fek it, I give up," he said. "Let's just go."

Torin proceeded outside. Oldavei agreed to help as he and Wilhelm turned the armoire on its side to get it out the door. Halfway through, the back of the piece hit the door frame. "Don't scratch it!" Wilhelm pleaded.

The guard next to the door stirred, sleepy eyes widening. "Hey! Help!" he yelled. Torin thumped him in the forehead with the pommel of his axe, knocking him out instantly.

"Hurry!" Torin urged. "Let's move!"

Oldavei, watching Wilhelm struggle to mount the armoire once again on his back, couldn't stop giggling. Torin trotted past the stables, balancing the keg precariously. Oldavei tripped on his blanket, which made him laugh even harder. Wilhelm had only made it about ten feet when two guards burst from the side door, and two more came running from the front.

All four were within inches of the bard when they suddenly rose several feet off the ground, kicking frantically, waving their swords but remaining hovering in place.

Torin, dumbfounded, turned to see Xamus just outside the tree line, one hand raised toward the guards. "Ha!" Torin blurted, "Knew you'd come around, fekker!"

Xamus was frowning at the flailing guards. "That was supposed to be a slow spell."

Oldavei came trotting by, cackling, blanket hiked up to his knees.

"Woohoo!" Wilhelm hooted, stumbling down the path, nearly bent in half under the ridiculously large armoire.

Xamus smiled, stifling belly laughs of his own as he followed them, their hysterical laughter ringing through the woods.

CHAPTER THIRTY-SEVEN

A MESSAGE

Wilhelm arrived in the storeroom a full two hours behind the others at the abandoned keep drenched in sweat, knees shaking, continuing to function by way of grim determination only as he eased the armoire down and collapsed next to it, lying flat on his back, moaning softly.

Wilhelm cleared his throat. "Look, uh . . . thanks for indulging me." He opened the doors on the cabinet to find shelves stacked with linens.

Torin chuckled. "Welcome back! You make one hell of a pack mule."

"He *is* an ass," Oldavei commented, drawing a snicker from Xamus. The ma'ii was seated with a portion of the blanket pulled over his head like a hood. "You think the guards got a good look at us?" he asked.

"What the 'Master of the House' will do," Torin interjected, "is ride out to Hearthvale tomorrow and lodge a complaint with the constabulary. He'll be told the brigands are 'likely long gone by now,' and that'll be the end of it." The dwarf grinned. "I have a bit of experience in these matters."

And Torin was right. Days passed with no contact from the master of the second keep. The group fell into a routine of gathering water, keeping watch, hunting, and drinking—a routine that, while comfortable, soon began to wear thin.

Xamus, still grappling with troubled sleep, became especially restless. He wondered how they would go about doing what Torin said they should do: ensure that Nicholas's death had not been in vain.

On the eve of the fifth day, the elf lounged, staring at the painting of the young man while Oldavei sat swaddled in his blanket, drinking from one of the grog bottles now filled with ale taken from the keg Torin had absconded with. Wilhelm drank as well, leaning against his beloved armoire, which he slept next to each night.

The elf sat transfixed, examining the painting's every brush stroke. He felt that the answers to his questions regarding the creator's intent were there; he just hadn't picked up on them yet. It was a puzzle to be solved, though he was still unsure why he was so determined to solve it.

"Time to relieve Torin yet?" Oldavei asked.

"Hmm?" Xamus said, then, "Oh yeah, I think so."

Xamus climbed to the top level of the tower and found the dwarf leaning on the ledge, looking out.

"There ya are!" Torin proclaimed, stepping away from the window. "Nothin' worth reportin'. Time now to see how much o' that keg's—"

A flapping of wings interrupted the dwarf's thought. They both looked to the window ledge, where a large black-and-white falcon alighted. "Falcon!" Torin spat, reaching for his axe.

"Wait!" Xamus said with an upraised hand. "I think that's Darylonde's falcon, from the druid refuge."

Torin squinted one eye. "What? Ah, maybe . . . " he replied, relaxing. "There's a scroll on its leg."

Xamus approached cautiously. The falcon made no move to take flight as the elf untied the hemp securing the scroll. He unrolled the small parchment and held it to the moonlight. "It *is* from Darylonde," the elf confirmed.

"Why can't he use a damned owl or something?" Torin groused. "What's it say?"

After a moment Xamus looked to him and said, "He's 'strongly urging' us to return to the sanctuary. Says the significance of the visions we shared has grown.'"

"Whatever the hell that means," Torin replied. The two agreed that they should discuss the matter with the others immediately. The falcon, not waiting for an answer, screeched and flew away.

In the storeroom, the conversation was brief. Wilhelm, Oldavei, and Torin had all grown weary of sitting still, and the sanctuary was certainly a safer option than their current hideaway. Thus it was unanimously decided that they would return to Kannibus Hills and see what Darylonde had to share. The group slept a final night in the keep, Xamus still tormented by night terrors. At first light he examined the painting one last time, committing every detail to memory. Oldavei packed his blanket for the journey, while Wilhelm ran his hand over the armoire's burnished wood, then wrapped his long arms around it. "Our time together was too short," he said. "Maybe we'll meet again some sunny day."

"Let's hit the trail," Torin replied with a scowl. "Before things get uncomfortable."

Despite a torrential rainstorm that drenched them and muddied the earth beneath their feet, the outlaws were in reasonably good spirits as they cleared the storm and entered the vicinity of the refuge halfway through their third day of travel. The closer they came, the more they looked forward to the cleansing, reinvigorating water, the tranquil setting, and the comfort, safety, and peace of the sanctuary.

This time around, no furtive figures emerged from the shadows to challenge them. The transition, in fact, once they reached a certain spot, was immediate: their surroundings were unfamiliar, and then, suddenly, they were familiar, like a warm embrace, as they discerned a path leading toward melodic birdsongs, a trail and foliage that opened like parting curtains to reveal the Grove of Lights.

Darylonde Talonhand stood before the pit of the Woodsong amphitheater as if aware of the exact moment they would arrive. He canted his head to the visitors' right as they drew near and said, "Same shelters as last time. Stow your things, and let's talk."

They did as they were bade. Upon returning, Torin strode directly to the Wildkeeper and said, "How the hell did your bird find us?"

"Your location was given to Goshaedas to know in a vision," Darylonde answered. "As was the revelation and circumstance of your friend's passing." The soldier's unsettling gaze swept over them. "I'm truly sorry for your loss. As it was told to me, Nicholas was a true warrior who acquitted himself admirably, exacting a heavy toll on the enemy. But his was only one battle in a much greater war."

"Mm," Torin said. "Thought you didn't take kindly to us lowlifes."

"I'll tell you this," Darylonde replied, his silver eyes drilling into the dwarf's. "I know all too well the pain of such loss and the burden you bear." He then turned and strolled to the tiered earthen seating of the amphitheater, where he chose a spot a few levels down. The outlaws took seats in a staggered formation and swiveled to face him as he continued.

"As you know, our spies have been tracking Children of the Sun activity," Darylonde said. "The cult is increasingly responsible for efforts to destabilize Lawbrand and sow upheaval throughout the realm." Darylonde paused. "Their influence shows no sign of waning . . ."

"And their ambitions appear to be limitless," a smooth, deep voice declared. All eyes turned to the lip of the pit behind and to the left of Darylonde, where a female human stood, draped in a cloak of raven feathers, wearing leather of gray and black hues, a bow and quiver slung on her back. Her hair was the color of fire, and her eyes were the serene blue of a crystal lake.

"This is Lara Raincaller," Darylonde said. "One of our most accomplished spies and . . . a close friend." The two shared a look. Lara came down to the floor of the pit and stood just before the Silver Spring, where the outlaws had viewed their reflections in their previous visit.

"I've learned quite a bit about the Children of the Sun over the last several months," Lara said. "As I mentioned, their craving for power knows no bounds. They've even gone so far as to solicit assassination. The incident in Sargrad, at the theater—we know you were there, that you fought the Night Devils. We know also of the Draconis Malisath. It may surprise you to learn"—her eyes swept the outlaws—"that the party who hired them to murder the Sularian clergy was none other than—"

"The Children of the Sun," Xamus said, eliciting surprised looks from both the druid and Darylonde.

PART THREE: WASTELAND

CHAPTER THIRTY-EIGHT
A STROLL IN THE WOODS

"Nicholas found out," Xamus said. The elf had also shared the information with the others, shortly after.

"Then you understand," Lara said, "that the Children are not simply *competing* with the Sularian faith for believers. They're looking to supplant the church entirely."

"No offense," Wilhelm said, "but why do the Wildkeepers and Goshaedas and all of you care? You got a good thing goin' here, why poke around in some religious war?"

"The world is far from perfect," Darylonde said. "But there is a balance. The Children threaten that balance. Their influence, if allowed to fester, could destabilize all of Lawbrand."

"And," Lara said, "left unchecked, the cult will in time endanger even the peace and safety of this sanctuary."

"That's why you're here," Darylonde said.

"Your note said somethin' about our visions . . ." Torin said. "So what is it you want from us?"

"It's not what *I* want . . ." Darylonde answered. They heard sounds then, creaking and groaning of wood, accompanied by the plodding steps of something big approaching. Darylonde and Lara both stood and moved to ground level, prompting the others to do the same, as Goshaedas marched forward from the nearby forest to greet them.

"Welcome back, travelers," the tree-folk intoned. "I mourn the loss of your friend Nicholas. Sadly, there will be many more if the Children are not stopped. I called you here because I have seen that your destinies and the fate of the Children of the Sun are interwoven. I know not exactly how . . . but it was my hope that I might persuade you to return once more to the Bear Mound."

The outlaws looked at one another hesitantly. "Last time around," Oldavei said, "we didn't see much, honestly."

"The substance of what is shown to you at the Bear Mound will not always be immediately clear," Goshaedas said. "But I believe that you come now to a crossroads and that through the sacred visions, your path will be illuminated."

The outlaws didn't appear convinced.

Goshaedas raised a spindly branch-hand. "There is no need to answer this instant. Rest. Rejuvenate. If you so choose, you will undergo the sacred ceremony tomorrow when the sun is at its height." The moss-crusted hollow that served as the tree-folk's mouth curved in a smile. "Be well, my friends." With that, Goshaedas turned and tramped away.

"I guess we'll . . . let you know," Xamus said to Darylonde.

The Wildkeeper shrugged. "Do as you wish."

"Do what you feel is right," Lara said, giving Darylonde an admonishing look. The two then nodded farewell and departed together.

Wilhelm looked to Oldavei. "Well? You were the one who had the biggest problem last time."

The ma'ii rubbed his chin. "I don't know . . . I'll do it if you all do."

Above them, wisps awakened and emerged from the canopy, spiraling down in greeting. With them came the faeries, and one in particular who landed with her large boots on Torin's shoulder.

"Wittabit!" Torin exclaimed. "How you been, girl?"

Wittabit leaned in and spoke in Torin's ear. "Ho-ho, you vixen!" the dwarf exclaimed. "She wants to buy me a drink. Meet here later," he said and began heading toward the Traders' Thicket.

"Right," Xamus said, "well, I want to take some time . . . go for a walk."

"We'll occupy ourselves," Wilhelm answered, with a look to Oldavei. Xamus took his leave and strolled through the refuge, hoping his memory would be capable of guiding him back to the out-of-the-way spot where he had practiced his fireball creation, where he had made a critical leap, in fact . . . thanks to the counsel of a specific druid, the satyr Amberlyn.

With a sense of palpable relief, he found the location and the very same stump where he had sat before. He went and placed his hand there, looking around, seeing that he was alone save for the birds that sang in the nearby trees. The elf lounged, rolled a smoke, lit up, and waited. Several minutes later he heard a voice not far behind him.

"I see you're making good use of what I taught you."

Xamus pushed off the stump and turned to see the druid. "What do you—" he started to say, then looked at the smoke and smiled. "Oh. Just occupying my time while I was waiting." He stubbed his smoke on the stump and stuck the remainder in a shirt pocket.

"Waiting for what?" Amberlyn asked.

"Not what," Xamus replied. "Who. I was . . . hoping I'd see you again."

At this Amberlyn giggled, her sapphire eyes twinkling. "So you came here? You could have just asked for me."

"Fair point," Xamus admitted with a smile. "I don't always do things the easy way."

The satyr's eyebrows raised on her slightly extended brow. "Oh I remember . . . you like a challenge."

Xamus nodded. "I sure do." His eyes lingered on hers for a long moment. Finally he said, "You were talking earlier about what you taught me . . . I've been wanting to thank you. It made such a difference . . ." He thought of the last fireball he cast, of Nicholas in Night Devil form, the assassin having become the thing he had most feared, there one instant and gone the next. Xamus's eyes watered. "More than you could ever know."

Amberlyn took his hand. "Let's take a walk," she said.

They strolled through the sleepy woods hand in hand, talking of many things: their likes and dislikes, their hopes and aspirations, until the conversation turned to family.

"Mine were lost when I was very young," Amberlyn said, "in a battle against the Howling." Xamus remembered the play they all watched when they last stayed at the refuge, a performance depicting the twisted nightmare-beasts.

"I'm sorry," Xamus said.

"I was raised here," Amberlyn continued. "The other Wildkeepers have been my family for almost as long as I can remember." She squeezed his hand and said, "What about you? What of your family?"

PART THREE: WASTELAND

"I never really knew them," he said. "Aside from my aunt. I had an uncle too, Galandil. A hero, I was told, but also considered reckless, dangerous, a nonconformist. In a way I guess I was influenced by some of those stories to go my own way, despite how it made my people think of me. I never really got along with the others of my kind. All they want to do is hide away from the world, while I want to see it. Experience it." He stopped, keeping hold of her hand, standing close. "Living under a shroud isn't really living at all."

Amberlyn reached up and removed his hat, putting it on her own head, perched atop her horns. She then ran her fingers over the tip of his left ear. "I'm sure your people miss you," she said. "And love you."

"They were glad I left," he said. "I was nothing but a pain to them."

"Really?" She eyed him skeptically.

"Speaking of leaving, last time you just kind of disappeared. I asked around, but they said you were gone."

"I leave again tomorrow," she said. "To keep watch for signs of the Howling's return."

"Ah," Xamus said in obvious disappointment. "I was hoping we could have more time."

Amberlyn gave a puckish grin. She leaned in and gave Xamus a long kiss that sent his heart racing. She pulled away, cupped his cheek in her palm, and said, "We have tonight."

CHAPTER THIRTY-NINE

SECOND SIGHT

Shortly after first light, Xamus, who had gone early to say his farewells to Amberlyn, returned to find the other outlaws had awoken and were discussing the second vision quest. They quickly concluded that there was no harm in undertaking the ceremony again.

"It's decided, then," Xamus said.

Torin, whose head was still clearing after a night of heavy drinking, said, "So . . . how'd everything go with that druid lady . . . ?"

The elf became acutely aware of eager eyes, all locked on him. "Amberlyn's her name," Xamus said. "It went well."

"You seem different," Oldavei said.

With a sigh and a shake of his head, Xamus walked away toward the Grove of Lights. "I'm gonna get some food."

"He does have a kind o' . . . glow about him," Torin said, falling in behind, along with the others.

"A spring in the step," Wilhelm observed.

Ignoring the running commentary, Xamus mused that he did feel . . . different after the time he spent with Amberlyn. During the short time he had slept, there had been no eerie dreams, and he felt more clearheaded than he had in a long time. He also found that he was already missing Amberlyn's company, even as he looked forward to the vision ceremony.

Hours later, as the sun neared its zenith, they ventured up the path to the stone-carved bear head and through its open mouth. They were accompanied this time around not only by Darylonde but Lara Raincaller, as they passed along the warmly radiant tunnels, hair clinging to their skin in the humidity, proceeding beyond the healing pools until they came once again to the cavernous, sigil-inscribed chamber with its steaming pit of stones beneath the resplendent shaft of light.

Darylonde led them to the pit, and as Xamus and the others removed their upper garments, the Wildkeeper did so as well. "The ceremony will take place largely as last time," he said. "With one exception: at the request of Goshaedas, I'll be joining you."

And now the group understood why Lara attended—to serve the function that Darylonde had served previously. All save the female spy sat cross-legged around the stones, closed their eyes, and relaxed. The ambient sounds of the cave seemed to amplify as they concentrated on long, controlled inhalations and exhalations through the nose and out the mouth as sweat began to collect and run down their heads and torsos. After an indeterminate amount of time, Lara approached and flung herbs onto the stones, causing a flash, more steam, and a blossoming cloud of violet haze.

The participants breathed in the mist, felt their bodies slacken, and as Lara began a low, rhythmic chant, they gave themselves over to the odd sensation of their bodies and minds separating from time and place amid a riot of color and light.

For some, the images that materialized before them were unsettlingly familiar: Xamus witnessed once again the nightmares from before, of the dracolich, of Nicholas disintegrating. Incongruously linked to this was the painting from the keep. Oldavei saw flame, roiling, twisting, coiling like a thing alive, all-consuming, assuming a serpentine shape and form—a display similar to that which had led to him leaving his kin, for it had betokened his death. For the others, the depictions were frustratingly cryptic. Torin was shown two piles of flat stones—funeral cairns—piled atop blood-soaked earth with an ornate weapon—a chop-and-maul, or sledge axe—laying behind, its blade coated in gore. Wilhelm found himself standing on a stage before a massive but empty arena, his mandolin smashed to pieces at his feet. All of the outlaws shared one single vision of a man with short-cropped brown hair dressed in olive-hued Children of the Sun robes, holding an expertly crafted scimitar, standing before a magnificent coliseum.

Darylonde's revelation was far different from the others: he saw at first the bodies of fallen soldiers, one part of a Wildkeeper patrol who had died in the war because of him, because he had been perimeter guard and missed the Howling's tracks. He relived his own torture, hearing once again the screams of his remaining
comrades . . . all part of an overall failure that tormented him endlessly. The image mercifully shifted, and he witnessed the outlaws facing down a single enormous reptilian eye; then he beheld them battling a colossal birdlike creature composed of living flame; finally he was granted several images of different times and places, of families composed of all the myriad races in the world eating, working, smiling, playing . . . living lives free of oppression.

When the ritual at last ended, the attendees slowly regained clarity. Oldavei, who was downright agitated, remained careful to appear calm. The others seemed perplexed, none more so than Darylonde, whose vision only affirmed Goshaedas's faith in a group of what he had considered to be well-intentioned but largely incompetent rabble-rousers.

Moments later, Lara accompanied the group outside and down the path as the outlaws compared their experiences. Wilhelm spoke of what he saw, as did Torin; Xamus mentioned the painting, but not Malis or Nicholas; and Oldavei spoke only of the robed figure, to which the others responded that they saw the cultist as well.

"So let's say Goshaedas is right," Wilhelm said as they descended the mountain path. "That our fates are tied to the Children. We all saw that same cultist . . . standing in front of an arena, right?" When the others answered in the affirmative, the bard continued: "Pretty sure that was the Grand Coliseum in Lietsin."

"There are substantial Children of the Sun operations taking place in Lietsin," Lara said. "There is also a strong Order-Militant presence there as a result."

"Sounds like a place we should stay farthest from, if we're smart," Oldavei said, with a sideways look at Darylonde.

"What about you?" Torin said to the Wildkeeper. "What'd you see?"

The soldier, who noted that the others had clearly not seen the same things he had, chose to keep the information to himself, at least for now. "Nothing of import," he answered.

"So where does all this leave us?" Torin said as they came to the valley of Oram's Rest, where Darylonde slowed, closed his eyes, and reverently placed his hand over his heart.

"Wherever you want it to," a voice called from near the mighty oak in the center of the breezy dale. It was Goshaedas. The tree-folk met them halfway. "You may stay here for as long as you like. Leave the Children and the law to do as they will. Or you may seek to untangle this knot that destiny has tied for you, knowing that in so doing, you place your very lives in danger. Take your time," he said, "and think on it."

The adventurers took Goshaedas's advice—they set the matter temporarily aside and passed the afternoon in leisurely fashion, then spent the night feasting, laughing, spinning tales, and drinking. On the stage, Wilhelm played to an adoring crowd that danced and sang along as best they could. Following the performance, the bard came and sat next to Lara Raincaller seated in the bottom row. He peered over his most recently purchased pair of tinted glasses at her and asked, "If I write you a letter, could you or one of your spies deliver it to Wallaroo?"

"I believe so," the spy answered.

After the evening's festivities tapered off, the outlaws gathered back at the clearing in the center of their shelters. Oldavei retrieved his blanket, and they sat on the cool grass and spoke.

"Well," Xamus said, "where do we stand?"

Torin spoke first. "I go wherever the action is."

Oldavei, still deeply unsettled but remembering also the conversation with Darylonde on his previous visit, regarding running, replied, "I said if we were smart, we would stay as far away as possible . . ." He offered a slight smile. "But no one ever accused us of being smart."

They turned to Xamus, who had been giving the matter a great deal of thought. The elf in turn looked to Torin: "You said you wanted Nicholas's sacrifice to mean something. Well"—his gaze swept the others—"this is how we honor Nicholas's memory."

All eyes then turned to Wilhelm, who offered a wide, toothy grin. "Oh, I'm in!"

"Getting into Lietsin won't be easy," Oldavei observed. "The Order-Militant will surely be on the watch for us."

"I've got an idea on getting into the city," Wilhelm answered. "A crazy-ass idea, the best kind!"

Oldavei snickered. "This should be good!"

In another part of the sanctuary, Darylonde came to a small clearing.

"Well?" a voice asked. One of the trees moved as Goshaedas stepped forward.

The soldier sighed. "I was shown a reminder of . . . what happened before," he said. "Of my failure." Before Goshaedas could offer some conciliatory response, the Wildkeeper continued, "But I won't deny it, I was also shown the outlaws doing incredible things. I saw a . . . different world. A better world." He fixed his silver eyes on the other. "I think maybe I'm supposed to be a part of whatever awaits them."

"I've long thought the same," Goshaedas said. "But it was a conclusion I felt you should come to on your own." He stepped closer. "I've watched you distance yourself more and more as of late. From me, from others, from Lara." Darylonde averted his eyes at the mention of her name. "I believe it would be good for you to take on this mission, to once again take part in something momentous. Especially if it presents a way for you to heal or maybe, dare I say, to forgive yourself."

Darylonde wondered if the old tree-folk was right. Maybe. The Wildkeeper would not just invite himself on the group's adventure, however. For a while, at least, he would continue to observe, see what kind of trouble they managed to get into . . . and, if necessary, help them to get out of it.

PART THREE: WASTELAND

CHAPTER FORTY

BAKER

After a few more days of tranquility, on the advice of Wilhelm in regards to timing, the outlaws said their farewells and struck out, crossing the Talisande via an old, structurally questionable rope bridge, then heading down out of the foothills and beginning what would be a relatively short trek across a stretch of the northern Tanaroch Desert.

Oldavei and Torin were well acclimated to the dry, harsh, barren conditions. Oldavei especially seemed in good spirits, the desert being his preferred environment. Xamus and Wilhelm were far less comfortable. The group had timed their travel with the hope of reaching their destination in the early morning hours, before the onset of the brutal midday heat. Despite their intentions, they had not yet completed their journey as the sun neared its apex.

They kept a watchful eye for scorpions, snakes, and roving packs of ma'ii (a threat that Oldavei said he may or not be able to talk them out of, should the situation arise) while they discussed Wilhelm's "crazy plan"—as much of it as he was willing to share, at least. He had not yet revealed, for instance, that he had sent a letter to his home in Wallaroo. Also, he had not explained why he currently directed them not to the sunbaked city of Lietsen but instead to the dusty crossroads town of Baker.

As they came within sight of the peak that overlooked the frontier outpost and the needlelike obelisk at its height, the party members grew more insistent on being informed. Wilhelm explained that his logic was simple: as Oldavei had pointed out, Lietsin was a highly secured metropolis with guards who would no doubt be on the lookout for them. Baker, not so much. There wasn't even a wall around the town. The bard's plan was to travel from Baker to Lietsin using an annual infamous desert event as cover—the Lietsin 100, a torturous off-road chariot race known each year for wrecked chariots, broken bones, and more than a few casualties. Though the race retraced the route taken by refugees fleeing certain death from Old Sularia nearly three hundred years ago, there was nothing in the event that paid tribute to that ancient pilgrimage. It was, quite unabashedly, a free-for-all cutthroat death race that terminated with a world-renowned citywide debauch known as Lietsinfest.

"We hide in plain sight!" Wilhelm enthused. "Slip in right under their noses!"

Oldavei frowned, still working through the logic. "If we're going to slip in with the racers, why are we heading to Baker and not waiting outside of Lietsin?"

The bard threw his hands out: "Because then we wouldn't get to race!"

"We're going to be *in* the actual race?" Oldavei asked. "In a chariot?"

"Yeah!" Wilhelm replied.

Torin and Xamus shared a look—the dwarf appearing especially concerned.

"I've wanted to run the Lietsin 100 ever since I was a kid," Wilhelm said. "And the festival at the end? I heard it's even better than Bard-In!"

"*This* was your plan," Torin said. "To run a fekking chariot race."

"It's nothin' we can't handle," Wilhelm said.

"We won't have to worry about Ironside killin' us," the dwarf continued. "We'll kill our damn fool selves before we get to Lietsin!"

"You'll warm up to the idea," Wilhelm replied. "You'll see when we get to Baker, and you can take it all in. This is gonna be epic!"

Torin huffed.

They came nearer the town, its mysterious, sigil-inscribed obelisk atop the craggy Searchlight Hill looming larger as they approached. Who created the monolith and why was lost to time. It was said, however, that a light shone from the stone monument long ago during the mass exodus of refugees from Old Sularia, acting as a beacon that led the haggard wanderers to shelter, rest, and relative safety. A later blessing upon that same hill by a Sularian priest led to the town's founding.

Sounds of bustling activity rose in volume as they rounded the base of the hill. A diverse throng of racers, promoters, mechanics, spectators, and townsfolk chatted, argued, and strolled among wandering packs of emaciated dogs and sand-swept, dome-roofed huts. The group was soon surrounded by scattered chariot pieces—many on wooden blocks—and the ubiquitous sounds of wrenching, ratcheting, assembling, and disassembling. Other sounds carried as well: the more distant pounding of hooves and clamor of wheels on the town's test track.

A couple of rough-and-tumble militia soldiers in mismatched leather armor, carrying spiked clubs, spoke to a small band of apparently agitated gnolls. One of the soldiers spared a glance at the outlaws, more specifically eyeing Oldavei, as they shuffled by, but neither guard gave any sign of recognition or alarm.

"This way," Wilhelm said, guiding them through the clusters of desert folk toward a section of town called Racers' Run, where teams worked on their chariots in garages or took them for test rides on the peanut-shaped test track called the Crash Circuit.

The outlaws found a spot free of spectators at the edge of the track near a row of garages called the Pits and observed an incoming chariot. It was a fairly standard affair, a finely crafted carriage detailed with bronze and tin decorations, inside of which stood three tall, thin men in formfitting head-to-toe leather, bright red with stark white stripes along the sleeves, long blond hair flowing gracefully behind them. The team, consisting of two passengers and the driver, held perfectly erect postures, chins thrust forward, seemingly oblivious to the spectators as they whipped along the track under the power of three white, feather-plumed stallions.

A trio of similarly dressed men, also with long blond hair, one of them in grease-coated coveralls, stood on the opposite side of the track. "Faster! Faster!" the tallest shouted, holding a small, ornate hourglass, intently watching the falling sands.

As the chariot shot past, Torin squinted his eyes against a cloud of dust and said, "Ain't they a pretty bunch?"

They walked south behind the backs of spectators lining the track and came to the Pits and its row of garages on their right; promoters and racers milled about outside the open bays while mechanics and engineers toiled within. The group moved nearer one of the garages, where three human female racers in pink jackets stood just outside, watching a small cluster of female mechanics working on a sleekly crafted, brightly colored, streamlined vessel. The coverall-clad women appeared to be installing some kind of bladed device into a panel on the carriage's right flank.

"Hello, ladies!" Wilhelm announced as they came to the women outside. "How go the prepar—"

"Mind your business!" one of them lashed.

Another removed a thick smoke from her mouth and yelled, "Keep it movin'!"

Recoiling slightly, Wilhelm threw up his hands and, with the others, slowly backed away and continued on. A commotion soon drew their attention, coming from farther down the row, where they viewed a small crowd gathered just outside of another garage. They pushed through the observers and witnessed two large muscular centaurs engaged in an argument with what appeared to be event staff. The horse-men were hitched to a conveyance of clearly inferior construction, with a dummy of a human figure mounted on the chariot floor. The dispute centered around several violations of race rules and regulations, related to both the transport and the draft animals, which in this case were not considered animals at all. The centaurs, seemingly unconcerned with rules, clomped away, brushing the outlaws as they parted the crowd, the wooden dummy in the carriage swaying unsteadily as they went.

The adventurers carried on to the end of the Pits. There, next to the last garage, a group of hunched robed and hooded figures busied about the oddest, most off-putting chariot any of the outlaws had ever laid eyes on. The large jet-black carriage held a position a few feet off the ground without the use of any wheels. Also, there was no apparatus for hitching and no animals in sight for the conveyance to be hitched to. Shimmering waves radiated off the chariot surface. Most disturbing of all, each of the outlaws found that they could not gaze on it for very long. The team members—if such they were—whisked back and forth around the vessel, speaking to one another via hisses and groans.

Wilhelm casually wandered to one of the frightening agents, who turned to him. Within the hood, the bard could make out only darkness. Wilhelm said, "Hey. So how does this thing . . . go?"

The wraithlike being answered with a prolonged combination of a screech and a wheeze. The other outlaws stood transfixed.

"Uh," Wilhelm replied. "Okay, how about this? What's it made of?"

"Black," the thing answered in a rasping vocalization.

"Black—black what? Black steel?"

"No!" the racer shot back. "Just . . . black."

At this point, the other wraith-beings had ceased their creeping and now looked to Wilhelm from the unsettling voids beneath their hoods.

"Okay. Thanks so much for your time." Wilhelm rejoined the others, and they set off, shaking away the chills that ran down their spines as they rambled alongside the track for a while longer, observing various other teams and chariots. In time they came to the southern turn of the track, where they stopped and cast their eyes back over the run.

Torin cleared his throat. "Well," he said, "I've had time to soak it all in."

"Yeah," Wilhelm replied. "Pretty amazing, right?"

"Mm," the dwarf said. "Couldn't help but notice there's maybe one minor detail you've overlooked."

"What's that?"

"You don't have a fekkin' chariot!" Torin barked, drawing the attention of several people nearby. The dwarf returned their gazes with a smile and a wave.

"Oh, that's not a problem," Wilhelm answered. "I got that sorted." He turned then to the south,

looking out over the desert, where a dust cloud presaged the arrival of another transport. "In fact
. . ." the bard said as thundering hoofbeats reached Oldavei's ears first, then the others'. They spotted
no less than seven great white buffalo, four in front, three in back, pulling a vessel so bright that the
sunlight reflecting off it was blinding.

"Here it comes now," Wilhelm concluded with a wicked grin.

PART THREE: WASTELAND

CHAPTER FORTY-ONE
RHOMAN

Many spectators came to look at the new arrival as the buffalo hauled it in. The gleaming-white chariot was a double-wide with exquisite gold filigree detailing. The reins were of the finest leather; the drawbar, shafts, and yokes were made from the rarest oaks of Mount Effron; and the set of four sturdy, thick wheels were silver plated with spokes and hubs of gold. The conveyance drew an immediate crowd, along with many appreciative responses and more than a few snubs.

The driver, a thin, smiling man with medium-length, wispy, tapered brown hair and large bright eyes—one of them drifting—stepped out. He wore a foreign-looking floral-pattern robe and sandals. The man locked his good eye on Wilhelm and said, "This must be yours!"

The outlaws looked at Wilhelm in raw disbelief. The bard chuckled and nodded. "That's my baby."

Oldavei ran his fingers through one of the buffalo's fur. "Buffalo are usually grazing animals."

"Don't underestimate buffalo, my friend," Wilhelm said. "They're extremely agile, and they can run as fast as a horse."

"Where'd this thing come from?" Xamus asked.

"Had it built," Wilhelm replied. "Took forever. When I decided to leave home, though, she just kinda reminded me of some of the things I wanted to leave behind. All the glitter and pomp and pretentious horseshit."

"It's not exactly subtle," Oldavei noted.

Momentarily lost in a reverie, staring at the chariot, Wilhelm snapped out of it and said, "Besides, I never had a team to run her with. Now"—he looked around at the others—"now I have all of you."

Torin grunted. Xamus went around to look at the chariot interior. Oldavei, still standing alongside one of the buffalo, turned and offered the largest pointy toothed grin any of them had yet seen. "This is gonna be fun," he said.

"Yeah! Woo!" the driver exclaimed from a short distance away. The others turned, having almost forgotten he was there. He stood with his legs crossed, right hand folded over his torso, holding the left arm at the elbow. He was smiling, nodding emphatically.

"Where did my family . . . find you?" Wilhelm asked.

"Oh, they put the call out for drivers, and I said, 'Look no further!' Or farther. Not sure which is—Anyway, I said, 'Right here!' 'Cause I'm an expert. Ex-pert," he overenunciated, "driver. Best in the business. Right here."

"What were you doing in Wallaroo?" Wilhelm asked.

"Oh, I got fired," the man replied. "From my last team. Yeah. Let go. Total misunderstanding. A lot of growling—" He growled and snarled, baring his teeth. "A lot o' that."

"Who'd you drive for?" Oldavei asked, fascinated, both by the man and his story.

"Gnolls," the driver answered. "One of their moms was on the team, not doin' much, really. I was tryin' to learn how to speak gnoll, you know, to fit in, so I said she should pull her weight. I said it in gnoll, and it came out like I wanted her to pull the chariot. Translation issues, it's hard to get some of those grunts just right. I shoulda just said it in common, but anyway, they got mad, kicked me out. You see this scar—" He started to pull aside the lapel of his robe.

"He does bring up a good point," Torin interrupted. "About a driver. Can *you* drive this thing?" he asked Wilhelm.

"No, man, I'd always planned on hiring a driver."

"You want us to enter a chariot race, and you don't know how to drive a chariot?" Xamus asked.

Oldavei giggled. "This just gets better and better."

Wilhelm turned to the stranger. "What's your name?"

"Name's Rhoman. I sometimes go by Rhomansky. Also Rhoheim. Or Rho. Anything, really, you can call me anything you want."

"You want a job, Rhoman?" Wilhelm asked.

Rhoman uncrossed his legs and held out one hand as if he were holding reins, making a whipping motion with the other. "Yah! Yah!" he said. "Hell yeah. I'm your man. Rho-man!"

Oldavei belly laughed. "We're all gonna die."

"Mm," Torin said, unconvinced. Xamus simply stood by, watching the spectacle with mild bemusement as some of the crowd began to depart.

The outlaws paid for a secure garage to lock the chariot in as well as stables for the buffalo. As day turned to night, the group, accompanied by Rhoman, sought out a particularly lively tavern called the Angry Axle in an area of town known as the Hub.

The Angry Axle was a loud and offbeat hole-in-the-wall, a favorite of rowdy locals, many of whom were honored in one fashion or another by the memorabilia that filled the place, ranging from trophies to mechanical pieces to chariot decorations. Two entire walls were dedicated to paintings of former winners, and above the bar hung a chariot that had apparently met some grisly racing demise—warped, scraped, and scarred, with large pieces missing. Lamps were situated throughout, casting both bright light and deep shadows that hinted at unseen dangers.

The group sat at a table in the middle of the establishment, halfway through their second flagon of Lightning Lager, as Rhoman dished some dirt on the surrounding racing teams. "Pink-jacket gals are the Lizzies," he said, bopping his head forward and back as if to a musical beat that only he could hear. In a corner, the women cackled at some joke, slamming the table with their fists. "You gotta watch 'em cause they are a little bit out there. They've won before, and they'll do whatever to win again. Half the wreckage in here is their doing."

Rhoman directed his still-bouncing head toward the cloaked wraith-figures seated in one corner, watching the room from beneath their hoods. "That's Team Necromancer," he said as one of the dark racers reached a gauntleted hand to their mug and sprinkled in some dark powder, causing an immediate puff of reddish steam. The necromancer raised the cup to unseen lips and tilted their head. "Reeeeeal creepy," Rhoman said. "They've won a few races too, and some of the folks they've raced against have just disappeared. Chariots and all! Nothin' left. We oughta stay as far away from them as possible."

Next, Rhoman indicated a table near the bar, where the group of long blond-haired men sat, along with gorgeous women whose hair was equally long and equally as blonde. All appeared to be drinking milk as they occasionally flipped their golden locks. "Team Lilihammer," Rhoman notified the outlaws. "The winningest of the bunch. Five trophies under their size-thirty-two belts." The driver stopped moving his head and looked forward. With the use of his good eye and his drifting eye, he was able to gaze at all of them. "They're the ones to beat, my friends," he said with great levity, then immediately resumed head-bopping.

"Okay," Wilhelm said. "Now we know what we're up against. We have a few hours tomorrow before the start to register. Whaddaya say?" He looked hopefully to Torin.

"I say you're all fekkin' touched in the head," the dwarf replied. The table remained silent. Torin looked to Xamus, who simply shrugged. The dwarf sighed and continued: "But if you're determined to add the wreckage o' that pretty chariot o' yours to the collection here . . . we oughta have a name, like the others."

Wilhelm smiled widely and clapped the dwarf's shoulder. "Told you you'd come around!" he said. "So, a name . . ."

"Wheels of Glory!" Oldavei said.

Torin shook his head. "Death on Wheels!" he offered. Silence followed. "No?"

"Team Rhoman," the driver said, then giggled as if it was the funniest thing he ever heard, his face turning red. "I—no, really I'm just—" He sighed, wiping away tears and clearing his throat. "Sorry. Yeah, that's not a—not a real suggestion." Oldavei stared at him, both amused and mesmerized.

A long silence then followed as they all attempted to come up with a name. Finally Wilhelm said, "Fek it, let's just get hamro, and maybe that'll—" His eyes lit up, as did the eyes of everyone at the table.

"Hamro," Torin said. "Does have a ring, don't it?"

"Team Hamro," Xamus repeated, nodding. The others nodded as well, all save for Rhoman, who looked to each of them in confusion. In unison, the outlaws raised their cups.

"Hamro!" they chorused, and drank. As they lowered their cups, Rhoman raised his, saying in a lone voice, "Yeah, uh, Hamro! Team Hamro!" He drank and pumped a fist as if reinforcing his endorsement.

CHAPTER FORTY-TWO

INTO THE STORM

It was an amazing sight: over seventy chariots lined up, three rows deep, just outside Baker's southern border in the predawn light. An enormous and highly energized crowd surrounded the starting line on three sides, leaving space in front of the chariots to the wide-open desert.

The first row was comprised of veteran teams and previous winners. Team Hamro, having been assigned number sixty-two, pulled into a vacant spot in roughly the middle of the last row, next to Team Centaur, hitched to their rickety conveyance. The horse-men paid the outlaws no mind, casting their eyes about as if on the lookout for event staff. Torin looked over to the straw-stuffed dummy with outstretched arms in the carriage, looking like a bedraggled scarecrow, leaning as if about to fall over, and shook his head.

Despite the spacious design of Wilhelm's double-wide, the fit for the team, they knew, would be tight. Rhoman sat in the very front, hands grasping the seven sets of reins. Torin, Xamus, and Oldavei had piled in behind and were already feeling crowded when Wilhelm came running up, having briefly separated from the group on some secret errand. He hopped onto the back of the chariot, dug into his travel bag, and pulled out items, which he began handing out.

"What—" Oldavei began.

"Goggles!" Wilhelm exclaimed. "Dual uses. One, keep dust out of our eyes; two—" He removed his hat and glasses briefly to don a pair. Goggles in place, he pocketed the glasses, put his hat back on, and cracked a wide grin. "Disguises! For when we get to Lietsin."

Torin sneered. "Desert dwarves don't wear goggles!" He shoved them back at Wilhelm.

Oldavei had already donned his. "How do I look?" he asked Xamus.

"Probably as ridiculous as I'm about to," the elf answered, putting on his set. Rohman turned and gave a thumbs-up, unaware that he had put his goggles on upside down.

Another chariot arrived in the empty spot next to them, one that looked to have been constructed out of farm equipment. Pulling the odd conveyance were two large ostriches. Three desert ranchers, one of them in coveralls, looked over at the outlaws and offered a wave.

Looking over his shoulder, Rhoman said, "A lot of these teams have at least one mechanic on board. Any of you, uh, mechanically inclined?"

In response to a collective shaking of heads, Rhoman said, "Well, just keep in mind, if we break down, we're fekked."

Another chariot passed behind them toward an empty spot—this one made from sturdy but well-worn, unpainted metal. The three men in the carriage wore ratty attire, and their soot-darkened skin looked as though it would never come clean no matter how many washings it received. Team Hamro immediately pegged them as miners, perhaps from Skarborough, an assumption given credence by the horses pulling the carriage, which resembled the pit ponies miners used to assist in their labors beneath the earth. The miners eyed the outlaws menacingly as they passed, exchanging whispers, clearly sizing up the team.

Just as the miners passed, a noise drew Team Hamro's attention—barking and growling coming from a gnoll standing between the centaur chariot and the double-wide. The dog-man pointed an angry, clawed finger at Rhoman.

"I did not mean to insult your mother!" Rhoman shot back.

The gnoll continued snarling, gnashing, and grunting, punctuating his tirade with a final bark before storming off.

"You could just speak common, you know!" Rhoman called after him. "That's what got me into trouble!"

A few more chariots had taken up remaining empty spots farther down the line, most of them fairly traditional, until the arrival of what the team would call the contraption. It had six wheels in total. The conveyance, occupied by three men whose fine suits and perfectly greased hair made the outlaws suspect they hailed from Sargrad, possessed two wheels. Towing the chariot via a metal arm was not a team of draft animals but rather one large mechanical apparatus with four wheels instead of legs and a long metallic horizontally oriented cylindrical body. A metal projection thrust up at a forward angle from the front of it, shaped to slightly resemble a horse's head. The top of the piece, however, pumped thick black smoke into the desert air. The driver held reins that connected to bars above the left and right front wheels in order to steer the metal monstrosity.

The contraption was incredibly loud—rattling, clanking, and occasionally emitting a sound like a cannon shot, accompanied by a brief billowing of smoke and a small gout of flame from the metal horse's smokestack-head. The entirety of it seemed as though it might fly to pieces at any instant, making the outlaws glad they were not positioned any nearer.

Just then a voice broke out, a race official yelling from a horn atop a tower situated at the right rear flank of the starting line.

"Racers!" the official proclaimed. "Ready your chariots!"

A host of cheers arose from the teams as well as the spectators. Farther down the line, the contraption blew a loud whistle. Rhoman whooped and swung his fist in circles, saying, "Get ready for the ride of your lives, boys!" Xamus, Oldavei and Wilhelm grinned like fools as the energy throughout the starting line built, creating a charge in the air. Even Torin felt a quickening of the heart. The buffalo team seemed to sense the impending event as they snorted and began stamping their hooves into the hard-packed desert earth. Many of the other draft animals did the same, resulting in tremors that rattled the carriage floors.

"Ready!" the official bellowed. The roar of the teams and the crowd heightened; the vibrations increased. "Get set!"

With an ear-to-ear grin Oldavei said, "I did mention we're all going to die, right?"

Just as the rim of the sun peeked over the eastern horizon, the official yelled, "Go!"

The first few moments were a chaotic free-for-all; in the initial burst, some chariots didn't even make it off the starting line, so determined was the charge of the animals and so poor the construction of the conveyances that here and there draft animals could be seen dragging shafts with no carriages attached, running with the group simply because that was the same direction the other animals were running.

The pack quickly separated into three parts: the most seasoned racers, including many of the previous winners, took the lead. Behind them came a second group made up of well-built chariots and capable teams, viable contenders for the title. Last was a combination of the weakest competitors—those quickly left in the dust, whose chances of making a strong showing diminished rapidly as the gap between them and the second group widened—and those at the front of the group, who chose to bide their time and preserve their energies, awaiting the perfect time to act. They remained behind the second group yet always within striking distance.

Team Hamro fared well at the outset, as the seven mighty buffalo muscled their way forward, easily overtaking the slowest competitors. The furious flight of the bovine coursers shook the carriage so violently that the outlaws were compelled to hold on to the handrails installed on either side. The buffalos' performance brought Team Hamro into an early spot at the rear of the second group. Despite the animals' extraordinary effort, however, it became quickly apparent that it would be difficult for the team to gain additional ground or improve their position due to the combined weight of the chariot and the number of its occupants.

A handful of racers in the third group did appear to be making progress, including the miners, the ranchers, and the contraption. It was the ranchers with their ostrich team who chose to make the first move. The large birds expelled a tremendous effort and in a sudden burst of speed closed the gap, swung round Team Hamro on the left flank—the ranchers once again offering a friendly wave as their chariot pulled ahead—and claimed a position two chariot lengths in front.

The pack had covered the first fifteen miles when Rhoman yelled, "That don't look good!"

The outlaws peered over his head to see a mass on the horizon, a cloud that grew steadily over the next few moments. "Sandstorm headed straight for us!" Rhoman warned as the monstrous dark wall rolled over the foothills in the south, a colossal bank of sand that blotted out the sky.

As the pack charged over the next several miles, the monster storm continued growing in size and strength. Team Hamro watched in fascination as the desert maelstrom engulfed chariots ahead. Many of the racers slowed as it came on, placing the team in a cluster of ten competitors when the gargantuan sand wave crashed into them.

"Goggles, goggles!" Torin prompted Wilhelm. The bard obliged, and the dwarf pulled on the eye protection just as the storm hit.

Visibility was immediately reduced to near zero; the buffeting wind shut noise out intermittently, causing sounds to reach them in detached, almost disembodied fragments. Fast-flying particles stung exposed skin like the prickling of a thousand tiny insects.

Rhoman turned to Wilhelm, who had moved up behind him and yelled, "This is where we make up some ground!"

"How?" the bard yelled back.

"By going even faster!" the driver exclaimed.

Wilhelm turned to Oldavei. "Our driver's crazy!"

"I know!" the ma'ii enthused giddily.

Fearsome snatches of noise—crashes, crunching metal, the frightened squeals of animals, the shouts of drivers and teams, came to them. At one point the ghostly pounding of hooves grew loud, seeming to come from right next to the chariot on their left side, before diminishing once again. Moments later they heard the chugging contraption and a loud boom, spotting at the same time a

PART THREE: WASTELAND

flash, presumably from the conveyance's smokestack. Later still came a cacophony of harsh sounds, followed by a terrifying sight, an object flying at an angle from their left out of the maelstrom—a screaming ostrich tumbling scant inches over their heads, causing all of them to duck.

"Agh!" Torin yelped. "Damned overgrown chicken!"

Rhoman yanked the reins hard right. The team held on; the rear wheel jolted from striking some object, and the carriage tilted precariously for an instant before righting itself.

Little by little, the storm began to dissipate, and visibility steadily improved. Sound grew more uniform. In the clearing dust, the team observed that they were now in the midst of scores of chariots, surrounded on all sides, the thunder of hooves nearly deafening.

"That was fun!" Rhoman said over his shoulder. "Now things get really interesting." The driver pointed ahead to where high stone canyon walls funneled into a narrow gorge. "I recommend drawing your weapons," he yelled.

CHAPTER FORTY-THREE
OFF-ROAD RAGE

The dust-caked outlaws, spitting dust and wiping sand from their goggles, unlimbered their weapons. As the chariots neared the mouth of the gorge, the cluster tightened. Rhoman endeavored mightily to keep the double-wide steady with the narrow cut directly in his line of sight so they would not be crowded out as two chariots closed in on either flank—burly, maul- and club-wielding hooligans in a stout carriage on one side; lithe, shifty-eyed, dagger-armed cutthroats in a sleek vessel on the other. For the next few heart-stopping moments, the outlaws' immediate world became a raging bedlam of clashing steel and red mist. Torin's axe exacted a swift and heavy toll; Xamus's graceful elven blade found a highwayman's neck; Wilhelm's longsword laid open a thug's chest, and Oldavei's sword sliced an incoming attacker's wrist.

The thug carriage slowed; the buffalo team shouldered left into horses pulling the lighter cutthroat craft, causing them to veer wildly and scramble to a stop before colliding with the gorge wall.

"Hahahaha!" Torin grabbed Xamus's shoulder and shook. "I guess chariot racin' ain't so bad after all!"

Team Hamro entered the gorge, the stones of the cliff face now within inches of their left side as Rhoman pulled alongside a carriage made from a fishing boat on their right. That conveyance whipped close enough that the wheels of the two transports briefly touched before drawing slightly away. One of the fishermen threw a net, which Xamus quickly sliced through, while another jabbed at Torin with a gaff. The dwarf grabbed and yanked the pole, jerking the wiry man over the side of his carriage. The fisherman released the gaff and gripped the rim of Team Hamro's chariot wall desperately as two of his teammates held on to his legs and attempted to pull him back. Their conveyance struck a rock, loosening their grip on the imperiled sailor, whose own hands broke loose from Team Hamro's carriage. The man fell face-first to the desert floor, screaming, the flesh stripping away before his panicked mates let go fully and the body tumbled to the ground, rolling, soon to be trampled by the horse team pulling the hooligan chariot. As that carriage ran over the fisherman, the impact sent it several feet into the air, temporarily dislodging the driver and two wounded thugs. The transport's wheels smashed as they impacted the ground once again, and the entirety of the conveyance burst to pieces.

Team Hamro and what remained of the fishermen emerged from the gorge. The sailors' driver managed to pull ahead slightly, swinging his horse team into the buffalo's flanks. The bovine chargers swung left up onto a shallow incline. Oldavei grabbed Rhoman's shoulder and clambered up onto the carriage rim, leaping down onto the rear of the fisherman's chariot just as Team Hamro's chariot gained level land. Rocks along the edge of the plateau forced Rhoman to pull away, and the outlaws were granted one final glimpse of Oldavei battling two fishermen before their line of sight was lost.

The raised tract of land was free of other racers, and with Oldavei's absence lightening the overall load, the white buffalo quickly gained speed. A sizable cloud of dust indicated the lead group ahead; Rhoman was able to close the distance to that cloud, and when a section of the plateau descended to bring them to the desert floor once again, Team Hamro found themselves close on the heels of the lead group, comprised of only a handful of teams.

Wilhelm, Xamus, and Torin all looked around for the fishermen's chariot and Oldavei, to no avail.

Not far ahead, the smoke-belching contraption surged to a spot near the Lizzies. The women shouted several expletives at the dapper racers before one of the females drew a crossbow and another used a pocket lamp to light a cloth bundle just behind the bolt head. The shooter yelled, "Fek you!" and fired the bolt into the wheeled, faux-horse apparatus. The well-dressed gentlemen screamed, and the Lizzies pulled away just as a terrific explosion erupted, incinerating the men instantly, destroying the carriage, casting metal pieces in all directions, shaking the earth below, and creating a blast wave that briefly sent the Lizzies' chariot up onto one wheel.

Rhoman swept out and around to the right in an attempt to pass the Lizzies. The women, still recovering from the contraption blast, didn't notice until the chariots were adjacent, at which point the crossbow shooter's eyes flew wide and she quickly began to reload. Wilhelm stepped up onto their chariot rim and leaped across, barely reaching the Lizzies' transport edge, dropping into the carriage and wrestling the crossbow from the racer's grasp.

The pink-jacketed driver, meantime, pulled one of two tall levers at her side. A small door flew off their carriage's right flank near the front. Within the exposed compartment, just above the hub height of Team Hamro's chariot wheel, was a pointed object that resembled a ballista bolt. Torin prepared to leap to Wilhelm's aid—the women having combined their forces against him—while the Lizzies' driver reached for the second lever . . .

Realizing what was about to happen, Xamus quickly focused, whispered the necessary words, and worked his fingers. The bolt launched from the Lizzies' transport, but the instant it left the compartment, the missile metamorphosed into a swarm of hornets. Torin reconsidered his jump as the rampaging insects attacked everyone inside the Lizzies' carriage, including Wilhelm, who gripped the pilfered crossbow—with bolt loaded—in one hand, holding the other arm in front of his face as he leaped back onto the Team Hamro chariot.

The female driver screamed and swatted frantically as the terrified horses crashed into one another, causing the three animals to tumble, the conveyance launching forward and up, sending Lizzies pinwheeling through the dusty air.

Team Hamro pulled ahead as the miners' chariot, having made a terrific push since the start of the race, quickly bypassing the Lizzies' wreckage. They pulled close to another transport that Team Hamro recognized as that belonging to Team Necromancer, the black carriage seeming to absorb rather than reflect the desert sun. A strange energy accompanied the wheelless conveyance as well—a shifting, indistinct miasma, the shape and form of which at times suggested a team of phantasmic creatures at the front. As the miners' cart-like chariot drew near, the mist enveloping the necromancers' carriage darkened and took on increasing substance until Team Hamro discerned tentacle-like projections unfurling from the stygian conveyance, wrapping around the miners' craft, even as slender, snakelike appendages coiled about the torsos of the miners themselves. The men, eyes wide to the point of bursting, emitted tortured cries unlike any the outlaws had ever heard issue from a human throat.

In a manner similar to the shape-changing of the vampires, the tentacle-wrapped men and their coach transformed from solid matter to intangible smoke, which was pulled by the tentacles and limbs back to the necromancers' sleek vessel. The smoky limbs vanished, and with that, the miners were gone as if they had never existed.

Wilhelm spoke in an awed voice, still staring at Team Necromancer: "What the fek was that? Did you see that?" Torin answered with a horrified groan as Xamus addressed his mental collection of spells, searching for something that might counter the eldritch powers of the black chariot.

Almost as one, the necromancers' vacuous hoods turned in the direction of Team Hamro.

"Oh fek!" Torin exclaimed. "Get us outta here!"

Rhoman urged the buffalo with both commands and reins. The driver's desperate attempts proved ineffective, however, as the necromancers' sinister carriage drifted ominously closer.

The necromancers came near, yet not close enough for any of the outlaws to make a jump. The nebulous mist formed once again as Xamus settled on a counterspell he believed might be effective. Wilhelm raised the crossbow he stole from the Lizzies; before he could fire, however, a dark, ropelike tentacle whipped from the black chariot and seized the weapon, turning it to a dusky, insubstantial haze that quickly dissipated. Torin had backed all the way to the opposite wall, horrified beyond the power of speech. Xamus focused intently, fingers moving rapidly; suddenly, two of the probing black tentacles turned to a greenish haze and diminished. It was working, the elf thought.

Just then an invisible constriction locked around his throat. Xamus's hands flew up, clawing at a noose that tightened despite its intangibility. Wilhelm looked to the elf, then to the necromancers, one of whom held out a gauntleted hand in a crushing motion. Xamus gurgled and turned purple, falling to his knees.

Rhoman tried desperately to pull away, but the Necromancers kept pace. Two more large mist-tentacles undulated from the impossible carriage, rolling toward the outlaws. Wilhelm drew his dagger and Torin readied his axe, both preparing to throw, when a missile—what looked like a fishing spear—flew from behind the black chariot and impaled the wraith, striking just below his extended arm, punching through the robes on the other side at a downward angle and lancing the lower extremities of the figure next to him.

Wilhelm and Torin looked to Oldavei, holding the reins of the fishermen's chariot, closing fast on the rear of Team Necromancer, already holding a second spear.

The invisible constriction around Xamus's neck vanished, and the elf concentrated once again on his counterspell; instead of targeting the tentacles this time—one of which was slipping toward Wilhelm while the other slid beneath the chariot to wrap upward—the elf directed his magical energies against the black carriage itself.

It was a more difficult, more substantial working, but the elf persisted, shutting all else out until naught but his own concentration remained.

The dark mist that surrounded the coach and formed the spectral coursers shifted to a greenish hue, weakened and diminished at last to nothing. An ear-rending, soul-searing screech arose from the necromancers as the carriage disincorporated, transitioning almost instantly from a tangible state to a green, amorphous mist that quickly evaporated, leaving no platform for the robed figures, who plummeted unceremoniously to the desert floor.

Team Hamro cheered, joined by Oldavei, who pulled up. Behind them, a smattering of teams charged, but none seemed poised to overtake.

PART THREE: WASTELAND

Ahead of them now was only one competitor: Team Lilihammer.

On the far horizon, shimmering like some mirage, were the structure tops and high walls of Lietsin.

"Go, go!" Torin urged.

"The buffalo are nearly worn out!" Rhoman replied. "They're givin' everything they got, but it won't be enough."

Team Hamro could feel victory within their grasp. As little as a day ago, none of them save Wilhelm had ever harbored aspirations toward racing chariots; now, here they were almost at the head of the pack, with only one team between them and total victory.

However, the distance between them and Lilihammer was too great, and though Team Hamro had gained ground, the buffalo were too tired to catch the champions, much less surpass them.

"I can try to take 'em!" Oldavei yelled.

"Gotta be a team!" Rhoman shouted back. "They'll disqualify ya!"

"There's gotta be somethin' we can do!" Torin said. Looking behind, he noted that there were no competitors in their immediate wake.

"I thought the plan was just to participate in the race," Xamus said loud over the pounding of hooves and jouncing of the wheels. "Not to win it."

"It ain't about winnin'!" Torin insisted. "It's about not gettin' beat!"

Xamus smiled.

Wilhelm was bent over, running his hand along the inside of the carriage wall next to Rhoman's legs. "Tell me it's still here . . ." he said to himself. He slid open a compartment door, said, "Aha!" and withdrew a strange device—what looked to be two barbed, three-hooked grapnels connected by a short chain.

"What the fek is that?" Torin asked.

"A little something I procured during travels in my younger years," Wilhelm answered cryptically. "A real-life artifact! I call it the Apparatus!"

"How's that supposed to help?"

"Just watch." The bard held one hooked end and let the other hang. Incredibly, that end extended all the way to the floor of the carriage, the chain magically lengthening.

Looking grudgingly impressed, Torin said, "Well, whatever you're gonna do, do it fast!"

The city of Lietsin had become more distinct now, a massive crowd visible outside the main gates lit by the final rays of the setting sun.

Rhoman had drawn Team Hamro to within two chariot lengths of the leader, pushing the buffalo to the absolute limits of their speed and endurance. Team Lilihammer faced front, paying their pursuers no mind, seemingly dismissive of any competition.

"Here goes!" Wilhelm said as he began swinging one end of the Apparatus in an arc over the others' heads. He whipped the chain and hook around until they made a steady humming noise, sighted his target, then cast. The grapnel sailed in an arc toward Team Lilihammer as the chain miraculously extended.

Two of the opposing team members had begun waving and pumping their fists as the city of Lietsin drew nearer. One of the long-haired racers casually glanced back and saw the Apparatus's barbed hooks descending toward the right side of the chariot. His bland expression turned to genuine concern as the grapnel struck the coach on the outside just below the rim. The man began shouting to his mates as the Apparatus end dropped, the chain catching on the axle between the right wheel and chariot wall. The hooks and chain wrapped around the axle, and within a fraction of a second reached a mass too great for the wheel to continue spinning; all at once it locked up, skidded, then burst to pieces.

The chariot toppled, bounced, and flipped. Blond hair swirled as bodies flew and tumbled amid a cloud of dust and gut-wrenching screams.

Rhoman pulled around the wreckage, bypassing the plumed horses that now ran aimlessly, pulling a shaft that furrowed the dirt.

Wilhelm moved to the back of the chariot and squeezed a portion of his end of the Apparatus, signaling the chain to reel in the newly freed opposite end. The grapnel bounced along the stony desert floor, the chain rapidly shortening until the end reached the bard's waiting hand.

At the same time, Oldavei came alongside. He balanced on the rim of the fishermen's chariot, holding the reins to the last second before leaping to join his teammates. The driverless fishermen's chariot peeled away, and Team Hamro looked to Lietsin, where they had drawn close enough now to hear the roar of the welcoming fans.

PART THREE: WASTELAND

CHAPTER FORTY-FOUR

LIETSINFEST

Rhoman brought the chariot to a stop outside the gates, dropped the reins, stood, and thrust his fists to the sky, screaming victory. The crowd, many holding huge banners or waving massive flags to congratulate the race champions, responded with a deafening roar. Some came to touch the winning chariot or run their hands through the buffalos' fur. They reminded the outlaws of the raucous Bard-In throng in both number and fervor, though many of them wore the light cloth and mismatched combination of accoutrements that was the hallmark of desert garb. They represented different cultures and seemed to cover mostly the young-adult age range, all with drinks in hand, exhibiting varying degrees of drunkenness as they shouted themselves hoarse. At the fringes, clusters of devotees dressed to emulate their favorite racing teams sulked and lamented their heroes' losses.

"Fans!" Wilhem enthused. "We have fans!" The adulations clearly gratified the bard, who basked in the limelight. Oldavei laughed in disbelief. Torin seemed unsure how to respond at first but quickly warmed up and began working the crowd, shaking his fist and shouting, "Yeah!" All the while, Xamus cracked a grin but did little more than tip his hat at a few of the more enthusiastic females.

The assembly was not made up only of revelers—armored, mounted Order-Militant milled throughout the multitude. Amazingly, their eyes seemed locked on the voluminous crowd, scanning the sea of faces for perhaps both Children of the Sun and—incredible as it was to consider—the outlaws themselves. The gate guards on either side of the entry and up on the walks of the gargantuan walls eyed the festivities with interest but gave no indication that they recognized the team.

Slowly, the chariot progressed through the open gates. Wilhelm leaned in to Torin. "Told you this would work!" The dwarf responded by slapping a meaty hand on the bard's shoulder, grinning widely.

Rhoman continued standing, reins in hand, whooping and hollering and gyrating all the while. Just inside the gates, raucous frolickers filled every inch of a widely expansive plaza, hoisting more flags and banners and giving breath to a cacophony of noisemakers.

To one side stood a grand outdoor stage. In the middle of the platform was a male gnome with slicked-back hair and a goatee wearing a perfectly tailored suit. Flanking him were two scantily clad females—one human and one satyr—striking provocative poses. A goliath banner, adorned with *Lietsin 100*, stretched above them. All along the front of the stage and on nearby banners, the words *Revel Inc.* were emblazoned. The gnome shouted through a bullhorn:

"Here they come! Ladies and gentlemen, our champions!" The crowd grew even louder as a race official in front of Team Hamro's chariot motioned for them to stop near the stage.

"Unless my eyes fail me," the announcer asked, "it looks as though we'll crown *new* winners this day!" The crowd exulted. "Come, you desert devils! Chariot champions! Join me on the stage!"

Wilhelm leaned and whispered to the others before they dismounted, "Just keep the goggles on!"

The gnome continued, "I am, of course, your ever-excited, always outspoken, gleefully gabby Master of Ceremonies . . . Grandmaster Plunk!" The outlaws, joined by Rhoman, climbed up to the stage. "And joining me now is—" Plunk pulled the horn away and held it in front of Oldavei. Wilhelm snatched it up and shouted, "We are Team Hamro!"

The audience went crazy.

"Team Hamro!" Plunk repeated, wresting the horn from Wilhelm.

The crowd chanted, "Hamro! Hamro!" as a third attractive female stepped up to the stage, holding a metal trophy, which she paraded in front of the gathering. "It is my distinct pleasure and the pleasure of our sponsor, as always, Revel Inc., to announce," Plunk said, taking the trophy, "here and to all the world that you"—he paused for effect—"are . . . the winners of this year's Lietsin 100!" The gnome then handed the trophy to the team.

The outlaws motioned for Wilhelm to take it. He did so, holding the giant metal chalice aloft with both hands as the crowd raged, while a man in a green feathered floppy hat and matching robes pushed to the front. "Make way!" he commanded. "Make way while there's still light!" Holding a stretched canvas and slate pencil, he stood at the foot of the stage, eyeing the team critically, his hand flying over the canvas.

Rhoman turned to the team and said, "He's doin' the sketch! Later he'll add paint and then—"

"Then, Team Hamro, you will be immortalized on the walls of the Angry Axle!" Plunk declared. The two females who had been standing with Plunk now moved to either side of Team Hamro, posing once again.

Torin, at one end, grabbed onto the satyr's waist. "Oh, I could get used to this!"

"There is also the matter of your winning purse," Plunk went on. The female who had brought the trophy and then departed now returned carrying what looked to be a heavy bag. Plunk motioned for her to take it to the team, which she did, handing the sack to Oldavei. The ma'ii immediately peeked in, then held it open for the others to see. Team Hamro cheered. Rhoman danced.

"I give you also these tickets," Plunk declared, "good for your choice of items at the Sand Markets!"

Torin accepted the tickets. Xamus laughed aloud at the insanity, and as the team stood waving at the crowd, waiting for the artist to sketch, he took a moment to observe the city he had heard so much of, spread out before him in the waning light. Directly ahead were a vast assortment of the Baker-style domed roofs. To the right, dominating the center of the city, he spied the upper tiers and flag array of the gargantuan Coliseum. Beyond that towered another obelisk, similar to that atop the hill in Baker, though a brilliant white light shone from the apex of this monument.

Xamus then scanned the gathering that filled the entirety of the plaza. An ocean of faces and, among them, the mounted Order-Militant. One of these, a man far across the crowd, glanced at the stage, looked away, then returned his attention to the team. He continued staring, giving Xamus an uneasy feeling.

The Master of Ceremonies' voice caught Xamus's attention as the gnome announced, "With these particulars addressed . . . ladies and gentlemen, it is my distinct pleasure"—his voice took on a scandalous tone as the crowd quieted, waiting—"to declare the official start . . . of Lietsinfest!"

The audience erupted. For so many, the long-awaited yearly moment had arrived. Robes came

PART THREE: WASTELAND

off several bodies to reveal colorful and skimpy festival wear beneath. Several of the Lietsin 100–related banners and flags disappeared and were replaced with multicolored Lietsinfest symbols and paraphernalia. Ornately costumed and painted dancers, acrobats and jugglers seemed to appear out of nowhere. Drums were heard throughout the plaza, accompanied by a plethora of additional musical instruments, and all across the city, giant cressets were lit.

"One final announcement before I let you go," the Master of Ceremonies piped, stepping to Xamus and handing him another handful of tickets, these bright red. "In one hour, you are invited to the Grand Coliseum. There, as the honored guests of Revel Inc., you will witness the spectacle of a lifetime . . ." He looked to the crowd. "The final, main event of our annual RevelSLAM!"

Again the crowd cheered. Grandmaster Plunk notified the team where to locate the stables and garage for the chariot, then expressed his expectation of seeing them at the arena. The team spoke briefly before leaving the stage, and it was agreed that Rhoman would see to the storage of the chariot and stabling of the buffalo, and then he'd meet the outlaws at the Sand Markets.

Immediately upon rejoining the crowd, drinks were thrust into Team Hamro's hands. Rhoman mounted the chariot, and as the outlaws began to work their way through the adoring crowd, voices rose once again from outside the gates.

"Another team's comin' in!" Wilhelm exclaimed. The bard's height allowed a better view than most, and he was the first to notice which team would be taking second place. "It's the fekking centaurs!"

After Rhoman pulled the Team Hamro chariot away, the outlaws joined all of the revelers in cheering the arrival of the centaurs, who appeared slightly overwhelmed but raised their fists in celebration nonetheless. Wilhelm noted that the faux-human carriage rider had at some point received a decapitating blow, straw jutting now from its neck hole.

Laughing hysterically, the outlaws made their way through the packed avenue into a part of the city called Old Town and on to the infamous Sand Markets, where Oldavei spotted some items and clothing among the vendors that originated from his own people. A mounted Order-Militant soldier rode nearby, looking over the crowd, causing the outlaws to squat down as if inspecting items arrayed on the blankets beneath the table.

When the soldier moved on, Xamus, still eyeing the rider warily, spoke to the others about Rhoman. Before long a consensus was reached. Half an hour later the driver, walking as if to a rhythm that no one else could hear, surrounded by adoring males and females of multiple races, at last found them among the vendors. As the group worked through yet another round of free drinks, Wilhelm said to the driver, "So hey, buddy, we need to have a little talk."

The driver's jubilant expression fell. "Are you firing me?" he asked.

"No, not—look, there's something you have to know," the bard said.

"Something we should have told you sooner," Xamus added.

"We're wanted," Oldavei said. "We're outlaws."

"And you don't need to be mixed up in our mess," Torin said.

"Oh," Rhoman replied, looking to each of them. "Oh, okay. Yeah, I, uh, I understand." He dug a key from his robe pocket. "This is for the garage. The stables, you can just—"

Wilhelm held up a hand. "We all agreed," he said. "First off, we want you to have this . . ." He handed the trophy to the driver. In it was a one-fifth share of the winning purse.

"The trophy? Serious?" Rhoman asked, eyes wide.

"Yeah, serious." Wilhelm said. "You got us here. More important, though, I want you to hang on to that key."

"But—" Rhoman began.

"The chariot's yours," the bard said. "I don't know how things are gonna go for us from here on out, but I don't see us drivin' that thing all around Lawbrand." He smiled. "It did what we needed it to do. You take it, make the most of it. Maybe go win a few more races."

Rhoman teared up. Holding the trophy cup in one hand, he threw the other around Wilhelm.

"You really are the best driver in the business," Wilhelm said.

"Ex-pert," Oldavei agreed. Each of them put a hand to Rhoman's shoulders.

Rhoman wiped at his eyes. Xamus nodded to the others. "We should lay low for a while, then get to the arena." To Rhoman, he said, "You should stay as far away from the Order-Militant as you're able."

Rhoman nodded, offered his final farewells, and departed to whatever adventures awaited him. Moments later the outlaws found the thickest part of the crowd, doing their best to blend in. At one point, Xamus noted a figure in a green sleeveless pullover. He caught only a glimpse of the man, who looked an awful lot like Darylonde Talonhand, before the figure vanished among the revelers.

PART THREE: WASTELAND

CHAPTER FORTY-FIVE
BLOOD ARENA

Team Hamro's celebrity status made the journey to the Grand Coliseum a balancing act between the outlaws soaking up the recognition wherever they went and taking full advantage of the many free drinks offered while also avoiding close proximity to the mounted Order-Militant, who maintained a significant, mobile presence throughout the city.

The group continued wearing their goggles at Wilhelm's insistence as they pushed through the more densely packed crowds in the middle of the city, a section known as Legends' Center. Nearing the colossal, circular, five-tiered arena with its arcades and statues, it took all of the team's willpower not to saunter into the Broken Chalice, a rowdy tavern packed to the rafters, and drink themselves blind.

"We can always come back after the main event," Xamus reasoned. "But the arena's where we saw the cultist in our visions. And the fact that our winning gained us access . . ."

"Yeah," Torin agreed, while they skirted a line of rough-looking characters of every stripe snaking around the arches of the Coliseum's bottom tier. "That's gotta be more than just coincidence. Should be fun to watch, in any case. You know about RevelSLAM," the dwarf said to Wilhelm. "These are the fighters?"

"These are the amateur hopefuls," the bard answered. "The more experienced fighters have been going at it all day—the arena has its own chariot races and battle royals where they pit gladiators against all kinds of nasty animals and shit. It's nuts, man! So now the main event's gonna have the seasoned fighters go against these amateurs, along with whatever else they wanna throw in the mix."

"This'll be fun!" Oldavei enthused.

"How do we get *into* this damn place anyhow?" the dwarf asked, just as someone nearby recognized the group.

"Hamro!" the drunken man yelled.

The outlaws smiled, nodded, and said thank you in response to all of the congratulations that followed from the revelers in the immediate vicinity. The throng had packed in tightly around them when a voice rumbled, "There you are!"

The outlaws put hands on weapons, preparing for the worst, when a thickly muscled, yellow-jacketed ogre shoved several festivalgoers aside and said, "Guests of honor! Follow me!" The ogre pushed more inebriates out of the way, ducking through an arch and hammering on an iron-banded door.

A gnoll, also wearing a yellow jacket, answered. "The guests!" the ogre informed. With a nod the gnoll allowed the outlaws in. The door closed with a boom as they passed through a short tunnel and entered a large, shadowy space filled with rough wooden beams and supports eerily lit by flickering braziers. Darker shadows and points of light hinted at various corridors and passages. Sounds of chains clanking, doors opening and shutting, and distant voices drifted to them, all of these overlaid by a more muffled noise: the words and anxious murmurings of a thousand spectators somewhere beyond the walls.

"Wait here!" the gnoll advised, turning and scurrying up a set of wooden stairs. Torin glanced down one of the passages, squinting to see a tall man with a spear and shield cross from one side to the other. Another man stepped into view then, a robed figure; firelight glinted off the blade he held, a finely crafted scimitar. The man nodded to someone Torin could not see, then moved out of view.

"It's him!" Torin blurted, discarding his empty mug and striking out.

"What?" Wilhelm asked.

"The cultist from the vision!" Torin called over his shoulder. The others looked to one another, and a tacit consensus was reached. They left behind their now-empty cups and followed the dwarf.

A door shut not far ahead. An instant later Torin turned right at an intersection, and they followed a short, dark passage to a barred wooden door. "Mm," the dwarf said. Outside the door, Grandmaster Plunk's voice could be heard. "After an exciting day of awe-inspiring entertainment, it comes to this. Prepare yourselves! For tonight's RevelSLAM main event—made possible by our proud sponsors, Revel Inc.—is about to begin!"

"We should go," Wilhelm said.

"I know I saw him!" Torin insisted. He looked to his left—an access way where a black cloth hung. Plunk continued working up the crowd outside while Torin pushed through the curtain. The group traversed a narrow wood-lined corridor to another intersecting passage, this one larger. Torin hooked right and walked a short distance to a thick-barred portcullis. Behind them, an inhuman screeching sound broke out from deep shadows, accompanied by loud bangs of something solid striking iron bars.

"Uh . . ." Oldavei said.

Outside, Plunk's voice announced, "And now, ladies and gentlemen . . . let the final battle commence!" The portcullis raised. From the shadows, a sound came of another iron gate lifting. Something rushed screaming from the benighted recesses.

"Go!" Oldavei said, running, joined by the others. The ma'ii shoved open a set of wooden doors, and the outlaws spilled out onto the sandy floor of the arena, engulfed by the deafening shouts of the bloodthirsty crowd.

Battle yells, death cries, and the clamor of all-out combat filled the open space. The outlaws had only an instant to register the presence of several other fighters engaging in combat, viewed by the blazing light from giant cressets atop high, thick poles as they rolled away from the egress. A monstrous creature emerged from the tunnel, eight feet tall, with scythe-like, hook-ended bone blades for hands, its body covered in spiky projections and carapace plates. Round, baleful yellow eyes peered out from a head like that of a giant raptor with a sharply pointed beak. It stormed forth on two thick legs and razor-taloned feet, screeching bloody murder, turning and attacking the closest target—Wilhelm, who was scuttling away on palms and heels. One massive claw-limb staked the floor, missing his groin by scant inches. Xamus began hacking at the massive beast while Torin and Oldavei faced off with another attacker—this a leather-armored, broadsword- and flail-wielding minotaur.

A spectator in the lowest seating section, just above the perimeter wall, shouted, "It's them! It's them, it's Team Hamro!"

PART THREE: WASTELAND

The nearby fans took up an immediate chant of "Hamro!" Soon joined by others, spreading through the seats until all of the Coliseum resounded with shouts of their name.

Torin ducked, the flail's spiked ball whizzing over his head and just grazing Oldavei, who sucked in his stomach as he leaped back.

As Wilhelm gained his feet, Xamus chopped and slashed, looking for a weak point in the monster's natural armor, with no result. The beast struck out with the back of one scythe, gouging the elf with serrated bone-teeth and launching him off his feet. He struck one of the stout cresset poles, dislocating his left shoulder.

"Is it—yes, it is them. Team Hamro!" Grandmaster Plunk blared from a horn, standing atop a podium that jutted out several feet into the arena a great distance away. "Truly a sight to behold! It seems that winning the Lietsin 100 was not enough for our intrepid thrill-seekers! They vie for the title of champions here in RevelSLAM as well! Is there no end to their ambitions?"

The freakish creature lunged at Wilhelm, beak open wide, providing at last a soft target for the bard, who rammed his longsword down the monster's throat. In the stands, the crowds went insane.

Not far away, the minotaur roared and slashed downward with his broadsword as Oldavei slipped to one side. Torin rushed in, axe raised—realizing too late that a centaur was charging in from the left, a spiked club poised to bash his skull—when the horse-man cried out, arching backward. His forelegs buckled and he pitched forward, crashing to the sand, an arrow jutting from his back. The distraction was enough for the minotaur to leap backward, temporarily out of Torin's axe range.

Meantime, unseen by the others, a figure vaulted a far wall from the lowest seating level into the arena, forward-rolling to a stand, running toward the outlaws—the very same archer who had fired the arrow that felled the centaur: Darylonde.

"Another startling development!" the Master of Ceremonies piped. "A new combatant has entered the fray and looks to be aiding Team Hamro!"

In midrun, the Wildkeeper nocked and shot another arrow, this time at a new beast that loped toward the outlaws—a giant owlbear. The arrow, which lodged high on one shoulder, had no effect whatsoever on the raging animal. Darylonde neared the outlaws, shouting "Circle up! Circle up! Back to back!" Wilhelm had just retrieved his sword from the fallen monstrosity when Darylonde grabbed his sleeve and pulled him toward Torin and Oldavei.

"When did you—" the startled bard began.

"Later!" Darylonde barked, drawing his longsword.

Xamus hurried back to the group, intending to work a sleep spell on the owlbear only to find that his dislocated shoulder affected his ability to perform the gesticulations necessary with his left hand.

"Keep your backs to each other and fight as one!" Darylonde commanded. The outlaws did as they were told as the massive owlbear rushed closer.

The minotaur circled the clustered outlaws, snorting, stomping the head of the downed centaur as he went, until his back faced the door Team Hamro had emerged from. "Separate on my mark," Darylonde ordered. The centaur lowered his head and surged in as the owlbear thundered forth from the other side. "Now!" Darylonde shouted.

The group broke apart, leaping out of the path of the owlbear, who charged straight through and into the surprised minotaur. The bull-man managed an overhead flail swing that penetrated the owlbear's skull, just before the rampaging beast swept claws as big as sickle blades across the minotaur's gut, spilling ropes of intestine onto the sand. Throughout the stands, the crowds erupted.

UNDER THE SUN

The minotaur fell to his knees as the owlbear spun, swiping, driving Xamus and Darylonde back; Wilhelm and Oldavei closed in on the beast's flanks while Torin chopped at its hind legs. The owlbear kicked, a glancing blow to the dwarf's torso that cracked two of his ribs.

Xamus and Darylonde continued hacking even as they retreated, their companions plunging blades into the beast from both sides. The owlbear, spiked ball still lodged in its skull, roared and reared up on hind legs, swiping downward. Xamus drove his sword one-handed to the hilt in the beast's wrist, the blade jutting from the other side. Wilhelm and Oldavei continued stabbing as Darylonde leaped in and plunged his blade between the ribs and up into the owlbear's heart. He withdrew his weapon and staggered back as the mighty beast fell, shaking the floor and dispersing a cloud of sand.

The crowd bellowed their delight. Xamus, still catching his breath, pulled his sword free and backed up, feeling the ground beneath him buck. He stumbled away toward the center of the arena, noting a twelve-foot-by-twelve-foot section of the floor rocking, scattering sand. Near the seam he noticed a lock chained to a thick staple as the giant trapdoor shuddered again. Something raged below their feet, trying to get out. Something immense that was, for now, mercifully, trapped.

Xamus turned to view the rest of the arena, where bodies lay strewn across the blood-soaked sand. Clusters of battle still remained: three combatants faced off against a fierce but grievously wounded, bare-chested ogre in one sector of the killing field, while in another, the robed cultist that Torin had spied earlier engaged against four opponents. His movements were a graceful dance as he deftly avoided one strike after another, his scimitar a swift and merciless equalizer, severing throat and vein until none but he was left standing.

"It's him," Torin said at Xamus's side, holding his injured ribs. "He's one of the so-called amateurs . . . don't look so amateur to me."

"The cultist from your visions," Darylonde said, now at the elf's opposite shoulder.

Before the Wildkeeper could continue, Grandmaster Plunk announced, "Ladies and gentlemen, Team Hamro, our Lietsin 100 champions, have survived thus far . . ."

As the crowd cheered, another voice broke in, a blood-chilling bass projection that the outlaws instantly recognized. "These are not champions," the voice declared.

Far across the arena, the Master of Ceremonies moved quickly away as Ironside stepped to the podium, his fur-lined hood hiding his features. "They are fugitives! And now, at last . . ."

He leaped over the low wall, landing on the arena floor, mace in hand.

"The hour of their judgment has come!"

PART THREE: WASTELAND

CHAPTER FORTY-SIX

DEAD TO RIGHTS

From eight access ways throughout the arena, mounted Order-Militant Peacekeepers entered and began forming a perimeter. The beleaguered ogre and his three attackers paused, casting their eyes about in confusion, unsure what to do. The cultist seemed to simply take in the situation as he moved to one of the cresset poles and waited. Ironside marched forward.

"Form up!" Darylonde commanded. Torin yanked the flail out of the owlbear's skull and joined the others, who once again put their backs to one another as they inched closer to the center of the Coliseum. The dwarf stuck his axe under one arm and ripped off his goggles, prompting the others to do the same. Darylonde substituted his sword for bow and arrow.

"You didn't have to put yourself in this position," Xamus said to the Wildkeeper.

"There are reasons for everything," the soldier said, without further explanation.

Above, they heard the screech of the dreaded falcon, Bolo. Its master stepped from a darkened doorway to a spot between two of the Order-Militant, near the befuddled ogre. The soldier-perimeter had fully formed now, at least a hundred strong. In the stands, the stunned crowd remained silent.

A few feet away from the outlaws, the trapdoor rocked from a heavy blow. A low rumble, akin to a growl, emanated from beneath.

Ironside drew up to a cresset pole ten yards away, with a knot of Peacekeepers close behind. "You have a great deal . . ." the Knight-Paladin intoned, lowering his hood, "to answer for." He bore scarring that fused a portion of his lips on the left side and extended over his nose and much of his forehead. An attempt to cover the damage inflicted by Nicholas's demise was evidenced by an iron plate, a kind of half-mask that covered much of the left side of his face. The eye that peered through the hole in the mask was stark white.

Wilhelm immediately began laughing. Xamus and Darylonde, on either side of him, looked to the bard as if he had lost his mind. He glanced back at them, shaking his head. "Sorry it's just—I mean his name's *Ironside*. What are the chances?"

The Knight-Paladin raised his left hand, then let it drop. A signal . . . followed by the sound of something cutting through the air from somewhere in the stands. Then an impact—an arrow in the center of Wilhelm's chest. The bard's hand flew to the shaft, a shocked expression on his face. He began to slump.

A chorus of gasps sounded from the spectators. At the podium, Grandmaster Plunk simply watched, fearful of providing any further commentary.

Xamus caught Wilhelm as Darylonde scanned the stands, arrow nocked. He sighted his target, took quick aim, and let fly.

Far away in the second tier of seating, Ironside's archer Enforcer, Daromis, had just enough time to react, dodging to one side as the Wildkeeper's arrow lodged in the thigh of a spectator behind him. The man cried out; the audience around the archer panicked.

Darylonde immediately grabbed another arrow, redrew, sighted Ironside, and fired. The missile sped toward the Knight-Paladin's left eye but turned to ash before hitting its target. The confused Wildkeeper cast his gaze about, spotting a haggard, long-haired crone emerging from between two Order-Militant riders.

"Witch!" Darylonde spat, then turned his attention to Wilhelm. Miraculously the bard was still alive, pulling away the arrow, which had made a small dent in the center of the cruciform symbol on his chain-mail shirt.

"Palonsus . . ." Wilhelm said, dropping the arrow. "Blacksmith makes one hell of a shirt."

It was a welcome but temporary reprieve, the outlaws realized, gazing at the numbers arrayed against them.

"They have us dead to rights," Oldavei said softly.

Torin looked to the trapdoor. "Never underestimate the power of desperation."

"Take them!" Ironside commanded. The Peacekeepers galloped forth.

Darylonde shot one arrow through the eye slit of an oncoming rider, then stowed his bow and retrieved his sword. Torin took two steps away, ignoring the excruciating pain in his side as he began swinging the flail with all of his might, smashing the ball and chain down onto the trapdoor lock. "What are you—" Oldavei began.

"Just tryin' to even things a bit," Torin gritted, bashing the lock again, causing visible damage. The Order-Militant soldiers closed in; Torin struck the lock once more, and this time it broke. "Look sharp!" the dwarf advised, jumping aside as the trapdoor burst open.

A twenty-five-foot-tall tyrannosaur exploded from the hole and thundered to the closest onrushing rider, twisting its head as it lunged, locking jaws on the horse's neck. The stallion's pained screams died abruptly as the massive theropod bit down, then whipped both rider and limp-necked mount through the air. The crowd exploded in jubilation.

Nearly half of the wide-eyed horses bucked and reared or turned tail and ran. The remaining half of the soldiers closed in, but their advance was disorganized, uncoordinated, the riders keeping one eye on their quarry while also maintaining a fearful watch on the rampaging behemoth. Oldavei took advantage of one stunned Peacekeeper's indecision by leaping up behind him, thrusting the tip of his sword up under the soldier's helm. He cast the body aside, took the saddle and reins, and began running among the other riders, cutting them off and turning them away, adding to the chaos and confusion to the best of his ability. As he engaged one mounted soldier, another rushed to his unprotected side. Before that rider's sword slash could land, however, a grapnel hook wrapped around his wrist.

Wilhelm squeezed the opposite end of the Apparatus, causing the magical chain to retract, yanking the soldier from his saddle. The bard dodged a swipe from another attacker, taking a gash on the shoulder for his trouble.

Several yards away, the tyrannosaur locked beady eyes on Ironside, lowered its gigantic head, and charged. Ironside surged forward, bellowing a war cry. The two met, Ironside clubbing the behemoth upside the face with a two-handed swing. The theropod reeled, thrashing its tail as it spun, catching the Knight-Paladin full force and catapulting him forty feet to the base of Grandmaster Plunk's podium.

PART THREE: WASTELAND

Throughout the stands, the crowd went berserk.

Suddenly, a dark, semitransparent globe appeared around the monstrous beast. Jagged forks of lightning-like energy shot from the outer limits of the sphere to the tyrannosaur, causing it to bellow in pain. The globe, only visible for an instant, vanished. In a shadowed recess not far away, a dark globe similar to that which had enveloped the tyrannosaur disappeared from around the crone's outstretched hand.

The crowds hushed while the theropod teetered drunkenly, as though it might fall, shaking its head. It stomped one foot to regain balance, seemed to collect itself, let loose a deafening roar, and bolted once again, driving into the thick of the mounted soldiers, unseating riders and toppling soldiers with wide sweeps of both head and tail.

Near the center of the arena, the wounded ogre, perhaps thinking that currying the Order-Militant's favor would be in his best interests, stormed in, wielding a spiked club the size of a small tree, preparing to drive Torin into the arena floor like a tent stake.

The dwarf turned to see a robed figure dash behind the ogre, slashing the back of its legs. The brute dropped to its knees and swept one arm back in a clumsy attempt to strike; the cultist rolled beneath the limb, shot to his feet, whirled, and swiped his scimitar across the attacker's throat, drawing a sheet of blood.

Where possible, apart from the tyrannosaur's havoc, the Order-Militant attempted to regroup and prepare for another advance. As the beleaguered outlaws steeled themselves for the next assault, the cultist said, "Follow me!" to Torin, then jumped into the open pit that the tyrannosaur had issued from. He landed several feet down, on some form of mechanical lift.

"Here!" Torin said to the others. "Here! Now!" He dropped into the hole, followed quickly by the others as the Peacekeepers charged in.

The robed fighter began working a crank, lowering the lift. "There are tunnels," he said. "A way out. I'll show you." The riders above, unable and unwilling to urge their mounts into the chasm, watched helplessly as the lift reached bottom.

Above, the outlaws heard the falcon, Bolo, screech. An upward glance from Darylonde revealed the raptor circling in the firelight. With a heavy sigh, he drew bow and arrow and aimed. "Forgive me, proud one," he said. "You are too great an asset to the enemy, too great a liability to us." He loosed, and the arrow flew true, skewering the bird's heart.

"Come!" the cultist said, striking off into a dark tunnel. The outlaws followed, Darylonde hesitating as the lifeless form of Bolo fell to the lift. The Wildkeeper knelt and brushed the feathers with his fingers before retrieving his arrow and rushing into the shadows.

CHAPTER FORTY-SEVEN
CARAVAN

Ambient torchlight provided just enough illumination for the group to see as they progressed through one set of tunnels after another, descending, pushing through earthen passages to a large, old wooden door. A few well-placed kicks from Wilhelm burst the door open, admitting them to a subbasement filled with crates of vegetables, fruits, and bags of nuts and flour.

"They use the passages to transport supplies to the Coliseum," the man said. "Food for both animals and spectators. Only few know of it, but it won't take them long to figure where we've gone. Come!"

He led them up a set of stairs to a basement proper, up to a food storage warehouse, and out a side window into a dark, narrow alley. "I'm Eric," he said. "Blessings upon you. This way." Crowds still filled the main streets, while a network of back alleys littered with refuse and passed-out drunks led them to the back door of a small domicile within a few blocks of the Sand Markets. Two large wagons with canvas bonnets sat to either side of the door, which Eric pounded on before turning to the outlaws. "You'll accompany us," he said. "To the desert, where we live. We only come here to buy, sell, and
trade . . . or in my case, to hone fighting skills."

Another cultist, a young robed woman with eyes of two different colors—blue and brown— answered the door, looking as if she had been roused from sleep and was none too happy about it. "Change in plans," he said to her. "We leave now. Send Rolf for the oxen."

The scowling woman moved away from the door. Eric entered and waved for the outlaws to follow. The quarters were small, with stacked double beds lining two walls. Much of the remaining space was occupied by food crates. A tall, burly man in underpants—presumably Rolf—was in the process of putting on robes as the woman rousted the other cultists, telling them it was time to go.

Eric addressed the outlaws once again: "They'll have the city locked down, but there's a guard whom we pay handsomely. He'll let us through a side gate." Rolf exited while the other cultists donned robes and the woman began carrying supplies to the wagon. "From there, we'll join our brethren. A glorious caravan, on a path to destiny."

Darylonde stood next to the door, appearing tense, on edge, waiting for the situation to devolve at any instant. Torin, holding his injured ribs, spoke up. "We're grateful to be sure . . . but why help us?"

Eric addressed the woman and one other cultist. "Leave empty space in the front!" he ordered, then turned to Torin. "You're clearly wayward," he said, eyes lighting up. "Lost sheep. But all outcasts are welcome in the heart of the desert. Our paths crossing tonight . . . brothers, that was no random occurrence. I see the hand of the Great Prophet in this. He'll show you a way to true freedom. A better way. The only way! In the wasteland you'll find new life and new hope. The light of the Sun touches all!"

"Mm," Torin replied. "Mm-hmm."

Eric joined the others in loading crates. Xamus looked to Oldavei, whose jaw clenched repeatedly, his eyes fixed on a blank spot on the wall. The elf recalled the riot at Innis, incited by Oldavei's loathing of the Children's oppressive ideology and his stirring of the crowd. Xamus put a hand to Oldavei's shoulder, snapping the ma'ii out of his trance. Oldavei returned Xamus's look with a nod of reassurance that all was well.

Torin drew close and said in a low voice, "Are we doin' this?"

The outlaws traded looks. "It may be the only way," Xamus answered, "to find what they're about."

They looked to Darylonde, whose silver eyes gave very little away. He said simply, "If this is where the visions led you, then this is the path."

"Before we go," Xamus said to Oldavei, "I could use a little of your expertise. My shoulder . . ."

"Of course," Oldavei replied. The ma'ii pulled Xamus to a corner of the room and worked his healing magic first on the elf, then on Torin's ribs. Eric seemed to take notice at one point in between loading trips, but said nothing. By the time Oldavei's mending was done, the oxen had been hitched to the wagons, and half the crates had been loaded.

"Let's get you in the wagons," Eric said. Wilhelm and Torin were deposited in a void that had been left at the front of one wagon, while Darylonde, Xamus, and Oldavei took up empty space in the other. Crates were stacked in front of them until the stowaways were no longer visible.

Moments later the wagons set out. Oldavei became anxious in the cramped space. Darylonde informed him to take deep breaths, close his eyes, and wait. The ma'ii complied. After what seemed an interminable span, the wagons stopped, and the outlaws heard an exchange of voices.

A few tense moments of silence and no movement transpired. The same thought passed through all of the outlaws' minds: Would Eric have given them up in exchange for clemency? But if so, why would he have led them from the arena in the first place?

Their fears were allayed a moment later when the wagons' motion resumed.

The transports proceeded east into the Tanaroch Desert, and once beyond sight of Lietsin's guards, it came to another stop. The group emerged from their hiding places and assisted in redistributing crates so they could fit in one wagon. They filled waterskins from a barrel lashed to the sideboards, and as they set off again, Eric joined them in the covered bed, sitting at one end, speaking animatedly.

"A whole new world is about to be opened to you!" he said. "You'll see, with fresh eyes . . . as though you've been blinded your entire lives. You'll see the light!" He looked to Oldavei, who sat near the front on the opposite side, leaned against one of the bonnet's wooden bows, arms folded, scowling.

Eric sighed, sweeping his eyes over all of them, eyes that suddenly seemed more grounded in reality. "Listen, I know how a lot of this sounds. I know what I sound like, and I know some of the things you must be thinking, because I thought those same things. I've had my doubts."

"Before you saw the light?" Xamus asked.

Eric sat silent for a moment. "Truth?" he said. "Some of the Children behave as if they're above everyone. I understand that. Sometimes that irritates me. They say a lot of things, and I don't know their minds. I only know my own mind, that I believe in the Prophet, and I believe in the principles of the faith. All I ask is that you give it a chance."

"And what of Taron Braun?" Torin asked. "Did he say the wrong thing? Is that why the Children wanted him silenced?"

"Braun?" Eric's eyebrows lifted. "Taron Braun was secreting coin away, buying property, following a path to his own glory at the expense of others, behavior that evidently carried over from his life before joining us. It's not a surprise that his indiscretions caught up with him."

So, Xamus thought, sparing a glance at Torin, now they knew why the cult wanted Braun dead. Interesting, though, that Eric tied the contract on Braun's life to past behavior. Either the swordsman was lying, or he had been lied to.

"You said the 'heart of the desert,'" Wilhelm put in. "What's there exactly?"

"A vast and beautiful oasis," Eric answered. "Sights beyond your imagination. And a community of believers. More than that, though, it's a place to find *answers*."

"There's nothing but ruins at the desert's center," Oldavei said.

"Not so long ago, there was nothing but ancient remains, as you say." Eric admitted. "Until the coming of the Great Prophet. He created life from lifelessness. Bounty from desolation. You'll see. And in seeing, you will know truth."

"Who is this prophet?" Darylonde asked. "Where does he come from?"

"Patience," Eric said. "All will be made known in time. Now rest. Stay hydrated. We've a long journey ahead." The cultist left the matter at that, and the group rode the next several hours in silence.

They had begun to nod off when the wagons came to a stop, rousing them. "The caravan we're joining is here," Eric said. "Filled with new believers . . . and seekers. Like yourselves." He hopped out, followed by the others. Rolf, the woman, and the fourth cultist had dismounted also. They found themselves at the base of a tall mesa. Several paces away, wrapping around the foot of the formation was a caravan, a host of wagons, stretching out into the desert to the west and out of sight beyond the mesa to the east. Eric approached the nearest wagon driver, a stout male gnoll in umber robes, and embraced him. The gnoll then warmly greeted the other believers in Eric's party.

"Say hello to our prospects," Eric said, indicating Darylonde and the outlaws.

The gnoll made a point of walking up to and touching the arm of each of them—causing Darylonde to pull away—gazing soulfully in their eyes as he said in a gruff voice, "Sun's blessings on you!" and "A new hope is yours!" He returned to Eric and said, "We're readying to go."

"We'll fall in behind," Eric said.

Oldavei looked to the wagon sitting in front of the gnoll's transport. In the back, he witnessed another ma'ii seated with hands in his lap, manacles around his wrists. The driver of that wagon, a barrel-chested, hirsute man in sapphire robes, quickly drew the back flap closed, then waved at the group, smiling and saying, "We're set to leave."

The two drivers both took their seats as Eric said to Xamus, "I'll ride in the other wagon for the remainder. I'm sure you have a lot to discuss."

The caravan lurched forward as the adventurers piled into their wagon once more, with Xamus and Wilhelm grateful to be shielded from the unforgiving sun. As their transport, the very last in the queue, joined the others, Oldavei told his comrades of what he had seen. "He looked to be a prisoner," the ma'ii concluded. "And the place we're going," Oldavei continued, "my people know of it. They call it Tanasrael, a temple city built in some forgotten age and fallen to ruin."

"My people spoke o' somethin' too," Torin said. "Deep in the desert. A mountain raised by sorcery that collapsed under the weight of its own evil."

"You think the two are related?" Xamus asked.

PART THREE: WASTELAND

"Could be," the dwarf answered. "Maybe this 'Great Prophet' rebuilt Tanasrael."

"Guess we'll find out," Wilhelm said.

Darylonde spoke from the front of the bed. "Wherever it is we end up, be ready for anything."

"When I said you didn't have to put yourself in this position," Xamus replied to Darylonde, "you said there were reasons for everything. What did you mean?"

The Wildkeeper didn't answer immediately.

"You almost died for us," Oldavei said.

"We are, each of us, bedeviled," Darylonde said. "By one thing or another. And I'm no exception. How we choose to confront these torments defines who we are. I believe my destiny is tied to all of this," he nodded toward the caravan. "Maybe even to all of you. If so . . ." he cast his silver eyes on all of them, a thick edge to his voice. "I will face that destiny head-on."

CHAPTER FORTY-EIGHT
MIDNIGHT RUN

The view out the back of the wagon bonnet changed little over the course of the following days. Always at sundown the wagons would circle, fires would be built, and the Children would sing their songs and dance and give praise to the Prophet, while Darylonde and the outlaws sat at their own fire and observed. Quite often these nights reminded Oldavei and Xamus of the compound they besieged in a time that seemed forever ago in their effort to return the wayward "missing youth" of Hearthvale. These thoughts inevitably led to memories of Nicholas. For Xamus these thoughts ultimately led down the same rabbit hole: of the battle at the theater, the summoning of Malis, and ultimately the death— or second death—of his friend at his own hands. Xamus would pass the evenings quietly, thinking of what Darylonde said, that each of them was bedeviled in some way. As a distraction, the elf found himself wondering what phantoms haunted his companions.

Eric would often visit their fire, sit with them and talk, though he gave little away in the form of information. One night, Oldavei asked Eric about the shackled ma'ii he had spotted in the wagon. That wagon was moved nearly to the front of the line upon the outlaws joining the caravan, far from their own wagon's position. Each night, however, it was repositioned once again in the circle, so that it sat far on the opposite side.

"A few of our prospects are particularly violent," Eric said. "Regrettably, they must be kept from the others and remain in restraints, for their own safety as well as the safety of others. Their aggressive and destructive tendencies will disappear, though, after they've spent time at the oasis. I know that because I've seen it happen with others time and again."

Later that night, wrapped in his beloved blue blanket, Oldavei found himself thinking about the cultist's words. The explanation made sense, yet he could not help wondering if Eric was being untruthful.

It was on the evening of the seventh day, just as the water barrels were nearing empty, that the caravan arrived at a rare destination in the endless desert—a waywell, a deep and expansive shaft, surrounded by a low stone wall with multiple bucket and pulley systems for extracting water.

The origin of the wells was a mystery. There were rumors, Oldavei explained, that they were built by the same forgotten race that built the city in the heart of the desert. It was also held that the water of the wells replenished through magical means, though no one had ever verified the claim. Whatever the case, the travelers all took full advantage of the accommodation. Water barrels and skins were filled, and later the wagons were circled with the well serving as the hub of the giant wheel they formed.

In the deep of the night while the caravan slept, a distant, weary howl stirred Oldavei from his sleep.

It was a sound the ma'ii knew all too well, the call of his people. He felt a sudden, irresistible pull—to the moonlit night, the desert, the light breeze, and the source of that vocalization. With slow and careful movements, he abandoned his blanket, moving furtively away from the cooling embers of the fire, past their wagon, out into the hard-packed wide open. When he had reached a sufficient distance from the wagon corral, his aspect began to morph and shift until he had taken on the form of the coyote.

He ran, feeling the rush of the wind, the earth beneath his paws, the euphoric sense of freedom and inner peace that he had not experienced in such a long time that he had almost forgotten the joy of it.

The wind shifted, and he followed a particular scent, one that lead him to a shallow rise, where a scrawny, bedraggled pack of his fellows idled in coyote form beneath the bright, full moon.

Oldavei came and touched noses with the leader. Following a great deal of sniffing-greetings with the other pack members, Oldavei found a vacant spot and shifted to his more oft-used form. The other ma'ii did the same, and within a short span, Oldavei was standing among five thin dark-skinned members of a tribe he recognized as Kawati, denoted by the color and markings of the leathers and the trinkets they wore.

The leader, tall with long, stringy black hair, said, "Tohtach," referring to the name of Oldavei's tribe. He then stared at Oldavei's forehead tattoo, putting him on guard. Realization crossed the other's features. "You're the shaman, Oldavei, yes?" He said.

"I'm no shaman," Oldavei answered. "I left that life behind long ago." He pointed to his forehead. "I'm an outcast."

The other ma'ii looked skeptical. "But you *are* Oldavei."

"Yes."

"Shaman or no, you look as though you carry the weight of the world on your shoulders," the leader said, putting a hand to Oldavei's shoulder. "I'm Ahdami." He introduced his tribemates, ending with a female, Norra—slender, with thick black hair down to her waist. She offered Oldavei a warm smile.

"We welcome you, brother," Ahdami said.

Oldavei gave a nod and a tight smile. "Well met, all of you." He searched for something else to say and landed on, "How long have you been following the caravan?"

"Five days," Ahdami said, then sat, cross-legged. Oldavei reciprocated, as did the rest of the tribe.

"We've been watching the Children for some time now," the leader continued. "Even more so recently, as more of our people have been taken."

"Taken?" Oldavei replied.

"By the Children," Ahdami said. "They've reconstructed the ancient dwelling-place Tanasrael, stone by stone, and they've done so on the backs of forced labor."

"Slaves," Oldavei said, thinking once again of the ma'ii in the wagon.

"They've taken my brother as well," Norra said in a soft-spoken voice.

"And it's not just us," Ahdami said. "Many desert dwarves have gone missing also. And as of late, this captive-taking has not only continued, it has increased."

Oldavei frowned. "But if the structures of Tanasrael have already been rebuilt—"

"There are rumors"—the leader broke in, leaning forward—"of mines beneath the main ziggurat. What they're after, we don't know. But we're trying to find out so that we can stop the subjugation of our people."

"You must come with us!" the female said, rising to her knees. "Escape now before you end in shackles too!"

"I . . . thank you, but I can't," Oldavei replied. "I have friends, and I can't leave them."

"We can take them too," Ahdami said. "Tonight. Now."

Oldavei shook his head, "If what you say is correct . . . me going to Tanasrael is the best way to find out what's happening. And why. Maybe I can help."

Ahdami nodded understanding, then stood. When Oldavei gained his feet the leader reached out and grasped Oldavei's forearm in the tradition of ma'ii greeting and parting. As he did so, he looked to Oldavei with something wholly unexpected: admiration. "We'll continue watching," the leader said.

"Don't take any risks," Oldavei answered. "Not yet, at least. Not until we know more."

The leader bowed slightly, then stepped away. Other members of the tribe came one by one and repeated the forearm grasp. The female was last. "Be careful," she said, gazing at him earnestly, her glittering eyes quickening Oldavei's pulse. "There's a dark power associated with the cult. We've all felt it. Stay safe! My brother, his name is Altach. If you see him or hear of anything—"

"I'll help if I can," Oldavei said. Norra's expression reflected warm gratitude.

As Oldavei set off down the slope, Ahdami called for him to pause. The leader came and spoke in a low voice. "Mah'wari came to us, after you left," he said, referring to Oldavei's shaman-teacher, his mentor, and for a time, something akin to a father. It was a name that caused immediate pangs of emotion, memories of harsh, bitter words spoken around the time of Oldavei's choice to leave the tribe. Ahdami continued, "He went to all of the tribes, asking after you. He seemed deeply concerned. I just . . . thought you might want to know."

Oldavei fought against the feelings that warred within him: guilt, anger, confusion, sorrow.

"Thank you," he managed, then took his leave. Several paces away from the rise, he shifted once again to coyote form, running over the hard-packed flatlands back to the caravan.

PART THREE: WASTELAND

CHAPTER FORTY-NINE

TANASRAEL

Over the next several days, the adventurers kept the news that Oldavei shared with them in close confidence. During overnight stops they conversed with Eric often, always probing gently, while at the same time attempting to give nothing away.

When nearly two full weeks had passed, the caravan reached its destination. The wagon line formed a half circle at the periphery of the oasis, and as it did, Xamus and the others detected an immediate change in temperature. Wherever they were, it was somehow cooler than the surrounding desert. The curious group emerged from the wagon, cast their eyes on the panorama before them, and were immediately struck silent.

An ocean of earth-tone-colored tents, ranging from sizes intended for only a few occupants to massive pavilions capable of hosting entire convocations, lay spread before them. Sprinkled throughout the assemblage were vendor stalls and hovel domiciles. At the center of all, a gargantuan, multitiered ziggurat dominated the scene. So large and commanding was the structure that it made all dwellings and shelters around it seem as little more than trifles; the massive edifice appeared, in fact, almost a city unto itself.

From its apex shone a gleaming beacon whose brilliance nearly rivaled that of the sun; solar motifs adorned the meticulously carved stone walls. At the foot of the mountainous construction a majestic platform sat, emblazoned with sun symbols and topped with monoliths similar to those seen in Baker and Lietsin.

The ziggurat and the multitude of tents surrounding it was truly an awesome sight to behold. Yet these were not what rendered the visitors speechless; what astounded them was the *water*.

It seemed to flow from everywhere, running through canals dug into the desert floor, springing forth in gushing fountains, and falling in streams from the upper reaches of the mighty ziggurat's various tiers. It sparkled, crystal clear, inviting and essential. The source of all life. And the sounds of it—gurgling, murmuring, and in some places roaring, served as a backdrop to all other sound. Because of that water, much of the color that met the visitors' eyes was not the harsh brown of the dry desert but a lush and vibrant green. Foliage flourished throughout Tanasrael in the form of expansive crop fields; dense, verdant thickets of tree and brush; and gardens, consisting of flora from all over the known world, spilling out over the ziggurat's ledges and down its walls. The gardens and waterfalls, combined with the sheer size and mass of the temple structure, made for a study in contrast, a spectacle both indomitable and beautiful.

Throughout the oasis-metropolis, a staggering congregation of Children sang, preached, conversed, prayed, and meditated, garbed in their light and multicolored robes.

"This is . . . impossible," Torin said. "It shouldn't exist."

"And yet here it is," Oldavei replied.

As the caravan drivers and attendants began unloading crates and carrying them into the city, Eric strode to the fore of the still-observing adventure spreading his hands. "Go, brothers, go and experience all that Tanasrael has to offer," he said. "All here are free—" This earned a veiled scowl from Oldavei. "And all here are welcome."

When Eric left, Darylonde said, "Be on your guard at all times," and led the way, advancing first not toward the tent grounds but instead to the expanse of fields to the east.

They maneuvered through a small crowd of chanting faithful, hands raised to the air. "Belief!" one frail woman shouted. "Belief sets hearts aflame!"

The group progressed to a large, rocky outcropping from which spewed a steady stream of pristine water. Enraptured-looking believers waded in the pool at the base of the stone. Earthen channels conveyed the water from the spring in multiple directions. Darylonde chose one path and followed the irrigation ditch to the edge of a tomato field.

He gazed out over the farmlands. There were not only crops but pastures with animals as well: horses, cows, bison, and sheep. "Astonishing," he said as the others came and joined him, "to see nature flourish here . . . small wonder that some of these faithful consider the prophet a miracle worker."

"Yeah, but somethin' don't feel right," Torin said.

Darylonde knelt, thrusting his fingers into the soil, retrieving fingers full of soft brown loam. He raised his hand and took a deep breath. "Your senses do you credit," the Wildkeeper said. "Something is indeed wrong. A strange energy permeates this land. One that I've never come into contact with."

"I feel it too," Xamus said.

"Something treacherous lies here," Darylonde declared, standing. "Something vast and deep. Breathing beneath our feet."

The outlaws, unsettled, looked down at their boots, then at each other. "Let's continue exploring," Darylonde said, and set off for the tent city.

They strolled along the avenues, chickens or dogs often darting across their path. The adherents they passed, who sat or stood with faces upraised and mouths engaged in prayer, came from every corner of the world. They represented all ages as well, though the majority appeared in the twenty-to-thirty-year range.

The party pressed onward, rounding the edge of the stone terrace with its soaring obelisks, gazing all the while with craned necks at the monumental ziggurat, feeling the spray of its gushing falls, catching the scent of its hanging gardens and marveling at the immensity of the steeply ascending steps.

On the western side of the behemoth structure, the group encountered larger and more crowded shelters. In one, they observed a tent with some open crates containing garments similar to those they had seen at the Children's warehouse in Skarborough—leather armor. A nearby crate contained a variety of weapons such as knives, short swords, and shields.

Elsewhere the faithful gathered, listening in rapt attention to preachers sermonizing in grand open-air pavilions. A wild-eyed female with fire-red hair declared in one tent, "The sun illuminates our hidden fears! Let them burn and you will be free!" In another, a portly, more subdued man asserted, "The Church and its pet guilds have held you down. Made you small! You are nothing but cogs in the machineries of their ambition!"

In some places Children rolled up robe sleeves and bit back cries of pain as smiths branded their naked skin with esoteric symbols. One of the recipients, a female gnoll, called out, "The day is coming, brothers and sisters! The day is coming!" just before receiving her brand.

PART THREE: WASTELAND

Deeper in, the group came to an open common area where several spectators had gathered, voicing encouragement for a disciple who was preparing to traverse a bed of glowing-hot coals in bare feet.

As the others watched, fascinated, Wilhelm found his attention diverted to a particular brightly colored tent not far away. It was huge, with flaps closed on all sides and no markings to indicate its purpose. The bard stole away to one entrance and stealthily pulled the canvas aside. He poked his head in, but before his eyes could adjust, a massive hand grasped his chain-mail shirt, yanked him inside, and threw him to the floor.

Wilhelm looked up to see an enormous barrel-chested ogre, draped in billowing robes, staring down at him, fists balled. "What do you believe in, boy?" the ogre demanded in a throaty voice.

"Uh . . ." Wilhelm began. The ogre reached down, hauled him to his feet, and swung a meaty fist into his gut.

Wilhelm doubled over, red-faced, suppressing the urge to vomit.

"What do you believe in?" the ogre challenged again.

"Nothing!" Wilhelm shot back, recovering, throwing a wild punch at his assailant's jaw. The ogre swatted the attempt away and batted the bard upside the head, openhanded.

Wilhelm staggered and caught himself on a writing desk topped with scrolls and texts. The ogre repeated his query.

Wilhelm answered, "I believe in faeries with boo—" The ogre swatted him on the other side of the head, sending him side-stumbling across the tent.

"What do you believe in?" the ogre said again.

Wilhelm threw a front kick. The ogre smashed a fist down onto his shin, causing the bard to cry out and grab his leg. "What the fek is your problem?" Wilhelm panted.

The ogre hoisted him up, lifting until the two were face-to-face, the bard on the toes of his boots. "What do you believe in?" the ogre asked again, his foul breath nearly overwhelming.

Exhausted, Wilhelm croaked, "Myself. I believe in myself, okay?"

The ogre's grip eased. He lowered the bard gingerly to his feet, then wrapped his tree-trunk arms around Wilhelm's shoulders and neck, pulling him in tight, not a crushing clinch but an almost paternal embrace.

He let go, and as Wilhelm pulled away, the ogre tapped him on the cheek. "Go in peace, brother," he rumbled.

"Yeah," Wilhelm said. "Sure." He left the tent, and after a few minutes of pushing through the crowd—and walking with a slight limp—he found the others, arriving just as the believer finished his walk on the hot coals.

Torin looked to Wilhelm and scowled. "What the fek happened to you?"

"You've only been away five minutes," Oldavei said.

"It's nothing," Wilhelm said. "No big deal, really."

Darylonde narrowed his silver eyes at the bard and was ready to pose questions of his own when horns sounded from atop the ziggurat.

Murmurs of excitement rippled through the faithful. As one they began moving in the direction of the massive structure. The adventurers looked around in confusion. Torin caught the robe sleeve of a passing adherent.

"What's goin' on?" he asked.

"The time has arrived," the dreamy-eyed acolyte responded. "To hear the words of the Prophet."

CHAPTER FIFTY

VOICE OF THE PROPHET

They jostled their way to a spot several feet away from the stone terrace, opposite the foot of the ziggurat. All eyes lifted to the apex of the mighty edifice, and there, a figure appeared to chants of "the Prophet" and "the Prophet speaks" from the faithful. The person stepped to the very edge of the peak, silhouetted by its brilliant, gleaming light. No features were readily identifiable at this distance, though it appeared the individual was thin and slightly hunched, bright robes rippling in a light breeze.

"Not exactly what I expected," Torin said.

Darylonde, whose sight was akin to that of an eagle, spoke: "It's a female," he said. "Ma'ii."

"The Prophet's ma'ii?" Oldavei replied.

"That is not the Prophet," a nearby adherent—a tall, thin man—said in a low tone. "To behold the Prophet would be overwhelming. Shayan Shibaar is the Voice of the Prophet. Her words are the Prophet's words, and we are blessed to hear them." A handful of other believers shushed the conversation, and the adventurers waited in silence.

Shayan lifted her arms; the voice that rang out was powerful and resonant, loud as if amplified by artificial means, though she held no horn. "The glory of the Sun touches all," the Voice of the Prophet said. "And we are all equal beneath it. It is the power of the Sun that spurs growth. Rebirth. It is the power of the Sun that awakens within us the abilities to go beyond what we ever thought possible—to do more. To *be* more. When called for, it is the fury of the Sun that purges. And it is the flame of truth . . ."

"That purifies the soul," the crowd answered in unison.

Torin looked to Xamus with raised eyebrows as Shayan continued: "We are, all of us, blessed. For we live in a time of hope, a time when the faithful will see society remade."

"Remade?" Wilhelm said in a low voice.

"There is a day approaching," the Voice of the Prophet said, "when all believers will be called upon to rise up and reclaim that which is rightfully ours." Darylonde's jaw clenched. His fingers curled into fists reflexively. The responses of the surrounding Children rose in volume. A current of energy seemed to course through the crowd as Shayan went on: "To reenter the cities of your birth, not as lost Children but as the Exalted, the Chosen—those who will bring light and, to any who stand in our way, a reckoning!"

Hands raised all around. Xamus looked about, noting the zeal in the Children's eyes, the beatific smiles on their faces.

"We will serve as the harbingers of society's transformation," Shayan said. "In the meantime there is much work to be done. Preparations to be made. Most importantly, we must stand united. Doubt, fear, subversion . . . these must be eradicated."

The Voice of the Prophet appeared to stare down directly at the adventurers.

"I don't like this," Oldavei said.

"Even now," the Voice continued, "here among us there are those who refuse to see. Those who resist the truth and hide from the light . . ."

The party looked around and found many of the nearby faces turned toward them. Darylonde, who already had his hand on his blade, pulled it slightly. The others reached for their weapons as well and began slowly backing away from the terrace. Several of the Children, eyes locked on the group, spoke in a synchronized monotone: "The flame of truth purifies the soul."

Shayan continued: "Among us today are those who sought out and killed our beloved followers and leaders. Those who incited violence against our faithful believers. Outlaws. Dissidents!"

"Let's get out of here," Darylonde said. He and the others turned away from the ziggurat, and as they did, the crowd behind them parted to reveal Eric, sword drawn, standing with ten other armed Children.

"We've been watching you," Eric said. "For some time now. Following your exploits."

On both sides, cultists moved away and were replaced by Children armed with swords, long daggers, and sickles. Torin looked behind them to see that a row of archers had ascended to the terrace, bowstrings drawn, arrows aimed their way.

Darylonde drew his blade as Eric continued: "You're clearly gifted warriors. Anarchists. The disruption of our operation in Skarborough, the assassination of Brother Braun . . . impressive. Yet they pale in comparison to your subsequent accomplishments: Talis, Innis, Sargrad. The glorious destruction and mayhem you've wrought, the utter disdain for authority you've displayed, these have elevated you in our eyes, in the eyes of the Prophet." He took a step forward. "You have an opportunity, right here, right now. I could have let you die in the Grand Coliseum, but I didn't. I brought you here . . . to open your eyes, to show you the light. The world is broken. We can make a better one. Join us."

"You're a bunch of fekkin' loonies!" Torin spat, drawing his axe.

Eric looked to Wilhelm. "You? Will you open your eyes to the truth?"

"I'm just fine bein' ignorant," Wilhelm said, baring his longsword.

When Eric looked to Xamus, in lieu of speaking, the elf simply drew his weapon.

Oldavei looked around them. "There's no play here," he said, looking to Xamus. "You know that right?"

Xamus glanced sideways and said, "Yeah, I know."

"If we die," Darylonde declared, "we die fighting."

"You," Eric said to Oldavei. "Surely you're the smart one."

Oldavei looked to Eric, then to his friends. He sighed heavily and unlimbered his scimitar. "Apparently not," he said.

"A shame," Eric replied. "If you deny the Sun, then the Sun will be denied to you. If you refuse to see the light, then you will be purified . . . by pain."

Eric looked up at Shayan. There, a signal was given, her arm extended, then dropped. "Take them," Eric said.

The party steeled themselves as the crowd closed in.

CHAPTER FIFTY-ONE
THE MINES OF GALAMOK

The Mines of Galamok were a subterranean tunnel system located beneath Tanasrael's ziggurat. There, in the maze of lamplit earthen corridors, shackled ma'ii, desert dwarf slaves, dissidents, nonbelievers, and outcast Children all toiled in twelve-hour shifts amid the echoing strikes of pick on stone.

It was here the adventurers were dragged shortly after Eric declared they would be denied the sun. Stripped of their weapons, equipment, and travel packs, each of them were bound in leg irons and fitted with collars made to prevent spellcasting and dampen any latent magical abilities. The keys for these shackles were kept in some secret place not carried by the guards. At the end of each work shift, they were relieved of their tools and escorted to iron-barred subterranean cells, given one meager ration of food and water, and left in the cool dark to await the coming of their next shift. Opportunities for them to see one another happened infrequently during shift changes or meal breaks, and occasions for them to speak to each other occurred even less so and never for all of them at once. Beneath the whips and heavy fists of their taskmasters, they chafed their palms raw and bloody, and with no sense of day or night, time's passage became a slow, open wound that bled their lives away. Days turned to weeks. Weeks turned to months. Hopes of escape diminished as the length of their enslavement stretched on seemingly without end.

The material they were driven to carve from the rocky depths was Bloodstone Shale, a remarkable substance that, once exposed to daylight, was capable of retaining the sun's heat and energy. It was a mineral that existed in various deposits throughout the Tanaroch, and one familiar to all of them but especially to Oldavei and Torin, though neither of them had encountered it in such abundance in one part of the desert. The vital question was, what were the Children mining it for? The adventurers understood all too well the shale's potential for devastation. A sudden release of stored energy could kill scores of people and easily raze walls of stone. This knowledge lent all the more urgency to their desire
for escape.

Guards, however, outnumbered prisoners two to one. And even if slave drivers in the immediate vicinity might be overcome, the only path upward was a single shaft with a wooden lift, operated on a pulley system, for raising shale piles hauled and dumped via wheeled carts. Anyone on the lift at any time who was not a guard would receive a large stone to the head from high above. And even if one could access the upper level, the sheer numbers of well-armed cultists there increased exponentially. Still, a few desert dwarves, unwilling to listen to reason, made desperate attempts at flight. Each time the would-be escapees' plans were quickly thwarted, and they were made an example of by being beaten mercilessly in front of the others.

The interminable confinement and grueling toil affected all of them in different ways. Wilhelm, born to roam and explore and express his soul through song and music, grew despondent; a vital piece of him, it seemed, went missing. While the captives had been allowed to keep their clothing, Wilhelm laid aside his hat and chain-mail shirt inside the tiny cell. One of the senior guards, a continually sweating, heavyset man named Gorman, had apparently been gifted the Apparatus as his own personal keepsake, and he wasted no opportunity to parade it on his belt as a kind of trophy, taking pleasure in asserting that the bard would never again possess the item he had so highly valued. At one point Wilhelm pocketed a piece of shale, which he sharpened with another stone. Rather than use it to slice a guard, however, Wilhelm put the improvised blade to the use of shaving his long black locks, leaving his scalp shorn but covered in nicks and cuts. And though he had sometimes sung in the first few months in an attempt to keep up the spirits of those around him, after the passage of half a year his voice fell silent, save for night whisperings shared with a spider he named Beauregard that spun a frail web in one corner of his iron pen.

The dampening collar had a particular effect on Darylonde, obstructing his extraordinary ability to *feel* nature—the sigh and roar of the wind, the springing of flora, the heartbeats of creatures nearby. It was as if a critical sense had been severed from him, an almost blindness that rendered him bereft. Shut off from the sky and forest, he retreated into the recesses of his tortured brain. His mind became a prison all its own as he replayed his darkest hours in a continuous cycle. He dwelled on his Wildkeeper comrades who died long ago, butchered in their sleep; he relived as well his time in the Howling lair, forced to listen to the death cries of the members of his patrol who remained, brutally slain, one after another, while he underwent torture. And though he tried, the soldier could not shut out thoughts of what came after, of what he had done, what he had *become* in order to escape. So preoccupied was he that there came points where he mistook one time period for another, venting rage at who he called the "Howling bastards," addressing in fact his confused Children taskmasters. Over the course of time, his hair grew to his shoulders, and his thick beard hung to the top of his chest. Late at night, captives in nearby cells—spaced apart to prevent quiet conspiring—would hear wails, whimpers, and frightful sleep mutterings from Darylonde's prison.

Lack of sunlight and open spaces did not affect Torin in the same way as Wilhelm or Darylonde. Being a desert dwarf, he was better equipped, mentally and physically, for a subterranean existence, especially in a clime like that of the Tanaroch. What Torin grappled with above all was quite simply rage—a rage not simply born of his incarceration and forced labor but of separation from people whom he had come to value as true friends, something that was relatively new in his life. Add to that the knowledge and sometimes direct observation of the beatings and mistreatment suffered by his comrades, and the dwarf's blood fairly boiled on a constant basis. He cursed and railed at the guards until his voice gave out; he struggled mightily against shackle and whip and endured near-ceaseless beatings with astonishing resilience. He channeled his ire into every strike of his axe, and through it all, he told himself that when the appropriate opportunity presented itself, he must be ready. As time dragged inexorably on, however, even his near-inexhaustible vitality began to flag.

Oldavei fared the best of them all. Within the first few weeks he identified Altach, brother of Norra, whom he had met the night of the caravan's stopover at the waywell. And whereas Torin had not carried on relations with fellow desert dwarf prisoners beyond general exchanges of information, Oldavei forged close bonds with fellow ma'ii prisoners. Together they formed their own pack, complete with secret hand and voice signals. They observed the methods and schedules of the guards, and they gathered intelligence over time. When occasion permitted, they conspired. Despite his outcast status, Oldavei found that the other ma'ii looked to him for answers, for leadership. Barred from the magic he seldom used anyway, Oldavei found that providing comfort, hope, and whatever wisdom he might possess to his fellows was a kind of magic all its own. He came to reexamine what it meant to be a shaman—musing that perhaps it had less to do with healing wounds, influencing through magic, and communing with spirits, and more to do with elevating morale, empathizing, uniting, listening, and guiding. And despite all the hardship he endured, he found in the mines something he had been missing for many years: the sense of purpose and fulfillment that came from connecting to his people once again.

Xamus endured the hardship in stride. As a long-lived people, elves simply did not *feel* the passage of time in the same way as other races. Though he hated the captivity just as much as the others, he was also possessed of an innate patience that for his companions simply did not exist, one that allowed him to retain clarity and control. He occupied much of his time with careful attempts to conquer the magic-suppressing collar he was forced to wear, without success. Each night, despite his best efforts, the powers of wild magic remained frustratingly beyond his reach. There was, however, that other energy source, the one that he and Darylonde and the others had sensed immediately upon their arrival, a kind of background vibration, ominous, yet present and lingering, it seemed, in recesses he was incapable of accessing. At roughly the six-month mark, following his work shifts, Xamus began concentrating on making contact with this enigmatic force. After months of attempts, he grew angry— furious. He lashed out mentally to the power that seemed to taunt him, and to his great surprise, that power responded. Only a taste of it was acquired, but it was unmistakable. Intoxicating and—for the briefest instant—nearly overwhelming. There . . . and then gone.

Xamus continued his pursuit diligently, with scattered instances of minor success. The sensation he experienced over and again when he made contact was of a presence, unspeakably immense, immeasurably potent—shifting, twisting . . . *coiling*. It was, he increasingly felt, the shadow of this thing that he touched sporadically and fleetingly.

During the lonesome nights, Xamus contemplated also the painting from the keep. Ofttimes the image came to him unbidden, and he bent all of his consideration to it, of the young man on the horse looking down at the suit of armor. What thoughts, Xamus wondered, were going through the man's mind? Had he come to don the armor, or was he preparing to abandon it? Above all, Xamus asked himself why he cared. To this also, he found no answer.

Through it all, he longed to reconnect with his companions. And as the length of their confinement reached the one-year mark, an opportunity finally presented itself.

Xamus, Darylonde, Oldavei, Torin, Wilhelm, and Altach all worked not only the same shift but the same section of dead-end mine. Though conversation was not allowed during their labors, when the time came for a meal break, the captives sat along both sides of the tunnel, facing one another. They remained quiet as they ate, until the bored guards wandered near the intersection of the main passage, where the picks had been set aside, and began a game of dice.

Given a moment alone at last, the group looked from one to another, noting the clothes that hung from thin frames, the sunken cheeks and bruised bodies. Darylonde, seated at one end near the tunnel wall, simply stared at his meal as he ate, while Oldavei kept watch on the dice game. When the distracted guards' voices grew loud enough, Torin addressed Wilhelm, who sat across: "The fek did you do to your hair?"

PART THREE: WASTELAND

"Cut it," Wilhelm replied thickly, with no further explanation.

"With what, a spoon?" The dwarf chuckled at his own joke, but it was a mirthless sound.

"I think we've all looked better," Xamus admitted. "What has me worried most is the Bloodstone."

"Yeah," Torin replied. "Same."

Xamus continued, quietly, "These lunatics keep talking about remaking civilization. Given what we've mined, on top of however much they dug up before, they might just—"

A lull in the dice game occurred. Oldavei cleared his throat, causing Xamus to fall silent. The captives immediately resumed eating. One of the guards looked back briefly before the game was resumed, and Oldavei gave a nod.

"They might just have enough by now to do it," Xamus finished.

Oldavei spoke up. "I want you all to meet Altach," he said.

The ma'ii was smaller than Oldavei, dressed in different colors, and with larger, brighter eyes. Those eyes swept the gathering as he gave a slight wave. The ma'ii then focused his attention on the dice game as Oldavei leaned forward, confiding: "He and the other ma'ii, they're on our side. There'll be an opportunity soon. Count the shifts, not with this one but starting with the next. During the sixth, you'll hear a call echoing through the tunnels. Assist if you can. Hopefully they keep us on the same schedule for a while, but if they don't, for any who are in their cells, we'll release you. When the time comes, just follow my lead. We may only have one chance. Understood?"

Oldavei waited for confirmation. Xamus said, "Understood."

"I'm with ya," Torin said.

Wilhelm, feeling the others' eyes on him, said, "Yeah, sure."

They next observed Darylonde, who offered no acknowledgment, mopping up the remaining bean paste on his plate with a hunk of stale bread.

"Darylonde, did you hear?" Oldavei asked, but received no response.

"Hey!" Torin blurted. The dice game at the intersection paused.

"It's okay," Oldavei said. "Just remember what I said. We'll make it through this. All of us."

"Meal's finished!" the first guard, a heavyset bald man, declared as he and others approached.

"We're still eatin'!" Torin protested.

The guard strode to where the dwarf sat and kicked, breaking Torin's clay plate and covering him in bean paste. The dwarf shot to his feet and immediately caught a punch to the gut that doubled him over.

Xamus moved to rise but found a sword tip placed just under the brim of his hat.

"Don't be stupid," the cultist, a young man with shaggy hair, said. Torin was hauled past and dumped next to his pick near the intersection. The others set aside their plates, quietly took up their tools, and resumed work.

When the shift was over, Xamus was shoved into his cell. He ate his second allotted meal and had just begun meditating when he received a visitor. The man was roughly familiar; he was the same one who had come to see the elf on a handful of occasions since the group's incarceration began, a man who many apparently looked to as a God . . .

The Prophet Tikanen.

CHAPTER FIFTY-TWO

TIKANEN

The Prophet had spoken with Xamus on five occasions over the course of the year. Xamus understood that Tikanen wanted the adventurers to join in his crusade despite their resistance. Such demands had been made to the others by Eric and were refused each time. Yet for some reason Xamus still did not fully grasp, he was the only one to be continuously courted by the leader himself.

Each time they spoke, the elf found himself struggling to reconcile the man with the myth.

The Prophet was clean- shaven with short, curly brown hair. His posture was relaxed. Aside from sunbaked, almost leathery skin that accentuated crow's-feet and other deep lines on face, his features were gentle and largely unremarkable. He was not a particularly striking figure or one who would stand out in a crowd. His light, youthful eyes belied the other indicators of his age. His attention seemed to always be occupied elsewhere; he rarely made eye contact when he spoke, and his voice, though full, was low and relatively monotone in delivery. The only sign of his elevated status was the robes he wore—layered and intricately patterned with sun rays and motifs. A large sun pendant hung around his neck on a golden chain.

He arrived with four bodyguards, including Eric, who kept a watchful eye on Xamus all the while. A chair was brought in, and the Prophet lowered himself into the seat. Xamus glanced at a wide scar, perhaps from a blade, on the back of his left hand. Tikanen was silent for a long moment, his gaze shifting about the floor while Xamus leaned on the wall opposite. At one point the Prophet drew in breath as if to speak, then remained silent for another moment before beginning. "There are many theories as to who I was before my ascension," he said in his restrained tone. "Very few know the truth, but I wish to share that truth with you now." The manner of his delivery made it clear that Xamus should feel as if a great blessing was being bestowed upon him.

"I was raised by stern but fair parents," Tikanen said. "Certain ideals were instilled in me throughout my upbringing: justice, order, truth. Almost from the time I could hold a sword, I knew what path my life should take. When I came of age, I set upon that path with single-minded determination, and I excelled, all the way to the fulfillment of my greatest ambition: to become a Knight-Paladin."

He paused, his eyes seeking a corner of the room as he reflected.

"I took no pleasure in harming others, but when circumstances called for violence I acted without hesitation. One day, I was forced to quell an uprising—farmers in Hearthvale who had suffered a particularly brutal season of drought and failed crops. These hardworking people reasoned that they paid taxes, and therefore the government should lend a hand. Demands were made, tempers flared; the local militia tried to maintain order, but the situation escalated into a large-scale revolt. I was called in to quell the insurrection by any means necessary. And that's exactly what I did. I and my enforcers. A score of people died before that rebellion was crushed. Good people. The youngest who perished beneath my blade was barely out of his teens."

Tikanen leaned back, gazing at the ceiling. "My actions weighed heavily on me. I questioned what I had done, the necessity of it. Yet when I voiced these concerns to my superiors, I was met with apathy. Their response made one thing suddenly and painfully clear: they simply didn't care. None of them. The farmers didn't matter. People didn't matter. They were simply game pieces, a means to an end. Parts to serve the greater whole, and if they dared upset the system, they were to be eliminated. I saw no justice in that, and I came to believe that those I had sworn fealty to were unworthy. Corrupt. But what could one man do? What could he hope to accomplish against the system? Even the symbol, the Lawbrand, that I had dedicated my life to, lost its meaning. I became soul-sick. Faced with an impossible situation, I made a

choice . . . to leave it all behind. And so I struck out with a single horse and a small wagon of provisions destined for the remotest place in the known world: the Tanaroch, fully expecting that I might die, leaving my bones to bleach in the sun. And I did come near to death many times, but something happened as my horse and I both took what I thought would surely be our final breaths— we arrived at a waywell. There, I drank, I refilled my water barrel, and I found my spirits invigorated. The water *cleansed* me. I was struck then by an epiphany regarding those who built the well, the ancients. I could sense their power and magnificence, and I knew without a doubt that my sojourn was not mere chance, that I was walking in the footsteps of gods. I knew that something waited for me beneath the purifying light of the sun . . . and I was right." He smiled. "I was right. Days later I came here to the ruins of a long-forgotten people, the Aldan Thei. A city of the gods. And I felt, immediately, the power that resided beneath the rubble." He paused once again, sitting forward, his eyes brushing for an instant Xamus's leaning form. "You've felt it too," he said. "I know you have. You've fumbled for it here in the dark."

Xamus remained silent. Tikanen continued, "It is a power capable of shaking the very foundations of the world. I . . . had never possessed any magical abilities. But when I found scrolls in the ruins, I set myself to the task of learning. I became the most dedicated pupil, and when I felt that perhaps I was ready, I reached out." The Prophet's voice took on a tone of wonder. "And it responded. To me. I channeled that power, directed it, to bring life to a lifeless city. Water, crops, livestock. I rebuilt Tanasrael."

"You?" Xamus said, interrupting for the first time, "Or slaves?"

Tikanen's eyes drifted. "There were those, early on, who came attempting to take what I had created. So, yes, I punished them. I set them to work constructing something greater than anything they had ever known or seen. And though they toiled in chains, they no longer lived a lie. Truth, you see, is the greatest freedom of all."

The Prophet seemed lost for a moment. Xamus found himself wondering: Did Tikanen honestly believe the drivel he was peddling?

The Prophet began speaking again as if he had never paused. "With the great temple standing tall once again, I rediscovered my sense of justice. My sense of self. When the time was right, I ventured back into civilization. I spoke *truths*, and I found that there were many, many who were ready to listen, who felt as I felt . . . that the world was broken. I brought them into the fold, and I taught them, and they in turn helped to shine the light of the sun into the darkest corners of the world. I realized the enormity of what was being created . . . an entirely new faith. One as pure as the sun. A faith of selflessness, a faith to reform a wayward religion. Sularia attempted to bridge the eternal with mortal hearts and minds, but we *are* the eternal. Inheritors of the Aldan Thei. Wielding the might of gods."

"But the church won't just step aside, will they?" Xamus answered. "It's why you hired the Draconis Malisath to eliminate the clergy. Like you had Taron Braun eliminated."

"The church is corrupt. Braun was power hungry and only pretended to see the light. Furthermore, it was you and your friends who killed him, which means you forfeit the moral high ground."

"You're just as much a slave to power as anyone," Xamus said. "Everything you're doing here is about control."

"There *will* be a reckoning," Tikanen admitted. "The decadent old world will burn, and a paradise will be built upon the ashes." His eyes moved to Xamus's boots. "You of all people should understand," he said. "Should appreciate the potential. You, an elf . . ."

So that was it, Xamus thought. And at last he understood, or thought he did. He stepped away from the wall, and while Tikanen did not react, Eric's hand closed on the grip of his sword. "I wondered," Xamus said, "why you came down here to speak to me. Only to me. It's because of my people's association with magic and your acquisition of it." He chuckled. "You come here seeking validation."

The response was immediate and took Xamus completely by surprise. One instant Tikanen was sitting idly, the next he was on his feet, just inches from the elf, yelling, "I seek no such thing!" as his eyes blazed fire. Though Xamus had no understanding of how it happened, he was displaced, colliding with the wall behind him, smacking his head hard enough to nearly knock him out. His legs gave and he fell to one side, the room spinning around him. Tikanen stood, posture fully erect, arms held out to his sides. Eric and the guards looked about the cell worriedly as the entire cavern briefly shook.

The small blinding fires of Tikanen's eyes dimmed, then disappeared. He dropped his arms, his posture slackening once again. "The wheels are in motion," he said, looking to the floor. "Civilization will soon be remade. I've given you every opportunity to bask in the light, but you repeatedly choose shadow."

Tikanen turned, making to leave, then paused. "If you continue seeking the force that dwells here, perhaps you'll gaze into the eyes of the serpent, as I have. Only then will you understand true power." He looked over his shoulder. "Auroboros. The World-Serpent. The Devourer. The Life Breather . . . the entirety of existence, of history reflected in its scales. That way"—he faced forward—"that way lies madness and oblivion. In the end all you can do is kiss the serpent on the tongue, ride it to paradise."

Tikanen left the cell, followed by his guards.

PART THREE: WASTELAND

CHAPTER FIFTY-THREE
BREAKOUT

When the time came, Wilhelm, Torin, Oldavei, Darylonde, and Altach were all on work shifts. Of the adventurers, only Xamus was in his cell.

Three shifts prior, Oldavei had briefly spoken to the elf, providing more details. At one point in the previous months, Oldavei informed him, a fellow ma'ii miner working a small side passage broke through to what looked like a natural cave. The hole was quickly covered by the worker with debris, and secret messages were sent among the ma'ii about the discovery. Later, Altach himself worked the same section of tunnel. While the guards watching over him were distracted by a diversion masterminded by Oldavei—two ma'ii fighting—Altach uncovered the hole and ventured into the space, an earthen void that extended beyond sight.

There, the ma'ii's extraordinary sense of smell served a critical purpose, for Altach detected scents drifting through winding natural corridors—outside scents of cactus and scrub brush arriving not from the worker tunnels but wafting through the subterranean warren. An indication that somewhere, those native passages accessed open desert. Unable to probe farther without raising suspicion, Altach returned, covered the hole, and later informed Oldavei of his discovery.

Afterward, secret discussions among the ma'ii took place. Decisions were made, and with Oldavei at the helm, a plan was devised. "The numbers above us are simply too great," Oldavei told Xamus during their brief conversation. "So we'll go where they are not—below." It was shortly after their discussion that Xamus began to see carvings on the corridor walls, a circle broken by vertical lines at top and bottom, horizontal on either side—the same as Oldavei's forehead tattoo. It served as a symbol of solidarity among the ma'ii.

It was three hours into the latest shift when Xamus heard the signal from his cell, a long, echoing, howl-like cry taken up by every ma'ii in the labor force and further amplified by those within their cells.

The first stage of Oldavei's plan was simple: overpower and neutralize the guards as quickly as possible and by any means necessary. As one, the ma'ii turned picks against their taskmasters. The desert dwarves, banished Children, and others who made up the rest of the workers quickly caught on and joined in the fray. The guards, having grown relatively complacent over the course of several months with no escape attempts, were blindsided by the coordinated attack.

Xamus could only watch and wait from his cell while, farther along the winding tunnels, Wilhelm rammed his wheeled cart into the nearest slave master, knocking him to the ground, swatting aside a frantic sword strike from Gorman, then swiping his pick across, striking the other man in the right temple. While the blunted metal tip did not puncture bone, the blow was sufficient to render the overseer immediately unconscious. Wilhelm took up not only the fallen man's sword but detached the

Apparatus from his belt as well, saying, "This is mine, fekker!" He then kicked Gorman in the head and used the pommel of the sword to knock out the second guard just as he reared up.

Violent acts of uprising unfolded throughout the mines. Down a long side passage, Torin gave voice to a deafening war cry as he quickly dispatched not just the two Children supervising him but a third as well. Not far away, a terrible instinct overtook Darylonde. His wide silver eyes gleamed as he tore into the guards closest him, breaking his pick near the top of the handle on a taskmaster's skull. As with Torin, Darylonde bellowed, but his was an unhinged, ragged vocalization of sheer abandon as he ripped into two subsequent guards with bare hands and teeth.

Within moments the first stage of Oldavei's plan was complete. The second phase—disable the lift to prevent reinforcements coming from above—was then implemented as prisoners nearest the lift used appropriated swords to slash the pulley ropes. While this occurred, other prisoners set about the plan's third stage: use picks and tools to snap the chains on their leg restraints.

After a flurry of activity and effort from the exhausted slaves, amid cries of "revolt!" echoing down the lift shaft, the final step was at last set into motion: use keys from the fallen guards to unlock and free the prisoners still in their cells.

Oldavei insisted on remaining behind to accomplish this task while the other slaves made their break for freedom. Altach refused to leave Oldavei's side, and it was the two ma'ii who released the cell occupants, including Xamus. Wilhelm joined soon after, opening his own cell and looking intently at the folded mail shirt with the hat lying atop it. After the slightest hesitation, he grabbed up the items and rushed out. At this same time, Xamus began hastily stacking a high pyre on the lift. Once done, he smashed a lamp on top to light it, preventing additional Children from lowering ropes to enter the mines and initiate pursuit.

Deeper in the mines, Torin was attempting to bring Darylonde back to reality. The Wildkeeper had backed into a short dead-end tunnel, holding a pilfered scimitar out in front of him, eyes apparently not registering that the dwarf was a friend. Torin went so far as to fetch a lamp, holding it next to his face. "It's me, see?" the dwarf said. "We're gettin' the fek outta here!" Darylonde was unmoved, his back to the stone wall, silver eyes gleaming, blade thrust forward.

Oldavei told the handful of newly released prisoners to continue on as he, Xamus, Wilhelm, and Altach came to where Torin stood. "Hey," Oldavei said. "I know you're hurting . . ." he stepped forward. Torin moved to stop him, but Xamus put out a hand. Oldavei continued to Darylonde's extended blade, reached up with his left hand, and wrapped his fingers over the top. "You told me that you were lost once, trying to figure out who and what you were," Oldavei said. "You only found the answer after you bonded"—Darylonde's eyes softened—"To your totem," Oldavei said. Darylonde shut his eyes tight, grimacing, as his grip on the sword loosened. Oldavei gingerly took the blade from the Wildkeeper, who seemed not to notice, keeping his trembling hands out before him. "I want to show you something," the ma'ii continued. With one smooth, deft movement, Oldavei slipped the black glove from Darylonde's right hand. The soldier's eyes flashed briefly as if he was set to attack, but his attention then focused on the extended talon-hand instead. "The spirit of the eagle left its mark," Oldavei said. "Focus on that now; let that spirit be your guide."

Darylonde looked to the others as if seeing them anew. He clenched the talon-fist, nodded slightly, and said in a shaky voice, "Let's go."

Oldavei grabbed a lamp of his own and took the lead, climbing into the earthen space where the others had fled. Altach, Xamus, Wilhelm, Darylonde, and Torin followed, crawling in a single line, the winding corridor forcing them to continue on hands and knees for several yards before expanding

PART THREE: WASTELAND

enough for them to stand and walk two abreast. The dwarf kept an eye on Darylonde, who stumbled along with his talon-hand clutched to his chest. They could hear the others fleeing ahead of them. At one point, Xamus paused, glancing down a shadowed side corridor. "What is it?" Torin inquired.

Without answering, Xamus struck off down the intersecting passage. The rest of the group, hesitating briefly, looked to each other and then followed, Oldavei in the rear, with Torin just behind Xamus, providing light. The new tunnel descended precipitously for several feet before leveling off and narrowing. Forced to hunch, the party rounded a corner and stepped over rubble through a transition space between natural cave and hand-smoothed stone. The room they entered was small, no larger than one of their former prison cells, connecting to an arched hallway. Carved into the walls and curved ceiling were sigils that Xamus regarded as being both familiar and peculiar at the same time; their style evinced elven qualities, though the language was not precisely elven. Or at least, not a form of elven that he recognized and could decipher.

"What place is this?" Altach asked Oldavei, his voice quiet and fearful.

"I don't know," Oldavei admitted.

"You feel that?" Torin asked.

Wilhelm was already rubbing his temple. "Yeah," he answered.

Darylonde's eyes darted about as if something monstrous might emerge at any instant from the darkness beyond the lamplight. They all felt, even through the dampening collars, the same energy that drew Xamus there, a thrumming vibration that reverberated through their bodies and exerted pressure inside their skulls.

Farther on they entered a cavernous chamber and stopped. Here, pilasters carved in a style similar to that of the ziggurat lined the walls, extending high up to arched ceilings. More of the runes were evident at various places throughout the ancient space. It was the enormous mosaic in the floor, however, that dominated their attention.

Lamplight gleamed off precious stones and gems, tracing the outline of a serpent with shimmering green scales, twined in a figure eight, consuming its own tail. A brilliant crimson jewel served as its eye. Myriad emotions coursed through the group at the sight of it: awe, exhilaration, wonder, dread, bewilderment, and most incredibly, both insignificance and omnipotence at once. It was the most off-putting, disquieting thing any of them had ever seen. Yet for Xamus specifically, it held a familiarity. He had beheld this symbol or one very much like it before—he was sure of it—long, long ago . . .

"Tikanen spoke of this," the elf said. "The World-Serpent. Auroboros. The power he wants to use to remake civilization . . . it has something to do with this. Whatever it is."

At that instant, a flood washed over them, a brief rush of energy that quickened their hearts and, for the briefest moment, made them feel as if liquid fire flowed in their veins. In that instant the great snake seemed to writhe before their eyes; flames appeared to dance across its scales and flare out like majestic, blazing wings as a striking glow enveloped it. For Oldavei this image was especially jarring, for it mimicked the vision he had beheld long ago that caused him to leave his tribe; it reflected also what he had seen during his last vision quest inside the Bear Mound. He took it as a stark message that his current path would ultimately lead to his undoing. There was another sensation connected to his observation, however, a brief, inexplicable feeling of utter invincibility. This, the others felt as well. Then, as quickly as it came on, the sensation vanished, and the unsettling pall fell over all of them once again.

"Tikanen can have it," Torin said, suppressing a shudder and spitting. He turned and set off back toward the earthen tunnel.

CHAPTER FIFTY-FOUR
MAH'WARI

The last stretch of the miles-long cave system was lined with a jumble of large, flat slabs, which the group was forced to clamber over in order to reach the egress, sheltered on the outside by large, thick brushwood.

Drenched in sweat and exhausted from both the battle and their long flight through the tunnels, the former prisoners issued forth on shaky legs to find all of the others nearby gathered beneath the golden hues of a dusky sky. The light, dim though it was, stung their vision; their eyes watered as much from their escape as from the waning luminescence of the sun they had been so long denied.

Once his vision cleared, Oldavei loped up a nearby rise, sniffing the air and casting his gaze about, a slight breeze cooling perspiration on the parts of his torso not covered by the vest. He spotted the light of the ziggurat several miles distant to the west but detected no sign of any Children in the immediate vicinity. Relieved, he leaned back, tilted his head to the sky, and released a long, victorious howl.

A moment later the ma'ii was pleasantly surprised to hear an answer—a pack of his brethren were nearby, and unless he missed his guess, he knew by the sound of the call who they were.

Oldavei led everyone east. They did not light their lamps at the onset of nightfall to better hide from cultist eyes. Roughly an hour later, beneath the moonlight, Oldavei and others spied the vagabond Kawati Tribe he had met a year before near the waywell. They were in coyote form running full tilt, coming to a stop and shifting to their ma'ii aspects as the groups converged.

Norra screamed in delight at the sight of Altach, rushing and enfolding him in her arms.

Oldavei and Ahdami grasped forearms, the Kawati leader beaming a pointy-toothed smile. "We had begun to think the worst," the leader said.

Oldavei noted how many of the pack there were. "One of you is missing," he said.

"We sent a runner," Ahdami answered. "There's a larger camp, another tribe just a few miles to the north. I'm sure you're hungry, thirsty, tired. But can you press on a little farther?"

"We'll push through," Oldavei replied.

"Okay," Ahdami said. "And . . . can we trust them?" He nodded toward the remainder of the freed slaves, referring especially to the desert dwarves, who often clashed with ma'ii tribes over various patches of the Tanaroch.

Oldavei considered for a moment, then said, "I believe so." Thin arms wrapped around his neck, a string of kisses pecking his cheek. "Thank you," Norra said, "for bringing my brother back to me. Thank you, thank you, thank you!"

The Kawati Tribe led them across the desert for nearly an hour, coming within sight of a rock formation as tall as a three-story building, expansive, roughly the shape of a boot laid on one side.

Scenting the air, Oldavei detected members of this separate ma'ii tribe at various places atop the formation posted as lookouts.

The group came around the toe of the stony boot to see, nestled in its instep, a ma'ii camp. Near the base of the wall, a fire had been built, with a semicircular rock barrier to block some of the light. Oldavei recognized immediately the colors painted on the animal-skin tents: it was his tribe, Tohtach.

Oldavei turned to Ahdami. "'Another tribe' you said."

"It *is* another tribe," Ahdami replied in mock defense, with a wry smile.

Mah'wari, Oldavei's shaman mentor, came running. "Cub!" he shouted. Slightly taller than the other tribe members, he was old, with a substantial gut protruding through the front of his vest. His trinkets jangled as he ran. Tears streamed down the shaman's cheeks as he engulfed his former student in a tight hug. "I'm so glad you're safe," he said over and over again. He pulled away, eyed the tattoo on Oldavei's forehead, sighed, then looked over the rest. He hesitated slightly upon sight of the desert dwarves. Noting the ma'ii prisoners who had suffered captivity alongside the dwarves, he came to a decision and said, "You're all welcome here. You must eat! Immediately! Come!"

As the larger group moved toward the camp, the desert dwarves hesitated. They watched as one of the Tohtach tribe members brought a clay cup of water and a small haunch of meat. Torin responded with an inclination of the head and bending forward at the waist, a gesture of deep thanks among the ma'ii. The dwarf then took his food near the fire. Seeing this, the desert dwarves looked to one other. Their tensions eased, and they approached the camp.

There, food—mostly desert hare—was made available, as well as water. An unlikely cooperation followed as one of the tribal members, aided by a desert dwarf who was versed in such things, took small bones from the fetishes of her fellows and assembled a lock-picking set. Various combinations of bone size and type were tried until the dwarf succeeded—first in unlocking the escapees' leg manacles, then finally, with more perseverance, their dampening collars.

With the collars removed, the former prisoners felt as though they could truly breathe again. Xamus concentrated and spoke a silent incantation, attempting to call forth a small fire orb. He found, however, that he was unable to do so. After having worn the dampening collar for a year, were the effects still lingering? If so, for how long? An alarming thought struck, that the collar may have caused permanent harm to his casting ability. He made a handful more attempts without success before resorting, out of desperation, to a fallback—casting his mind in search of that other magic, the mysterious and ominous Auroboros. That energy, however, remained out of reach as well. The consternated elf made a mental note to inquire later with Oldavei and Darylonde regarding their own magical capabilities.

Introductions were made as everyone relaxed near the fire. Tales of the escape were told, and many tribal members came and spoke at Oldavei's side, friends he had not seen in a number of years. As the night deepened, exasperated ma'ii, disavowed Children, and desert dwarves all fell into a heavy sleep beneath the starlit sky. The Kawati tribe slept as well, while the adventurers conversed with Mah'wari, speaking of what lay ahead.

"We can hide you," Mah'wari said, his attention focused especially on Oldavei. "We've known for some time that our kind were being taken. The Tohtach have become adept at avoiding the robed strangers. We can take you in, keep you safe . . ."

"We're still wanted," Oldavei said. "All the more now. Wanted by the Children, wanted by the Order-Militant. We'd only endanger you and the others."

"You alone could go with them," Xamus said. "You deserve it. You saved us. All of us . . ."

Darylonde, seated at the edge of the firelight near the stone base, flexed his right-hand glove.

"You could be with your people," Xamus continued.

Mah'wari nodded. "He's right, Cub. We'd be happy to have you back." When Oldavei did not respond, the old shaman pointed to Oldavei's head and said, "That tattoo need not define you."

"The tattoo?" Torin said. "What about the tattoo?"

Oldavei glanced to Darylonde, whose silver eyes returned his gaze placidly. "It means outcast," Oldavei said.

"Who put that on you?" Torin asked, sounding indignant.

"I gave *myself* the tattoo," Oldavei replied. "I ran. From my fate and from my people. I labeled myself an outcast." His eyes swept the other outlaws. "It's not something I'm proud of." He looked to Mah'wari. "And I understand what you mean. At least I do now. This tattoo will no longer define me or my actions. But the destiny I've been running from, whatever it is"—he gestured to Xamus, Wilhelm, Darylonde, and Torin—"that destiny is with them."

Though Mah'wari's eyes dropped in disappointment, he nodded understanding.

"Right then," Xamus said. "So . . . where *do* we go from here?"

"I'd say we could take refuge with my people in Red Bluff," Torin said, "But again, we'd only be puttin' them in danger."

"I have to warn Goshaedas," Darylonde said, seeming to have recovered himself. "Now that we know more of the Children's intent. The danger is far greater than we realized."

"I feel the same," Xamus replied. "I don't wanna speak for anyone else, but I'll go with you, if that's agreeable."

"It is," Darylonde answered.

"It would be nice to see the refuge again," Torin added.

"Whatever, man," Wilhelm said. "Let's just get the fek outta the desert."

"Makes sense to me," Oldavei concluded.

"So be it," said Mah'wari. "We'll talk more tomorrow. For now, rest."

PART THREE: WASTELAND

CHAPTER FIFTY-FIVE
THE CROSSING

The next day, with the rising of the sun, the Kawati Tribe said their goodbyes.

"What will you do?" Oldavei asked Ahdami.

"With any luck, we'll begin to heal," the leader answered.

Altach came and embraced Oldavei. "I owe you my life."

"I'm happy to have helped," Oldavei answered.

"You're the finest shaman I've ever known," Altach said, stepping away.

Oldavei prepared to answer, to say that he was not a shaman, but thought better of it. Norra then came and kissed him on the lips. "You have my gratitude forever," she said.

While a blushing Oldavei shared final words with the Kawati, Torin addressed the band of two-score desert dwarves who now prepared to depart. Reclusive and stoic by nature, the dwarves had kept mainly to themselves over the long year. Now, many who had at one point given up all hope of escape looked forward to laying eyes once again on their mighty home-mesa, to gazing out from the Sunforge at its top and bathe again in its spring-pools.

Torin felt a twinge of envy as he watched the dwarves leave for home.

A brief conversation was held with the remaining former captives, dissidents, and former cultists—a few gnolls, eight humans of varying ages and backgrounds, and one gnome. It was agreed that the Tohtach would shepherd them northwest, within short traveling distance to Lietsin.

With a strategy formulated, the tribe decamped and began the long desert crossing. Tohtach scouts ventured well ahead, two more flanked the formation by a mile each, and one other kept a fair distance behind. All would raise a signal if Children search parties or caravans were detected.

The going was tough for those who had spent a long, brutal year in the mines, but they pushed hard, eager to avoid recapture.

Over the course of several nights, Oldavei spoke to Mah'wari, and in that time, many old wounds—on both sides—were mended. And while no alarms of pursuit were raised, on the fifth day, warning was given by a particular howl from the rear scout: a colossal sandstorm arose from the south. Its size, strength, and speed easily outmatched the maelstrom encountered by the outlaws in the chariot race. Within an hour the travelers were overtaken, forced to huddle and shield not just from the biting sand but from gale-force winds. Sizable pebbles struck like missiles hurled from slings, raising welts where they hit exposed skin. One of the former Children, a human male, was knocked unconscious by a sharp-edged rock.

Indeed the power of the desert tempest caused Xamus to question its origin, suspecting that perhaps it was conjured by the Prophet and sent to slow their journey. The storm raged for a full hour before driving on to scour the lands due north. Scouts in all directions howled an all clear, and the long march continued.

Three days later they reached an unmarked and unremarkable patch of desert. To the north lay Baker and beyond, Kannibus Hills. To the west, Lietsin. It was time for the group to separate, for the adventurers to head north while Mah'wari and his tribe escorted the remaining former prisoners closer to civilization. The outlaws were given travel bags filled with rations as well as waterskins. Scimitars taken from the guards hung from each of their hips. The tribe gifted Torin an axe they used for cutting firewood. The dwarf accepted it with thanks, though he lamented deeply the loss of his own fine axe. Indeed all of the party members were saddened by the absence of their prized weapons—blades that were, in many ways, extensions of themselves.

Well-wishes were shared all around, after which Mah'wari held Oldavei for a long time, as if unwilling to let him leave. Finally he separated and said, "You've come so far. I'm so proud of you. You will go on to do great things, to lead with wisdom and courage. To honor those who came before and inspire those who will come after. I love you, Cub. I cherish you. When I die, I will think of you so that your face is the last one I see. And I will die happy."

Mah'wari gave Oldavei's shoulder a final squeeze, locked eyes with him one last time, then set off with the others. Oldavei wiped away tears and for the next hour watched the Tohtach tribe as he carried on with his comrades, looking over his shoulder until the tribe had gone completely out of sight.

For the remainder of the journey, they reverted to their old travel strategy: resting during the day, venturing at night. The farther they trekked, the more anxious they became to deliver their dire warning, to drink the rejuvenating water of the refuge, to greet once again old acquaintances. Xamus found himself warmly anticipating a reunion with Amberlyn, while Darylonde hoped that Lara would be in the sanctuary and not off on some mission. Even Torin greatly looked forward to seeing Wittabit.

Several more days saw a depletion of food and water, forcing the party to conserve to the point that hunger and thirst became constant companions. Through it all, conversation was minimal. Wilhelm kept his hat and mail shirt stowed in his travel bag and remained uncharacteristically silent. Torin groused. Darylonde often seemed lost in his own thoughts. Xamus remained introspective as well, quiet on the outside while his mind whirled, his contemplation dominated more and more often by recollections of the grandiose and terrifying World-Serpent mosaic beneath Tanasrael. On separate instances, the elf asked both Oldavei and Darylonde if they were capable of accessing magical abilities. The ma'ii said he could not but seemed relatively at ease. The Wildkeeper replied that certain magical druidic pathways remained closed to him, but he ended the discussion at that and offered no further details.

One night, seated by the fire, Xamus took a stick and drew the Auroboros symbol in the dirt before him. He stared at it for many long moments, determined to focus on nothing else until he could recall where he had seen it. Finally, all at once, it hit him: a memory of the elven refuge he grew up in. He was in the library looking for new books to read. He pulled out one large tome, and there on the cover was the symbol raised from the leather cover, painted with a material that caused the serpent scales to sparkle like gems. Before young Xamus could even crack the cover, however, his teacher Illarion rushed over and took the book away, saying such knowledge was not for him.

The next day, when Xamus had returned to the library and looked for the book, it was nowhere to be found. That had been only one of a hundred instances that shaped Xamus's enmity for his superiors

PART THREE: WASTELAND

and for the refuge as a whole, but he had forgotten it . . . until now. But what did it mean? Surely his people's possession of the book was no coincidence. He asked himself how much the elves knew of the World-Serpent and why they had been so keen to shield him from it.

Xamus wiped the dirt image away with his boot and went to sleep.

On the journey's final stretch, the party pushed beyond their physical limits, finding that the periods of rest they afforded themselves provided increasingly diminishing returns. They reached a point where every step was a burden, and they began to wonder if there would be no end to the odyssey. Then, at last, they came within sight of lights to the northwest.

Baker. It seemed now a lifetime ago since they had traveled to the small desert border town to participate in the insane chariot race.

While it was tempting to go to those lights, they knew that cultists would no doubt be waiting for them, lurking around every corner and hiding in every shadow. The consolation was that while Baker's enticements were off limits to them, their proximity to the outpost town meant that the outlying hills of the forest were nearby also. And so it transpired that they soon beheld the mammoth shape of the Barrier Peaks blotting out an entire swath of northern sky. Their spirits rose slightly, knowing that Kannibus Hills was now only a few days away.

After a half day of rest in the woods of the low hills, the party refilled their waterskins at a trickling stream and advanced aggressively, arriving at and crossing the creaking, swaying rope bridge they had traversed on their journey from the refuge to Baker over a year prior.

They decided that after one final partial day of rest, they could make a push for the sanctuary and reach it in one go. With their food rations now fully depleted, Oldavei offered to hunt, but the others unanimously agreed that because they were so close, they would wait and eat at their destination.

After a thirty-six-hour hike, as the light of a new day tinged the sky, with their bodies set to collapse, the adventurers topped a rise within sight of their goal. Darylonde stopped, gazing ahead, an expression of grave concern on his face.

"Something's wrong," he said.

From behind the opposing hill, they beheld a peculiar purple haze rising into the air.

CHAPTER FIFTY-SIX

FLASHPOINT

As they moved nearer the refuge, coming around the base of Bear Mound, it was Darylonde who noted the absence of sound. No morning birdsong. No creatures stirring in the bushes. He summoned final reserves of strength and ran, coming to Oram's Rest, falling to his knees at the sight before him: the great oak at the center of the dale was a blackened husk of its former self. Though the fire had burned away on the outside, the tree itself had split open vertically, revealing purplish glowing embers at its core. To Oldavei, Darylonde, and Xamus, it was a sight that indicated an attack of arcane magic.

As the Wildkeeper wept openly, Oldavei noted that the air was still, the smoke of the tree-fire rose directly upward, and the familiar breeze of the enchanted valley was nowhere to be felt.

"Lara," Darylonde said, struggling to his feet, running past the tree. The others followed, coming to a scene of slaughter: three druids lying on the grass, dead. To one side, the manticore, also slain, a sword rammed through its chest. A decapitated human lay alongside the beast, still clutching the sword grip, the soldier's helmed head lying near the base of a tall cyprus. The armor denoted the corpse, as well as a handful lying farther away, as Order-Militant Peacekeepers.

Xamus came to one of the fallen druids, gazing down at a once-familiar face, the skin now dried and brown, empty eye sockets pointing skyward, mouth slightly open, lips that he had kissed now peeled back from yellowed teeth, white horns curling from pale hair, a female satyr that he adored and might have come to truly love, given time. Amberlyn lie dead—and had been so for many months, judging by her state—a single arrow shaft protruding from the center of her chest. Xamus recognized the fletching as that used by the Enforcer Daromis. The elf knelt and pulled her close.

Darylonde raced ahead while the others surveyed the enemy corpses. The bodies of some bore multiple puncture wounds, injuries Oldavei suspected were caused by massive thorns, one of the many natural attacks employed by druids, as he had learned from the Woodsong stage play. More of the dead bore slash wounds, likely from the manticore. The remains of another were little more than blackened coal inside the armor. And yet another was instantly identified by the clothing, the long leather glove on her left hand and the long hair that had somehow remained jet black: the falconer's corpse was nearly hidden among a nest of vines, many of which were intertwined about her limbs and torso, one thick section wrapped around the woman's neck. Purplish-black skin stretched over her cadaverous face.

An outcry drew the attention of Torin, Wilhelm, and Oldavei, who ran through the woods, passing ruined structures and more bodies until they came to the Grove of Lights. Upon arriving, they were appalled by the scene that greeted them.

The delicate lattice work of Woodsong's stage canopy had collapsed along one edge. Dried-out cadavers lay everywhere. In the center of the stone-slab stage, a sizable tree lay on its side, pieces of it having been chopped off and piled around. In the amphitheater pit, three emaciated dead, one Order Militant and two druids, befouled the Silver Spring. Among the dead also were much smaller corpses that Torin mistook at first for debris. Upon closer inspection of one, his heart sank as he realized he was looking at faeries whose wings were gone, whose skin was black and smooth, like polished stone.

Darylonde went to inspect the hacked-up tree while Torin searched among the deceased fairies, finding at last on a lower step across the amphitheater a tiny form that he recognized as Wittabit. He reached down gingerly and scooped her up, her rigid body feeling far heavier than it should. She appeared to Torin as a tiny statue or figurine carved from onyx. Her eyes were closed, mouth open in a scream of extreme pain. Tears ran down the dwarf's face as he contemplated just how one of her kind might be killed, suspecting that the Enforcer crone's magic may be to blame.

On the stage, Darylonde trembled as he pulled away chopped bits of wood to see what remained of Goshaedas, a wide gash across his face, several deep cuts having opened a void in his chest. Elsewhere on his trunk, the venerated tree-folk bore scorch marks, such as might be left by a flaming-hot brand.

Oldavei walked among the bodies on the ground level while Wilhelm stepped down into the pit, shaking his head in disbelief. Oldavei's voice broke as he said, "I'd guess this happened six months or so ago, judging by the bodies."

Torin lay Wittabit down, pressed his forehead to her, then straightened and said, "This is us. This is our fault. All o' this! Ironside killed everyone tryin' to get to us!"

A heavy silence hung in the air.

Oldavei stepped down near Torin. "We don't know what might have—"

"No!" Torin said, drawing close, a finger held to the ma'ii's nose. "Maybe we could have stopped them if we'd been here. But we weren't." He turned and wagged his finger at Wilhelm. "Because o' you. You and your 'crazy ass idea'! Your fekkin' chariot race led us straight into that hole. For a gods-damned year!"

"We all agreed to follow the vision," Oldavei said.

"Stay outta this, fekkin' ma'ii!" Torin growled.

"What does that—" Oldavei started but was interrupted by Wilhelm yelling, "My plan led to the arena, to Eric!"

"And straight into a trap, ya useless fekker!" Torin fired back.

"'I go where the action is,'" Wilhelm quoted, closing on Torin, eyes wide. "You remember saying that, asshole? 'Cause I do!"

"Yeah?" Torin replied, "Why don't you go write a song about it, *bard*!"

"Maybe I will!" Wilhelm yelled.

"Good!" Torin shot back.

"I have the perfect title," Wilhem held up his hands as if the words were displayed before him. "I'll call it 'Keep the Faith!'"

A year's worth of pain and anguish capped by the discovery of the decimated refuge and the death of Torin's beloved fairy boiled to the surface. The dwarf flew into a murderous rage, roaring and launching himself at Wilhelm, putting all of his weight into a punch that caught the bard under the jaw, knocking him flat on his back.

"Don't—" Oldavei blurted, but Wilhelm was already up, shoving him out of the way, throwing a retaliatory left that wobbled Torin but failed to drop him. The dwarf threw a series of follow-up blows to Wilhelm's ribs as the bard wrapped his arms around Torin's head, and the two whirled, tussling, ripping at clothing, cursing and kicking. Oldavei tried once again to break up the fight, mistimed his approach, and was sent reeling by an accidental collision with Wilhelm's spinning elbow.

Wilhelm kicked Torin in the chest, but the dwarf absorbed the impact, grasped the bard's boot, stepped back, and wrenched, twisting Wilhelm's ankle. He let go and threw a kick of his own to the bard's opposite knee, causing Wilhelm to fall to one side. He then loaded up and let slip a vicious right that wheeled the bard 180 degrees, causing him to fall unconscious into the edge of the Silver Spring. Torin went and stood over Wilhelm, huffing, ready to continue the beating.

Oldavei yelled, "Stop!" He ran and shoved, knocking the dwarf off his feet.

He pulled Wilhelm free of the argent water, looked to Torin pleadingly, and said, "Haven't we lost enough? Do we have to lose one another too?" He knelt with a hand to Wilhelm's chest. "All we have is each other."

The fire of rage dimmed in Torin's eyes, and an expression of contrition crossed his face.

Darylonde, who had been praying over the remains of Goshaedas the entire time, stood and shouted, "Lara," over and over until his voice grew hoarse. He set out then to look for her as Xamus arrived at the amphitheater, carrying Amberlyn in his arms.

The outlaws—including Wilhelm, once he regained consciousness—searched the refuge in its entirety, with Darylonde exhaustively exploring the tunnels, nooks, and recesses of the Bear Mound. In the end they found no sign of the druid spy, leaving Darylonde to believe that she had, thankfully, been away on some assignment when the attack took place.

Neither was there any sign of Palonsus near his anvil or anywhere else in the vicinity. The sanctuary was, however, littered with other bodies. In the marketplace, the Traders' Thicket, the corpses of some vendors were discovered still within their stalls. All of the bodies belonging to residents or welcome visitors of the sanctuary were brought to the Woodsong stage, where they were placed with the remains of Goshaedas. When Oldavei inquired as to the Order-Militant cadavers, Darylonde replied, "Let them rot where they fell."

As night came on, no wisps lit the Grove of Lights. No birds sang, no drums beat as the outlaws sat on the earthen steps.

"Hey," Torin said thickly, looking to Wilhelm, whose face bore bruises and swelling. "I, uh . . . I just wanted to say I'm sorry I knocked you around like that."

"It's fine," Wilhelm answered flatly. Silence followed.

"I don't know about any of you," Oldavei said. "But I can't sleep here tonight."

"We're not staying here," Darylonde said.

"Where do we go then?" Torin asked.

"Maybe there's only one place left," Xamus said. "After all we've done. We've failed. Something I never admitted to all of you . . ." He passed his gaze over the others. "It was me who summoned Malis, looking for a way to stop Dargonnas. The destruction that followed wouldn't have taken place if not for my recklessness."

"Are you fekkin' serious?" Torin blurted. "Was it more of your 'wild magic' horseshit?"

"No," Xamus replied in an even tone. "It was intentional."

"Everywhere we go . . ." Wilhelm said, his voice somewhat distant. "All we do is fek things up . . ."

"There's no way you could have known—" Oldavei began, but Xamus held up a hand.

"Don't. I failed. We all have, over and over again. Maybe the only thing to do now is leave it all

PART THREE: WASTELAND

behind." He looked at their surroundings. "There's nothing left for us anyway. If the Children of the Sun wanna burn it all down, let 'em. Let Ironside and Tikanen have at each other while we go where we can't cause any more harm or pain." He pointed to the north. "There. Across the Barrier Peaks. The Northwilds. Where no living thing has been for as long as anyone can remember."

"We've no idea what's beyond those mountains," Torin said.

"You," Oldavei said to Darylonde. "You fought along the peaks. Do you know what's on the other side?"

"I've heard myths," Darylonde answered. "And tales told by Palonsus with what I judged to be varying degrees of truth depending on the amount of alcohol consumed. This much I do know: it's a forgotten land. Steeped in history and magic and shadow."

The group silently considered. "Maybe it's the perfect place then," Oldavei said. "For people who have nothing more to lose."

"I admit," Darylonde said. "A part of me has always longed to witness its mysteries for myself."

Oldavei and Xamus looked to Torin, who sighed and gave a slight shrug.

"What do you think?" Oldavei asked Wilhelm.

"Die here or die there," Wilhelm replied. "What's the difference?"

With that, the group gathered what supplies they needed, including warm clothing, daggers, and other weapons from the dead Peacekeepers. They stocked up on food and water, and Torin availed himself of a flask and alcohol, an indulgence that had remained unavailable to him for a very long time.

Darylonde came to the stage, spoke words in an ancient tongue, then used flint and steel from one of the fallen soldiers to set the pile of bodies aflame. Xamus said his final farewells to Amberlyn, and Torin did the same for Wittabit. The group collectively gave their thanks to Goshaedas and to the sanctuary itself for providing comfort to them in their darkest hours. The fire quickly climbed to Woodsong's bough canopy, with the raging conflagration sending thick plumes of smoke into the blushing sky as the outlaws set out for the north and the great unknown, leaving their old lives burning behind them.

PART FOUR

THE NORTHWILDS

CHAPTER FIFTY-SEVEN

THE SEA OF BONES

Far above the party, the Barrier Peaks thrust skyward like the spine plates of some behemoth reptile.

The group traveled in daytime and slept at night, unconcerned with any chance of pursuit. Despite this, Darylonde seemed alert and on edge. On the first night, as they crowded around the campfire and passed Torin's whiskey flask, the Wildkeeper left, then came back with a straight limb two inches thick. He split it vertically and began silently whittling. On the second night he stripped inner bark from a small tree, tore thin strips from the larger band, and twisted them into a string. By the end of that evening he had fashioned for himself a new bow.

The following day Darylonde collected fallen crane feathers, along with what small limbs he could find. Those limbs, however, were becoming more and more scarce—later in the day it became obvious that the trees were increasing in size the higher they trekked. That night Darylonde set about creating shafts and fletching with what wood he had.

Each of those nights, Xamus attempted to draw upon his wild magic without success. His concern grew that the dampening collar had inflicted long-lasting or even permanent harm to his casting abilities. On the third night, while Darylonde sharpened and attached stone heads to his arrows, Xamus sought with both mind and spirit the magic of the World-Serpent. And for the briefest flicker of time, he sensed a fleeting presence, a shadow among shadows. But it was gone in an instant; he had been scarcely able to detect it, much less access it.

The next day Oldavei remarked, "Have we gotten smaller, or has everything else gotten that much bigger?" The trees had increased so much in girth and height that they caused the group to feel tiny by comparison. Even the distant gush of roaring water seemed impossibly loud and overwhelming as the outlaws climbed ever higher.

Through it all, the hours of daylight decreased. The ascending slope grew steeper; the air cooled and thinned, causing each party member to fight for every misting breath. In time the volume of titanic trees decreased slightly, giving over to behemoth rock features one hundred times the size of the largest factory edifice any of them had ever seen.

The hikers found themselves shivering more frequently as a persistent, frigid wind cut through their clothing and chilled them to the bone. Also, the greater the heights they achieved, the more they felt a strange kind of *otherness* coupled with a mild discomfort and trepidation, as though unknown forces frowned upon their presence.

A light but steady snow began to fall, driven sideways by the biting wind, as they came at last to the middle peak's summit. Here were patches and drifts of snow, and where the ground was not covered with powder, it was as rigid as stone. They approached a vast gorge where sheer cliffs rose steeply on either side, a wide expanse that cut through the center of the peak and provided the only traversable route between the southern territories and the Midlands and realms of the north.

Howling gale-force gusts whipped through the winding cut, littered with tumbled stones ranging from the size of small carts to enormous boulders that blocked half the gorge. Fallen gargantuan trees also barred their path at various points, leaning from the cliff wall or lying flat, with immense roots that snaked and twined like the tentacles of some petrified leviathan. Here and there the gap narrowed to where the sheer sides were just a few yards away in either direction.

The journey through the pass took nearly a full two days, with the group forging constantly against a headwind that numbed their faces to the point that speech was uncomfortable. As they neared the end, scattered bits and pieces became evident. These grew to piles until, at the mouth of the gorge, the group could not take a step without crunching them beneath their heels . . .

Bones.

At the outlet of the gorge, an expanse of skeletons, whole and in pieces, covered nearly every inch of ground. A light snow flurried as the travelers stopped, taking in the spectacle that lent this place its gruesome name: the Sea of Bones.

"Heard tell it was a cataclysm in the north, drove all the races to this pass," Torin said, his beard coated in powder.

"Plague was what I heard," Oldavei replied through numb lips.

"Cataclysm," Torin insisted, white puffs expelling as he spoke. "Some kinda catastrophe. Either way, everybody in the north ran as far and as fast as they could, and they all got squeezed together here at the start of the pass. They all tried to get through at the same time. Scared, panicked, they fought, killed each other in the thousands. Ogres and human knights fared okay. Halflings, they say, damn near got wiped out. Dwarves got scattered; a lot died. The least fortunate, they're the ones we're standin' on now. The survivors, they went through and went on to found the 'shinin' realm' of Lawbrand."

A pensive expression settled on Torin's face as he said, "Never knew much about my parents, but I know they came through here. Sometime before they had me. Hard to say what that musta been like."

Oldavei found himself imagining the crush of bodies, the pain, suffering, and death. A sadness fairly saturated the area; the shaman found it curious also that the bones, having existed here for hundreds of years, remained in place remarkably well preserved, as if nature itself observed the site as a monument.

They spent a moment in silence to honor the fallen, then recognized the vista before them—dense, enormous woods and at a greater distance the plains of the Midlands. It was a view that, so far as they knew, no southlander had seen since the mass migration from north to south.

Eager to escape the bone-chilling temperatures of the summit and the desolate gloom of their environs, the travelers progressed at a steady pace down into the thick timber.

All during their descent, they experienced the strange sensation of being interlopers in a foreign land. The north simply *felt* different from Lawbrand. This perception grew with every step as they ventured finally to an elevation beneath the snow line, where they made camp and built a substantial fire.

For the first few hours the adventurers eyed the shadows warily, as if waiting for unspeakable monsters to emerge. Over time, they relaxed enough to judge that they were in no immediate danger.

Darylonde sat, eyes closed, meditating. Wilhelm took a spot separate from the others and simply

PART FOUR: THE NORTHWILDS

stared into the flames, while Xamus appeared to be taking in the sights, smells, and sounds around them. Oldavei sat next to Torin, who poked at the fire with a limb and accepted from the dwarf a silent offering—a pull from his flask. "I wanted to ask you something," the ma'ii said in a low voice, handing the flask back. "When we were at Kannibus Hills, you said 'fekkin' ma'ii.'" Torin's jaw clenched as Oldavei continued. "It wasn't so much what you said; I know tempers were flaring. But it was the way you said it. As if . . . my people had wronged you."

The dwarf took a drink and continued prodding the coals. Oldavei waited. Torin cleared his throat and said, "After my parents came through that pass, they went with the other dwarves and found a spot in the desert, started diggin' and buildin' what would become Red Bluff. Took a long time, and while that was goin' on, families made do by livin' in little shanty camps around the mesa. I was a baby when the camp was attacked"—he looked at Oldavei—"by ma'ii. My parents and some others were killed."

"I'm sorry," Oldavei said. "I had no idea."

"Course not, how could you?" Torin said, jabbing at the crackling cinders. "When I got a little older, I wandered a bit, got lost in the desert, and it was a ma'ii tribe that took me in, fed me. Let me stay for a while, and they told me that sometimes, some o' your kind get . . . stuck, I guess, between coyote form and ma'ii form."

"Ravenous," Oldavei said. "Those who are trapped in Ravenous form are more animal than ma'ii. Primal, feral, driven by base instincts."

"It was them that killed my parents," Torin said. "So I know it's not the same. What I said to you was just . . . somethin' I said in the moment. I was mad. Been that way a lot lately. I didn't mean nothin' by it, it just came out."

Across the fire, Xamus began whispering, gesticulating . . .

"I understand," Oldavei said. "Going into the desert, then coming here through that pass and through the Sea of Bones, it must bring back a lot."

Before Torin could answer, a massive fireball—the diameter of a wagon wheel—erupted in front of Xamus, causing the startled elf to scramble backward as it launched across the campfire at Wilhelm, who was forced to roll to one side to avoid being struck as the orb raced past. Fortunately the projectile hit a giant boulder and not a tree, dissipating in a shower of spark and flame and leaving a black scorch mark on the stone.

"What the fek?" Wilhelm shouted.

"Sorry," Xamus said as Wilhelm paced back and forth, rubbing the stubble on his head.

"I've been trying for a while, and it . . . caught me by surprise." Xamus continued: "But don't you understand what this means? Whatever those collars did to us, it's not permanent."

"I don't fekking care!" Wilhelm yelled, face red, eyes watering in the firelight. "I just—I've had enough, man, I can't take this shit anymore!" He grabbed his belongings and stomped away from the camp.

"Hey, don't—" Torin said, getting up.

"Let him be," Oldavei said, standing. "Where can he go? He just needs to cool off."

Torin exhaled heavily, looking clearly worried. "I shouldn't have thumped on him like I did."

"It'll be okay," Oldavei said. Torin sat back down with a grunt. Oldavei walked around to Xamus and said, "So your wild magic's back. That's good news."

"That's not exactly what happened," Xamus replied.

Darylonde, who had been quietly meditating throughout, opened his eyes and looked to Xamus. "Go ahead," the Wildkeeper said. "Tell him. I've felt it too."

Oldavei sat, looked enquiringly at Xamus, who said, "I reached out for the wild magic, but I couldn't make it work. I got frustrated, so I tried something else, to connect with the powers of the World-Serpent. The Auroboros. And as you could clearly see . . . it answered."

PART FOUR: THE NORTHWILDS

CHAPTER FIFTY-EIGHT
TRIAL BY COMBAT

Wilhelm didn't know where he was going. He didn't know what he was doing. Nothing, it seemed, made sense to him anymore. What was it that the time in shackles had taken from him? Some part of himself, he realized, was missing, and he had no idea how to get it back. And though he knew he had been foolish to abandon his friends, he had no desire to return to them at the present.

He walked aimlessly, for how long, he had no idea. At some point he stepped out from the trees onto a moonlit sward. He tromped onto the grass, then stopped as he spotted something large step out from the opposing tree line, roughly ten yards away.

It was a bear. Wilhelm was three-quarters its size, only coming up to its shoulders. It stepped onto the turf and stopped, gazing at the bard with soft brown eyes and a curious tilt of the head. Wilhelm found its gaze unnerving, but the animal showed no immediate signs of aggression, so he didn't reach for the cultist scimitar on his hip. For the moment, he simply stared back with his own head tilted. He continued to do so until he finally grew uneasy enough to blurt, "What's your problem, bear?"

Wilhelm nearly passed out from shock when the bear answered, in perfect common, "Nothing, what's your problem, *human*?"

* * *

The outlaws awaited Wilhelm's return for another two hours before exhaustion overtook them and they fell to a deep slumber.

Even Darylonde, who volunteered to take first watch, found himself nearly asleep on his feet as a sickle-blade moon emerged from behind wispy clouds. A twig snapping somewhere beyond the firelight dispelled his drowsiness and brought him to an instant state of awareness.

Bow held at the ready, arrow nocked, Darylonde padded into the shadows. A tiny figure darted from behind one tree to another; the Wildkeeper took one more silent step and froze, detecting a presence far to his right. Only then did he realize he had been lured into a trap as he felt a sting on the right side of his neck. He pulled away the dart, having just enough time to wonder if it was poisoned as his body fell limp and he blacked out.

Xamus, Torin, and Oldavei all awoke to find themselves bound with hemp rope to long wooden poles carried at each end by pale halflings, naked save for leather loincloths, their skin bearing crude tattoos and scarification, their bodies pierced in various places. Darylonde was tied to a stake as well, though he was still under the effects of the tranquilizer dart.

Torin, being transported alongside Xamus, said to the elf, "Remember that 'Screamin' Hawbutt' at

Bard-In?"

"Yeah," Xamus answered. "Looks like there's a whole tribe of them. Xu'keen, right?"

"Yeah," Torin confirmed.

"They could have killed us," Oldavei called from behind them. "But they didn't."

"Wonder if they got Wilhelm too," Xamus said.

The group was hauled along a trail through mammoth trees to a clearing where dome-shaped wattle huts surrounded a raging central bonfire. Seated halflings banged on drums made with stretched skin while females danced in a slowly moving circle around the blaze, their long, wriggling shadows stretching and rotating like the spokes of a wheel.

The outlaws were lowered in an open space between shelters and untied from the poles, their wrists and ankles remaining bound as they were sat up facing the fire.

A particular xu'keen more heavily muscled than the others with a bronze circlet on his right bicep and long, spiky white hair approached and spoke to the captors. Words in a foreign tongue were exchanged. The newcomer's blue eyes ranged over the captives.

"Have you seen our friend?" Xamus asked. "A tall human."

The apparent leader looked to one of the captors; more words were exchanged.

"No friend," the leader said. He poked a finger to his chest. "Raka."

"What is it you want from us, Raka?" Oldavei asked.

Raka stepped up closer to the group. "You come through our land," he said in broken common. "You pay price."

"What price is that?" Xamus asked.

The leader thumped his chest. "You fight!" he said. "You fight me!"

"We're not looking for a fight," Oldavei said. "We're just passing through."

"You pay price!" Raka repeated. "You fight! Now choose," he said.

"Choose?" Oldavei asked.

"He wants us to choose who's gonna fight him," Torin said, exhaling in exasperation. He locked eyes on the halfling. "Me, okay? Let's get this over with so we can move on."

Moments later they were taken to a separate clearing not far from the blazing xu'keen fire, where a circular space twenty-five feet in diameter was demarcated by freestanding torches. Here Torin's bonds were removed, and he was handed a simple club and an oval oxhide shield. Xamus, Oldavei, and a very confused but finally awake Darylonde stood close by. Oldavei began explaining to the Wildkeeper what he missed.

Raka entered the space, teeth bared, breathing heavily, each exhalation accompanied by a low growl. Carrying a studded club and a hide-shield with tribal markings, he began pacing from one side to the other, never taking his eyes off Torin.

"This should be easy," Torin said, assessing his opponent, who stood nearly half his own height. "I'll get it over with quick."

Despite Torin's bravado, Oldavei felt apprehension. These xu'keen were clearly savage and accustomed to violence.

The crowd of xu'keen behind Raka parted. An elaborately crafted chair made of wood with roots twining decoratively all around and woven to fashion a high back was placed at the boundary between the two largest torches. A squat, potbellied halfling carrying a staff laden with fetishes and ornaments stepped up in front of the throne. A multicolor feathered dress adorned his crown. All of the surrounding xu'keen lowered to one knee, heads inclined. The outlaws' captors kicked each of them in the crooks of their knees, one of the xu'keen saying, "Kneel to King Varl!"

Raka turned and knelt. He then stood, along with the others, and resumed pacing as Torin was shoved into the ring.

The king eased into his seat, lifted his staff, turned it crosswise, and held it at chest height. The surrounding halflings waited. Not far away, the steady pounding of drums continued. Raka strode back and forth like a caged tiger, staring intently at Torin. Finally, King Varl lifted the staff to head height and shouted a command.

The onlookers roared as Raka rushed Torin, clearing the space between them with astonishing speed, leaping at the last second, clobbering the dwarf upside the head so hard that, for an instant, Torin was out on his feet, the ground swaying beneath him.

"This is why you never underestimate an opponent," Darylonde remarked from the sidelines.

Torin, now taking the threat much more seriously, thrust up his shield just in time to deflect a follow-up blow, the impact of the club rattling his arm. He answered immediately, kicking, his heel stopping just short of his opponent. Raka jumped and spun; Torin leaned back far enough to avoid being bashed in the temple. The dwarf then advanced, swinging repeatedly with all of his might, but the halfling was far quicker, easily evading each strike.

But Torin would not be denied. He continued pressing the attack, feeling suddenly invigorated, as if suddenly drawing energy from the ground beneath his feet and the air in his lungs. He growled, feinted a side swing, and then switched quickly to an overhead swing.

The enemy rolled out of the way, but just barely. Overextended, Torin received a crushing blow to his right shin that sent lightning bolts of pain through his system and swept his leg from beneath him. The dwarf rolled onto his back while Raka flew to a mounted position, spittle flying from his gnashing mouth as he attempted repeatedly to smash the butt of his club against Torin's forehead.

Fury boiled Torin's blood. He blocked with his shield and heaved up, wrapping his club arm around the back of Raka's neck. He pulled his foe down, planted both boots, then arched his hips explosively, turning and rolling to a top position. This he followed with a vicious headbutt before tossing both shield and club to the side. He then closed the xu'keen's neck in a vise grip with his left hand and began raining down blows with his right.

Raka could only snarl and thrash at first, unable to bring either shield or club to bear.

"That's enough!" Oldavei yelled from the perimeter. "He's finished!"

Torin took no notice. As the beating continued, Raka's resistance grew weaker. His eyes bulged; blood poured from his nose. Nearly all of his front teeth were broken, and his face turned blue.

The crowd was so intent on the fight that none noticed Oldavei, bending down to untie his feet. An instant later the ma'ii rushed out and looped his still-bound hands around Torin's right arm, pulling the dwarf from atop Raka. "It's done!" he said, inches from Torin's face. "It's done!"

For the second time, the ma'ii watched primal fury abate in the dwarf's eyes.

"Away!" King Varl barked, motioning for Oldavei and Torin to withdraw. The drums ceased; the spectators quieted. Varl stepped into the ring, gazing down at the limp, battered body of Raka.

"I want to know," he said in a harsh and gritty voice, "if you've killed my son!"

CHAPTER FIFTY-NINE
DELIBERATIONS

"I can't believe I'm talking to a bear," Wilhelm said, still utterly confounded. Hearing the dracolich speak in Sargrad had been one thing—that had been some otherworldly creature of mystery and magic. But for all of his years and all his travels throughout Lawbrand, Wilhelm had never heard any of the animals speak.

They conversed at the edge of the tree line while the bear—whose name was Froedric, Wilhelm learned—lounged with its back against the base of a giant fir. Wilhelm was seated just a few feet away, one knee drawn up, chewing on a blade of grass.

"I wonder," he said. "Before we came through the pass, I ate those mushrooms . . ."

"I assure you I'm quite real," Froedric answered, his voice rich and resonant. "And if it's any consolation, I've never interacted with a human."

"How is it that you talk?" Wilhelm asked.

"Same as you, I suspect," Froedric answered. "I was taught by those who raised me."

The two had been chatting for quite some time, covering a number of topics. Wilhelm had talked a bit about himself as well as the others, and he informed the bear that he and his party were strangers in the land who had spent a year enduring forced labor in the deserts of the south. He had also spoken briefly about the Children of the Sun.

"You told me in the beginning that you had to 'get away' from your friends," Froedric said. "Why was that?"

"I don't know, man," Wilhelm said. "Everything just crashed down on me, I guess."

"I can tell," Froedric said. "You're a free spirit, and that freedom was taken away. On top of that, you're a natural-born performer who's had no opportunity to perform for a long time. Music and song are expressions of the soul. So, while you're no longer in the mines, I'd wager that your spirit still feels shackled."

Wilhelm was astounded at the bear's assessment.

"Yet nothing is so bad as it seems," Froedric continued.

"How so?" Wilhelm asked.

"I can't help but notice that you still have a voice," Froedric answered. "And I have no doubt that a musical instrument may be acquired, given time. I predict, my friend, that it won't be so long before melody once again lifts your heart and buoys your soul."

Suddenly overcome with emotion, Wilhelm wiped tears from his cheek. "That was, uh . . . exactly what I needed to hear," he said, laughing at the absurdity of it all. What world did he find himself in where it took a talking bear to set him straight? Whatever the case, he suddenly felt as though an immense weight had been lifted.

"I'm glad to have been of assistance," Froedric said. "I suppose now the question is, what are you going to do next?"

★ ★ ★

Raka fortunately survived.

King Varl sat on his throne a few yards from the fight ring outside a grand, stoutly constructed wooden structure flanked by two xu'keen guards. Currently, the patriarch was occupied with upending Torin's whiskey flask.

"Mm," the king muttered appreciatively, pulling the flask away.

Xamus, Torin, Oldavei, and Darylonde all sat on the ground a few feet distant, surrounded by what they assumed was nearly the entire tribe. Released from their bonds, the outlaws chewed on strips of dried meat provided by halflings at the king's behest.

"I just wanna say again—" Torin began, but Varl waved the comment off.

"You fought good," the king said. "Fought better than Raka. Made me think of myself in younger times." He tossed the flask back to Torin, who was disappointed to find it completely drained. "That drink I like. What you call it?"

"Whiskey," Torin replied, stowing the empty container.

"Ehh, whiskey is good," Varl said. He reached to a small wooden stand with a basket of meat strips on top, pulled one out, and began chewing on it. "So . . . you win fight. You go where you want. Where you go?"

The group shared looks. "We're not sure," Oldavei answered.

"You come from where?" Varl asked.

"South," Torin answered. "Lawbrand."

"All that way," Varl said, leaning forward onto his staff, swallowing a mouthful of dried meat. "And you don't know where next?"

"It's a fair point," Torin admitted. "You might say we just needed to get away."

"This meat's tasty," Oldavei said with his mouth full. "What is it?"

"Last fighter who lose," Varl said flatly.

And while Oldavei and Torin chuckled, the king's expression never changed. The snickers died out. Torin turned and pretended to cough, expelling the small amount he had in his mouth.

Xamus cleared his throat. "How long have your people lived here?"

"From the time of the Crossing," Varl answered, retrieving another meat strip. "Our tribe didn't get through the pass. Many died. We're all that's left."

"Sorry," Xamus said.

"Don't be," the king replied. "Death, life, all part of the Great Circle."

"Do you know of something called the Auroboros?" Xamus asked. "The World-Serpent?" The elf had come to believe that Auroboros energies saturated this land. Its presence, now that he had connected with it, was undeniable. And if the xu'keen had been here since the Crossing, maybe they knew more about what the power was and where it came from.

"Heard stories," Varl said, and his expression changed, turning to a very clear unease. He hesitated before going on: "Old xu'keen tell young. When young get old, they tell others. On and on. My father-

father say that Auroboros eat the sky, break the world. It's why all the people run south. Not good to talk of."

Xamus thought of what Torin mentioned earlier, about a cataclysm in the north causing everyone to flee.

"We'd like to learn more," Xamus said.

"We would?" Oldavei interjected.

Suddenly a horn call rang out. King Varl looked in the general direction of the sound, then addressed the party. "Had my tribe looking for your friend," he said. "Nothing south. If he was close, we know. If not south"—the king pointed to the north—"friend must be that way. Maybe Auroboros that way too. Just know that Auroboros eat the world." He ripped away a piece of meat with his teeth. "Maybe it eat *you* too."

PART FOUR: THE NORTHWILDS

CHAPTER SIXTY

THE THOUSAND SPRINGS

A pale sun that provided only dim light reached its zenith. Darylonde had picked up Wilhelm's trail, following it north for several hours through mammoth woodlands to a clearing in the region's foothills. He crossed the grassy field and knelt, examining impressions in the grass, then the area around the tree line, appearing troubled. Oldavei frowned as well, sniffing the air, then lowering to all fours and smelling the ground.

"What is it?" Xamus asked.

"Bear prints," Darylonde answered.

"You don't think—" Torin began, clearly worried.

The Wildkeeper shook his head. "There's no sign of a fight. Even if the bear would have dragged him away, there would be indications." He inspected the area carefully in a widening radius before returning and saying, "I can't find his tracks, only the bear's. It doesn't make sense."

"I only get traces of his scent," Oldavei said, setting out deeper into the woods. The others trailed, Darylonde on the lookout for tracks or marks of passage. They continued on until a wide stream crossed their path, flowing generally north to south. There, Oldavei lost the scent completely.

"Which way?" Torin asked.

"Hard to say," Oldavei admitted. "But I think we should continue north. If Wilhelm heads south, he should run into the xu'keen, and they'll send him this way."

"Or stick him in the ring," Torin said.

"Raka won't be fighting again very soon," Xamus said, and though it wasn't intended as an admonishment, Torin's face fell.

The party filled their waterskins and traveled upstream to where the land spread out into vast rolling plains with another enormous mountain range farther ahead. The tranquil prairies of the Midlands exemplified unspoiled nature such as no one in the group, including the Wildkeeper, had ever experienced. The nearest comparison was Kannibus Hills, but somehow the colors, the scents, and the *feel* of their surroundings were augmented to a degree that surpassed even the druid refuge. Darylonde and Oldavei sensed the magnificence on a much deeper level than the others, but Torin and Xamus recognized without doubt that they were in the presence of a setting more vibrant and alive than any they had ever known.

Coupled with the grandeur and purity was a sense of isolation within the seemingly endless wide-open plains. There was also, in between distant birdcalls and beneath the babbling of the stream, a profound silence, a complete and total absence of sound, which suggested that outside of this place, the adventurers had been unknowingly accustomed to some background noise that they automatically tuned out, one that in this enchanted realm simply did not exist.

To Xamus, the only reasonable explanation for what they were experiencing was the existence of some unimaginably powerful magic. These surroundings, however, seemed to run counter to what they had thus far heard—and what Xamus himself had experienced—regarding the Auroboros. Whatever was happening here, the elf felt that it was somehow connected to the World-Serpent, but also detached, perhaps even some kind of inversion.

Oldavei recovered from his trancelike daze and began scenting the air once again. Darylonde regained presence of mind as well, searching for tracks but finding none.

"Again, just traces," Oldavei said, loping along.

Hours later, as the sun descended from view, the adventurers followed the stream through more heavy timber to another expanse, a location that brought them once again to a standstill. Here was unbounded splendor, coupled with relics from some ages-old conflict: vines, lush vegetation, and dazzling flora had overtaken toppled and broken siege engines and hulking, monstrous weapons of war. The scene was a study in contradiction, a stunning display of unparalleled beauty and unchecked annihilation. It was impressed upon every member of the group that countless lives had been lost here, that the resplendent flora sprouted from soil once drenched in blood.

Here also was water in abundance—streams, eddies, gushing waterfalls at the periphery, and dotting the landscape, a multitude of pools, perceived by each of them to be battle craters now filled with pristine argent liquid reminiscent of the Grove of Lights' Silver Spring. Will-o'-the-wisps flaring to life in the waning daylight called to mind the sanctuary as well and made Torin's heart ache in remembrance of Wittabit.

While all who observed the spectacle were awed, Darylonde especially was rendered speechless and brought to tears. Here, the Wildkeeper felt a far deeper connection to nature than at any other time of his life, including the ritual in which he received the talon-hand.

So caught up in the moment was the Wildkeeper that he did not detect the multitude of animals until they began to emerge: fauna of every kind, ranging from the smallest mice, squirrels, and chipmunks to badgers, wolverines, boars, jungle cats, wolves, and lions to herbivores such as deer, elk, and bison to the largest of them all, an assortment of massive bears, black and grizzly. And for many of the beasts, there were tentative and alert young as well.

Next, a living cloud seemed to pass overhead as flocks of birds fitting every size and description from starlings to crows to mighty eagles filled the sky. They squawked and cawed and circled and whirled before settling on branches and jutting pieces of siege machinery.

The arrival had been sudden enough that all of the party members were caught completely off guard. The amazement they had already felt was now compounded, it seemed, a hundredfold. Superseding that incredulity was a growing sense of alarm, for the outlaws were surrounded, most definitely outnumbered, and every single beastly or avian eye was fixed menacingly on them.

A tiger and a panther padded forward, low growls building in their throats. Wolves also advanced, teeth bared. One of the larger black bears took two steps and raised up on hind legs.

Each adventurer slowly reached for their weapons.

Just then a roar sounded, reverberating through the trees, sending birds flying and small critters scurrying, turning all eyes westward. An enormous grizzly stepped from the timber into the waning light. On its back sat Wilhelm, wearing his chain-mail shirt and hat, smiling broadly, looking very much like his old self.

PART FOUR: THE NORTHWILDS

"He's back!" Torin blurted, clearly relieved. He turned and shook a grinning Oldavei by the arm. "He made it!"

"Hey!" Wilhelm yelled to the party, "Looks like we showed up just in time!" The cats and wolves backed off, and the black bear retreated as the grizzly lumbered across to a spot just a few feet away from Xamus, who was nearest the middle of the field. "Say hello to my new friend, Froedric," Wilhelm said.

Xamus eyed the bard and bear quizzically and said, "Okay . . . hello, Froedric."

"Pleased to meet you," Froedric answered.

Torin stumbled to them with a befuddled look and said, "You gotta be shittin' me!"

CHAPTER SIXTY-ONE

ASTERIA

"These travelers are no threat," Froedric called out.

With this endorsement given, the surrounding wildlife once again approached the adventurers, this time relaxed, docile, and curious. Many of the birds came and landed on the soft grass or on the backs of other animals, eyeing the party inquisitively. Then, nearly all at once, the animals spoke.

"What are they?" one wolf asked another.

"Good question," answered an old gray wolf.

"People-folk?"

"Thought they were all gone," the other answered.

"One's a dwarf," a tiger put in.

"Where do you come from?" called out a black bear.

A crow stepped up. "Are there more of you?"

A higher-pitched voice, this from a squirrel, asked, "Why are you here?"

"Okay now," Froedric said. "Let's give them a minute. I'm sure they're just as taken aback as we are." The grizzly's observation was apt, as all of the outlaws save Wilhelm—who watched with empathetic glee—stood silently dumbfounded.

"Follow me," Froedric said. "There's someone I want you to meet." The inquisitive animals walked or flew along as the outlaws followed Froedric, with Wilhelm still mounted, navigating pools and passing along a stream through the field into northern woods. A short trek led them to a clearing where cotton seeds drifted like snow, and wisps darted among the branches of smaller trees bearing leaves varying in color from the autumn hues of orange and red to the verdant greens of summer. All manner of flowers, including numerous varieties that none of the party, including Darylonde, could identify bloomed here in an explosion of colors—white, pink, purple, and yellow. Near the northern boundary, crystalline waters flowed to a rock formation, cascading down two horizontal outcroppings to a low, stony basin. Standing at the lip of the rocky bowl, drinking, was a horse larger than the outlaws had ever seen, a mare, with a long mane, feathering on the ankles, and a pristine, shining-white coat.

The horse lifted her head, revealing a single, spiraling pearlescent horn thrusting from a thick forelock. Mesmerizing eyes of emerald green regarded the outlaws as the unicorn turned and strode forward, sharply defined thews rippling with each step.

"Honored guests," Froedric intoned. "I present to you our esteemed guardian and caretaker, Asteria."

Without fully knowing why he felt the urge to do so, Wilhelm dismounted, removed his hat, and gave a sweeping bow. "Honored, your grace!" he said. Then, straightening, he placed a hand to his chest. "I am the humble bard, Wilhelm."

One by one, the others introduced themselves. Asteria's eyes locked briefly on each of them as two more unicorns, thickly built stallions, emerged from thick foliage.

"Welcome," Asteria said. And to the ears of the guests, her voice sounded as smooth and as soothing as a gently coursing river. "As Froedric said, I am a caretaker, tending this and other refuges across the Northwilds." She stepped forward, turning her head to one side. "As you've no doubt gathered, we don't often receive visitors of any kind, let alone people-folk. What brings you here?"

Xamus stepped forward. "We're . . . outcasts from the south. We come here seeking knowledge of the past."

"And what knowledge would that be?" Asteria asked.

"The Auroboros," Xamus said.

Asteria recoiled. The two males stepped forward. The entire mood of the gathering shifted to one of suspicion.

The larger of the unicorn stallions said, "Such talk is forbidden."

Xamus put up his hands. "I meant no disrespect. We just want to come to a better understanding."

Oldavei stepped forward. "If the subject is forbidden, we understand completely and beg your forgiveness. It won't come up again." He looked to Xamus, who nodded.

The beasts seemed appeased by this and visibly relaxed. After a moment Asteria said, "Your journey has clearly been a long one. You may stay for a time. Replenish your strength. Acquaint yourselves with the Thousand Springs. When you've rested, be on your way."

"Yes ma'am," Oldavei said.

Asteria and the stallions walked across the field and back into the shaded woods. Torin beelined for Wilhelm, swatting him on the arm, saying, "Hey! I'm glad to see you're okay. You had us worried. You had *me* worried."

Wilhelm gave a slight shrug and tilt of the head. "Ah, I just needed to get my head straight. Which I did"—he looked to Froedric—"with a little help."

Froedric began conversing with Wilhelm and Torin, joined by some of the nearby animals. Not far away, an old gray wolf approached Oldavei. "You!" he said in a weathered voice. "There's something about you . . . we can all feel it. You have a deep connection to the wild, yes?"

"Well . . . yeah," the ma'ii replied. "Yeah, I do." Many of the nearby animals, including more wolves and several of the jungle cats closed in, fascinated.

"There's more, though," the wolf continued. "Something else that I can't—"

Oldavei dropped his travel pack and sword belt. Xamus, knowing what was coming, stepped away as the ma'ii underwent his transformation. Gasps resounded among the wildlife. Beastly eyes widened, and paws shuffled backward.

When the change was complete, Oldavei, now in coyote form, gave a short, pleasant bark. The gray wolf laughed, shaking his head. "Incredible!" Murmurs rippled throughout the other animals as Oldavei padded forward, touched noses with the wolf, then began moving among the gathering, sniffing incessantly.

Xamus laughed and began walking back in the direction they had come, when a pleasant voice called: "You're an elf, unless I miss my guess."

Xamus glanced to a low branch near the edge of the clearing, where a great horned owl sat, pinning him with its gaze. The nearby bears and smaller critters drew in, suddenly eyeing Xamus as if he were an oddity among oddities. "An elf?" said the black bear.

"Thought the elves were gone," said a small voice at his feet, slightly garbled. The squirrel held a half-eaten nut, the remaining half still in its mouth.

"It's true," the owl continued, swooping around to land on the black bear's back. "We thought elves had gone extinct in ages past."

Oldavei, still in coyote form, ran past, along with jungle cats and a pack of wolves, heading back toward the prairie. Xamus continued walking as well, with the bears and owl alongside. "Some of my people survived," Xamus said. "They live in seclusion, in an enclave called Feyonnas."

While Xamus continued conversing, Darylonde had already stepped back through the timber to the prairie, seeking a particular animal, one he had glimpsed only briefly as he had followed the others to meet Asteria. In that instant the Wildkeeper had been struck by an aura of immense power and wisdom radiating from the creature. As he reemerged in the open plain, Darylonde spotted the subject of his interest—a great bald eagle.

Perched atop one corner of a toppled siege engine, overgrown with lush foliage, the bird of prey spread its wings, covering a span of seven feet, shifted its talons for better purchase, and then folded its wings. Darylonde drew within a few paces, dropped to one knee, and bowed his head. "Greetings, mighty one," he declared.

"Mighty?" the eagle responded in a female voice, mature with a slight grit. "I don't know about all of that."

"Don't listen," a young female golden eagle added, landing on a lower protrusion of the wreckage. "You're addressing Arakalah, Queen of the Eagles."

"Then I am honored," Darylonde said, rising. "I'm Darylonde."

Arakalah lowered her head. "I sense that you are blessed by our kind."

Darylonde reached up and solemnly removed his glove, revealing his talon-hand.

"Ooh, would you look at that?" said the younger female.

"Indeed," Arakalah said, "you have been marked. Yet I also discern that your spirit is tethered. Why is this?"

Darylonde considered. "I've seen and done terrible things. I've failed, repeatedly, and I've lost loved ones because of it. In the midst of it all, I believe I've lost my way, lost my connection to sky and wind and the heart of the wild."

"Hold out your arm," Arakalah said, and the Wildkeeper complied, understanding that she meant for him to hold out his talon-hand. The majestic wings flared briefly, and in an eyeblink, the queen was positioned on Darylonde's wrist. She closed her eyes and inclined her beak . . .

And Darylonde felt an immediate rush, a merging of mind and spirit. The unspeakable magnificence of the creature was fully impressed upon him even as Arakalah peered into the thoughts and memories of the Wildkeeper. After a brief displacement of time and place and body, the connection was broken, and the queen relocated to the wreckage peak.

"I see that your faith has been shaken," the queen said. "But know this: quite often what we deem lost has been in front of us all along, we simply lose sight of it. And despite all that's happened, despite all of your doubts, you *are* one of us, Darylonde of the talon-hand. I invite you to join us in flight, take to the wind. Soar as you once did."

"Your sage advice is well taken, and I thank you with all of my being," Darylonde answered. "Yet I

PART FOUR: THE NORTHWILDS

am not able. I simply don't have it in me to do so."

"What you mean is that you're not ready," Arakalah answered. "This is a choice you have to make on your own. You'll know when the time is right. And you'll know where to find me. Be well, Darylonde." With that the queen spread her wings once more and took flight. Watching her ascend, a small piece of Darylonde's spirit was lifted also. The Wildkeeper donned his glove as the chill of night came on and looked to the golden eagle.

"Have you ever seen a proper campfire?" he asked.

"No, but I'm intrigued," the eagle answered.

"A fire it is," Darylonde said, and within moments, that fire was made using the remains of an old ballista. At first the animals were afraid, having known only the dangerous and deadly fire caused by lightning strikes. Once they learned the flames were contained, the surprised and delighted wildlife all gathered round. Flasks of water instead of whiskey were passed, and Torin found himself strangely appeased, not missing the alcohol as he normally would. Fruits and nuts were also shared, and as with the food in Kannibus Hills, these were filling and scrumptious.

Oldavei, now back in his ma'ii form and having spent several hours chatting with the animals, took a spot next to Xamus, sticking his nose nearly to the elf's cheek, drawing a sideways glance.

"What's with you and the Auroboros?" Oldavei asked, pulling away. "Why do you keep asking after it?"

"Its presence here is undeniable," Xamus answered. "I know you've felt it too."

Oldavei nodded. "I think we've all felt it, in some way or another."

"I wanna know why it's so intense here. And I wanna how it works. 'Cause that's what Tikanen has tapped into; that's what he's going to use, along with his army and the Bloodstone and other weapons, to 'remake society.' So I'm thinking . . . that if we can at least understand it, maybe we can find a way to counter its power."

"Understand it or wield it?" Oldavei asked with a pointed, maybe even accusatory look, one that warned against such a pursuit.

Before Xamus could answer, a badger near the fire called out, "Tell us more about the south!" looking in Oldavei's direction.

"Yes, tell us stories!" a bear cub piped.

Oldavei looked back and smiled. "We might be able to spin a yarn or two . . ."

The beasts cheered in response. The youngest animals came closest to the fire while Oldavei launched into a tale. Across from the ma'ii, Wilhelm sat next to Froedric, holding the pencil and small parchment squares that he had kept in his pocket and not removed since well before the group's journey into the desert. At various points throughout the night, he wrote while the fellowship shared stories and laughed. During this time in the presence of this magical place, the outlaws began to heal and to regain some semblance of the former selves that had been taken by their year in the Mines of Galamok.

CHAPTER SIXTY-TWO
DENIZENS IN THE DARK

Xamus awoke to a majestic, spiral-horned horse head peering down at him.

"Good morn," Asteria said.

Xamus sat up as the other outlaws who had slept near the fire began to stir. Birds sang morning songs from the nearby woods. Froedric, who had slept near Wilhelm, lifted his head and gave a deep yawn. Smaller critters began busily collecting nuts. Many other animals came to the tree line to hear what Asteria had to say.

"I understand you better," the unicorn said, "from the stories you told and the time you've spent here." Xamus was surprised, as he had not seen Asteria or the other unicorns throughout the previous night.

"I believe your intentions to be good," Asteria continued. "And so I'll tell you this: there is a race, called drow, similar to your kind," she said, still looking at Xamus specifically.

"I've heard of them," Xamus replied, a slight edge to his voice. There were stories among his kin of a hatred that stretched back centuries.

"Some, it is said, still live to the northwest, beneath mountain peaks that rise like horns—the Twin Cliffs. These drow may possess the knowledge you seek."

Xamus was unsure at first how to respond. Many tales existed of the drow, some of them conflicting, but all agreed on the detail that their ancient civilization had died out and was no more. Could the drow truly still exist? The elf finally stood and said, "You have my warmest thanks."

"Safe journey to you and yours," Asteria replied. "Whatever it is you learn, use that information wisely." With that, the guardian stepped gracefully away in the direction of the clearing where the group had first
met her.

The rest of the animals bid farewell to the travelers. Froedric volunteered to guide them through the woodlands to the edge of the Old Lands.

Fully provisioned with fruits and nuts, the party set out, navigating the towering woods and winding streams, stopping to refill their waterskins. When the day was three-quarters gone they arrived at a place where the trees formed a wall, like sentinels to the north and south for as far as the eye could see, a barrier where the timber gave over to open fields.

Wilhelm stood in front of Froedric, silent for a moment.

"You okay?" the bear asked.

"Tryin' to find the words to say, 'Thank you' without just sayin', 'Thank you,' 'cause that don't seem like enough. I was down, man. The lowest I've ever been."

Torin clenched his jaw and looked away. Froedric's boulder-like shoulders lifted in a shrug. "You'll find your words, I've no doubt. And you'll put them into a song. And that song will outlast all of us." He swung his head toward the others. "Now go, all of you. I hope you find what you're looking for. And if you come back this way, I hope you stop in and say hello. Maybe build us another fire."

The bard leaned down and placed his cheek atop Froedric's head. The others said their goodbyes, and the group pursued a course to the northwest, with Wilhelm taking one final look over his shoulder at the bear, who lifted his head in farewell, turned, and vanished into the timber.

Over the remainder of the day, the air grew cooler, and the colors of the environment became steadily less vibrant. Grassy fields turned to rocky earth; tall firs, cedars, and pines disappeared entirely, replaced by mostly dead gnarled oaks; twisted, decaying weeping willows; and an odd, unidentifiable tree species with knotted roots that burst up from the earth several feet away in multiple locations, looking like small, strange arboreal creatures issuing from subterranean lairs.

They soon witnessed remnants of a civilization: tumbled blocks and piles of stone that must have, at one time, formed walls and indomitable structures. They also observed statue remains—naked bases among long, thin stone features, perplexing at first, until the group found also rocky representations of abdomens and thoraxes and realized that the rubble had once been statues of either giant spiders or some other arachnid god.

That night they camped in a shallow depression, aware once again of the absolute silence; the difference being that here, unlike the Thousand Springs, the silence was eerie and unsettling, broken only by the sigh of a mournful wind. Despite the desolation, the travelers remained aware of the World-Serpent's power, its energy a constant presence, though they spoke little of it.

After a fitful night's sleep, they set out as the sky lightened, though the sun remained veiled behind dim gray clouds. Indications of civilization continued, broken by long stretches of what was now slatelike earth covered in dust and detritus. Feeble shrubs clung to a kind of half-life, struggling through cracks in the stony ground. Near midday the travelers spotted two rocky needlelike peaks resembling the fangs of some great serpent.

A faint zephyr stirred hair on both body and head just enough to elicit shivers as, several hours later, the party came at last to the base of the Twin Cliffs. A massive stone gate construction bedecked the slanting mountain wall, its carved frame branching out to form the legs and head of a gargantuan arachnid. Closer observation revealed spider motifs carved into the stygian feature as the group stood at the doorless, yawning mouth, ten yards wide and fifteen yards tall. Within the abyssal opening they saw only the ground extending for several feet before surrendering to inscrutable shadow.

Shaking off the feeling that the opening resembled a gaping maw prepared to swallow them whole, the party advanced. A second portal came into view several steps later, where massive double doors had once stood, but now only hinges remained. Here their eyes adjusted to a wan violet light, the origin of which was unclear.

The dust-covered floor was tile that must have, at one time, been stunning, black with speckled white marbling that resembled star swaths. Farther on, the space led to an open gallery overlooking a cavernous chamber lit by enormous purple gem chandeliers and freestanding gem-topped posts. To either side, marble staircases wide enough to accommodate five people abreast swooped to the bottom floor. Beyond, dark stone humanoid statues rose to the lower edges of the vaulted ceiling. Elegant bridges crisscrossed in the distance.

Taking to the steps, the group observed meticulous details in the walls: workings in a spider motif, thin legs tracing intricate lines with purple jewels forming arachnid abdomens. Also at various places along the walls, they beheld marks of conflict—scratches, scrapes, and missing gems. At the bottom of the stair, on a chipped and scarred pilaster, a crude image of the Auroboros had been carved.

Their footfalls reverberated on the rubble-strewn floor as they neared the statues they had observed from above. Here they noted more details, such as pointed ears similar to Xamus's but slightly longer.

"They are a bit like you," Torin said to Xamus.

The elf stayed silent, recalling the chamber beneath the ziggurat in Tanasrael with the strange sigils that appeared elven yet not elven. Drow markings? Whatever the case, Xamus experienced a tense, visceral reaction to the surroundings, owing no doubt to the venomous stories that circulated among his people, yet the magnitude of animosity he felt caused him to wonder if perhaps there was more— some form of rancor that ran blood-deep and persisted through the generations?

A light, echoing sound reached their ears, like the scuffling of feet. Torin's eyes darted to shadowed recesses. "I don't like it," the dwarf said, shuddering slightly. "Ghosts, like as not."

"Maybe a Wailing Widow or two," Oldavei said.

"Shut it!" Torin retorted.

"Hello?" Wilhelm called out, his voice repeating throughout the corridors before fading.

Darylonde, looking grim, drew his self-made bow and nocked an arrow. Hands hovered over weapons as they continued on, observing several smaller chambers that lined the cavern boundaries. Wilhelm broke suddenly from the group and stepped into one.

The others entered to find a large room where scores of dust-covered items had been haphazardly relocated or discarded—ornate chairs, tables, and fixtures, half of them smashed or broken, but also among the items, musical instruments. Wilhelm stood before one in particular, still intact, resembling in some ways a mandolin, though with a square body of polished wood, featuring points and scrolls, a decorated strap, far more strings, and curious crystals at various places along the bridge, neck, and headstock.

"Just look at it," Wilhelm said with awe, reminding the party of his preoccupation with the armoire in the Hearthvale Foothills. "It's beautiful, man, fekkin' beautiful." The bard lifted the instrument delicately, wiped away dust, and plucked a few strings, eliciting sounds that rang throughout the subterranean complex.

"You should take it," Xamus said, somewhat surprised at the callousness in his voice.

Wilhelm remembered what Froedric had said about a musical instrument being "acquired" in time. Had the bear somehow foreseen this?

Torin, standing at the entryway, said, "The mutt wants us."

Wilhelm slung the instrument and followed with the others to join Oldavei, who was pointing down another wide, stone stairway. "I hear people moving down there," he said, leading them down. Lining one wall were faded paintings in lavish but weathered frames, three times the height of an average person, portraying regal-looking figures with dark skin, white eyes, and white hair.

At the next floor they came to a domed concourse and, directly across, a doorway through which a long table with a tattered cloth and dusty candelabra was visible. Standing on the far side of the table was a male figure who appeared like those in the paintings: long white hair, white eyes, and dark skin. He wore formal though ragged attire, and his eyes were fixed on something deeper in the room that the others could not see. Now, however, they could hear what Oldavei had heard: feet moving across tile.

The group moved to a vantage point that allowed a view of the entire room. It appeared to be a royal chamber, yet all that had once been regal and magnificent was now neglected and time-worn. A long table mirroring the one the travelers had already seen ran along the left wall. The middle portion of the room was an open space. Near the far end a male and female drow danced, moving in a slow, circular embrace. Overlooking the dance area in the back of the room was a throne, carved to represent a gargantuan arachnid, with the abdomen forming the seat, legs splayed to either side, the forward portion of the body angled upward as if the creature were preparing to climb a wall, its thorax and head forming the seat back. Within the throne a female figure reclined. Her meticulously styled hair was snow white, her luxurious black dress gray with age. She supported her head on one hand, elbow on the carved armrest, seeming preoccupied with some other place or time, interested in neither the dancers nor the visitors who stood at the chamber entry.

The male drow stationed opposite the group at the table finally acknowledged them, first with a tepid glance, then with an equally tepid greeting. "Who are you? Why are you here?"

When Xamus did not immediately answer, and no one else spoke up, Oldavei said, "We come from the southlands, wishing to learn more of the north." The ma'ii chose his words carefully. "We hope to know more of the culture here, the history."

"The Queen-Majestrix does not converse with strangers," the drow answered curtly. "Be gone."

Oldavei was preparing to respond when a low female voice boomed from the back of the room: "You!"

The dance ceased. All eyes turned to the female drow on the throne. She pointed a black-nailed finger and commanded, "Come here, elf!"

CHAPTER SIXTY-THREE

TIETLIANA

The dancers scurried away to the shadows. The party, along with the male drow, stood before the Queen-Majestrix, leaned forward in the throne, white eyes gazing intently at Xamus. "What is your name?"

"Xamus Frood, your Majesty," the elf replied, working to keep the tension from his voice.

Tendons stood out in the matriarch's neck. She balled her left hand into a fist. "I knew it! That face . . . never thought to see that face again."

"I'm . . . sorry, Majesty, I don't follow," Xamus said.

"Nothing much left of our glorious Alash'eth, City of Midnight," the queen answered in an abrupt change of subject. "Nothing but mice and roaches and ghosts and the whispering wind. Which are you?" She looked them over. "Mice I should think."

The group remained awkwardly silent.

"Why have you truly come here?" the queen asked.

"To learn," Xamus said, "what happened in the north. What happened here."

"What happened here . . ." She glanced to Wilhelm as if noticing him for the first time. "The aethari."

"Pardon?" Wilhelm answered.

"You have the aethari," the queen said.

Wilhelm remained silent and utterly confused, until he realized she was referring to the musical instrument he took. "Oh! Uh, yeah. Yes. Sorry. I will put this right back where I—"

"Don't bother, no one uses it," the matriarch waved her hand and shifted her attention back to Xamus. "What happened here. Yes, you *would* want to know. Your people have a history here, your bloodline . . . Frood . . . and mine. Creppit. Tietliana."

Xamus replied, "I'm sorry, what—"

"Tietliana Creppit. My name, little mouse. Not that it matters. Xan'gro, another name, one that matters more." Xamus recalled the name Xan'gro being spoken of with great derision in his home enclave. "Auroboros," the queen continued. "Yet another name and the reason you're here. Chasing ghosts. What happened . . . what happened is the world tried to eat itself. It's happening again, isn't it? Steward!"

"Yes, Queen-Majestrix," the male drow answered.

"I shall require travel shoes. Something comfortable."

"Travel?" the steward's shock was evident.

"And a canister of water," Tietliana answered, still staring at Xamus.

"Surely you don't mean—" the steward began.

"I've sat here far too long, haven't I?" the matriarch replied. "In this very spot. The day has come at last. The hour has struck. It is time." She rose, seemingly with no effort or preparation, simply moving from a seated position to standing in an eyeblink.

The steward let out a small yelp and fell to his knees. "I'll . . . assemble a retinue."

"I go alone," the queen answered.

"But Majesty—"

Tietliana's head whipped toward him. The steward, still genuflecting, looked up in abject terror. "Right away, Your Eminence," he managed before standing and practically running from the chamber.

The party was ordered to wait at the spider gate. They conversed, trying to make sense of what Tietliana had said and what it was, exactly, that she intended to do.

The queen emerged moments later with a very old but well-made water canister slung over one shoulder, her shoes hidden beneath the hem of her ornate dress. She scanned the surroundings briefly, took a deep breath, then sighed heavily and ripped her dress along one side to allow freedom of movement. "Been a few hundred years," she said with a mischievous glint in her eye. "Let's see how out of practice I am." She set off toward the southwest.

The outlaws hesitated, unsure if they were meant to follow. "Come!" Tietliana said. They looked to one another, Torin shrugged, and they fell in behind.

Tietliana set a brutal pace, never appearing to fatigue, hardly ever speaking, or, in fact, acknowledging their presence as they trekked across the remains of the empire. The queen's footing was always sure, and if she was ever disoriented, she never indicated it. In fact, it seemed that the very act of traveling by foot was, to her, a perfunctory one, as she moved unerringly through a physical world in which she seemed only half present at any given time.

They had ventured beyond the desolate gray slate ground into regions of brown, arid earth littered with dead, dried flora. It was well into the night when Wilhelm stumbled and, out of breath, stayed down for a moment. The others called to Tietliana, who had kept on. She returned, gazing down at the bard ambivalently.

"Rest," she said. "Yes, of course you require rest."

The relieved outlaws made a fire. All the while, the queen stood on a low rise nearby, still as a statue, gazing toward the north. At one point she called out, "Elf! Come here!"

Xamus did as he was bade.

Tietliana turned to him and stared for a moment, then put a hand to his face. Her skin was cold and dry.

"Tell me about your parents," she said.

Xamus hesitated before answering. "Didn't know 'em."

"What of your home?" the queen asked.

"I come from a refuge," Xamus replied. "Founded by wood elves during the Golden Reign. Abandoned and forgotten, then reinhabited by my people a few thousand years ago. Now it's just a place where they hide away and pretend the rest of the world doesn't exist."

"You resent them," Tietliana said. "For staying secreted away. Did these elves tell you why they fled the north?"

The elf's jaw clenched. "The drow turned against them."

"Do you hate me?" the matriarch asked, and in that instant, Xamus could feel the sorcerous power emanating from her; she stood, wreathed in an aura of menace, eyes drilling through him. A seething animosity built up within Xamus, but it was he who looked away, striving to contain his rising fury.

"You do hate me," Tietliana continued. "As you should."

Just then, the notes of a melody carried to them, seeming wholly out of place in the deserted land. Xamus and Tietliana both looked to see Wilhelm plucking on the aethari.

"Have you played an aethari before?" Tietliana called.

"No, never," Wilhelm stopped and answered.

"Yet you play as if you were born to it." The queen swept her white eyes back to Xamus. "Isn't that curious." She resumed gazing north. "Keep playing, bard. It pleases me."

For a moment there was only the soft, lilting sound of Wilhelm's tune as the drow and elf stood side by side. "Hatred can be a very powerful thing," Tietliana said. "Destructive. All-consuming. You may embrace it, wield it, but time and again the same question repeats: If hatred consumes all, then what does it leave behind?"

Xamus remained silent. "Go," Tietliana said, a note of melancholy in her voice. "I wish to be alone."

Once again Xamus complied. He and the others, fatigued from their long travels, fell asleep in little time. The ever-wary Darylonde woke at various points, spotting Tietliana, standing in the exact same spot, her eyes trained upward as if admiring the stars as they traced their path across the night sky. With the coming of dawn the queen had not moved, so far as Darylonde could tell.

After the first few hours of trekking, as Xamus, Darylonde, and Wilhelm lagged slightly behind Torin and Oldavei, the bard asked Xamus in a low voice: "Why do you think a queen would bother to escort us wherever it is she's escorting us to?"

"I've wondered that myself," Xamus admitted. "Guilt, maybe, for things the drow have done? Maybe something else. I don't know."

"Keep an eye on her at all times," Darylonde advised. "Trust no one."

Presently they began seeing signs of civilization, but the rubble here was more massive in scale than the remnants of the drow empire. Chunks of masonry the size of wagons lay strewn across the landscape. In time they came to a ridge overlooking an expanse that spread as far as the eye could see and beheld the time-lost debris of a metropolis, the immensity of which, in its heyday, would have put any Trade-City in Lawbrand to shame. Now nothing remained but a sprawling field of masonic ruin— toppled towers, collapsed domes, fire-charred walls—with a single, behemoth edifice at its center.

The fortresslike construction, still partially intact, displayed an architectural style reminiscent of the Cathedral of Saint Varina in Sargrad—only built of stone rather than steel and glass—and was so immense that, like the ziggurat of Tanasrael, it seemed capable of housing a small city of its own.

"Come," Tietliana said, striding toward the ruins.

They picked their way through the dust and monolithic stones to an open spot just a few yards from one massive wing of the structure. The group looked and listened, noting an absence of birds or even insects. Nothing moved, not even a light wind. Also, no plant life or vegetation of any kind existed here. The eerie silence of the desolate city was stifling, almost preternatural.

While the queen stood, eyes fixed on the structure's crumbling spires, half-demolished walls, and broken, fragmented flying buttresses, Darylonde continued scanning their surroundings, unable to shake a feeling that something moved among the debris.

"This," Tietliana said, indicating the structure before them, "was the Sanctorium. Seat of authority here in Torune, birthplace of the Sularian church. This city"— her eyes swept the devastation—"was a bastion of order. But that righteousness was a lie. Torune's holy lords were in league with powerful sorcerers far to the north. Secretly, the two powers ruled all of northern civilization, using fear, lies, and prejudice to keep the populations in line and advance their own interests."

These were the most lucid words the queen had yet spoken. But Darylonde had stopped listening. His sense of unease grew to a certainty: something was watching them. Stalking just out of sight. The Wildkeeper crept away unseen.

"What happened here?" Xamus asked, though he already suspected the answer.

"The Auroboros happened," the queen replied. "Torune was destroyed. The few who survived fled south." Tietliana's eyes locked on Xamus. "I told you, hatred consumes all. And the question: What does it leave

behind . . . this is the answer." She swept her hand in an arc. "Waste, misery, and ruin." She leaned in. "Or perhaps a city in the cliffs, forgotten, populated by mice and roaches and ghosts and whispering winds."

Darylonde slipped stealthily among the debris, his senses in a state of alert and awareness that somehow, in this place, surpassed his already extraordinary vigilance, as though he were developing some kind of extra sense, an ability to perceive danger without the aid of sight, sound, smell, or touch. Bow in hand, the Wildkeeper stopped, noting the danger before it appeared, directing his bow to a massive block of stone atop a nearby pile, nearly two stories high. There he observed a creature, hairless but wolflike in form, multilimbed and deadly silent, a living silhouette with shadow-tentacles writhing from its shoulders. It bared daggerlike fangs, its sinister eyes gleaming with intelligence and malefic intent.

Darylonde loosed an arrow that passed *through* the heart of the beast.

This was no flesh-and-blood foe, the soldier realized. This enemy was magical in nature, capable of shifting through reality, and so Darylonde relied on his heightened sense, immediately nocking another arrow and firing, not where the beast leaped to a lower mound of rubble and then vanished, but to the empty space a few feet before him. There the shadow-creature materialized, an arrow buried in the center of its chest as it fell to the ground and dissipated in a kind of black mist.

The Wildkeeper's senses then alerted to multiple enemies—a rapidly tightening circle.

"Weapons ready!" Darylonde shouted as he fled back to the others. "We're under attack," he yelled, running from the ruins and closing distance to the group, who were already unlimbering weapons.

"Nonsense," Tietliana said. "There hasn't been a living thing in this land since—" She stopped, as the shadow-beasts emerged one by one without a sound and the group found themselves suddenly fully surrounded.

CHAPTER SIXTY-FOUR

THE WILD HUNT

"Beware!" Tietliana announced as the shadow-beasts closed in. "For your eyes cannot be trusted." The queen shut her own eyes as one of the attackers, perched on the ledge of a Sanctorium window-void, leaped and vanished in midair. Seconds later the beast appeared just a few feet above the matriarch, who spread the fingers of one outthrust hand, whispering words of power and shredding the lupine form of the enemy into smoky, tattered ribbons.

Darylonde relied on his newly honed extra sense to guide arrow shots to their targets. It was a strategy that met with mixed success; inexplicably, sometimes repeated shots on the same mark were needed, as his hyperawareness proved not to be one hundred percent accurate.

A berserker fury overcame Torin, who created distance between himself and his allies, taking no chances as the circle tightened, slashing at every inch of empty space around him. The rampaging dwarf cleaved one shadow foe the instant it materialized, just seconds before its glistening fangs reached his throat. Additionally and quite by accident, the dwarf dispatched a second shadow-wolf that was in the midst of lunging for Wilhelm, nearly striking the bard in the process. A third adversary opened a wide gash on the dwarf's right shoulder before Torin destroyed it.

Wilhelm, with a cultist scimitar in his left hand, had taken up the Apparatus in his right and fixed his attention on one fallen structure in particular, a massive jumble of precariously heaped stones where several beasts hid in shadowed recesses, awaiting their opportunity to attack. Wilhelm whirled one end of the device over his head, then cast, playing out the magically extending chain to the far edge of one horizontal slab. The bard yanked with all of his might, dislodging the already teetering monolith, bringing the entire mound crashing down like some colossal, masonic house of cards. The ground trembled beneath the party as goliath stones toppled to the earth, pulverizing and dissipating many of the arcane attackers as they attempted to flee.

At the very start of the melee, Oldavei shifted to coyote form. He darted among his fellow combatants, slashing, biting, and ripping into enemies as they appeared. Though he suffered wounds of his own, he moved so rapidly and with such strength and agility that no enemy claw or fang was able to achieve a kill strike.

Though he brandished an Order-Militant longsword, Xamus attempted to tap into the Auroboros energies that he felt in such high concentrations to effect a magical defense. He endeavored to do what Tietliana seemed to be doing—using arcane abilities to obliterate the creatures. He attempted to follow the late Amberlyn's advice, to be the "eye of the storm," but he soon discovered that the magnitude of the forces he called upon were often beyond his ability to manipulate; moreover, he was failing at identifying where the beasts would reappear after they vanished. At one point, the queen saved his hide by destroying a shadow-wolf that nearly had its jaws closed around the back of his neck.

As the battle at last wound down, one of the attackers the elf targeted, rather than disincorporating, actually *grew* in size. The beast bounded forward, disappearing, reappearing, increasing in mass until the thing that bore down on Xamus was one and a half times larger than the raging tyrannosaur the group battled in Lietsin's Grand Coliseum. Coyote-Oldavei sprang for the creature's jugular, but the action proved unnecessary, as the monster was unable to hold its enlarged form; even as the gaping maw yawned, the massive shadow-wolf shuddered violently, then exploded in dark-mist rivulets.

And with that, the assault was concluded.

Tietliana opened her eyes and assessed the scene. "Looks as though you all survived," she said.

Oldavei resumed ma'ii form and immediately rendered aid to Darylonde, who had received a swipe across the ribs. The shaman was pleasantly surprised to find that his efforts yielded immediate and dramatic results: the injury was instantly healed, with no sign that it had ever existed.

Next, Oldavei saw to Torin's shoulder. "What the fek were those things?" the out-of-breath dwarf asked Tietliana.

"The Wild Hunt," the queen answered. "They exist in shadow form and jump between realities. Their attack was unexpected. Nevertheless"—she looked to Xamus—"your response served to illustrate a lesson."

"What lesson is that?" the elf asked.

Just then, Torin howled. Oldavei, who had been in the midst of healing the dwarf's shoulder wound, found that not only did his attempt at restoration fail, but that two more similar wounds appeared: one across Torin's left arm and another on his right thigh. "What the fek kinda healin' is this?" the dwarf protested.

Tietliana continued, looking to the ma'ii and dwarf, "It illustrates that the serpent has no master." She gazed back at Xamus. "You attempt to control the uncontrollable. You were nearly eaten for your trouble."

Xamus wondered—did Tietliana allow the last massive wolf-beast to get so close to him to prove a point?

Despite the dwarf's objections, Oldavei tried again with a great deal more thought and concentration, and successfully mended the wounds. Only then did he tend to his own injuries.

"Yet, while the serpent has no master," Tietliana continued, "the Wild Hunt does. An old acquaintance, one who's aware of your presence here, and of your questions. Clearly he disapproves. Move!" she commanded Torin and Oldavei as she strode to a space farther away from the Sanctorium. She raised a hand; a one-foot-long chunk of stone levitated, passed between the shaman and dwarf, and settled to the dirt, standing on one end. Two more small pieces of debris floated from nearby piles and lowered to the earth. Tietliana pointed to a roundish chunk and said, "This is us." She indicated the second stone, tall, with an angled face. A piece broke away in the top-middle, leaving two hornlike projections. "There, the Twin Cliffs. And here"—she gestured to the thin, taller piece—"Gil'galar. The Spire of Perdition. Where the commander of the Hunt resides. More answers lie there as well, if you intend on finding them."

Overhead, a dark cloud bank obscured the sun. The party studied the stones in silence until Torin spoke up. "Where's Mitholme?"

Tietiliana motioned; a rocky corner piece sailed over and plunked down west of the stone representing the Spire. Torin stood near the piece, contemplating.

"You wish to visit your ancestors," Tietliana said.

"I heard stories about the mountain fort," the dwarf replied. "Always wanted to see it. More than that, though, the last vision I saw, in the Bear Mound . . . showed me a particular axe connected to Mitholme, legendary among dwarves. The Axe of Dominion. I didn't think much of it then 'cause I figured Mitholme would be impossible to ever see or get to. But here we are."

The adventurers looked one to another. "If you saw the axe, then it must be important," Oldavei said. "And despite all that's happened and wherever the visions may lead us"—Oldavei glanced at Darylonde—"they do serve a purpose. A critical one. I understand that now." He looked to the chunk of stone. "We could go to Mitholme first, then the tower."

"There's nothin' says you lot have to go with me," Torin replied and received several looks of chastisement. The dwarf squinted one eye and grinned in response.

"Be warned," Tietliana said, "the dwarves care little for anyone outside their mountain. I will *not* be going to Mitholme. Yet our paths may cross at the tower, if you live long enough to see it. Now gather, all of you."

Unsure of what was to come, the group complied, congregating in the midst of the stone map she had created.

"It has been quite a long time since I've had this much entertainment," the queen said. "Gallivanting, confronting peril!" She smiled for the first time since they had met her, and she looked specifically at Xamus. "I bid thee farewell, little mice." The queen stepped away, gestured grandly, and once again the elf felt her power wash over him. He felt also a wall of energy shoot up on all sides, carrying dust particles into the air. Outside the invisible barrier, the world began to shimmer and distort, as if viewed through water. There was a flash, a vertigo-inducing sense of displacement, and a painful twisting of the stomach that caused all of them to grimace and shut their eyes.

When they opened them, Tietliana was gone, as was the Sanctorium and the entire city of Torune.

PART FOUR: THE NORTHWILDS

CHAPTER SIXTY-FIVE
MITHOLME

It quickly became clear that they were atop some highly elevated stretch of land. Here were signs of life: shrubs and sparse grasses among the rock and stone and clay ground. Farther away in all directions, they observed the tips of tall trees. A strong, cool wind ruffled their hair and chilled their skin. Above, the sky was clear and blue.

Each of them registered their new surroundings slowly, struck silent in disbelief. Wilhelm managed to speak first. "She fekkin' . . . moved us. Relocated us."

"Teleportation," Xamus said, having heard of the spell but never experiencing it directly. A thought struck him: "Huh, that's it. That's how Ironside and his Enforcers ended up ahead of us or right behind . . . the crone. She teleported them, I'd wager that's it."

"Yeah," Oldavei said, still taking in the landscape. "That may be."

"Never seen anything like it," Wilhelm said. "My guts still don't feel right."

Darylonde, for his part, appeared deeply disturbed and remained silent.

Torin strode up a short incline to look out from a rocky ledge. "Yeah, she moved us alright . . ." The others walked up by his side. "Straight to the gates of Mitholme."

Directly opposite across a narrow ravine, they spied behemoth iron gates set into a mountainside, adorned with angular dwarven runes. Elsewhere across the surface of the mountain, crude fortification-like sections had been carved out: turrets, buttresses, and bartizans. The gates and several parts of the mountain bore old scars of combat—missing chunks of rock and scorch marks. Here and there, small pieces of siege machinery still littered the ground.

The group climbed down and across the shallow valley to a wide stretch of stony earth that led to the base of the formidable gates.

"How do we get in?" Oldavei asked.

Far to the right, beyond a cluster of stone outcroppings, a massive jet of steam shot into the sky.

"Heard about that," Torin said. "When they moved into the mountain, they had to deal with eruptions from the lava, so they capped the lakes and diverted magma and steam. Over there must be a vent."

The wind shifted, and Oldavei took several quick sniffs. "That's not all that's over there," the ma'ii said. All eyes turned to the stones.

Darylonde nocked an arrow and yelled, "Come out from there!"

A short, squat figure emerged. Though he sported a full beard, it was not long or braided like Torin's. His hair was dark, as was his skin, but not sunbaked like Torin's—he was coated in what looked like soot, enough to obscure any tattoos. His style of dress was similar to Torin's, though his grubby kilt was red, and he wore beat-up armor, mostly leather with metal accoutrements, such as iron pauldrons. In his left hand he carried a single-bladed axe. Slung on his right shoulder was a large sack.

"Just tryin' to get a closer look is all," the young dwarf called. "Who the fek are ya?"

"Travelers," Oldavei called back, as the stranger clambered down the rocks. He reached the ground and came within several paces, eyeing the group cautiously, regarding Torin with the keenest interest. Darylonde, judging that the dwarf didn't pose an immediate threat, lowered his bow.

"Oi, you're just a pup," Torin remarked.

"You don't look so old yourself," the youth answered. "Where you from?"

"The south," Torin answered.

"Didn't know any dwarves made it to the south," the youth said. "Kroeger'd be gobsmacked to see you."

"Who?" Torin asked.

"Kroeger's our leader," the young dwarf answered. "I'm Brakn. Why're you here?"

"I just want to learn more about my people," Torin said.

The youth considered. His gaze swept over the group's weapons. "You're fighters," he said.

"We've seen our share," Wilhelm put in.

"Could use fighters," Brakn said. He cocked his head toward the gates. "You wanna see inside?"

"Yeah," Torin answered.

"Follow me," Brakn said, climbing back the way he came.

The party followed, surmounting the stone clusters to a high swath of wet, stony land, where lichen and moss filled cracks and formed thick patches. Torin caught up to the youth and said, "We're not goin' through the gates?"

"Gotta sneak in," Brakn said.

"Why?" Torin asked.

"'Cause I had to sneak out," Brakn said, as if stating the obvious. He had stopped, looking toward a large hole in the rocks several paces away. "No one leaves the mountain," he said. "Not supposed to, anyway."

The others caught up. Darylonde looked into the youth's sack to see a collection of pine cones and acorns. Brakn noticed the Wildkeeper's interest. "I collect 'em," he said. "Trade 'em. Damn near impossible to find in the mountain. The acorns with the caps are the rarest."

"Mm," Darylonde replied.

"Now we just gotta wait for a bit," Brakn said.

"Wait for wha—" Wilhelm began, when a column of steam, three meters wide, shot up from inside the hole and persisted for a few seconds before dissipating, peppering them with a fine mist.

"Ah yeah," Brakn said. "Now we go."

He led them to a section of the hole's rim, grasped the rock, and lowered his foot inside. "Rungs'll be warm, but not too bad," he said, and the others took note of the metal hand- and footholds that had been bolted inside the vent.

They descended for several minutes, coming at last to a horizontal section of tunnel that led, so far as they could tell, deeper into the mountain. A few paces away from where the rungs ended, set into the wall, was an iron door with a portal window and a handwheel. A vibration arose in the wet ground. "We better hurry," Brakn remarked, setting to work turning the handwheel.

The shaking increased in intensity, as the anxious party members gazed down the dark recesses of the tunnel. A low rumble reached their ears, and suddenly Brakn seemed to be taking way too long at his task. "Need any help with that?" Torin offered, keeping an eye on the tunnel.

A heavy clunk sounded. "There it goes," Brakn said, yanking the thick door open. The group hurried inside as the entire tunnel shook. Brakn shut the door behind them and had just begun turning the interior wheel when the rumble became deafening and a torrent of steam shot past, visible through the porthole.

"Oh yeah, that woulda cooked us for sure," the youth said as he continued straining until a bolt latched with another clunking sound. He reached to a chain fastened to the wall and wrapped the free end around the wheel. "Right then, off we go," he said, grabbing up a lantern that sat, lit, on the tunnel floor.

This passage, the party observed, was dry. Soon they began to hear distant sounds: rattling, clanking, and clinking and an occasional faint, echoing voice. Farther on, an opening appeared through which a handrail was visible. Brakn motioned for them to stop, set down his lantern, then raced ahead. Just outside, he leaned over the handrail, looked both ways, then waved for them to come. Torin took up the lantern.

They came to a metal walkway overlooking an expansive, dimly lit thoroughfare. Unlike the rough-hewn walls of the tunnel, here the walls were smooth, much of them coated in grime and soot. Large dust particles floated through musty air that smelled of burned matches. Throughout the interior, a thin reddish haze hung.

Brakn took the lantern and urged them toward a set of stairs. A fair distance ahead, the party could barely make out the interior side of the massive gates, as well as shadowy forms of the goliath machinery that operated them. They reached the floor and crossed the wide-open space, passing unused equipment and large, abandoned mechanical constructs. Opposite the gates, the concourse continued deeper into gloomy shadow. Along the walls to either side, pipes ran, both large and small. Some rattled and clanked. Somewhere, steam hissed. Faint, almost disembodied voices carried through the murk.

Thus far, Torin was greatly disappointed. The tales he had grown up with painted a far different picture, of a bustling, lively dwarven society in the heart of the mountain, a mighty fortress-city. What then, was this? Where was the grandeur? Where were the people?

Brakn led them along the wall to a doorway, down another set of stairs, and finally into a large room, presumably a machine shop, lit by two small sconces at either end, with grubby tools and mechanical pieces lining the walls and piled along the edges.

In the center of the space, a handful of dwarves gathered around a metal table, upon which lay what looked like architectural plans. The dwarves were dressed much like Brakn, with the same cruddy skin. One of them was young, while three were gray-haired, and one, a dark-haired dwarf with a bald pate, appeared to be just past middle-age. Wide eyes and open mouths greeted the entry of the group; a few of the dwarves stumbled back; one gasped.

Brakn went near the table and indicated the bald dwarf. "This is Kroeger," he said to the travelers.

"Who the fek are they?" Kroeger responded in a gritty, incredulous voice.

"Travelers from the south," Oldavei said.

"A dwarf from the south!" one of the gray-hairs, a female, said.

"Dragran's flock survived," voiced another old dwarf, a male.

It was a name Torin had heard among his people, a highly respected, fearless dwarf leader who shepherded the others through the Barrier Peaks long ago.

"Deserters," another old male said, and Torin found that he was receiving looks of both disbelief and derision.

"You went outside," Kroeger accused Brakn. "And you brought strangers into our home."

"I brought warriors," Brakn argued. "So clearly I should be rewarded, not punished." He offered a lopsided grin.

"What is it you want?" Kroeger asked Torin.

"I wanna learn about my ancestors," Torin answered.

"Mm," Kroeger considered, scratching at his beard. He looked to the others, and something unspoken passed between them. "I'll tell you anything you want to know," Kroeger said. "But the information comes at a price."

CHAPTER SIXTY-SIX

THE BARGAIN

"As my young friend pointed out," Kroeger said, "we're in need of warriors."

They all stood now around the metal table, many of the dwarves still openly staring at Torin.

"Kazrak Anvilgar," Kroeger said. "Been nearly a year now since he usurped the throne, butchered the old guard, enslaved our engineers, and overtook the Deeps. Now he rules from the heart of the mountain, drunk on power, a tyrant."

"We do our best here at the Antechamber to keep things running," said the female. "But our knowledge and experience are limited. Kazrak seems not to care."

"Can you not unseat him?" Torin asked.

"There's a resistance," Brakn said proudly. "Kroeger leads it."

"Such as it is," Kroeger lamented. "We're few in number, and Kazrak wields fire magic as readily as he swings an axe. He's already killed a score of others who rebelled after the coup. Those of us who remain devise strategies in secret." Just then a steam whistle blew. Kroeger looked to the doorway, contemplating. He glanced at his fellows and made a choice. "Come," he said, rolling up the plans. "It's mealtime."

At the thoroughfare, Brakn looked for any signs of their oppressors before motioning that it was safe. "Kazrak's goons like to perform 'surprise inspections,'" the youth relayed as they crossed to another doorway and down a flight of stairs.

The next room they entered was once a great hall, a place where Torin would expect to see raucous dwarves congregated around a massive table, singing and shouting and laughing and feasting. There was, however, no center table. Muck-encrusted dwarves huddled in small groups against the walls, consuming bread, soup, and water. Bedding indicated that this space was used by many as makeshift lodging.

Upon seeing the travelers—most especially Torin—many of the dwarves voiced shock; some stood; a few began to approach. Kroeger put up a hand. "Finish your food, all of you," he said. "There'll be time to talk afterward."

The residents complied, though they continued to stare openly and murmur among themselves. Snippets reached the party's ears:

"Have they come to save us?"

"Vengeance . . . vengeance is here!"

"I had nearly lost all hope."

"The dark one scares me," said a child. And Torin observed fear in the eyes of others as well. He understood that though he was kin to these dwarves, he was also a complete stranger.

Echoing a similar sentiment from his own side, Kroeger said, "We are the outcasts," as they walked toward the end of the room, the dwarves from the machine shop trailing. They passed a dejected-looking male missing half of his left leg. "Kazrak banished the sick, the young and unruly, the old and infirm, the injured, or, such as in my case, those he just plain didn't like."

"Do you have weapons?" Torin asked.

"Picks, shovels, pipes, wrenches, and whatever else we could put together from what we have around us," Kroeger answered. "Any real weapons were taken directly after the coup."

"There was an axe I heard tell of," Torin said, as they stepped around a white-haired female who appeared to be sleeping. "A legendary blade . . ."

Kroeger threw Torin a sideways glance and said, "The Axe of Dominion."

"That's the one," Torin confirmed, experiencing a frisson of excitement.

"Lost," Kroeger said flatly. "So far as we know."

Torin's hopes fell. They approached a short table at the end of the room bearing a steaming pot, a pile of bread, and several cups. Behind the table stood a portly dwarf, his left arm missing just below the shoulder. He stood with a ladle ready to dip into the pot.

"At the start of every day," Kroeger said, "Kazrak's guards bring us rations. Just enough to keep us going. We don't have much, but you're welcome to my portion."

Torin put up a hand. "We have all we need," he said, looking to the other outlaws, who nodded agreement.

"Very well," Kroeger said. The one-armed dwarf served up a bowl of soup, then used the ladle to push the bowl across the table. The leader tucked the plans under his arm and took the bowl along with a hunk of bread, which he stuck in his mouth, and a water cup. The outlaws moved aside to make way for the other dwarves.

Torin drew close to Kroeger. "You said you devise strategies."

"Mm," Kroeger answered around the bread. He moved to a clear space on the floor, put everything down, pulled the plans out, and unrolled them. The party formed a circle and sat, looking at what appeared to be a schematic of the Antechamber. Kroeger devoured the bread in two bites as the other dwarves from the shop received their meals and sat nearby.

"We've thought about attacking the guards," the leader said. "Even if we defeated them, we'd come up against Kazrak's golems."

"Golems?" Xamus asked.

"Iron golems," Kroeger said. "Dread machines under the despot's control. Picks and shovels are useless against them. My latest plan involved this." He pointed to a set of parallel lines on the plan. "An old, out-of-use tunnel from the earliest days of construction. It's—"

"I found it!" Brakn announced from where he sat.

Kroeger nodded in begrudging recognition. "Just so. As I was saying, it's walled off on Kazrak's side, in the Deeps. I thought if we could break through the wall, maybe free some of the engineers, there might be a chance of destroying the golems. All the same, there would still be Kazrak himself to contend with. A hopeless situation, it seemed. But . . . with seasoned warriors on our side, maybe, just maybe there's some chance at success. Help us, and I'll tell you all you wish to know of your ancestors. I'm afraid it's all I have to offer."

Torin looked to each of his comrades.

Xamus spoke first. "Knowledge of the dwarves, the history here, it's all related. I'm in if you're in."

PART FOUR: THE NORTHWILDS

Oldavei, who had been glancing about the room, said, "These people need our help. They should have it."

Wilhelm spoke next, looking at Kroeger. "You call yourselves outcasts. We know a thing or two about that. I'm with Oldavei." He put a hand on the ma'ii's shoulder. "We gotta do the right thing."

Everyone gazed at Darylonde expectantly. "I don't know that it's wise to involve ourselves in such matters," the Wildkeeper said. Then, reading the reactions of the others, "But I can see that I'm in the minority on this."

Torin looked to Kroeger and grinned. "You got yourself a bargain."

CHAPTER SIXTY-SEVEN
INTO THE DEEPS

For the remainder of the evening, the travelers held court within the center of the Great Hall, telling tales and answering questions regarding not only life in the south but life outside of the fortress-city in general. The stories were met with much excitement as the dwarves—excepting curious youths like Brakn—had not ventured beyond the gates in centuries.

Torin related as much as he knew of the Crossing and the subsequent establishing of Red Bluff, with the audience hanging on his every word. Despite this, he still detected a sense of unease, the notion that he was one of them and yet still an outsider. And from a select few among the older dwarves, he perceived thinly veiled animosity for being a descendant of those who "deserted" Mitholme during the catastrophe.

Shortly after, the outlaws ate and drank from their own provisions as they sat with Kroeger and his top rebels and outlined a plan. Once all parties agreed on a strategy, the visitors passed a restless night of sleep in the tomb-like hall.

They were up shortly before the start of the new day. In preparation for the confrontation, Torin was provided an old maul typically used for driving spikes. Though it was an unfamiliar and unwieldy weapon, the dwarf had little doubt it would serve its purpose.

At the appointed hour, Wilhelm, Darylonde, and Oldavei, along with eleven dwarves who were capable of wielding improvised weapons, strode along the wide thoroughfare past abandoned machinery and old rattling pipes and approached a massive steel barrier—one of many fire doors meant to be used in emergencies to prevent the spread of an inferno closed now to form a division between the outcasts and the oppressors. The rebels stationed themselves outside the door and awaited the guards who would deliver the day's rations.

Oldavei spoke words of encouragement to the dwarves, some of whom were visibly terrified. He considered using his magical abilities to bolster their confidence, but with the instability of the omnipresent Auroboros, he thought it safest to use such methods only when absolutely necessary.

Two levels down, through a tiny maze of short passages, Torin, Xamus, Kroeger, Brakn, and the remainder of able-bodied dwarves entered a dusty old tunnel. Kroeger, holding a giant pipe wrench, walked next to Torin and just behind Brakn, who held a thick iron bar in one hand and a lamp in the other, raised to guide their path. A few minutes in, Kroeger said, "We've got a walk ahead of us, so go ahead and ask me what you want to know." Xamus, walking close behind, drew nearer.

"My biggest questions," Torin said, "are about how Mitholme came to be. What led the dwarves to lock themselves in the mountain? And what led to the split, to Dragran takin' our people through the pass?"

"It's quite a lot you're askin' me to boil down," Kroeger answered. "But I'll do my best. Long ago there were the elves and the drow. Two powerful races. The elves and us dwarves got along; it was dwarven hands, see, that built most o' their cities and monuments. Dwarves worked for the drow too, but the difference was the drow looked down on all 'lower races,' dwarves included. To the drow we were nothin'. Less than nothin'! But as it turned out, the elves weren't good enough for the drow either. Them drow got it in their heads to be the *only* powerful race in the land. They took the elves by surprise, damn near exterminated the lot." At this, Torin turned and looked back at Xamus, whose mouth was a thin straight line, his jaw clenching.

Kroeger continued: "After that the drow built Alash'eth, the City of Midnight. They outlawed the use of magic for any save themselves. And eventually, when they deemed us dwarves no longer useful, they sent orcs and goblins to wipe us out. Thus began a war called the Undersiege, a bloody and devastatin' conflict for our people. Dwarves fought like hell, but that war was ultimately a losin' proposition, so the ancestors dug tunnels all the way past the northern borders. At the height o' the conflict, they fled and blew the tunnels behind 'em."

Kroeger looked around at the hand-hewn walls of the corridor. "They escaped into the wilds and came to this mountain. It was an unstable and dangerous place at first, prone to geothermal eruptions, until the ancestors capped the lava pools and channeled away the magma and steam. With that done, they carved out the rest of what they hoped would be a lastin' home. Mitholme."

Kroeger fell silent as they rounded a bend in the passage.

"And the catastrophe?" Torin prompted.

A dead end materialized in the lamplight. "We're here," Brakn said as they came to stand before a wall of brick and mortar.

"It'll have to wait," Kroeger said. "Your friends will have their hands full any minute now."

Torin looked to Xamus, who nodded and took a step back. The dwarf hefted the maul, said, "Right then, let's get it done," and took a mighty swing.

Two levels up, Wilhelm and the others fell silent and made ready as heavy ratcheting and scraping sounds issued from the fire door. There was a final clunk, and seconds later the massive barrier swung slowly, steadily open.

For a brief instant, the twenty lightly armored dwarven guards on the other side, holding sacks and pots and water jugs, were frozen in shock. Darylonde chose the biggest, toughest looking of the bunch and sent an arrow straight into his throat. The astounded oppressors threw down their provisions and drew axes as Wilhelm shouted, "Let's fekking do this!" and charged, Oldavei at his side. The emboldened outcast dwarves rushed forward, their battle cries joining the resounding clash of steel on steel.

At this time also, Torin, Kroeger, and Brakn succeeded in demolishing enough of the brick wall to allow their group to pass through. Deep clanging sounds echoed from above as they took to nearby staircases and raced up two levels, coming to a wide-open space lined with steam-venting pipes of all sizes running vertically and horizontally, with chains of varying thickness dangling and festooning from the high ceiling.

The group scarcely registered the presence of dwarves Torin assumed to be engineers—deeper in, their ankles chained, working on various machines—as the assault team's main focus was drawn to the origin of the clanging sounds: seven iron golems stomping their way toward the rapidly unfolding battle just out of sight at the fire door. The golems stopped upon somehow detecting Torin and the others' approach and turned to face the threat. They were roughly humanoid in shape, slightly taller than Xamus but thick and clumsy, made from rusting parts, with dome heads, their cylindrical bodies housing furnace-chests in which flames roiled behind small, barred windows. The extremities of their long arms varied between spiked clubs and massive cleaver-like blades.

Xamus drew from the energies he detected in the bowels of the mountain itself, attempting to extinguish the chest-flame of the nearest golem, believing that to be the power source of their animation. The elf's first attempt was successful: the flame vanished, and within seconds the iron enemy, in the midst of rushing toward them, fell flat onto its face. Xamus's second attempt backfired: rather than dissipating, the flame within the metal torso erupted, blasting the golem to pieces and sending deadly shrapnel in all directions. Miraculously, the largest chunk lodged in the back of the next-closest automaton. A smaller but no less lethal fragment flew so near Torin it split the strip of sandy blond hair atop his head.

Torin, in midcharge, was steered off course by the force of the blast. Nevertheless he plowed ahead to the golem with the chunk in its back, which was now balancing on one leg, attempting to recover its footing. The dwarf swung and connected the maul head to the inside of his iron foe's supporting knee, destroying the joint and bringing the heavy body crashing to the floor.

With three of the arcane assailants neutralized, Brakn, Kroeger, and the rest of the outcasts bellowed their defiance and leaped into the fray.

At the same time, the scene outside the fire door was a bedlam of blood and screams. The scimitars of Oldavei and Wilhelm dispensed swift and furious havoc while Darylonde skewered targets of opportunity with feathered shafts. The outcasts performed competently, only one of them—the one-armed ration dispenser—suffering a major cut to the stomach, and another rendered unconscious by a blow to the head.

Within just a few moments, the floor was painted crimson and littered with the bodies of the oppressors. Oldavei took a moment with the one-armed dwarf, concentrating with all of his might to bring only healing properties to bear from the unstable Auroboros, fearing the outcome if his ministrations went astray. Mercifully, such was not the case. The one-armed dwarf gave thanks and joined the others; Oldavei chose not to press his fortune and, after checking that the unconscious dwarf's heart still beat, followed after the group, which pressed now farther into the Deeps toward the echoing cacophony of melee.

In the course of the battle against the golems, a pipe valve had been destroyed, allowing a continuous plume of hot steam to vent halfway across the floor. Of the seven iron constructs, only two remained. Torin, in a cyclonic rage of devastation, had singlehandedly dispensed with three of the automatons, a shocking display for his rebel kin. To the oldest among them especially, witnessing such prowess and courage in a "low-born" dwarf was a surprising, humbling, and enlightening experience.

As the battle wound down, Xamus used his abilities to harness one of the automatons and force it behind two large pipes before once again attempting to extinguish the golem's flame. This time the conflagration expanded, billowing out of the chest-window, tendrils of fire emanating from the construct's joints and seams. It bashed its way out from behind the pipes and ran full tilt toward Xamus, who attempted, with increasing desperation, to magically snuff the flames.

Xamus had backed up against the opposite wall, ready to dive out of the way, when Torin rushed in, a primal scream on his lips as he struck the flaming death-machine broadside with such force that he crumpled the torso and separated it from its limbs.

PART FOUR: THE NORTHWILDS

The outcast dwarves, now joined by their fellows from the fire door, raised a cheer and bashed the final golem to bits. Wilhelm stepped around the steam plume, smiling at Xamus. The bard's eyes then widened, looking over Xamus's shoulder. There came a terrible whooshing sound, and the entirety of the thoroughfare lit up. Wilhelm rushed to the side, as did Torin and most of the others, save for three of the dwarves, including the one-armed male, all of whom were engulfed by the enormous fireball—three-quarters the width of the avenue itself—that sped past the fiery golem debris, through the steam gout and on down the passage, from the direction of the engineers toward the fire door.

A thunderous voice bellowed from deeper in the mountain: "Which one o' you fekkers wants to be the next to die?"

CHAPTER SIXTY-EIGHT

KAZRAK

The rebels stayed close to the walls as they rushed forward, outlaws in the lead, followed closely by Kroeger and the majority of the other outcasts, while a band led by Brakn remained behind to free the engineers.

Deeper in, the rebel party arrived at a massive gorge, spanned by a metal walkway three meters wide, with waist-high railings running along each side. The air stung and the heat was oppressive, carrying sparks in rising waves all along the chasm, where magma flowed deep below in a slow current. In the center of the bridge stood a dwarf with blazing eyes and a face framed by wild, flickering flame forming both hair and beard. In one hand he held a double-bladed axe, the blades enveloped in fire, in the other, a jewel-encrusted heater shield. His armor consisted of both leather and plate, with massive spiked pauldrons and, beneath, a bright robe that hung lower than a kilt, with accents of flame along the hem, visible just above iron greaves.

The outlaws, stepping cautiously to the center of the thoroughfare, were not fully prepared for the visage of the fire dwarf, clearly an old and powerful being touched by elemental forces.

"Got word out, did ya?" Kazrak rumbled. "Brought in mercenaries to fight your battle, ya fekkin' ninnies! And a deserter dwarf among 'em! You've no pride at all. Makes no difference to me! Which one o' you tosspots has the stones to—"

The fire dwarf's taunt was cut off by Torin's war cry, as he set off at a dead sprint, bounding onto the span, gripping the maul shaft with both hands and leaping in with an overhead strike. Kazrak was caught off guard by the attack's suddenness but recovered quickly enough to raise his shield; Torin's blow shattered the center gem and rattled the mage's arm to the shoulder.

Kazrak swung for a decapitating blow that Torin ducked, answering with a thrust from the butt of the maul shaft that struck the mage in the forehead and sent him back two steps. In the close proximity, Torin could feel the heat, emanating more from his foe than from the lava far below, the roiling flames of hair and beard raising sweat on Torin's skin and forcing him to squint as Kazrak brought his axe down in an overhand arc. Torin slipped aside at the last instant, leaving the fiery blade to strike sparks off the bridge floor. He kicked his enemy's wrist, causing Kazrak to lose his grip. The mage swung his shield and rushed, driving Torin to the railing, then brought the point of the shield down onto Torin's foot.

Bellowing his rage, Torin purposely loosened his grip on the maul handle, allowing the head to slide down to his hand. He threw a hooking blow around the shield, striking the exposed ribs beneath Kazrak's outstretched arm with the maul head, eliciting a pained outcry from the mage. Kazrak yanked the shield away and spun to once again face his adversary. Torin switched the maul to his left hand, then tucked and rolled for the center of the bridge, grasping the handle of the fallen axe, the flames of which had now died out. Once on his feet, Torin charged in, swinging wide with the axe, forcing Kazrak to raise his shield, but it was a feint; Torin abandoned that strike and committed to a swing from the opposite side with the maul.

Kazrak snatched the incoming wrist. The heat was nearly unbearable as Torin glanced at his enemy's eyes, witnessing only depthless pits of fire. The mage's gauntleted hand began to glow; intense heat seared Torin's skin. He kicked the shield away to create space, then brought the axe out, over, and down in a tight sweep, severing Kazrak's right arm at the elbow.

The mage's scream was deafening. He stumbled back, tossed the shield, then ran to the railing, glanced down, and vaulted over. Torin heard his enemy's boots strike metal, and when he reached the railing and looked below, he sighted another bridge, one level down, running diagonally across the gorge. Kazrak's left gauntlet shone bright red as the mage clasped that hand over his bleeding stump, crying out in pain while the heat cauterized his wound. The mage then ran deeper into the bowels of the mountain even as Torin leaped down after him.

Even though the impact buckled Torin's knees, he was instantly back up and in pursuit, dimly registering the sounds of his comrades as they jumped also, followed closely by Kroeger.

Limping due to his injured foot, Torin followed the sounds of Kazrak's clomping boots. They navigated a maze of catwalks and metal staircases, rails covered in condensation, passing gargantuan gears and valves, massive flywheels, rattling pipes, and shuddering boilers. Torin's stripe of hair, wet with humidity, fell and clung to his scalp. The party's clothing stuck to their skin, and every intake of air burned both nasal passages and lungs.

All the while, intermittent calls from Kazrak reached their ears: "Burn it all down, and you with it!" and "Take all o' you with me!" and "All drown in lakes of fire!"

"What's this shithead up to?" Wilhelm called out.

Kroeger moved up past Darylonde just behind Torin and said, "Crazy fekker means to shut the vents and open the magma caps! All it takes is one to cause a chain reaction. He could flood the whole damned mountain!" The group increased their speed, coming to a vast earthen chamber where a great metal lid, taking up an area as large as Kannibus Hills' Grove of Lights, capped what was most assuredly a giant lava pool, evidenced by the eerie red light that radiated from porthole windows in the cap and lent the entire scene an infernal cast.

A metal staircase on the near side ran up to a catwalk that stretched over the cap and connected to a perpendicular walk on the far side. This in turn led past a massive lever attached to a series of giant gears against the chamber wall and farther to a tunnel that the group assumed accessed yet more lava caps. Steam-venting pipes ran along the boundaries of the space in all directions.

Kazrak had already crossed the walkway to the far side. Torin raced up the steps but stopped as the fire dwarf called out, "Stop right there!" having reached the enormous lever, ready to pull. "You take one more fekkin' step and I'll—"

The threat was cut short as an arrow fired by Darylonde penetrated one flaming eye, lodging itself halfway to the fletching. The shaft caught fire as the mage's hand fell limply from the lever; he collapsed first to the handrail, then down to the catwalk, and within seconds, his entire body erupted in a tremendous blaze.

CHAPTER SIXTY-NINE
A TOKEN OF GRATITUDE

For the second time in just a few days, the outlaws found themselves in a throne room, this time the royal chamber of the self-crowned and now deposed king, Kazrak.

The vacant, stone-carved throne sat on a dais at the back of the massive space. Before it, end on, lay a table the size of which none of the outlaws had ever seen, spread now with food and drink once hoarded by the doomed dictator: roast pig from hogs bred in the royal pens and honey mead from the king's brewery, a keg of which sat now in the center of the table.

Torin's foot felt just fine; minimal effort on Oldavei's behalf had been necessary to heal it. He held a place at the head of the table, back to the throne. The other outlaws sat to his right, and to his left, Kroeger and the rebels. The remainder of the seats were taken by grateful Mitholme dwarves, including the freed engineers.

"The drow fell to the orcs and goblins and a dark power in the north," Kroeger said, continuing the history lesson he had begun in the tunnel. "The Sularian faith rose to prominence. Humans became the dominant race. Terrible wars were fought—good and evil, light and dark. But according to the legends, it wasn't always so easy to tell one from the other. In one final battle at Auroch'Thiel, Sularia and a ragtag army of rebel races fought to the bitter end, leavin' both forever weakened. Common people regained power throughout the land. For a time, all seemed well. And then . . . word spread of a terrible threat from the north, a storm of magic with the power to undo the world. Panic spread throughout the realm. Some of our people, including the Dwarf Council, believed that sealing the gates was the best course; others wanted to flee south. In the end it was Dragran who led nearly a third of the old clans away, earnin' him the eternal ire o' the council and many others who remained behind."

Torin's eyes traveled down the table to some of the older dwarves. Those who had looked on him initially with enmity now regarded him with steely-eyed respect.

"You proved somethin' to us," Kroeger said to Torin. "To all of us. That there's no such thing as a lowborn dwarf." He raised his mug. "To friends, to warriors, to victory!"

Shouts of jubilation filled the room, and mugs were emptied.

Brakn, who had departed a few moments earlier, now returned with a large object wrapped in cloth. Kroeger reached over and pulled Torin's plate of pork away. The surprised outlaw withdrew his mug as Brakn set the object on the table before him.

"What's this?" Torin asked.

"Have a look," Kroeger said as Brakn retook his seat.

The other travelers stared in anticipation as Torin took up the bundle and unwrapped it to reveal an axe—the axe from his vision. A chop-and-maul that was, in a word, stunning. Beautifully crafted from the leather wrist strap, ornately detailed pommel, and blue leather wrapping along the haft to the metalworking and azure gems at the shoulder, and on to the two heads, hammer on one side and axe blade on the other. A deadly sharp spiked tip protruded from the eye at the top.

"The Axe of Dominion," Torin said, awestruck.

"Oh damn," Oldavei said.

"Now that's an axe," Wilhelm added. Xamus and Darylonde both eyed the weapon with admiration.

"I heard tales," Torin said, "that this axe once belonged to Bronjar Barrowulf, mentor of Dragran."

"You heard true," Kroeger said. "When I told you before that the axe was lost, I lied. I wasn't sure of your intentions at first. I had to know that you were helpin' us for the right reasons. I know now that you were. It's been said that picks and shovels used by the ancestors when they tunneled their way to freedom were melted down and used in the axe's creation. It represents strength, defiance, resilience, and ultimately, of course, dominion."

Torin hefted it, amazed at the precision, the perfect balance. It felt more than comfortable in his hands; it felt familiar, like a beloved item that he had lost and only now rediscovered.

"It's yours, if you want it. Along with that . . ." Kroeger motioned to the area behind Torin. The outlaw turned and realized with a sudden jolt that the leader gestured to the throne. "And the crown that comes with it," Kroeger finished.

Oldavei turned and spit out a mouthful of mead. "King?" he said to Kroeger, wiping his chin. "Him?"

Torin chuckled. He considered for all of ten seconds and said, "I think not." Reluctantly, he pushed the axe toward Kroeger. "I'm grateful for the offer, but I've never been good at stayin' in one place for very long. I was born to roam, not stay locked up in some mountain. No offense," he said, glancing around the table. "Besides, I've a feeling"—he looked to his fellow travelers—"that me and these lowlifes haven't reached the end of our journey quite yet."

Kroeger's disappointment was plain. As was that of many of the others. "I'm sorry to hear that," Kroeger said. Nevertheless, he pushed the axe back to Torin. "You should take this. As a token of our eternal gratitude. We've not seen a dwarf display the kind o' courage embodied by Bronjar in a very long time. None here are so worthy of the axe as you."

"You're sure?" Torin asked.

Kroeger met the eyes of several of the other dwarves and, after hearing no objections, said, "We're sure." He raised his empty mug. "Now someone bring another keg!" One of the gray-haired men farther down the table took the old keg away.

Torin picked up the axe once more, running his thumb along its razor edge.

"Where do your travels take you next?" Kroeger asked.

"A tower in the northeast," Torin said.

"Where that magic-storm originated from," the leader replied.

"There's more we need to learn," Xamus put in. "Understanding what happened may be the only way to prevent history from repeating."

The conversation continued until the old dwarf brought a new keg, at which point Kroeger grabbed Torin's empty mug, took his own to the keg, and said, "Come the morrow, I'll take you through an old tunnel that leads in the direction of the tower." He topped both mugs and brought them back. "Should save you hours of mountain climbing. Meantime"—he plopped Torin's now-full mug back on the table, spilling mead.—"we celebrate!"

CHAPTER SEVENTY
GIL'GALAR

With the onset of the new day, the travelers followed Kroeger through a long-neglected tunnel. For several hours they trudged with the radiance of Kroeger's lamp lighting their way. After a time they began a steady incline that seemed to last forever before finally arriving at a thick, rusted door.

Kroeger withdrew an ancient key ring from his belt, trying several before landing on one that finally caused the bolt to slide with a piercing screech. The door swung open on creaking hinges, and sunlight temporarily blinded the group.

One by one the travelers emerged onto rocky terrain not far from a low ridge. The cold stung, and a strong wind tossed their hair. Torin turned to Kroeger, who stood in the doorway, pointing. "Straight that way," he said. "I doubt you'll miss it."

"You could come with us, you know," Torin said. "No need to stay cooped up all your life."

Kroeger shook his head. "Thank you, but no. Besides, I'm told our new council held a vote last night; it's me they want to sit the throne."

"I've no doubt you'll make a fine king," Torin replied.

"Fare thee well, Torin Bloodstone," Kroeger said, putting his right hand to Torin's left shoulder.

Torin mirrored the gesture. "And you, Kroeger Stonefury."

The travelers walked away as the door creaked shut with resounding finality behind them.

The remainder of the day was spent negotiating mountain passes through thickening woods. They camped the night in a quiet, narrow valley, where Wilhelm played the aethari and continued his songwriting. Through it all Torin sat smiling, axe on his lap. At one point when the bard stopped playing, Oldavei said to the dwarf, "You look happier than I've seen you in a long time."

Torin was silent for a moment, then replied, "Me bein' born in the south, away from Mitholme, my parents choosin' to come through the pass, all of it—I guess on some level it must have bothered me. I didn't even realize. Mom and Pop, I never even knew their names. The few others who knew them from the journey south were killed in the attack . . ." Oldavei nodded, pain etched on his face. "But goin' to the mountain, seein' dwarves like Kroeger, Brakn, and the others, I guess it gives me some idea of what my own folks musta been like. So I guess, in a way, I think I know them a little better now, and that gives me some kinda peace I didn't know was missin'."

Oldavei nodded, smiling. "Good. I'm glad that we all went."

The fire popped. Wilhelm said to Darylonde, "That was one helluva shot. Kazrak."

The Wildkeeper stared into the fire. "In that moment," he said, "I remembered, with perfect clarity, my purpose: to protect others. Even if my people are no more, that purpose remains. I wonder if perhaps I'm starting to find my footing once again."

"I hope so," Wilhelm said. "One step at a time. Next step . . ."

"Next step, the tower," Xamus replied. "I've felt it ever since we left the tunnel. Tugging, almost like a magnetic pull."

"I felt it too," Wilhelm said.

"Same," Torin said.

"Yeah," Oldavei agreed.

"Almost like it knows we're coming," Darylonde said, drawing looks from the others. Wilhelm played no more, and the company bedded down for the night.

Hours later they awoke to the noise of something massive crashing through the timber a fair distance away. They waited on edge, marking the sounds of passage until the tramping faded and whatever had caused the disturbance apparently moved on.

With the dawn they were off again. Near midday, they came to a mountain peak and what at first appeared to be a monumental outcropping of stone, but upon closer observation proved to be the ruins of some ancient fortress, outer walls toppled, the whole of the edifice overgrown with tree, vine, and brush.

The outlaws persisted through the first half of the day, coming at last to a summit overlooking a wide trough to another, higher peak, this wreathed in mist, but a mist unlike any the group had ever seen: it was multicolored, consisting mainly of violet, jade, and cyan shades, with lightning-like flashes within. Through the haze they glimpsed intermittently at its center the upper portion of a tall, wide shadow that they assumed to be the Spire of Perdition. Upon the observation, each of them felt a quickening of breath and pulse in addition to the increasing draw of the energies swirling about the epicenter of Auroboros power.

A two-hour climb brought them to a forest shrouded in the strangely colored mist. It was here that they began hearing occasional, indecipherable whispers, something that set Torin especially on edge.

"Fekkin' ghosts," the dwarf said, attempting to see in all directions at once. The air held a charge, and there was a vibration that each of them felt in their chests. A barely detectable hum pervaded their surroundings.

At the edge of the mountain rim, the tree line opened onto a wide, vast stretch of flat land. There at the center, unmistakable, was the colossal black tower, Gil'galar. The spire ascended into the many-hued fog, tapering near the top, with long projections from the battlements that extended out and then upward, resembling clutching fingers. Jagged, unnatural bolts of lightning appeared, curving around the tower in blinding flashes.

At a distance from the base of the tower, the party discerned the remains of buildings. Most remarkable of all, however, was the fact that large pieces of the structures, as well as what looked like chunks of the ground itself, hovered, rotating slowly, not only around their own axes, but as time revealed, around the tower as well. Another curious effect was observed: the longer any member of the group stared at the tower, the more it seemed to alternately blur, shift, or shimmer, at times fading to a point of near transparency.

The vibration and hum felt within the outlaws' bodies increased as they proceeded forward, their every hair standing erect. The disembodied whispers continued, seeming to come from the mist itself, which now darkened as if night had fallen all at once. Periodically, shouts reached their ears, some echoing in the distance, some so close that all eyes snapped to the perceived source only to find that no one was there. Torin had broken into a sweat, his heart hammering in his chest, pulse racing. Weapons were held at the ready at all times.

"Where's our friend the queen?" Wilhelm asked. "Thinking she might be useful to have around. She did say she'd meet us here, right?"

"She said 'our paths might cross,'" Torin corrected. "How would she even know we're here?"

"Not much about her would surprise me," Wilhelm answered.

"Maybe she's in the tower," Xamus said.

As they pressed through the outlying ruins, the outlaws marveled at the floating masses. Though many were partially obscured by the mist, one of them—a piece of earth the size of a house—floated so close overhead that they could make out individual roots dangling from the soil before it passed on.

As the whispers and voices persisted, they soon spied familiar shadow figures; the Wild Hunt peered at them from among the wreckage. The group prepared to defend against an assault similar to that which took place at Torune, but several moments passed with no aggression, the dark shapes only moving silently among the debris, glowing eyes watching from shaded recesses.

"Why aren't they attacking?" Oldavei wondered.

"Maybe their master told them not to," Xamus answered.

They directed their steps to the base of the gargantuan tower, with Darylonde keeping a watch for any advance on the part of the shadow-beasts. A half mile from the spire, they observed what at first appeared to be a moat, but as they drew closer, the travelers realized that the ground directly surrounding the base was almost completely missing. A ring girdled the foot of the structure, one quarter-mile wide, wherein the earth simply fell away. The precipice of the abyss was a ragged, crenellated line of turf and stone. Coming closer to the edge, they perceived that the chasm faded to dark, unknown depths, and peering across, they noted parcels of mass of varying sizes moving along inside the ring just slower than walking speed in a circular motion around the base. The tower itself, stretching a great distance in either direction, appeared to be composed of monolithic stones—black, though this seemed to be not so much a result of coloration as of absorbing light rather than reflecting it.

"How do we get across?" Wilhelm asked as lightning flashed overhead. Torin still looked around them, expecting a spirit to materialize out of the mist at any instant.

As if in answer to Wilhelm's question, a finger of land slowly came into view on their left, hovering inside the ring. Roughly three meters wide and flat across the top, it took up space from nearly the outside of the gulf to the inside, capable of providing a natural bridge.

The party watched and waited as the island approached. Torin said, "Alright, fek it!" then ran to the edge and leaped, clearing the gap and landing on the hovering span. The other outlaws quickly followed, one after another, with Darylonde jumping last. Having all made the leap, the party members smiled at first, then realized that they were standing on something that was apparently held up by nothing but arcane magic. They took a few more hesitant steps, then quickly ran the span's length and jumped once again onto the belt of land surrounding the tower base.

An arcade similar to that of the Lietsin Coliseum, but three times larger and displaying a wholly unique architectural style, spread all along the foot of the spire. The company passed through one of the arches to an inner wall and walked for several moments before coming to a wide opening leading into what they assumed was the tower's main floor. Items and portions of items—furniture, statues, grand vases, columns—all floated and drifted within the expanse, which continued on in every direction into obscurity. The closest landmark, the opening behind them that looked out onto the chasm and mist, appeared to recede more quickly than their walking speed warranted, and upon different viewings, seemed to move in relation to where they were. Looking up gave no indication of the tower interior, revealing only hovering objects and deeper shadow.

Here the voices overlapped, and as the outlaws attempted to pinpoint their source, nebulous light anomalies appeared on all sides, manifesting at first as floating orbs, then morphing into humanoid shape. Torin gasped as a score of these closed in and took the form of tall, wraithlike monstrosities in hoods and dark, tattered, flowing robes. The shrieking phantoms attacked as one, and the travelers responded without hesitation. Skeletal hands slashed, and where those limbs passed into and through the outlaws' bodies, a soul-chilling freeze resulted that slowed their movements and sapped their strength. Though largely incorporeal, the specters proved tangible enough for blades to affect, though the effort took repeated hacking and slashing in quick succession, coupled with a singular focus of will and intent. Xamus channeled the vibration he felt throughout his body and met with success, blasting two of the phantoms with arcane energy, inducing bellows of anguish before the spirits disincorporated altogether.

Torin proved less fortunate; he chopped at one wraith but allowed two others to grasp him at either side. His vision blurred, his movements became sluggish, and he felt his very life essence begin to ebb. Vaguely he heard the cries of Oldavei and Wilhelm as they engaged his attackers. The dwarf had sunk to the floor, swimming in and out of consciousness, seeing the faces of his comrades above him. He experienced the sensation of being submerged in a kind of nothingness, but it was his friends, especially Oldavei, through word and laying on of hands, who brought him back at last to full awareness.

"I said it before, I'll say it again; I fekkin' hate ghosts!" Torin proclaimed as the others helped him to his feet.

With the wraiths eliminated, the outlaws looked around, seeing only floating objects, the opening they had entered through having vanished altogether. It was at that moment they heard a ragged voice call from above: "Might as well make peace with the ghosts. You'll join them soon enough."

CHAPTER SEVENTY-ONE

MALEVOLENCE

The outlaws looked up to see a figure descending. Long, stringy white hair obscured the face but suggested the newcomer was drow. The vestments—green leather jerkin, leather breeches, black-and-violet stole—were tattered, ripped, frayed, and faded with age. Many of the rune plates on his necklace were cracked or broken. The skin was hidden by what looked to be strips of gray cloth covering an emaciated and hunched frame. In the left hand, the stranger held a staff. Dangling from the right hip was a longsword.

Just by looking at the individual, Torin was unsure whether it was another wraith or not. Chills ran up and down his spine nonetheless.

"It's about time you arrived," the haggard visage remarked in a weathered male voice, booted feet touching the floor soundlessly as the outlaws backed away. "As you might have guessed"—he spread his arms—"I don't get many visitors."

"Who are you?" Xamus asked.

"Why does it matter?" the drow replied, his face remaining veiled by the scraggly white hair.

"Are you the master of the Wild Hunt?" Oldavei asked.

"Yes!" the drow answered, a smile in the voice.

"Are you the master of this tower?" Wilhelm asked.

"Quite the inquisitive bunch, aren't you?" the drow said, taking a step forward. As one, the outlaws stepped back.

"You released the storm," Xamus said.

"I did!" the stranger replied. "The Auroboros. It's why you're here. So many questions, but what's to tell you that hasn't already been said? It is primordial power, older than the world itself. Infinite as the universe." He raised his staff. The headpiece glowed softly, and a warm blue self-illuminated, transparent dragon appeared a few paces in front of the caster. The dragon resembled that which was portrayed on the tile mosaic floor beneath Tanasrael and on the book that Xamus's mentor forbade him from reading. It swam through the air as the travelers now all stumbled away. "It is all things at once," the stranger said. "Life, decay, love, despair, energy, and entropy." The dragon looped and twined, forming a figure eight as it began consuming its own tail. "It is inside everything and everyone. It is a perfect monster of energy and destruction, and it will writhe and coil through Creation long after this world has passed away."

The caster stood staring at the serpent, mesmerized.

"I had friends," he said. "A merry band, not unlike yours. I was"—the voice fell—"a great hero. Xan'gro." His tone brightened again. "A name that would ring through the ages! My friends . . .

Alrich, Jehnra, Robert, Bronja"—he looked to Xamus—"and Galandil. We, all of us, drew on the World-Serpent's power."

Xamus was thunderstruck at the mention of Galandil, his own blood somehow connected to all of this madness. And now, so many years later, for a direct descendant to be standing at the epicenter of where it all began seemed an impossible coincidence.

The illusion continued consuming itself, the head moving along the body in a loop. Xan'gro reached out and touched it. "We tapped the Auroboros, and it consumed us."

"My uncle . . ." Xamus said.

"He turned against me," Xan'gro said. "They all did. All I wanted was to make the world right again. Clean the slate and start anew. I unleashed the Auroboros in its rawest form against the unwitting masses."

The head of the illusion broke free and lunged outward, fang-lined mouth open. The travelers prepared their weapons, but the replica proved harmless, expanding to a gargantuan size, fading as it grew, until it vanished altogether.

"People . . . corrupt, flawed, incapable of self-governance. Pathetic. They screamed and fled in terror. The Auroboros ate away reality and unmade both land and sky. It was, in a word, glorious." Xan'gro's tone grew dark. "Alas my comrades didn't share my vision. They accused me! Attacked and betrayed me! But of all the betrayal, it was my dear friend Galandil's that hurt the most. Not happy with simply eliminating me, he gave his own life to reverse the storm. Turned the World-Serpent back upon itself. Twisted its power, forced the energies to *create* rather than destroy, breathing new life into the Northwilds, gifting the animals with speech and sentience. Ridiculous!" Xan'gro raised his sword, gazing at the blade. "There was to be a reckoning, but instead, civilization . . . worthless, flawed, decadent civilization, was allowed to endure."

Xamus reflected morbidly that the drow's rhetoric—of a reckoning, remaking a broken world, destroying decadent society . . . all sounded eerily similar to the nonsense Tikanen spouted.

Xan'gro faced Xamus. "You came to the north pursuing a deeper understanding of the Auroboros." He brought the softly glowing headpiece near his face, lifting his head to reveal a few strips of cloth beneath the hair, wrapped around what appeared to be little more than a skull. "This is the true cost of the Serpent's power. The utter ruin of body and soul. I did my best to employ it, but in the end, it was *I* who was unmade, saved only by my own foresight, by self-transformation at the precise instant of my death, resulting in the lich that stands before you now." The drow laughed. "You know what's funny? I'd do it all again. Kiss the serpent on the tongue. No such fate need await you, though. Because you remind me of them, because of your uncle"—he locked eyes on Xamus—"I'll spare you that agony! Instead of a slow and painful demise, I'll give you the distinct honor"—he drew the sword at his right side—"of dying quickly by my hand. The gift of termination at the end of my blade, Malevolence." The longsword was ebony from pommel to tip, featuring a hilt crafted to resemble a spider's legs and a small skull at the center of the cross guard.

Torin didn't wait for the lich to say any more. The dwarf rushed in, Axe of Dominion primed for a killing blow. Before he could reach his target, however, the headpiece of the drow's staff glowed brighter; Torin was lifted up by an invisible force and spun so that he was parallel to the floor, hovering, kicking, flailing, and cussing up a storm.

Xamus whispered, gestured, and was ready to cast a bolt of lightning when all sound was suddenly cut off. The elf's vision was distorted slightly by some transparent barrier; he reached out and felt the obstruction, though he could not see it. In fact, probing all around him, he discerned that he was trapped inside some invisible sphere.

Wilhelm doubled over, clutching his stomach, undergoing the most intense abdominal pain he had ever felt. Surrendering to the irresistible urge to vomit, he opened his mouth wide, spewing a swarm of tiny insects.

Oldavei charged, stumbled, and fell to all fours, undergoing a forced transformation, but only reaching the halfway point between ma'ii and coyote—the state of the Ravenous—before turning to ma'ii again, then repeating the process, a painful ordeal that left him writhing on the floor.

Darylonde nocked an arrow and raised his bow, but the light on Xan'gro's staff grew so bright that it turned everything white as snow; the brilliance then died, replaced by impenetrable black, and the Wildkeeper realized with sudden dread that he had been struck blind.

"It's adorable that you deem yourselves fit to challenge me," Xan'gro said, seeming genuinely enthused.

Xamus determined that the invisible sphere was shrinking steadily around him; Torin began rising into the air. Wilhelm fell to all fours, still disgorging a stream of bugs. Oldavei thrashed in his ever-changing state. The drow continued: "This is the most fun I've had in a very, very long time." Darylonde, who had been waiting for the sound of Xan'gro's voice, loosed an arrow. Unseen by him, Xan'gro tipped his staff, and the missile flew up and embedded in a hovering chair. "But here is where your adventure ends," the drow concluded.

He lifted the staff and sword high. Sorcerous power rippled forth in waves. But before he could unleash his final attack, there came a sudden flash, following which the lich was engulfed in a dark, crackling globe of arcane energy.

Xan'gro yelled and arched back. Torin fell with a heavy thud. The sphere around Xamus ceased to exist. The torrent of insects no longer issued from Wilhelm, and those that remained in the air fell dead to the floor. Oldavei assumed and held his ma'ii form, catching his breath . . . and Darylonde's vision began to clear. They all looked to see Tietliana several paces away hovering a few feet off the floor, one hand extended, that hand enveloped in the same dark energy that tormented Xan'gro.

A wraith, similar to those that accosted the party earlier, materialized and lunged for the queen. Tietliana diverted her attention long enough to eradicate the specter, but it was all the distraction Xan'gro needed to dispel the queen's magic. Even as the outlaws moved to renew the attack, more wraiths appeared and engaged.

"Not very sporting of you, cousin," the lich said.

"How far you've fallen," Tietliana said. "How wretched you've become!" She gestured, and the darkness around her began to collect into a massive shadow form that dashed toward Xan'gro.

"You've no right to judge me!" Xan'gro spat. He canted his staff; dark tentacles emerged from the floor, wrapped around the shadow-charger, and pulled it down and out of sight. "You and the rest, scuttling like roaches in dark corners. We could have been gods!"

The outlaws continued their attacks on the ghosts as Tietliana raised both hands, answering, "And what a deplorable god you would have been!" A glowing ball of energy the color of amethyst formed above her head and launched toward Xan'gro. A radiant blue-white beam shot from the lich's staff, lancing the queen's projectile, dissipating it and continuing to strike the queen herself in the center of the chest. Tietliana cried out and dropped to her knees.

Xamus, in the midst of slashing two wraiths, watched Tietliana fall. He heard Xan'gro call to her:

PART FOUR: THE NORTHWILDS

"How did you think this would end? Facing me in the heart of my sanctum?" And Xamus realized the lich was right—he clearly understood the Auroboros on a deeper level than any of them. Any magical attacks Xamus or Tietliana might levy against him would surely prove futile. But if he could tap the World-Serpent for a tangential use, a spell he had not yet attempted . . .

Xan'gro strode to within a few paces of Tietliana, who was on her knees, one hand to the floor, the other clutching her chest. A thin, wavy line of blue light extended from the lich's staff to the queen.

Xamus eliminated the wraith in front of him even as another advanced. He closed his eyes, whispered, gesticulated with his free hand, felt a keen pain in his guts . . .

And then suddenly, he opened his eyes to find himself standing just behind Xan'gro. The lich sensed it, but too late; Xamus's scimitar was already penetrating Xan'gro's back, skewering his darkly enchanted heart, the tip bursting through his chest.

For the briefest instant, an image flashed within Xamus's mind of another far older time, of an elf who looked much like him with jet hair, black leathers, and cloak—Galandil, his uncle, driving a longsword through a prelich—though just as insane looking—Xan'gro.

As quickly as the vision appeared, it was gone. The lich's arms fell, and what remained of his cursed body turned to ash. The staff and sword dropped and clattered.

Upon dispensing with the final wraiths, the other outlaws turned to see the tableau of Xamus standing over Xan'gro's remains and Tietliana still on her knees, drawing deep, ragged breaths. They ran over, Oldavei moving to assist the queen, who pushed him away.

"Back!" she ordered, still fighting for breath. "Been a long time coming. Long ago I helped Xan'gro, aided in his efforts to understand the magic that would result in the Serpent-Storm, never thinking he would be insane enough to attempt it." Her eyes became distant. "All of those lives consumed . . . at long last now . . . my tithe has come due." The floating objects nearby began to swirl madly. Darylonde, casting about for any sight of the exit, perceived only darkness. "Stand there," the queen said, nodding her head to the open space next to her. As the outlaws clustered, they witnessed pairs of glowing eyes emerging from the umbra on all sides—the Wild Hunt.

"You don't have to do this," Xamus said, even as Tietliana balled one fist, creating a barrier around them. Their stomachs tightened. More and more of the red eyes, hundreds of them, appeared in the dark. "Very sweet of you, little mouse, but have no worry," Tietliana said with a hint of a smile. "Time now for me to rest."

The last thing the outlaws saw before they teleported away was the Wild Hunt rushing in.

CHAPTER SEVENTY-TWO
LEAP OF FAITH

The outlaws found themselves on a wide, grassy dale. Behind them and on one side lay the edge of a thick forest; on the other side, sheer cliffs; and in front, an open expanse leading to wooded slopes, foothills, and mountains. There among the range of peaks, they observed a flat-topped summit capped by an otherworldly mist where lightning flashed intermittently; in the center, a dark fingerlike projection barely visible in the final light of day.

"She did it again," Wilhelm said, holding his stomach.

"You don't think she—" Oldavei began.

Xamus shook his head. "No way she made it," he said.

"She didn't want to," Torin remarked. He turned to his left and looked to where the sun was setting behind mountain peaks. "She brought us south," he said. "At least a day's journey, if not more."

"We should make camp," Darylonde said. They ventured south near the tree line, collected wood, and kindled a fire. Darylonde stood, gazing silently at the cliff less than a mile away, a stony mass nearly as tall as the highest spires of Sargrad's Cathedral of Saint Varina.

The other outlaws settled in, ate and drank from their provisions. Wilhelm removed his hat and ran fingers through the hair that was just now starting to coat his head. "Never shoulda cut my damn hair," he mumbled, then fell silent and set about writing lyrics.

"Well," Torin huffed. "Now what?"

"I'm worried," Xamus said suddenly. "I'm worried that Tikanen's gonna do what Xan'gro attempted: set loose the full power of the Auroboros. And I don't know that there's anyone who can stop him."

"He can let it loose on Ironside all he wants," Torin said. "Him and his Enforcers. Save us the trouble, after everything those fekkers did."

"We did plenty of things too," Oldavei replied. "You said it yourself before we left the south. What Ironside did at Kannibus, he did because of us."

"Let's not start all that again," Torin said with a quick glance to Wilhelm, who was still writing.

"All I'm saying is that maybe we have a responsibility, especially knowing what we know now, to do everything we can to stop the cult and stop Tikanen."

"What are you suggestin'?" Torin said. "Go back? We left for a reason."

"Oldavei's right," Xamus said. "I know that I said we should leave it all behind, but we have a greater understanding now. If the Auroboros power goes beyond Tikanen's control, he could potentially wipe out *all* life. Including here. He could destroy everything we've ever known. Nothing and no one in this world would be safe."

"What do you propose we do?" Wilhelm asked without looking up.

"We can warn people, if nothing else," Oldavei said. "Make them listen, make them see."

Torin sighed heavily. "I'd love to see all those bastards get what's comin' to 'em. The Church. The system. Ironside . . . Tikanen's cult too, for lockin' us up and takin' away a year of our lives. Fek 'em all, I say. If the plan involves crackin' some skulls, then you got my attention."

"I'm with him," Wilhelm said while scribbling. "Fek Tikanen. He took too much from us. No more."

"So it's agreed then," Xamus said. "Whether for different reasons or not, we're agreed we should go back." He looked to the Wildkeeper. "Darylonde, you been listening?"

"The innocent deserve our protection," Darylonde replied, still fixated on the cliff.

"Right then," Xamus said. "We're in accord."

It was several minutes later when Darylonde came to the fire. He and the others remained silent, and it wasn't long until fatigue overtook them and the party drifted to sleep.

With dawn's arrival they awoke to find the Wildkeeper nowhere in sight.

"Wonder where he went off to," Oldavei said.

"Probably just answering the call of nature," Wilhelm replied, rolling his bedding. Torin chuckled.

"I'm just gonna have a look around," Oldavei said. Remembering that the Wildkeeper had spent so long staring at the cliff, the ma'ii headed in that direction. Away from the camp, he shifted into coyote form. Nearer the base of the cliff, as the wind changed, he caught Darylonde's scent. Looking up, he could just barely make out Darylonde's shape, standing at the edge amid tall ash and fir trees.

Rather than fearing for his friend, Oldavei understood immediately that Darylonde was preparing to undergo the druidic ritual he had discussed long ago, the ritual in which the Wildkeeper had received his talon-hand. Oldavei stopped, sat back on his haunches, and loosed a long, encouraging howl.

Standing atop the cliff, looking down, with an Order-Militant dagger in his right hand, Darylonde heard Oldavei's call of support. He did not doubt that his comrade believed in him. The most important question was whether or not he believed in himself.

The answer for many long years now had been no. Ever since his failure in the war, the lives lost, the parts of himself that he lost along the way. But then, days ago—that spark, that reflex, with no hesitation, when the opportunity came to end the fire dwarf Kazrak . . . he saw the shot, and he took it. And that single act reminded him of his purpose, that his true *worth* came in protecting those who needed it, who deserved it. But in order to do that on a large enough scale to matter, he would need to be his best self. And he could not do that if he continued to wallow in self-pity and self-recrimination. Where he and the others would go from here, there would be no room for fear or doubt. And he understood now that his past failures should not erase the promise of what he might accomplish in the future—the *good* that he might still do before his own end came.

The Wildkeeper regarded the dagger.

So yes, that was the question: Did he believe in himself? He felt finally, after so very long, that the answer might be yes.

Darylonde lifted the razor-sharp blade and began cutting away, first at the hair on his head, then at the facial hair he had left untended in the Mines of Galamok. As he cut, he tossed the shorn hair to the wind. When he was done, he sheathed the dagger, content that he once again resembled his former self. He then gazed over the edge of the cliff.

The Wildkeeper knew that if he were to truly believe in himself again, it would be necessary to demonstrate his unshakable faith. And so here he was, staring down at certain death.

"I am not afraid," he said to the sky and the wind. "I have no wings, but I will fly."

With that, the Wildkeeper closed his eyes and leaped.

For a heart-stopping instant there was only the wind in his face and the rapidly approaching earth. Then a deafening sound—high-pitched screeches and the thunderous beating of mighty wings engulfing him in a furious tempest. His descent slowed, a result of the buffeting force of the air created by his sudden companions keeping him aloft. Briefly he heard the voice of Arakalah, the Queen of the Eagles, conferring upon him her blessing. And with it, all fear and doubt washed away. Darylonde was one with the mighty raptors, his spirit soaring in an exhilaration beyond words. Tears brought on by the beatitude of the moment blurred his vision.

The power of the fierce wind created by his winged brethren cushioned Darylonde all the way to solid ground, where he touched down softly and gave his thanks to the departing multitude.

Oldavei, now in ma'ii form, approached, his heart warmed by the look on the Wildkeeper's face, an expression he had not yet seen cross those features: peace.

The largest of the eagles stayed, settling onto the branch of a tall pine tree.

"It gladdens me to see your faith reaffirmed," Arakalah said to Darylonde, who stepped to within a few paces of her perch.

"I was lost for so long," Darylonde said in a heavy voice. "But my path is becoming clear again. Thank you for your wisdom and guidance."

"The path was there all along," Arakalah offered. "You just wandered away from it for a bit."

Darylonde turned to Oldavei. "And thank you for supporting me."

"No more running for either of us," Oldavei replied.

Just then, the other outlaws approached, travel bags slung. "There you two are," Wilhelm said, glancing at Arakalah. "Everything okay?"

"Never better," Darylonde replied, sharing a look with the grinning Oldavei.

"Then it saddens me to be the bearer of unwelcome news," a female voice informed. An eagle who had not been present in the convocation came and landed one branch away from Arakalah. It was the female golden eagle Darylonde had befriended when he and the queen had first met.

"Kenna, what's wrong?" Arakalah asked.

"A flood of darkness descends from the northern mountains," the eagle replied. "Shadow-beasts, more than a thousand, are on the run and heading this way."

"How long?" Darylonde asked.

"A day at the most," Kenna answered.

Oldavei exchanged dire looks with the others. Xan'gro's lapdogs, now raging and masterless, were left to run amok. The Wild Hunt, hungry for vengeance, looking for prey and ready to destroy anything and everything that lay before them.

"We must prepare," Darylonde said.

CHAPTER SEVENTY-THREE
THE GATHERING STORM

The reunion and pleasantries between the outlaws and the animals of the Thousand Springs was short-lived. Talk turned quickly to preparation for the onrushing flood of the Wild Hunt.

The travelers stood in the clearing where they had first met Asteria, the Caretaker and her male unicorn companions receiving a full account of the threat from Kenna, who delivered her report from a spot near Arakalah on the edge of the stone basin, sunlight glittering off the pristine water behind them.

After giving the warning careful consideration, Asteria said, "I want scouts and ongoing status updates."

"My eagles will see to it," Arakalah said. "Kenna—"

"I'll organize rotating patrols," the eagle answered, taking flight.

"This is our fault," Darylonde said.

"He's right," Wilhelm admitted. "If we hadn't been snooping around, if we hadn't killed that drow or lich or whatever the fek he was—"

"The shadow-wolves have long been a threat to our kind," Asteria said. "While their attacks were infrequent and brief, I always suspected they might descend someday in greater force."

"Still, not all at once," one of the stallions interjected. "Over a thousand, when we number in the hundreds . . ."

"I want to help you," Darylonde said.

"We all do," Torin added.

"I appreciate that," Asteria said. She then stepped toward Xamus. "And you, did you find the answers you were looking for?"

"We learned a lot," the elf replied.

"And do you intend to use any of that here?" Asteria asked.

Xamus glanced at the others. "Depending on how bad things get, on how many there are, it might be unavoidable," the elf replied.

"We don't need them," the second stallion said.

"Please," Darylonde implored. "I have experience in warfare, organizing defenses . . . what's coming is likely beyond anything you've faced, but if we do this right, you'll never have to fear the Wild Hunt again."

Asteria chuffed and asked, "Froedric, what say you?"

The bear's brown eyes widened in obvious surprise at being consulted. "These people-folk have my trust," he said solemnly.

Asteria then addressed the eagle queen. "Arakalah?"

"Darylonde will guide us true," the queen answered. "I have no doubt."

"Your confidence in me is humbling," the Wildkeeper replied, then gazed pointedly at Asteria. "But not misplaced. I will do all that I say. I will protect you and teach you and your kind how to protect yourselves, if you'll let me."

After a moment's hesitation, Asteria said, "So be it."

"Asteria—" one of the stallions began to protest, but the Caretaker cut him off.

"My mind's made up, Bolden," she said. Then, looking from Xamus to Darylonde, "Don't make me regret it."

And so it was decided. From there, Darylonde oversaw the defense preparations. Work was done quickly but efficiently, maximizing the daylight, with reports from eagle patrols coming in every hour. Darylonde conducted inspections of the siege equipment and chose a handful of ballistae, mangonels, and one stone-thrower that were the least degraded. Once the foliage choking the old machines was cut away, Darylonde directed the outlaws in the process of making them battle ready. One of the toppled siege towers was likewise repaired to a functional status, raised to its original height of three stories and relocated to the southeastern corner of the fields.

At this same time, bulwarks were formed at strategic locations within the dense timber east and west of the springs' open grassland. In many cases, such as the east, with its rolling hills and rushing falls, a mixture of stone, earth, and wood, erected through the combined efforts of bears, moles, and beavers, composed the obstructions. To the west, in the open spaces between towering tree trunks, wooden remains from the battlefield were hauled in on the backs of bison or dragged behind. The wood was then used to create barricades, with earth and timber behind. The line of bulwarks projected outward from the northernmost end of the field at seventy-five-degree angles on both sides, with the purpose of creating a funnel. Though the beasts were no doubt capable of phasing past the walls, it was Darylonde's hope that the sight and thickness of the barriers would be enough to direct their charge onto the battlefield and prevent them from flanking the defenders.

Throughout the day, Darylonde provided specific instructions to groups of the animals concerning the coming battle, defensive strategy, and his expectations so that the roles of every group were understood and agreed to. In the waning light, the siege machinery was positioned along the pastures' southern edge, facing the springs. The latest eagle report had the marauding pack still several hours away. Asteria gathered all of the sentient creatures before the machinery, and Darylonde, standing on the base of a mangonel, called out:

"Either this night or come the dawn, the enemy will be upon us. We will, all of us, be tested. Not everyone will survive . . . but know that if you die, your life was given so that others might continue to live, and so that the young would be given a chance to grow old in this miraculous and sacred place. I'm an outsider, but I'll give my blood, sweat, and final breath to see it so. As will my friends. No one of us can move mountains on our own, but

together . . . I believe we will overcome the impossible."

With that Darylonde fell silent, and the animals dispersed. Asteria offered a brief nod of the head and walked away.

Before the Wildkeeper departed from the mangonel, Arakalah came and landed on the wooden frame. "Good speech," she said.

Darylonde bowed. "Gratitude, my queen."

PART FOUR: THE NORTHWILDS

"Just do us all a favor and don't get yourself killed," Arakalah answered before taking wing.

Darylonde stepped from the weapon and approached the outlaws. "You all know your places," he said.

"We do," Wilhelm answered.

"Good," the Wildkeeper nodded and gave each of them a pat on the shoulder.

"See you on the other side of this," Xamus said.

"Just so," Darylonde replied. He proceeded then to the siege tower, up the ladder and to the top.

Wilhelm took up a spot next to a mangonel and looked over to Froedric, who waited on the opposite side. "Ready to stomp some shadow-wolf ass, bear?"

"Ready, human," and Wilhelm could hear the smile in his friend's voice.

Fires and torches were lit. The outlaws and the animals hunkered down, watched, and waited.

An hour later the first clouds began rolling in.

CHAPTER SEVENTY-FOUR
BATTLE OF THE THOUSAND SPRINGS

The defenders slept only briefly throughout the long night, some of them not at all.

The rain that had begun as a light drizzle just past midnight built to a downpour that set the torch and bonfire flames guttering and raised gouts of liquid throughout the field's myriad pools. Lightning rendered the scene in stark relief, with booming thunder following directly behind.

Although the sky had begun to lighten, black thunderclouds continued to cast a dismal gloom as the first of the shadow-wolves rushed onto the field, their coming foretold a half hour before by the latest eagle report.

Torin, Xamus, and Wilhelm stood in between their designated siege machines. Before them, ranks of defenders, all drenched to the bone, anxiously waited. Behind the siege engines, on a low rise, Asteria watched, flanked by the unicorn stallions who ground their teeth in nervous anticipation. Overhead, hundreds of birds of prey formed a maelstrom of their own, whirling, screeching, and preparing to attack.

The thirty-odd shadow-beasts charged across the field, and for the most savage of the protectors—the badgers, wolverines, jungle cats, and boars—it was all they could do not to rush forward to meet them, but Darylonde's orders had been specific, and they held their ground to the last, when the enemy was less than five paces away.

And here, more of Darylonde's strategy came into play, as the animals had been counseled to rely not on their sight but on their senses, on wild instinct to guide their fangs and claws. The attackers, he had informed, could only inflict their own wounds when they became tangible, and not before; up until that last instant, however, they may transition between solid form and vapor, vanishing and instantly relocating.

The animals had heard, and now they obeyed. They waited like coiled springs, and in the very last instant before enemy teeth closed on jugular veins, they lashed out explosively and ripped their foes to shreds. In short order, the forerunners were decimated, with only one casualty on the protectors' side.

Any celebration was short-lived, however, as the bulk of the Wild Hunt stormed onto the northern section of the field. The black tide surged forth, a great and terrible mass of darkness and death with no end in sight, most of the beasts phasing through or around bonfires or over pools, some toppling torches and splashing through the shallower springs.

Darylonde leaned over the wall of the siege tower and yelled, "Ready!"

Wilhelm took up the trigger rope of the mangonel he stood beside. Xamus grabbed his rope and stepped away, ready to pull. Behind them, Torin held the much longer rope of the stone-thrower.

"Make ready!" Arakalah screamed to her avian comrades, keeping a sharp eye on the siege weapons.

Darylonde held one hand up over the sidewall of the tower, watching the field. Lightning flashed. Thunder boomed. The Wildkeeper dropped his hand and screamed, "Loose!"

Wilhelm, Xamus, and Torin pulled. Tension was released; the stout arms of the mangonels snapped up and crashed into their blocks, hurling two-hundred-pound stones into the hammering rain. At the same time the counterweight of the stone-thrower swung down, the arm roared upward and launched a three-hundred-pound boulder from its sling.

"Now!" Arakalah called.

The gargantuan missiles sailed through the deluge, their flight concealed—as planned—by the raptors, who obscured the stones right up to the second of impact.

Here the greatest advantage enjoyed by the Wild Hunt—sheer numbers—proved to be their biggest weakness in the initial onslaught; the shoulder-to-shoulder, nose-to-tail crush of bodies made them disinclined to phase a short distance away, as there were no empty spaces to phase to. Also, the bulwarks created in the woods to east and west achieved their desired effect as shadow-wolves flooded in on both sides, repelled by the barriers as intended, adding to and compressing the stampede.

With the lack of warning, very few of the attackers disincorporated in place as the great boulders crashed down, cratering the soaked earth, bounding, arcing, and smashing again, barreling forth and annihilating droves of invaders.

Once the projectiles were loosed, Torin abandoned the stone-thrower, which would take far too long to reload to be of more use. The dwarf and Xamus feverishly cranked back the arms of the mangonels while Froedric and a black bear rolled up the next boulders and with the outlaws' help nudged them into the buckets. Wilhelm took up a position behind one of the ballistae. Torin and Xamus, their work done at the mangonels, did the same while the bears took the mangonels' trigger ropes into their mouths and awaited the Wildkeeper's command.

"Loose!" came the shout from Darylonde; boulders flew, accompanied by the quaking rumble of thunder as the projectiles once more wreaked their havoc among the dark and relentless tide.

Froedric and the other bears took up positions at the front line. From the tower top, Darylonde terminated larger enemies with arrow shafts. Between shots he yelled, "Ballistae!"

The animals who stood in front of the ballistae checked to ensure they were out of the line of fire. Wilhelm, Xamus, and Torin all yelled, "Clear!" from their positions behind the massive weapons.

"Fire!" Darylonde screamed.

Triggers were released; spear-tipped bolts, four feet long, sliced the air, raced over the field, and bored long holes through the enemy ranks.

"Ready for close quarters!" Darylonde yelled, firing his last arrow.

Wilhelm, Xamus, and Torin drew weapons and raced to the front line.

Froedric and the other bears reared up on hind legs. All along the line of defenders, bodies tensed, fangs bared, and hearts hammered. Wilhelm, Torin, and Xamus all took several quick breaths and tightened their grips on their swords.

The gleaming eyes and fangs of the invaders sped toward them in the murk. Lightning flashed, illuminating the onrushing torrent of multilimbed, lupine forms.

"Now!" Darylonde shouted.

The front line surged to meet the assault. There was no clash of blade against blade, only the war cries of the outlaws and the growling and huffing and snarling of the animal defenders as they waded into the dark and deadly current.

Arakalah and her avian comrades harried the shadow-beasts from above, diving, lunging, raking with talon and gnashing with beak, enticing many of the enemy to assume solid form to defend, leaving them open to attack from the protectors. This left the birds at grave risk, and more than one of them fell prey to the tentacle-like limbs on the invaders' backs, including Kenna, who dove too near one of the extremities and was squeezed to death.

Wilhelm, Xamus, and Torin pressed forward, blades flashing and slicing, carving the enemy to amorphous pieces. Froedric and the other bears charged as well, and it was not uncommon for a single ursine swipe to shred three of the enemy at one time, though the bears made for larger targets and were also absorbing severe damage.

Torin stormed ahead, the Axe of Dominion a blur of motion in his hands as he whirled and slashed in every direction in a constant state of motion that allowed his foes no angle of attack for any significant length of time. His eyes blazed with battle lust. As with the others, Torin felt the power of the Auroboros thrumming in his veins, making him an unparalleled force to be reckoned with. The disadvantage of his furor was that in the heat of the conflict, he drew no distinction between friend or foe, making his comrades just as vulnerable to his whistling blade as the enemy, something Wilhelm learned when Torin's axe came near enough to glance off the upper sleeve of the bard's mail shirt.

Though Wilhelm moved away, he too was swept up in the frenzy of the moment, overcome by a sensation of near invincibility that drove him deep into enemy ranks but also left him open to multiple strikes. Nonetheless, the sword and dagger he took from fallen Order-Militant soldiers at Kannibus Hills exacted a monumental toll.

Not far away, Xamus found himself struggling against the upswelling of Auroboros energies within him, powers that threatened to suddenly erupt, with or without his participation. The scales were tipped when a shadow-wolf vanished and reappeared in an empty space next to him, locking jaws on Xamus's wrist and causing him to drop his sword. A dagger to the throat dispatched the beast, but what came after was not of his own doing—he felt the Serpent-force like a pressure requiring instant release; he shut his eyes, planted his feet in the rain-soaked earth, and faced the enemy as a wave of energy exploded outward. The Serpent-force ripped through the attacking swarm, cutting a swath across the entire length of the field with the effect of a mammoth, invisible plowshare cleaving a top layer of soil. With the blast expended, Xamus, out of breath, reclaimed the dropped sword with his opposite hand and peered into the rain, feeling deep and immediate regret at the sight of several avian defenders falling from above the furrow he had unintentionally created in the enemy masses.

Darylonde's scimitar made short work of a shadow-beast throng that swarmed the siege tower. He gazed out over the battlefield, eyes roving to the north, not yet seeing what he desperately hoped for. As with the other outlaws, the Wildkeeper felt the surge of the Auroboros. In his case, the greatest concentration he was subjected to was not from the land but from the storm overhead, and as the storm intensified, so too did the Serpent-force. Even now, as thunder boomed, he felt the furious energy of the tempest raising the hairs on his skin. Then, in an instant, the powers of the maelstrom were unleashed. Lightning arced down in jagged forks all across the beast-army, incinerating entire clusters. A bolt struck also the upright arm of the stone-thrower, splitting it in half, sending a long, heavy section of timber down toward the combatants, including an unaware jungle-cat defender.

Wilhelm, spotting the threat, reacted immediately, darting to his right, diving into the flank of the panther, the two of them barely getting clear as the sheared pole toppled, raising miniature waves on either side and destroying a score of attackers. In the tower above, Darylonde whispered a prayer of thanks, knowing that the Auroboros energy had somehow channeled *through* him.

Atop the low rise behind the siege machines, Asteria and her companions clashed with a small pack of attackers who had managed to bypass the defenses. The three fought bravely, kicking, stomping, and goring, suffering grievous wounds all the while, none more than Bolden, who withstood repeated biting from enemies that relocated from the ground to his back, clamping down on his crest and slashing at his neck.

Darylonde observed the assault on the Caretaker and her comrades. He took one last look at the northern end of the field and in a flash of lightning witnessed at last what he had been waiting for: a tapering in the heretofore endless stream of shadow. He reached for a horn that he had slung on one shoulder, brought it to his lips, and blew. With the signal given, he then leaped from the tower onto the frame of the stone-thrower and then to the ground, rushing to Asteria's aid.

It had been torture for Oldavei to hide along with his wolf allies behind the bulwarks in the forest to the west of the field, awaiting the call from Darylonde. The ma'ii in his coyote form, along with the wolves, had made short work of any stray shadow-beasts that phased through the wall, but those incidents did little to appease his overwhelming desire to join the melee and fight alongside his friends. Long before the assault began, however, Darylonde had convinced the shaman that his involvement in the battle and the timing of his and the wolves' arrival was key. The same was to be said for the bison who held positions inside the forest along the eastern edge of the Thousand Springs.

With the sounding of the horn, Oldavei led the charge from the tree line into the western flank of the surge, taking the invaders completely by surprise, fanning out, ripping enemy chargers to inky ribbons, and driving a deep wedge into the rampaging throng. Oldavei especially relied on his heightened instinct, sensing the presence of enemy beasts as they disappeared and reappeared, leaping over the backs of his fellows in some cases to thrash attackers the instant they materialized.

On the eastern side a very similar episode unfolded as the bison tore through the marauders, goring and trampling, hooves pounding the mud and grass and quaking the earth. In the space of just a few moments, the herd fully wiped out a third of the enemy that remained. Despite suffering heavy casualties, the bison never slowed their advance, only halting once they met Oldavei and his lupine compatriots in the center of the battlefield. The two groups then spread outward once again to take up the width of the field, turning their combined attention northward to what remained of the rear assault force, losing more of their own but nevertheless laying waste to every enemy in their path. To the south the line of defenders who had advanced over nearly a quarter of the field destroyed the final shadow-wolves, and with that, the battle at long last ended.

As the deluge tapered off, the blood of fallen defenders continued to stain the earth, including that of Bolden, who succumbed to his injuries before Oldavei could reach him and administer aid. Darylonde spoke words of tribute over the fallen unicorn, as did Asteria. The Wildkeeper then accompanied the Caretaker as she stepped out onto the rain-and-crimson-slicked pasture.

Xamus's heart was heavy at the sight of the fallen birds, several of whom represented losses he himself inflicted through the use of the Auroboros. Asteria's gaze lingered briefly on him as she assessed the carnage and destruction the battle had wrought. Scores of dead littered the field from end to end. Some animals still cried out in pain. Oldavei, back in ma'ii form and ignoring his own wounds for now, tended to the most severely hurt, steadily watchful of his practice, ready to abort at the first sign of worsening an injury rather than healing it.

"Arakalah!" Asteria called. The eagle, missing a few feathers now from her left wing, came and landed a few steps away. "Will you go to my alcove and retrieve the acorn? You know the one."

The queen glanced at Darylonde. "Yes, of course," she said, taking wing.

The surviving animals all gathered around Asteria. Froedric, limping from an injured foreleg, came and stood next to Wilhelm, who bled from wounds that were many but superficial. A battered and bloodied Torin hobbled his way to the inner circle as well.

"We paid a heavy price," Asteria said solemnly. "But after all these years, the enemy has been defeated." She looked to Darylonde. "Thanks to you. I don't believe we would have survived without your knowledge and leadership . . ." She turned her gaze to Xamus, Oldavei—who was treating a terribly maimed black bear—Torin, and Wilhelm. "Likewise, we would not have triumphed without your courage and determination. And so I thank you."

Overhead, the clouds at last broke. Sunlight reflected off the spring water and bathed the pastures in a warm and golden hue.

Arakalah flew back, holding an acorn in her talons.

"Darylonde," Asteria said, "hold out your hand."

The Wildkeeper complied. Arakalah dropped the nut into his open palm and landed nearby as Asteria continued. "As a means of expressing my gratitude for all that you've done, I gift you this sacred acorn. Its power is great. Even as death is but one revolution in the great cycle, the acorn will bring forth *new* life, wherever it is needed most."

With tears streaming down his grubby cheeks, Darylonde clutched the acorn to his chest, speaking his thanks for the gift and knowing exactly where he wished to plant it.

PART FOUR: THE NORTHWILDS

PART FIVE

UNTO THE ENDING
OF THE WORLD

CHAPTER SEVENTY-FIVE

LAST STOP AT KANNIBUS HILLS

The journey south, including the crossing of the Barrier Pass, occurred over the course of several days without incident. Wilhelm wrote all the while on what he called his "anthem." At various points throughout the course of the journey, when Xamus slept, he found his mind revisiting the painting from the keep in the Hearthvale Foothills—the young man on horseback staring at the suit of armor. Still, after all this time, Xamus grasped for its meaning. Each of those mornings he awoke wondering why the image continued to vex him.

The journey afforded ample time also for discussing the powers of the Auroboros, and specifically how it operated through some of them at the battle of the Thousand Springs. In that conflict they had been relatively fortunate that the energies did not cause more casualties on their own side, but the encounter also provided irrefutable proof that none of them possessed the means to control or direct the power of the World-Serpent. And while the Auroboros's influence was less concentrated when they returned to the lands of the south, they still sensed that power, like a pack of ravenous wolves waiting just beyond the campfire light. Xamus especially found himself wondering what form the World-Serpent would take through the vessel of Tikanen—would he also manifest some monstrous Serpent-Storm to scour the face of the world? The elf thought not, though he couldn't put his finger on why. Yet whatever form the cult's wrath took, Xamus had no doubt that it would be just as terrifying, powerful, and destructive as that which the insane drow Xan'gro had unleashed.

On top of it all, Xamus's thoughts were increasingly occupied with something else: his people in Feyonnas and the enclave he had once called home. Following all that he had seen in the Northwilds, the elf noted that he viewed his kin in a different kind of light. Having a better understanding of what his ancestors struggled with, of the powers arrayed against them in the north, caused a large degree of the animosity he held against the inhabitants of Feyonnas to subside. A small measure of bitterness remained, however, as well as questions. He understood now why his mentor Illarion might have wanted to keep the knowledge of Auroboros from him, but the biggest unanswered question of all was simply this: How much did the elves of Feyonnas know about the World-Serpent? Given that they possessed an entire tome dedicated to it, Xamus suspected that they knew a great deal.

Despite resting each night, the group maintained a brisk pace, and each of the outlaws was travel weary as they traversed the foothills of Mount Effron in the shadow of the Bear Mound. Here Darylonde noted once again the silence of the woods and was reminded of the scene that greeted them when they last came to Kannibus Hills, producing a melancholy that was only heightened by the sight at Oram's Rest and the burned-out husk of the ancient oak, along with the continued absence of what had once been an enchanted, ever-present breeze that Darylonde often thought might have been the spirit of old Oram himself.

The Wildkeeper led them to the Grove of Lights, where nothing of Woodsong remained but the stone stage and the earthen, tiered pit. Darylonde descended, stepped to the center of the open space where the Silver Spring had once been, and there he knelt, retrieved, and set aside the sacred acorn gifted by Asteria and began scooping up soft dirt. Though the others wished to help, they sensed, without the Wildkeeper saying as much, that it was an act he wished to conduct on his own. They stood at ground level, watching silently and reverently as Darylonde dug a two-foot hole, gingerly placed the acorn inside, and returned the displaced soil.

Oldavei turned then at the scent of someone approaching from the trailhead of the southern woods, hand on his scimitar grip. All eyes fell on the newcomer. Darylonde, who was in the midst of ascending the earthen steps, shouted, "Lara!"

The Wildkeeper ran to the druid and embraced her, then pulled back, gazing into her eyes. "I thought I'd lost you," he said, voice breaking. The druid appeared fatigued, unkempt, even aged since the last time the group had seen her. "I'm so glad to see you," Darylonde said.

"I wasn't here when it happened," Lara said, looking forlornly toward the open pit. "But a part of me died with them. With this place." She returned her attention to Darylonde. "And you? Where have you been? How have you escaped Ironside and his Enforcers this long?"

Thus began a lengthy recount held in the seating area of the former amphitheater, wherein Darylonde and the others relayed to Lara their experiences from the time they had last seen her before departing for Baker to the present day. Most importantly, they spoke of the Auroboros and the dangers it posed.

Lara sat silently at the end of the telling and gave careful consideration.

"Our concern," Xamus said, "is that Tikanen will attempt something similar to what Xan'gro did."

Lara nodded. "You've missed quite a bit since you left. Lawbrand is already burning. Weeks ago, the Children, with their unparalleled zealotry, marched out from the desert to begin their righteous war."

"So it's begun," Wilhelm said.

"Are we too late?" Oldavei asked.

"Lietsin has been under siege for two weeks and seems primed to fall. If it does, I believe the Children will march on Tidesfar next, maybe try to commandeer its fleet. And after that . . . they could sail unopposed to the capital and bring ruin to the very heart of Lawbrand."

"The cathedral," Xamus said, to which Lara nodded.

Wilhelm rose and began pacing. "Fek me," Torin said. Oldavei placed both hands atop his head.

"The local constabularies are no match for the might that's being brought against them," Lara continued. "Tikanen has priests—the Ash'ahand—who wield flame spells beyond anything I've ever witnessed. There are strange armored soldiers as well—Ash'ahar. And the cult uses enormous siege engines that launch massive, exploding projectiles."

"The Bloodstone Shale," Torin said. "Just as we feared."

"Where are the Knight-Paladins in the midst of all this?" Darylonde asked.

"The Order-Militant's been recalled to Sargrad to protect the capital. In doing so, they've left the Trade-Cities to fend for themselves."

"Sons o' fekkin' bitches!" Torin spat. Wilhelm's hands curled into fists.

Xamus looked to Oldavei. "You said it yourself, we need to make them listen. Make them see. Maybe there's still time to do that. I think I know where to begin . . . but it'll be the most dangerous thing we've ever done."

"That's saying a lot," Oldavei replied.

"I don't care how dangerous it is," Torin said. "I've had my fill of these cultist fekkers. Time to put 'em down like dogs."

Wilhelm nodded. "It's time for us to get into the fight. No matter how bad it gets."

Lara glanced at the center of the pit. "I'll be damned," she said, standing up and walking to where a single willowy stem sprouted from where Darylonde had planted the acorn. The sprout bore three leaves at the top, leaves which appeared to be that of a beech tree, the same tree type that Goshaedas had been.

"I didn't think there would be any new growth here," Lara said. "Ever again."

Darylonde went and stood next to Lara. "Even as the world falls to pieces," he said softly, "hope blooms."

PART FIVE: UNTO THE ENDING OF THE WORLD

CHAPTER SEVENTY-SIX

TRUTH BE TOLD

Throughout the Cathedral Square at Sargrad, at the foot of the gargantuan Cathedral of Saint Varina, a detachment of very anxious Order-Militant Peacekeepers on foot and horseback waited at the ready. The late afternoon sun reflected blindingly from the glass and polished steel of the cathedral. The streets, normally overflowing with citizens and travelers, were empty save for roving soldier patrols. Shopkeepers huddled nervously behind closed doors.

Near the court's center, a crackling sound attracted the attention of two foot soldiers. The air became energized, and it seemed as though an invisible hand pushed from above, causing the men to move aside. In the next instant, the outlaws appeared, nearly six feet above the paving stones, floating for just a second in midair before falling heavily to the ground.

Xamus stood with a slight groan, holding his stomach.

Torin rose, leaning forward with both hands on his knees. "What the fek do you think we are, birds?"

"Didn't go one hundred percent according to plan," the elf admitted. "But I got us here."

Xamus was surprised that the spell had worked at all. There were, he understood, a thousandfold ways in which it could have gone wrong, but asking all of his companions to think of and focus on the space in front of the cathedral as he spoke the words and opened himself to the Auroboros—inviting the wolves to the campfire—had miraculously carried them across the realm from Kannibus Hills to Sargrad in an instant. The elf didn't know whether to be relieved or not. Time would tell.

The surrounding Peacekeepers, initially thunderstruck to see five strangers suddenly appear in their midst, drew weapons and circled the group.

"Tell your bosses," Wilhelm called out, "that the most wanted criminals in Lawbrand . . . the ones Ironside kept looking for but could never actually *catch* . . . are here to see 'em!"

The soldiers hesitated, looking to the nearest Marshall-Captain on horseback, who appeared unsure of how to proceed. He finally pointed to a Peacekeeper near the steps. "You, go!"

"And make it quick!" Torin shouted.

The outlaws waited, facing the cathedral. Moments later the massive iron-strapped doors opened. Ironside stepped into the light.

"How's the face?" Wilhelm called.

A breeze blew through the square, flicking the Knight-Paladin's gray-streaked hair and the fur-fringed cape that hung on one shoulder. His good eye, along with the white eye behind the half-iron mask, fixed on the travelers as he descended the wide steps and strode into the plaza, flanged mace slung on his back, sunlight reflecting off his silver Lawbrand breastplate.

Several more Peacekeepers exited the cathedral and staged on the landing at the top of the stairs.

Darylonde caught movement from the corner of his eye and looked up and to the right to see the archer Daromis taking a position on a shop roof, bow at the ready. Between two shops on the left side, soldiers parted to make way for the humpbacked crone, hobbling forth in a squatting position, her bent, withered arm held close to her chest, leaning with the other on a gnarled wooden staff.

Shopkeepers on either side of the square and thoroughfare leading to the cathedral waited at their windows, watching and listening.

Ironside stood with his thick arms folded over his barrel chest. "So," he said, "you lawless shits have finally had enough of life on the run."

Xamus stepped forward. "Yes, we broke your laws," he said. "And maybe we deserve justice for all that we've done, but for right now, if you high and mighty assholes want Lawbrand to survive, you'll listen to—"

"I've heard plenty," Ironside said. "Kill these—"

"No!" came a commanding female voice from a balcony high above the giant cathedral doors. There, in her dark robes, stood the Grand-Justiarch of the Sularian Church, Laravess Kelwynde. As all eyes watched, six red-robed Cardinals appeared as well, flanking her, three to each side.

"I know these men," she said. "They saved many of us from the Malisath at the Theatre Massacre. Whatever else they might have done . . . I will hear what they have to say."

By way of answer, Ironside turned his head and spat.

"We've been to the north," Xamus said. "There we've seen the remains of a once-mighty place, a city that would have made Sargrad look like a quaint village. There's nothing left of it but rubble. Because of power wielded by one crazed individual. A drow, who unleashed a force that scoured the north and would have destroyed the entire world if he hadn't been stopped."

"Does your history lesson have a point, or are you stalling for time?" Ironside interjected.

"The *point*," Xamus continued, "is that the very same power is being used against Lawbrand even now by the Children of the Sun and by their leader, Tikanen. We know this because we spent a year enslaved by the cult beneath the ziggurat at Tanasrael."

Citizens began entering the square, many having left their homes upon hearing the exchange. Shopkeepers exited their stores as well, stepping tentatively into the thoroughfare.

Xamus went on: "As we speak, Lietsin is under siege. A city is burning, and its citizens are dying while you cower here in safety and look to your own survival."

"It's pathetic," Wilhelm said.

Oldavei spoke next. "The people of Lawbrand look to you," he said, "to both lead and to serve. To protect."

Torin called out, "You're nothin' but a bunch o' whores!" This drew gasps from the citizenry and an eyebrow lift from the Grand-Justiarch. "Sold out to power"—he stared at Ironside—"and your own delusions o' grandeur!" His eyes swept the Peacekeepers. "If any o' you fekkers had an ounce of honor or courage . . . you'd be on the front lines right now."

"And you're the worst of them all," Darylonde accused, gloved finger pointing at Ironside. "How many hundreds of civilians died as you hunted us across the realm? How many murders have you committed in the name of the church? You slaughtered"—here his voice broke, his teeth bared as he continued—"an entire community of peaceful druids . . ."

"It's not my fault they broke under questioning," Ironside answered.

PART FIVE: UNTO THE ENDING OF THE WORLD

"You butchered them to exact revenge," Darylonde answered. "On us! For evading you, for making you look foolish. You went beyond your jurisdiction and outside your mandate in order to heal your wounded pride. You exemplify everything the church claims to abhor."

"Maybe the Children have it right," Oldavei said. "If the church has truly fallen so far, maybe civilization does deserve to burn."

"Enough!" Ironside yelled.

"Not yet," Grand-Justiarch Kelwynde said.

"Matters of the military are *my* purview!" Ironside bellowed to the balcony. "These are nothing but lawless scum! Thieves and insurrectionists!" His blazing eyes locked on the party. "You know nothing of honor or courage. Everything I've done I'd do a hundred times over, in the name of justice."

The Cardinals, clearly shocked by the damning admission, looked to the Justiarch as Ironside turned to the outlaws and continued: "Now the time for justice has come. You've been judged and found guilty, and I'm very happy to announce that your sentence is death. Execute them," he said, looking to the crone, then up at Daromis. "Now!"

Though Daromis had an arrow nocked, he did not aim. Conflict raged across his dryad features. The crone, as well, hesitated, shifting weight from one foot to another, trembling slightly and making mewling noises.

"Fek's sake, I said kill them!" Ironside bellowed. Still, the two waited, unsure.

"You!" Ironside yelled to a Peacekeeper standing to his right, a young man who looked to be barely twenty. The soldier tightened his sword grip, but stayed in place, looking up to the Grand-Justiarch, who stared back in silence.

Ironside clenched his teeth, growled, and threw a straight left punch that smashed the man's nose through the open-faced helm and sent him crumpling to the ground.

As one, the outlaws advanced, weapons drawn. Ironside turned to the party, drew his mace, and took two steps, weapon held high—but Wilhelm was there, one hand on the Knight-Paladin's wrist, arresting the blow. He thrust his scimitar up under Ironside's upraised arm. Oldavei circled quickly behind, shoving a dagger into the Knight-Paladin's lower back. Torin snarled, lunged, and buried the Axe of Dominion high on Ironside's left thigh. The dwarf stepped back, leaving the axe lodged, as Darylonde came and wedged his sword up and under the silver the breastplate and mail on the left side. Xamus stepped forward and plunged a dagger—taken from one of Ironside's own soldiers at Kannibus Hills before the group left for the north—into the Knight-Paladin's throat.

Ironside's terrified eyes bulged, looking to either side for aid from his Enforcers or Peacekeepers. A single spurt of blood issued from his mouth as his body turned to dead weight. The outlaws retrieved their weapons and stepped away. Ironside fell back onto the stones, his horrified gaze fixed skyward as blood began to pool beneath him.

For a moment, there was complete silence and stillness. Soldiers looked to one another; a few on each side looked to the nearest Marshall-Captain, who nodded. The Peacekeepers moved to detain the outlaws, but the Justiarch's voice froze them: "Take no action unless I order it!"

Xamus wiped the dagger blade on his dungarees. "You can arrest us if you want," he called out, looking up at the Grand-Justiarch.

"They can try," Torin said, stepping to Xamus's side.

"Or"—he turned and scanned the crowd of Peacekeepers, citizens and shopkeepers—"you can do the right thing: focus on what's important and defend your people from annihilation." The elf spared a glance up at Daromis, then looked over at the crone.

No one moved. All eyes looked expectantly to the Justiarch, who said, "'Order' means nothing if the innocent perish in its enforcement." Her eyes turned to Ironside's bloody corpse. "I feel that justice has been served. Let them go."

The outlaws turned and walked down the center of the thoroughfare, shoulder to shoulder, Peacekeepers moving out of their path. The citizens and shopkeepers made way as well, staring at them in awe as they passed.

At the cross street, a familiar carriage pulled up. The door opened, and Archemus Strand leaned out.

"Are you *determined* to get yourselves killed?" the old man said. "Never mind, get in!"

PART FIVE: UNTO THE ENDING OF THE WORLD

CHAPTER SEVENTY-SEVEN

PASSAGE

"How'd you know we were here?" Wilhelm asked, seated at the carriage window, squeezed against Torin and Darylonde.

Strand sat directly across, along with Xamus and Oldavei. "Have you forgotten so soon?" the old man replied, grinning. "I have spies all over the city. Nevertheless, I wasn't jesting a moment ago—I truly believed I'd arrive to find you dead."

"We had to come," Xamus said.

"The druids have spies also," Darylonde informed. "It's their belief that if Lietsin falls, Tidesfar will be next."

"The Bohen Dur monks and I came to the same conclusion," Strand replied. "Piotr and the others are on their way even now to assist in Tidesfar's defense." The carriage jostled. Strand cleared his throat. "I should say, I was very sorry to hear of your friend, Nicholas. He was a good man."

"Yes he was," Xamus said.

Strand continued: "I heard tell of your further exploits, including the performance at RevelSLAM, but not much after."

Oldavei spoke up: "Let's just say we learned enough to understand what kind of power the Children of the Sun wield. All of Lawbrand is at danger if they're not stopped. We mean to oppose them in any way we can."

"I assume you'll want to go to the bay, then," Strand said.

"We have access to immediate transport," Wilhelm replied, smiling widely at Xamus.

"We were lucky today," the elf replied. "In more ways than one. We may *not* be so lucky the next time I try to teleport us." He turned to Strand. "Yeah, take us to the bay. We'll charter a boat."

"No need for a charter," Strand answered. He stuck his head partially out the window. "Driver! To the Front Bay, quickly!"

"Sir!" came the answer.

The carriage made good time. As they pulled close to the docks, Strand said, "Slip ninety-nine. You'll recognize the boat and captain." The outlaws thanked the old man and exited. "The monks and my people will do everything in our power to assist in the war effort," Strand said. "You have my word."

The outlaws offered thanks, said farewell, and proceeded to the designated slip, where they found a familiar single-masted cog, the *One Fine Day*, and her curly-haired captain, Chopper.

"Hello friends," Chopper called from the boat. "Come aboard, hurry! Word's just come in: the walls at Lietsin are breached; the city has all but fallen." The outlaws boarded as Chopper began untying the mooring lines. "We're for Tidesfar, then?" he asked.

Xamus confirmed while Wilhelm helped with the ropes. Moments later the *One Fine Day* was sailing for open water.

The captain offered his condolences for the loss of Nicholas as the party gathered near him at the helm. "There've been reports," Chopper said, "of enormous, unnatural sandstorms blowing across the Bay of Tidesfar for the last two days."

Xamus remembered the raging sands that followed them out of the desert following their escape from Tanasrael. "The cultists," he said.

"But why send sandstorms over—" Oldavei began.

"To keep the ships from putting out to sea," Wilhelm said.

"Lara was right," Darylonde concluded. "They're coming for the fleet."

"How long?" Xamus asked Chopper.

"To Tidesfar? Three days, but if the dust storms are still blowin'—"

"Just get us as close as you can," Xamus said.

The group discussed some initial strategies, and with the setting of the sun retreated to the hold, where they reacquainted themselves with Chopper's beloved grog. "It's been far too long since we've all gotten hamro!" Torin announced happily.

"Hamro," Wilhelm chuckled. Xamus rolled a smoke, and the others partook of pipe-weed with the captain. Further alcohol consumption led to nostalgic recollections from their first meetings—"I knew I was in trouble the minute you said you couldn't ride a horse," Xamus said to Oldavei—to the various adventures they had experienced and all the colorful personalities they had encountered along the way. "Rhoman," Oldavei recalled fondly. "Crazy dust-runner! That man was my idol."

Late into the night they lay in their hammocks, joining with Chopper in the singing of sea shanties while Wilhelm played the aethari, until they passed out, grog bottles still in hand.

The next morning, Wilhelm found Xamus at the boat's aft on the port side, elbows on the handrail, seemingly lost in thought while Chopper manned the helm nearby.

"Ugh," Wilhelm said. "All that grog and smoking gave me a damn headache."

"That just means you didn't drink enough!" Chopper called as the bard joined Xamus at the rail.

The elf seemed not to notice as he stared out at the water. Wilhelm waved a hand in front of his face. "What's got you so preoccupied?" he asked.

"It's that stupid painting," Xamus admitted. "From the keep."

"The kid on the horse lookin' at the armor?" Wilhelm asked.

Xamus nodded. "Haven't been able to stop thinking about it, and I'll be damned if I know why."

Wilhelm leaned on the rail and looked out. "Art's intensely personal, man. It means what you want it to mean, you know? It can be different for everybody. It could even be different depending on what's going on in your life."

Xamus considered. Was he projecting himself into the painting? Were the questions of the painting related to his own questions about the enclave and the choices he made? Did he feel that the young man had turned his back on his home and his family, and if so, did that mean the piece conjured some kind of subconscious guilt associated with Xamus leaving his people? This in turn made him think of the book with the Auroboros symbol on the cover that his mentor had withheld from him in the library—just one of a hundred things that had driven Xamus away. But again, it caused him to wonder just how much his people truly knew of the World-Serpent. And whether or not that knowledge would

PART FIVE: UNTO THE ENDING OF THE WORLD

be helpful in their fight against Tikanen.

He turned to Chopper and said, "We're making a stop before we get to Tidesfar. I'll show you where."

"Aye, aye," the captain replied.

"Where we goin'?" Wilhelm asked.

"To a place that doesn't exist," Xamus answered.

CHAPTER SEVENTY-EIGHT
HOMECOMING

Three hours later at low tide, at a location indicated by Xamus, the *One Fine Day* beached.

"If you don't hear from us when high tide comes," the elf said, "don't wait around. We'll find our own way from here."

"In case we don't see you," Oldavei said. "Thanks. For everything."

"I can't say it's been boring," Chopper said with a wry smile. "Good fortune, my friends."

The outlaws disembarked and began hiking inland, with Xamus leading the way. They passed into the lush Illian forest, accompanied by musical birdcalls as they traversed the soft earth, coming at one point to a gnoll camp composed of huts with hide stretched over wooden frames. Thankfully, the dog-people were nowhere to be seen. Skirting the settlement, the party pressed on, observing at times ancient stones and rubble grown over with moss and vine. "The remains of ancient peoples," Xamus said. "There are ruins throughout the forest. Different civilizations, including, some say, the Salamar empire of Ax'oloth."

Thus far, the elf had explained only that the people of his enclave of Feyonnas might hold knowledge that could aid in their battle against the Children. Deep in the forest, after a few hours of trekking, the outlaws trailing Xamus perceived that they had perhaps crossed some invisible barrier. Birdcalls cut off in midtune. The ground changed texture beneath their feet. Insect noises ceased, and the very air felt different—heavy and still, yet charged with some form of energy. And while sound seemed muted, colors here appeared more vibrant, appearing in variations among the flora that had not been present elsewhere in the forest. High above, glowing sprites darted among the branches and leaves, cavorting amid the narrow sunbeams that pierced the canopy.

"We've come to the Leywild," Xamus advised. "A kind of between place."

"Between what and what?" Torin asked suspiciously.

"The world you know," Xamus answered, "and a piece of another world, maintained by magic, hidden from outsiders."

"Your home," Oldavei said.

"The enclave of my people," Xamus answered.

In time they came to a what looked to be simply a wooded hillside. Closer observation revealed a network of thorned bough and vine interlaced with bountiful buds and blossoms set against the earthen face, forming a roughly circular pattern twice Wilhelm's height and four times Torin's width.

Here Xamus kneeled, whispering the words of his elders and reaching out to touch leaves draped inside the circle before him.

Small creaking and groaning sounds arose as the boughs moved, loosening, disentangling; foliage laid over the space inside the circle pulled back and away, disclosing not a hillside but a descending, stony corridor. With one look at the others, Xamus said, "Come on," and plunged in.

The passage was only dimly illuminated, though no light source was immediately visible. The tunnel continued down, flattened for several paces, then rose steadily.

"They'll know we're here," Xamus said over his shoulder. "Not sure what kind of reception we'll get."

What began as a pinprick of sharp light slowly took the shape of a terminus as they steadily advanced, emerging at last into bright sunshine and the soft gush of nearby waterfalls.

They walked to the edge of a grassy earthen terrace that offered a stunning view of the enclave in its entirety: pathways wound among glistening lakes and pools that appeared to glow with an inner light. Domed and peaked structures of varying sizes, built in an architectural style altogether foreign to the group, save for Xamus, dotted the landscape. Splendorous gardens bloomed in abundance, particularly in the center of the community. All along the periphery, thick limbs extended and wove together to form elevated spans and walkways between enormous trees that housed smaller domiciles in their leafy branches. To the group's left, a domineering structure, as elegant as it was massive, jutted from the mountainside between cascading falls.

The sanctum, bounded on all sides by cliff and forest, gave every impression of a place tucked away from the world, existing in seclusion and what appeared to be relative peace, though each of the outlaws could now feel an underlying presence . . .

"It's here," Darylonde said. "The Auroboros."

Heads nodded all around. "I never felt it before," Xamus said. "Or maybe I did on some small level, and I just didn't understand what I was feeling."

"I'd say there's a great deal you don't understand." A female stepped out from a side path that led from the giant building between the falls. Her head was adorned with a decorative tiara; silky blonde hair, parted on either side by pointed ears, flowed onto her shoulders and down her back. She wore an intricately patterned, layered robe that reflected the sun's rays.

"You made your choice long ago," the woman said, her harsh expression mirroring her tone.

"Hello, Shallandra," Xamus said.

"You traded knowledge for reckless and childish pursuits," the female continued, eyes locked on Xamus, ignoring the others. "You left. You turned your back on your people, and you denied your heritage."

"I tasted freedom," Xamus answered.

"Something the rest of us have sacrificed," Shallandra shot back, "for the greater good. You are, and always have been, selfish."

"The knowledge I sought here was denied me," Xamus replied with an edge to his voice.

"You speak of the book," a smooth male voice broke in. Xamus's former mentor, Illarion, stepped from a path opposite that which Shallandra had taken. The teacher wore robes similar to the female's but simpler in design. His hair was as long as his colleague's but a rich, dark brown. His eyes were the iridescent green of emeralds.

"Had I allowed you to keep the tome, would you have even read it? Or would you have skimmed the pages, looking for a shortcut, as you always did? How many times did I tell you, you cannot just 'feel your way' through magic. It requires time and careful study. Dedication, patience . . . all of which you lacked. You would never listen; you always knew better. I took that book away from you because you were simply not mature enough to grasp its secrets."

Xamus felt a familiar anger well up within him; here he was being scolded once again like some misbehaving child, and yet, the elf had to admit . . .

"There's truth to what you say," Xamus replied.

Illarion lifted a brow.

"I was prideful," Xamus continued. "And yes, I was selfish," he looked to Shallandra. "I was frustrated with being caged in this refuge. So I left, but I never *denied* my heritage. I simply chose not to draw attention to it."

"And now you've returned," Shallandra said. "Accompanied by strangers, no less." And here she passed her gaze briefly over the others.

"I've returned because I've gained knowledge," Xamus said. "I—we, have been to the north. We know now what happened long ago—with Xan'gro and Galandil, the Black Tower, the Serpent-Storm. I've . . . changed. I've *learned*. A lot. About the Auroboros, the World-Serpent, what it is, what it's capable of." Shallandra and Illarion shared a look. "What happened before is going to happen again, if we"—he gestured to his friends—"don't stop it. And to do that, I believe we're gonna have to channel the Auroboros, despite the knowledge—the acceptance—that we aren't proficient enough to control it. And so we came here, hoping that maybe you could provide some guidance."

The other two elves remained silent, contemplating.

Torin cleared his throat. "It's a shitty world out there," the dwarf said, earning a slight widening of the older elves' eyes. "But it's one worth saving."

"I leave this to you," Shallandra said to Illarion before turning and walking back the way she came.

Illarion lowered his head for a moment. "Your return was foreseen," the teacher said. "As were the events you describe."

"Visions," Xamus said.

"Just because we shelter here does not mean that we are blind. Something else you never understood."

Xamus bit back a retort as Illarion approached. "Hold out your hands," he said, holding his own out, palms up, to demonstrate.

With only a brief hesitation, Xamus complied.

Illarion whispered, gestured. A thick tome materialized on top of Xamus's palms, growing heavy as it solidified. Once fully manifested, Xamus recognized the serpent symbol on its leather cover, scales glinting in the sun.

"You say you've changed," Illarion spoke, indicating the book. "I invite you to prove it."

PART FIVE: UNTO THE ENDING OF THE WORLD

CHAPTER SEVENTY-NINE

A DIRE WARNING

The outlaws spent the next five hours in the Library of Atesh'ar, one of the largest tree constructions in the refuge, composed of multiple structures, some peaked and some domed, with shelves upon shelves of books, tomes, and scrolls lining the inner walls, and open balconies facing the enclave, where the day's light had begun to wane.

Xamus sat at a table and read aloud to the others from the Auroboros book. It was an eye-opening and astonishing read, chronicling not only the history of the Serpent power in the north—the only part Xamus skimmed, confirming several points of which he was already aware—but a parallel history as well, one that the elf had remained completely unaware of over the course of countless years. Long before Xan'gro's unleashing of the Serpent-Storm, when the drow began their purge of the elves in the north, a handful of families fled; they ventured into the Tanaroch Desert, happening upon the ruins of a forgotten race—the Aldan Thei—at Tanasrael. Beneath the desert sands they created the Auroboros mosaic, meant as a warning to any who would dare attempt to channel its energies.

The refugees then traveled to the Illian Forest, where they employed magic to hide themselves away from the world. That much, Xamus had known; what he had *not* known—and what was most surprising of all—was that the elves tapped Auroboros energies buried deep beneath the woodlands to accomplish their incredible feat.

Those magical workings sparked fearsome repercussions, chief among them being that elves within the sorcerous field could not age or reproduce. The nearly immortal elves would never die but instead spend eternity in a kind of timeless stasis. It was one of the many things that Xamus found unacceptable about "life" in the refuge.

He understood now that the ramifications were a side effect of channeling the World-Serpent's energies.

When he explained all of this to the others, questions were raised.

"Were you not born here?" Wilhelm asked.

Xamus answered, "When the drow slaughtered the high elves, my family didn't flee with the other survivors. For whatever reason, they stayed in Old Sularia and hid among the humans, took the name Frood to better blend in, moving from place to place, keeping their true nature hidden for centuries. I would have been very young when the Breakwar came, and later, when the Serpent-Storm hit and wiped everything out. I don't remember any of it. What I do know is that everyone in my family except my aunt—Sevestra—was killed in all the chaos. She saved me and took me south. We traveled around for years, living like vagabonds . . . while Lawbrand and its cities took shape."

Xamus smiled wistfully. "I can still remember her face, her smile. Her eyes were kind but sad and always tired. She told me often that after all the hardship and loss, she just wanted me to be safe. We'd heard rumors of Feyonnas, that others of our kind had created a refuge for themselves. After a lot of searching, she found the Threshold and brought me through. I was amazed to see this place. But the first night we spent here, when I awoke, she was gone."

"Why?" Torin asked.

"I found out later that she told Illarion that Feyonnas was not for her. I think once she knew I was okay"—his voice softened—"she just wanted to be done with life. The thought of being trapped here with her grief forever was too much. I never saw her again."

"How old were you when you came here?" Oldavei asked.

"I was an angry, bitter eighteen- or nineteen-year-old, at least the way humans figure age."

"That was hundreds of years ago," Wilhelm said, incredulous.

"Time doesn't pass the same here as it does in the outside world. I lived here a long time, but I never really felt like I belonged. And on some level, I always blamed this place and these people for Sevestra's loss. Eventually I just left, put Feyonnas out of my mind, and never looked back. By the time I met you lowlifes, I'd been on my own in Lawbrand for twenty or so years."

"Gonna start callin' you Grandpa," Torin said.

"Great, great grandpa," Oldavei added with a smile.

Xamus shook his head and looked down at the book. "It always seemed ridiculous to me for the elves to go on maintaining a spell that isolated them, kept them from aging or living any kind of a real life, that prevented them from reproducing. But now I know . . ."

"They were trying to contain the Auroboros," Darylonde said.

Just then the lilting strains of a soft melody reached their ears. In response to the others' looks, Xamus said, "The flowers of the Singing Gardens make music at the end of each day when they blossom to the moonlight."

"Beautiful," Wilhelm said, eyes closed serenely.

Presently, a chorus of voices lifted in accompaniment to the soothing melody of the gardens. These voices seemed to come from everywhere, though the majority could be heard to the east of the archives. Xamus rose and crossed to the arched open-air windows of the balcony facing the largest structure in the refuge, the Shrine of Nar'lithyl. The others soon joined him, looking out to where a host of elves had congregated on the earthen terraces near the top of the structure and along the grounds at its base, their voices raised in a haunting, dirgelike lament.

"I always thought this ritual was sad and pointless," Xamus said. Now, from his reading, the elf was aware that his people used the nightly song to offer up their darkest thoughts and inclinations, some of the most intimate pieces of themselves, meant to appease the serpent, to prevent it from rising to overtake the sanctum in its entirety. The full weight of it hit him, causing emotions that he had locked away for scores of years to swell. He brushed away a tear on his cheek as Oldavei laid a comforting hand on his shoulder.

Even now, as the outlaws watched, they discerned ephemeral energies of varying colors, emitting from the gathered singers, swirling and eddying before drifting down *into* the ground and out of sight, beneath the shrine where, Xamus now knew, the Auroboros existed in its greatest concentration. It was something he had never seen before, as many times as he had watched or participated. It was as if his eyes were truly open for the first time, and he was literally seeing the refuge in a new way.

"There was so much I didn't know," Xamus said. "So much I didn't grasp . . . or care to. I have a greater understanding of sacrifice"—the elf lowered his head—"of what these people sacrifice every day."

"Not just 'these people,'" Illarion said from just a few paces behind them. The outlaws turned. "*Your* people."

Xamus lifted his chin slightly. "Yeah," he said. "My people."

The teacher looked over to the table where the tome sat. "You read the book."

"Yes," Xamus answered.

"So you know there is a way," Illarion said, "to gain some degree of control over the Serpent."

Xamus nodded. There was a section at the very end of the tome that spoke of the elven tattoo artists, the extraordinarily talented Tir'Assar—the very same sigilists whose tattoo art adorned Xamus's body—and something called the Mark of the Serpent. "Of all the chapters in the book, that section was the most ambiguous," Xamus said.

"And with good reason," Illarion replied. "The Mark is capable of conferring a measure of control over the Auroboros to the bearer, that is true. But it is something that must only be taken as a last resort . . . once done, it cannot be undone. Once accepted, it cannot be denied."

"If it can help us corral the Auroboros, it's worth it," Torin said.

"You don't understand," Illarion said. "To control the World-Serpent will take all that you are, every ounce of your being. You will become, in some respects, godlike, but your extraordinary capabilities will be short-lived, for mortals were never intended to command such power. The force of the Auroboros will turn inward and begin to consume itself, eating away at the bravest hearts and devouring the most courageous souls. It is only a matter of time. What I say to you very plainly is this: if you take the Mark, you *will* die."

CHAPTER EIGHTY
THE PIT OF SCALES

"You know how many times I've been told I was gonna die?" Wilhelm whispered to Torin, the two of them trailing as Illarion led the group along a dimly lit passage.

They were descending beneath the Shrine of Nar'lithyl. Here a secret place existed far below the structure, a location hidden from Xamus all the years that he had lived in the refuge. The earthen corridor plunged downward in a constant winding curve. "I wouldn't be too worried," Wilhelm continued. "Besides, we still have to pass the test." Illarion had explained to them that before receiving the Mark, they must undergo "the Ritual."

The concentration of Auroboros energies in the subterranean space was dizzying, even more pronounced than it had been in the Northwilds. Hushed voices drifted through the twisting tunnels, accompanied by a steady *thump, thump* as the party proceeded, noting that the walls were covered in large slabs of overlapping shale, along the surface of which a mysterious, eerie light passed in waves. The glittering stones reminded Xamus of the World-Serpent's skin, causing him to suspect they were also the source of the grotto's name: the Pit of Scales.

The repetitive beat became more pronounced as they arrived at a larger chamber, where Oldavei's rapid sniffing detected a smell of sulphur. The cavern was brightly lit by a glowing pool in the center. In response to a gesture from Illarion, the outlaws circled the pool, staring down at the swirling yellow liquid. Deep within, barely visible, long, thin shadows appeared to glide and sweep.

"Here," Illarion advised, "you may or may not see a vision; the outcome will determine if you are fit to receive the Mark."

"We've undergone similar vision quests," Xamus said. "Among the druids."

"Then you have an advantage over the few who came before you," Illarion replied. He motioned to the ground. "Sit." The group complied. "Gaze into the pool."

The outlaws peered into the mesmerizing liquid, adjusting their breathing as they had done in the past at the Bear Mound. The surrounding voices faded; the travelers' heartbeats synchronized with the thumping that reverberated through the chamber as they became lost in the churning light and shadow of the pool.

The vision that flashed suddenly before them was shared by all: a multilimbed tree, nearly incomprehensible in its enormity, with gleaming stars in place of leaves, hovering in an ethereal mist. The World-Serpent, motionless at first, stirred and began to coil slowly around the enormous roots— consuming its own tail in the process—constricting, choking, causing stars to fall from the boughs above. Reflected in the shifting Auroboros scales, the observers beheld elf-like beings in varying forms of attire, some light-skinned, some dark. They chanted with raised hands, eyes closed, seeming to be at once both slave *and* master to the World-Serpent.

In an instant the outlaws were ripped from the revelation, the image of the tree and Serpent replaced once again by the mysterious pool before them.

"What the fek was that?" Wilhelm asked.

Illarion was silent at first. He must have borne witness to the vision as well, for his features were clouded by a mixture of disbelief and unease. Finally, he said, "The vision augured one possible future, a glimpse into the Heart of Creation and a foretelling of what will befall, should the Serpent reawaken: the world, like the stars of the Celestial Crown, would surely fall. Creation would be undone."

"Who were the people?" Wilhelm asked.

"The Aldan Thei?" Xamus offered. "Everything started with them . . ."

"Correct," Illarion confirmed, a hint of surprise in his voice.

"Okay," Torin said, "so did we pass or not?"

"I believe your destinies are tied to the Serpent," Illarion answered. "Your previous interactions with the Auroboros have already established a connection, brought you into an alignment. That bond will be strengthened should the Mark be given. But you must accept it with full knowledge of the consequences."

The outlaws stood. Xamus looked to the others. "Save the world and die trying . . . or sit by while it all burns . . ."

"And die anyway," Oldavei said.

Xamus looked to Illarion. "I'll take the Mark," he said.

"As will I," Darylonde said.

"And I," this from Torin.

"Fek it, I'm in," Wilhelm said.

"There's no other choice," Oldavei added with grim resolve.

"Follow me," Illarion ordered, proceeding farther along the tunnel.

As the outlaws complied, Torin said to the others, "So about the other visions? At the Bear Mound, what was that all about?"

"Most, at first, were guidance," Darylonde said. "Illuminating the path to get us here—the chariots, the caravan, the ziggurat. The next were a mixture of guidance—Eric at the Coliseum—as well as images of things that we clung to desperately: fears and doubts and the burdens that weighed us down."

"I saw the vision that drove me from my people," Oldavei said. "Death by fire. Many of the things we saw, they're the things we had to let go of to find peace. My people have a belief that when we die, the things we hold on to are the things that follow us from this life to the next."

"We're not gonna die," Wilhelm said over his shoulder, walking just behind Illarion.

Torin thought of his vision, not only of the Axe of Dominion, but of the funeral cairns representing his parents, his unknown lineage, a lingering concern that was eased by his time at Mitholme.

Darylonde considered the images he saw, of his dead patrol, his tortured comrades, the nightmares he had forced himself to move past when he had once again taken his leap of faith in the Northwilds.

Wilhelm thought of his own vision at their second visit to the Bear Mound, of the empty arena, and wondered what it was that *he* was still holding on to.

A realization came over Xamus. "I was wrong about the painting," he said to Wilhelm. "I thought the young man was dwelling on the past, grieving for the life and home he was leaving behind. I thought the boy was me or some version of me . . . but he isn't. He's all of us. Not caught up in the past but looking to the future, ready to embrace an all-new responsibility, to turn his back on childhood and reckless youth, to let go of what came before and focus on the task ahead."

"Well, look at you gettin' all profound," Wilhelm said. Xamus smiled. "Like I said, man, the most important thing about art isn't what the creator intended but what the observer takes away from it."

Illarion glanced back but said nothing as he led them to a larger chamber, where the same yellowish, radiant liquid from the pool cascaded down the far wall. Two massive stalactites projected from the stony roof, reaching down and curving inward to resemble giant fangs. Standing beneath these was an elf. More specifically, a Tir'Assar.

The Tir'Assar were among the oldest and most gifted artists in the known world. Recipients of their tattoos were considered living canvasses upon which the sigilists rendered their masterworks, expressions not only of their own style and expertise but also of creativity in its purest form, heedless of expectation, reception, or critical analysis.

The elven artist was especially tall, bedecked in elegant, layered red robes, his long hair meticulously styled, high on top, falling in gently sweeping waves to waist height. He bore shining piercings in his nose, ears, and lower lip. His facial features were made up, and his green eyes were bright. At his feet were various ink bottles filled with glowing liquid. In his right hand was a tattoo needle.

"Welcome," the sigilist said in a deep voice that carried over the gushing of the water. He gestured to the empty space at his side. "Come and embrace your fate."

PART FIVE: UNTO THE ENDING OF THE WORLD

CHAPTER EIGHTY-ONE

THE MARK OF THE SERPENT

One by one, throughout the night, they lay on the hard, wet stone and received the Mark.

The tattoos were the same and yet unique. All were of the Auroboros in a figure eight, consuming its own tail, yet the style of each reflected either the personality or culture of the recipient, sometimes both. Torin's tattoo was angular and sharp in the dwarven style. The colors of Oldavei's Mark were the muted, desaturated hues of his desert people. Darylonde's Serpent was intricately detailed and by far the most realistic in appearance. Wilhelm's was the most expressionistic, exaggerated and abstract in feature and proportion. Xamus's was smooth and elegant, rendered in the elven style of sweeping strokes and rich colors.

Upon completion, all of them felt a staggering surge of energy as well as a connection to the timeless power that slumbered beneath their feet.

"How do you feel?" Illarion asked Xamus.

Xamus's senses were sharpened; his thinking was clearer than it had ever been, his thoughts moving almost too fast for him to keep up with. He extended his hands to either side; there was a deep groan from the stones as the entire tunnel expanded slightly, then contracted. He looked to Illarion.

"Godlike, if I'm being honest," he replied. Looking to the others, Xamus discerned that they were experiencing similar revelations.

"Each of you now holds power beyond your imagining," Illarion said. "The Mark is an impossibly heavy burden. You must steel yourselves and be mindful of your consciousness. One errant thought, one violent musing, could cause those forces to lash out and do irreparable harm, however unintended. You must maintain control of the Auroboros at all times. Traditionally, recipients of the Mark are taught to be extremely judicious with its use. Especially in the early stages."

"We probably won't have the luxury of being judicious," Xamus replied.

"If the powers are used too often and too fast, the bearer's distress and eventual demise will likewise be hastened," Illarion advised.

The outlaws shared somber looks.

"I think we all understand the risks," Xamus said. "But it doesn't change what we have to do."

Illarion looked to each of their faces, witnessing unshakable determination in each and every one. His own features conveyed respect as he turned and led them back toward the shrine.

The otherworldly ink burned slightly but steadily as the group followed the teacher, their tattoos shining brightly in the dark.

"So," Illarion said to Xamus, who walked next to him. "What now?"

"Now we face the Children of the Sun," Xamus replied. "There's no time to rest. I worry that we've spent too long here already. If the cult claims the navy at Tidesfar, Sargrad will surely fall. If the capital is taken, Lawbrand is lost."

Illarion nodded as they emerged from the tunnels into the lower levels of the shrine. "Go to the terrace where I greeted you," the teacher said. "There's something I wish to give you before you leave." With that, he broke away to an adjoining hall and disappeared.

The party waited only a few moments beneath the starlit sky before Illarion rejoined them, a long cloth-bound bundle in his hands. He came and stood before Xamus.

"Sevestra had this among her things," the teacher said. "She asked that I not give it to you until I felt that you were ready. When you left, you gave no warning; even if you had, I would not have bequeathed this to you, for I felt that you did not yet deserve it. Seeing the transformation that has come over you now, my opinion has changed."

Illarion pulled the cloth from the bundle to reveal an elven short sword. "Go on," he said.

Xamus seized the grip, held the scabbard with his left hand, and drew.

"It's part of a set," Illarion said, "that belonged to your uncle Galandil. Its name is Sorro'mir, and the time has come for you to have it."

"Sorro'mir," Xamus said. "Dawn's Whisper."

The sword was a masterpiece of design, with a leather-wrapped hilt, curved blade etched in sigils along the ricasso, and a golden, minutely detailed filigree cross guard. As Xamus held the weapon before him, the moon reflected a beam of light from the blade onto his astonished face.

"Thank you," Xamus said in a heavy voice as he sheathed the sword.

"Before you leave again," Illarion said, gazing intently, "there's something I want you to know. Whether you chose to see it as such or not"—he put a hand on Xamus's shoulder—"Feyonnas is and always will be your home."

Emotion welled within Xamus. Unable to find his voice, he simply nodded in response and wiped at the corners of his eyes. A moment later the travelers said their goodbyes and proceeded to the passage leading to Illian Forest.

As they came to the Threshold, all save for Xamus were surprised to see daylight through the canopy. Xamus spoke up. "As I said, time doesn't pass the same in Feyonnas as it does outside."

The group quickly made their way through the forest, but when they exited the timber into the clearing near the coastline, the *One Fine Day* was nowhere to be seen. Oldavei looked to the sun, which was nearing the mountaintops to the west.

"It's fine," Xamus said. "I would have asked him to depart anyway. I can get us there faster, and I can do it accurately." He looked down at his tattoo. "I know I can."

"Everything's different now," Torin said, looking at the Mark on his own forearm.

"Fortunately," Xamus said, "Tidesfar is a place that I've been to. I can clearly remember the lumber highway that leads in from the north. That's where I'll take us so we can assess."

There was a moment of silence, accompanied by a sense of heaviness, of finality.

Xamus ran his eyes over the others. "If we are facing the end of the world, or potentially our own end, I'm glad to be doing it with you. My friends."

Darylonde's stern voice answered, "We're not friends." The others looked to him, and in a softer tone, he said, "After all the shit we've been through, we're brothers."

The group formed a circle. Xamus spoke: "Amberlyn told me that magic is both order and chaos. Like a storm. To control wild magic, I had to be the eye . . ." He paused, looking down at his tattoo,

PART FIVE: UNTO THE ENDING OF THE WORLD

feeling the energy crawling over his skin. He stepped to the center of the circle and put out his hand. One by one, the others did the same, stacking their hands atop his. Xamus looked to each of them in turn, then said, "It's time now to be the storm."

The elf whispered words of power, and in an instant the party winked out of existence.

CHAPTER EIGHTY-TWO
THE SIEGE OF TIDESFAR

Due to a northern wind, portions of the unnatural sandstorms had been blown from the Bay of Tidesfar inland. So it was that when the group appeared on the dirty highway outside the main gates, they found themselves surrounded by a thick, dusty haze.

Surrounding the road was a clearing, featureless for many yards in each direction, giving way to stump-riddled earth where trees had long ago been felled for the local lumber mills. Beyond the clear-cut, a thick forest rose on all sides, broken only by the wide ribbon of highway that extended to the north, through the trees, and out of sight.

In the west, the sun was a crimson orb burning through the dust.

Several yards to the south, they heard the clatter and voices of restless troops. Tidesfar defenders, barely visible in the clouded distance, stood arrayed before the gates and stout wooden palisades that formed the fortresslike walls of the city.

A hulking shadow approached, and the party moved to greet it. "Seems the wind blew in some desert trash!" a rumbling voice intoned, though it lacked true malice.

The group soon recognized Molt Thunderhoof, the gladiator minotaur they met at Bard-In. He was shirtless, a gigantic wooden maul slung on his back. He carried a flagon in one hand and reeked of ale.

"Well shit," Torin said. "Didn't expect to see your drunk ass here."

"I'm sure you heard that Lietsin fell," Molt said. "*My* Coliseum is now in the hands of that stinking cult. I'll be damned if I just stand by while another city's taken."

"We're of the same mind," Wilhelm said.

"I hear you're no strangers to the Coliseum yourselves, *Team Hamro*." Of the party's looks Molt said, "I knew from the descriptions it had to be you muttonheads!"

"We do get around," Oldavei answered.

They drew nearer the gates to find a motley assortment of defenders: lightly armored Tidesfar Mariners—the local constabulary—formed the front lines, backed by unarmored citizens—shipwrights, barkeeps, longshoremen, traders, and able-bodied locals. Archers packed the ramparts. The outlaws were introduced to a score of Molt's fellow gladiators, rugged individuals wearing very little in the way of armor, carrying an assortment of weapons. The warriors, accustomed to fighting in the arena, bore the wounds and grim countenances of grizzled soldiers who had witnessed the true horrors of war, no doubt from their experiences at Lietsin.

"What have you done?" a voice called. Xamus turned to see Piotr approaching. Two sickles hung on his belt in place of the sharpened sticks he had carried in Sargrad. He strode right up to the elf, grabbed his wrist, and held it with the Serpent Mark facing upward. "This will consume you. All of you!"

PART FIVE: UNTO THE ENDING OF THE WORLD

The monk's fellow Bohen Dur—many of whom were those freed from the Draconis Malisath prison by Nicholas—came closer, visibly concerned.

"It's not Night Devils we're up against this time," Xamus said. "It's something far worse. The cult's leader uses this same power, and he's intent on destroying civilization, period. He'll burn it all down if we don't stop him. So we're gonna fight fire with fire. But we're doing it with eyes wide open. We know the risks and we know the responsibility."

The expressions of the Bohen Dur softened. Piotr contemplated Xamus's words, passed his gaze over the other outlaws, then backed up and bowed in respect. "It will be our honor to fight at your side." The other monks bowed as well.

"Thank you," Xamus said.

"What of Sargrad's forces?" Torin asked Piotr. "The Order-Militant?"

"There has been no word from them that I'm aware of," Piotr answered.

"Coward sons o' bitches!" Torin replied.

Someone yelled, "Ho!" Torin turned to see a cluster of the desert dwarves the outlaws had liberated from the mines at Tanasrael. Along with them came a larger contingent of Red Bluff dwarves, all girded for war. Torin was glad to see the former prisoners, who had regained lost weight; they greeted the outlaws with determination in their eyes and fire in their bellies. Foremost among them was a dwarf whose name Torin remembered was Donigan. He was gray at the temples of his otherwise dark hair, carrying a war helm beneath one arm. "I've two years of slave labor to repay the Children for," he said. "Many of us do. And we've convinced some of our kin that if the cult wins—"

Donigan stopped, distracted. Torin realized what he was staring at and drew the axe from his back. "The Axe o' Dominion," he said, as the other Red Bluff dwarves gathered round, awestruck.

While Torin launched into a brief tale of the axe's origin, Xamus looked out over the entirety of the ad hoc army. It was an impressive assortment, though he estimated they numbered less than five hundred.

"Do we know how far out the Children are?" Xamus asked Molt.

"I've been told they're close," the minotaur replied.

Darylonde knelt, frowning, placing a hand to the hard earth. "Closer than you know," he said.

Soon, all of the protectors felt the ground vibrating. Distant noises carried to them: snapping, crunching, crashing. The vibrations became more pronounced, and the sounds rose in volume. All eyes turned north, to the highway-cut that was a light patch at the center of the shadowy forest. The din increased to a deafening pitch as bright spots flared to life amid the dark woods. Sparks rose; timber popped, cracked, split, and toppled heavily to the earth, sending showers of embers into the dust haze as the horizon exploded in a wall of fire.

Figures strode through the flames, impervious, clad in dusky, heavy-plated armor, swords in one hand, shields in the other. They composed a formation six rows deep, stretching nearly as far as the eye could see to either side, marching down the low grade as the sheer intensity of heat behind them turned the once dense forest to ash and smoldering ember. Xamus conjectured that these may be the soldiers—the Ash'ahar—that Lara Raincaller had warned of.

Through the ashes came the next wave of troops, garbed in the now-familiar desert colors of the Children. Some among them, adorned with purple hoods and more ornate regalia, drew the attention of the outlaws, who detected extraordinary magical capabilities. Xamus supposed these to be priests that Lara had described, the Ash'ahand. The robed cultists numbered easily twice as many as the armored soldiers.

The ground continued to shake more violently as silhouettes of behemoth, lumbering contraptions emerged from the smoke. So far as the outlaws could tell, the machines were stone-throwers, but these made the one from the Thousand Springs seem miniscule; they were more like rolling buildings, easily three stories high, forming a cityscape across the horizon. As the massive contraptions eased to a stop, the earth at last ceased quaking. For a moment, the only sound was the persistent gush of wind and sand.

"How many, you figure?" Molt asked Torin, as a murmuring spread through the ranks of defenders.

"A few thousand," Torin answered.

The minotaur took a pull from his flagon. "Mm, hoped I was seein' double!"

Oldavei could feel the fear of the protectors as statements of doubt and despair passed between them.

A lone figure strode from somewhere at the back of the Children's ranks, advancing to a spot several paces in front of the armored troops.

"Defenders of Tidesfar!" the voice yelled.

"Eric," Xamus said at the same time the other outlaws recognized the cult leader.

"This transfer of power can be accomplished without bloodshed," Eric continued. "You see what it is you're up against. You have no chance of success. The purging of Lawbrand has begun. Lietsin defied us, and we ground that city to dust. But"—he fanned his finger at Tidesfar—"you may still count yourselves among the chosen! Throw down your arms, swear your allegiance to our master, the Prophet Tikanen, and you have my word . . . you will be spared!"

The murmurings fell silent. A palpable fear hung over all. Many of those gathered looked to each other in hopelessness; Mariners looked to their captains, who seemed as much at a loss as everyone else. The disparity in numbers was clear for all to see. Any hope of victory seemed impossible. The silence dragged on.

"I'll have your answer!" Eric yelled.

Then a slow, harmonious melody began, originating from Wilhelm's aethari. The bard stepped out and began walking a few paces away from the front line. He noted his Serpent tattoo glowing intensely and felt the Auroboros funneling through him; he focused the energy, transmuted it, a perfect expression of vitality and will and passion. He joined his voice to the chords, strong and resonant and crystal clear:

When all that's left is dust and fire, when all else burns away
We rise and face the bastards down, charging back into the fray

Mariners and citizens frowned in confusion at first, taken aback by the bard's display. They looked from one to the other tentatively, then directed their full attention to Wilhelm. Across the vast divide, even Eric seemed caught off guard, unsure how to respond.

We've been kicked and chained and beaten down, lost good friends along the way
But we spit into the bastards' eyes, though it be our final day

The pace and intensity of the chords changed, building slowly throughout the remainder of the song, while Wilhelm paced from one end of the line to the other. As the volume and tempo rose, the protectors experienced a stirring in their hearts. Tired limbs surged with renewed vigor. Pulses thundered. Courage, such as none of them had ever known, welled within. They felt emboldened, empowered, and much like the bearers of the Mark, nearly invincible. Only the monks were unaffected by Wilhelm's tune, as they relied on their own inner strength and kept a quiet mind that did not invite outside influence.

We have no creed, we heed no laws, nothin' holds us in its sway

We stand for one another, though it be our final day

By the time Wilhelm completed his song, the spirits of the defenders soared. They whooped and howled and struck their swords against their shields and taunted the opposing forces. Wilhelm stood, back at the center, gazing at the aethari.

"That's the tune you've been writin' since the Northwilds?" Xamus asked.

"Yeah, go figure," the bard answered, having suddenly gained a clearer understanding of what it was he had to let go of: the notion that fame defined his worth. The fear of the empty arena. He smiled suddenly, took the instrument by the neck, bent down, and smashed it to pieces. The defenders cheered.

"Your master can go fek himself!" Wilhelm screamed across the open space. "You want Tidesfar, come and take it!"

The line erupted in defiance, joined by the archers on the wall.

"Get ready," Xamus called. The outlaws spread out across the front line.

The answer from the other side came quickly: creaking sounds carried across the divide. The stone-throwers' towering beams whipped up, launching apocalyptic projectiles, six-hundred-pound boulders of compressed Bloodstone that burned and crackled within iron rings—the Children of the Sun's "perfect bombs"—trailing sparks as they hurtled through the ruddy haze.

CHAPTER EIGHTY-THREE
BLOOD AND FIRE

The Children of the Sun began a slow march across the divide.

"Forward!" Torin yelled. The line surged, beginning with Torin and the Red Bluff dwarves, then Molt and the gladiators; next came Oldavei, Wilhelm, joined by Piotr and the monks, and Darylonde at the opposite end, with Mariners and Tidesfar citizens sprinkled throughout. Xamus remained, allowing the defenders to flow around him like water rushing past a rock as he focused his newly enhanced abilities on the meteoric rain of Bloodstone Shale.

No words of power were needed; thought and action were one. The elf concentrated on the three boulders in his immediate line of sight, and with a slight gesture, the smoldering missiles slowed and hung in midair. At the same moment, to either side, projectiles impacted with devastating effect. Screams pierced the mist as timber walls exploded. Xamus maintained his concentration amid the sudden chaos and, through force of will, sent the three flaming stones *back* the way they had come.

Smoke and fire billowed along the wall as Xamus set off at a full run, teleporting midstride. One second he was behind the defenders, the next, he was at a spot just ahead of them, continuing his sprint, observing now the oncoming frontline attackers at closer range, noting the magma-like fissures in their overlapping plate armor, the smoke wafting from chinks and seams, the sawblade design of their shields, and the sorcerous light that burned within their helms.

Two of the three Bloodstone boulders that had reversed course came screaming back, striking deep in the cultist ranks, detonating on impact and tossing scores of flaming, robed cultists through the air. The third projectile obliterated the base of the stone-thrower that launched it, sending the upper two-thirds crashing down into the enemy formation.

Eric stood, grinning, scimitar in hand as Xamus rushed to meet him, Sorro'mir still in its sheath.

Just before reaching Eric, Xamus teleported past, materializing between the cult leader and the Ash'ahar. He thrust his arms out, and an invisible battering ram seemed to hit the attackers' line, scattering them like toy soldiers and rending armor to pieces.

Xamus spun, Sorro'mir appearing in his hand as Eric launched an all-out assault. The Serpent-energies lent Xamus superior speed, however, enough to make up for the elf's relative lack of sword-fighting skill. The duel was over in mere seconds as Xamus parried a flurry of slashes and answered with a thrust of impossible speed, plunging his blade into and out of Eric's chest before the other could mount any defense.

Eric appeared utterly stupefied, only grasping the matter in his final seconds of life, his eyes falling on Xamus's Serpent tattoo as he sagged to the ground.

Molt shot past and tore into the advancing forces, wielding his maul with bone-shattering strength, though Xamus wondered whether flesh and bone actually existed beneath their opponents' mysterious armor. The minotaur's fellow gladiators collided with the soldiers; one of them miscalculated the strength of his sword, breaking it against the attacker's seething chest plate and losing his head as a result.

Xamus gestured; several paces ahead, an unseen force opened a hole in the enemy lines. The elf teleported into the void and raised his hands, sending the combatants in his immediate vicinity straight up into the air, nearly to the height of the siege engine tops; he then dropped his arms, driving the mute soldiers to the earth, smashing their dusky armor to bits. A sudden dizziness then overcame the elf, and he took a step to steady himself. He wiped sweat from a feverish forehead and refocused his efforts.

At the western flank, Torin, having raced ahead of the Red Bluff dwarves, leaped impossibly high, Axe of Dominion poised overhead. He plunged down amid the Ash'ahar, cleaving one soldier from helm to codpiece, hitting the earth with enough power to punch a crater, spraying dirt and foes in a wide radius. The dwarf turned the axe in his hands, orienting the blades parallel to the ground, and as his fellows watched, astonished, he jumped from the pit and spun, rotating with such speed that he blurred, transforming into a whirlwind before their disbelieving eyes. The living cyclone cut a path through the dark legion, chewing up metal plate and spitting out shrapnel, reaping scores of enemy forces at a time.

The Red Bluff dwarves, led by Donigan, capitalized on the advantage and pressed the attack deeper into the ranks of robed cultists. There, however, one of the priests emerged, chanting. Fire enveloped her outthrust hands and spewed forth in a blazing jet, incinerating Donigan and over half of the dwarves within seconds, leaving only drifting ash behind.

Torin slowed to a stop, voicing a battle cry. He imagined a tether of energy connected to his axe and flung it outward, the whirling blade severing the upper half of the female priest's head. Torin then yanked, returning the axe to his hand. As he uttered a silent prayer for his fallen kin, he tasted blood running from his nose, even though he had not yet been hit. The Auroboros energies burned like fire in his veins, raising a sheen of sweat. Spurred by rage and vengeance, Torin pressed on, aided by the few remaining Red Bluff dwarves and several incoming Mariners.

In the moments before Torin and Xamus engaged the enemy, Oldavei transformed midrun from ma'ii to coyote. As he narrowed the distance to the attackers, he continued channeling Auroboros abilities to increase his size, and by the time his animal form clashed with the frontline Ash'ahar, he was ten times his normal mass. He clamped his enormous jaws on his adversaries, ignoring the pain of their sword strikes against his legs and their jagged armor in his mouth, flinging his head, sending foes sailing while he slashed with claws that shredded dark armor like parchment.

As a contingent of Tidesfar Mariners and unarmored citizens arrived on Oldavei's heels, a furious melee resulted in the mortal wounding of a female constable, a longshoreman, and a lumber mill worker. Oldavei paused, surrounded by a greenish aura as he manipulated the powers of the World-Serpent to heal all three victims before their hearts ceased beating, restoring them to perfect health. He bit the head and right arm off one attacker but was forced to briefly relent, feeling a sudden stiffness in his joints, heat racing through his body. His tongue lolled, and foam gathered on his drooling lips. Shaking off the afflictions, Oldavei summoned his strength and tore once more into the raging cultists.

At the same time Oldavei transformed to coyote form, Wilhelm closed distance on the enemy, running ahead of Piotr and the monks, swinging the Apparatus in increasingly swift revolutions until the arc of its spin was nothing but a blur. As the Ash'ahar came within range, the grapnel ripped them to shreds; Wilhelm plunged onward, creating a wide expanse of armored body pieces and pairs of legs that tumbled unceremoniously to the dirt.

Slowing and retracting the Apparatus, Wilhelm snatched up one of the sawblade shields and whipped it into the cultists, slicing both armored and robed foes in half and cutting through the thick beams of a siege engine at the rear before the disc sailed out of sight. As Wilhelm prepared to engage the next closest enemy, the foe whipped jerkily to one side, moving like a puppet on strings, attacking a fellow Ash'ahar. Not far away, another armored enemy did the same.

Piotr and his fellow monks drew up alongside Wilhelm, hands extended, their faces set in concentration as they controlled the actions of their enemy puppets. Mariners and citizens poured in as well, crossing steel with both Ash'ahar and robed cultists.

All across the field, cries rang out, blades clashed, blood poured, and the dying stumbled among the already dead as sunlight struggled to penetrate the crimson haze.

The siege engines reloaded with impossible speed. Thick beams shot up with a heavy groan and lobbed a second volley of Bloodstone Shale through the smoke toward the palisades. There, archers abandoned their posts as scores of boulders struck and exploded, pulverizing entire sections of the defensive wall and reducing the gates to ash and kindling.

"We gotta take out those throwers," Wilhelm yelled to Piotr over the battle din.

On the eastern flank, at the same time Oldavei morphed from ma'ii to coyote, before reaching the Ash'ahar, Darylonde cast out with his extra sense, detecting the charges and energies in the dusty air. He harnessed those powers to create a terrifically augmented bolt of lightning. Multiple jagged forks crashed down in a blinding flash, leaving nothing but smoking chunks of armor where a hundred enemy troops had once been.

As the remaining masses attempted to close in, giant roots punched up through the ground, wrapping around the torsos and extremities of the attackers, withdrawing seconds later and taking scores of the enemy with them.

Cultists made room as a priest stepped forward, an orb of fire rotating between his outstretched hands. The ball flew, increasing in size, set to engulf the Wildkeeper. Darylonde cast his mind to the roiling flame, sensing its natural energy, and with the aid of the Auroboros, commanded the conflagration to harmlessly disperse. He then drew both bow and arrow in a motion too fast for the eye to follow and sent a shaft straight through the stunned priest's heart.

As Tidesfar Mariners flooded the scene, Ash'ahar troops, whose formations extended to the tree line, swung round. Darylonde focused more powerful druidic magic on the nearby stumps of the clear-cut. Two of the severed trunks sprouted stems that exhibited decades of growth within mere seconds, resulting in full-size tree-folk. Though animated, the servants possessed no minds of their own, existing only to follow the imperative given by their creator: to destroy the enemy. Moving forward on trunk-legs, the arboreal minions thrashed the Ash'ahar with their thick limbs, grasping, constricting, and ripping the armored soldiers apart.

A brief vertigo gave Darylonde pause. His skin radiated heat; he found it suddenly difficult to catch his breath, and he tasted blood trickling from his nose onto his lips. Pushing past the fever, taking several deep breaths, the soldier nocked another arrow and called upon the wind to lift him up, providing a higher vantage point to see over his allies and identify cultist targets.

The Bohen Dur utilized their abilities to swipe cultists to either side without laying a hand on them. At the same time, Wilhelm drew upon the Auroboros to mirror Oldavei's achievement, growing exponentially, until his height equaled that of the siege engines. Moving at reduced speed but with colossal strength, he stomped cultists beneath his gargantuan boots, oblivious to the sword strikes of his foes as he lumbered to the line of stone-throwers, smashing one beam in half just as it sprang upward, sending the Bloodstone boulder careering into the road midway to Tidesfar, where it exploded harmlessly.

Wilhelm lifted the broken contraption and tossed it overhead into the adjacent throwers to the east, leaving only two standing. He then turned and began thrashing and kicking his way through the line, scattering wood and debris in his rampage, lifting two boulders from their slings in each hand at the westernmost flank and tossing them into the scurrying enemy ranks, well clear of any allies, blasting cultists into oblivion.

In the midst of a hearty, deafening laugh, Wilhelm clutched at his heart, a sudden, seizing agony blooming in his chest. He diminished until he was once again his normal size, then fell to hands and knees, disgorging a stream of bloody sputum.

A vortex whipped through the robed cultists who attempted to close in on the bard, leaving a trail of blood, viscera, and tattered remains. When the whirlwind ceased and took the form of Torin, the coughing dwarf came to Wilhelm, his lower face caked with his own blood, lifting the bard to his feet.

"Not givin' up yet, are ya?" Torin quipped hoarsely.

"I'm fit as a . . . fekkin' fiddle," Wilhelm answered. The two then reacted to a sound from the north, gazing out over the mounds of scattering ash to spy several ranks of Children reinforcements one hundred yards away and closing steadily.

Marching at the front of the newcomers' lines were Ash'ahand priests, one of whom formed a fireball overhead and sent it streaking across the divide, gaining size until it equaled that of the yellow globe atop the House of the Rising Son Inn.

Before it could strike, however, the blazing orb swooped up, arced over, and sailed in the opposite direction; the priest raised hands in an apparent attempt to arrest its flight but to no avail. She screamed before the fireball hit, igniting her and six Ash'ahar to either side. Despite the inferno, the armored soldiers continued marching. The priest did not.

Wilhelm and Torin turned to the sound of hammering hooves as Sargrad Order-Militant riders burst onto the field from the west. Foremost among them was Daromis, mounted with the crone seated behind, the cause, no doubt, of the fireball's stunning reversal. As the five-hundred-strong cavalry tore into the flank of the Children's forces, Daromis pulled alongside Wilhelm and Torin and said, "We came as quickly as we could."

Torin huffed. "Lucky for you, there's enough to go around."

Daromis nodded and set off for the enemy.

Several yards away, among the scattered corpses of the attackers' decimated front line, a bloodied dockworker turned back to the palisade and witnessed a knot of Children, led by a priest, making way toward the city gates.

"They're at the gates," he yelled, pointing, drawing the attention of Xamus.

A moment before the longshoreman witnessed their progress, the male Ash'ahand and four robed Children, armed with scimitars, advanced on the destroyed gates. During their approach, surviving archers who attempted to strike down the group were immolated by a casual wave from the priest.

Among the wreckage, a cluster of Tidesfar citizens waited defiantly. At the very front stood a white-haired man, barely capable of holding his rusted sword aloft. Behind him, men and women of similar age assumed ready stances, along with a handful of boys and girls barely into their teenage years.

The dark-eyed priest smiled and raised his hands. On each, fire danced from palm to fingertip, but before the flames could fly to their target, an arrow punched into the side of the cultist's head. The dark eyes rolled back as the priest crumpled.

The remaining attackers turned to see a magnificent white stag bearing down on them. Lara Raincaller, sword now in hand, rode into their midst, blade flashing, parrying and countering with ease, making quick work of the outmatched zealots. As the last of them fell, Xamus teleported to the area, Sorro'mir held at the ready. He wiped blood from his nose, looked to Lara, and said "I see . . . you have things well in hand."

"I wish the circumstances were better," Lara said. "But I came to issue a dire warning. Our agents have confirmed that Tikanen is at Tanasrael preparing a spell of unparalleled magnitude."

"What kind of spell?" Xamus asked between ragged breaths.

"I'm told he calls on the power of the sun," Lara answered. "To make his armies invincible."

PART FIVE: UNTO THE ENDING OF THE WORLD

CHAPTER EIGHTY-FOUR

SUNDOWN

The battle between the Children's reinforcements and the defenders, now bolstered by Sargrad cavalry, raged on.

After speaking to Lara, Xamus removed Wilhelm, Torin, Darylonde, and Oldavei—now back in ma'ii form—from the conflict, teleporting them to an open spot just inside Tidesfar's main gates. Lara, along with the citizens she saved and a small group of fellow druids, stood guard just outside as a last line of defense.

"With the Peacekeepers here and the damage we've already done," Xamus said, covered in sweat and blood, heart hammering in his chest, "there's a chance . . . of turning this battle around. But if what Lara says is

true . . . if Tikanen could work a spell to make his people invincible—"

"We have to go," Darylonde said simply, his normally bright silver eyes now a dull gray, perspiration running down his pale face.

"I know it's asking a lot," Xamus said, looking to his friends. Oldavei's head hung, his shoulders slumped, a grimace of pain and determination on his face. Wilhelm held one hand to his stomach, the other resting on Torin for support as he tried to maintain focus. The dwarf, having been unable to catch his breath, continued to inhale and exhale in heavy, wheezing gusts, chest rising and falling in tandem. "The energy it'll take to stop Tikanen . . ."

"We know," Oldavei said.

"Darylonde's right," Torin rasped. "We . . . gotta go."

Wilhelm nodded. "Let's finish this."

Darylonde turned to see Lara, now unmounted, approaching. He glanced back at Xamus, who nodded. The Wildkeeper broke away and met the druid, whose features expressed great concern.

"Your friend told me about the tattoos," she said. "That they're . . . affecting you." She eyed him critically. "It's more than that, isn't it?"

Darylonde let out a shaky sigh, turned his head and coughed, then gazed once again at Lara. "I won't be coming back from this," he said. Tears burst onto Lara's cheeks. "If I could . . . put sands back in the hourglass, there's one thing above all else . . . that I would do differently." He put his left hand to her face. "I was a fool to have ever let you go."

Lara fought to keep her voice even. "I seem to remember telling you the same damn thing."

"You were right," Darylonde said. He embraced her then as tightly as he could. After holding her for a long moment, he looked to the others, who had gathered in a circle. "It's time," he said, kissing her cheek, then pulling away and returning to the group.

Xamus put one hand out, and the others reciprocated. Darylonde met Lara's eyes one final time, and in the very next instant, they were gone.

The five appeared high atop the ziggurat at Tanasrael, not far from the structure's eastern edge. Below, thousands of chanting voices could be heard coming from legions of the faithful assembled at the base of the mammoth edifice. Several yards away at the center of the roof, ten cultist bodyguards, wearing distinctive sleeveless robes, surrounded columns that stood in a square formation atop raised steps. Whatever had cast the light that they had seen shining from the structure before was seemingly not present now. In the middle of the platform, on a high, rectangular dais, Tikanen held a position with his back to the party, hands raised to the sky, murmuring some repeating incantation, echoed by that which came from the crowds below. The prophet was silhouetted by the sun hanging low in the west. Incredibly, the orb appeared far larger than it should be, occupying a massive swath of the horizon, sending shimmering waves rising from the paved roof, an oppressive heat that caused the outlaws to fight even harder for every inhalation.

Upon sighting the newcomers, the bodyguards drew wide-bladed scimitars and rushed to engage.

"Gotta . . . save our powers," Xamus said, drawing Sorro'mir. "Take 'em the old-fashioned way."

Despite their exhaustion, the group proceeded with a practiced ease borne of experience and familiarity. Darylonde, the veteran soldier, put an arrow immediately through the heart of the cultist he judged to be the biggest threat, then slung his bow, bared steel, and faced off with the next-strongest-looking opponent. Wilhelm and Torin, whose fighting styles were particularly omplementary, coordinated their offensive, with Torin attacking low at Wilhelm's left while the bard maximized his reach advantage and kept his strikes at chest height. Xamus filled the open space left by Darylonde's elimination of the first bodyguard, keeping the Wildkeeper on his right and focusing his efforts on a single opponent. Oldavei took on coyote form, darting as rapidly as possible in his weakened condition among two foes, always on the move, keeping the enemy distracted until Xamus, having dispatched his own adversary, reduced Oldavei's attackers to one. Oldavei then leaped and closed his fangs on the final cultist's jugular.

The entire battle lasted less than a minute. The outlaws suffered only minor wounds, save for Oldavei, who received a wide slash to his ribs on the left side. Now back in ma'ii form, he waved away the entreaties of the others, not willing to use his healing abilities until Tikanen was dealt with.

The party struggled across the roof, intending to attack the cult leader directly. As they neared the templelike feature, however, they found that what appeared to be a wave of rising heat was in fact an invisible barrier. The group circled the columns only to confirm that the shield encompassed the Prophet entirely. They stood before him on the western side, but Tikanen seemed unaware, eyes closed, hands raised, mouth moving with utterances of conjuration. They felt the heat on their backs from the impossibly large sun as they forced air into their lungs and tested the shield with their weapons without success. Then, the cult leader's voice boomed inside their heads, though the prophet's eyes remained closed and his chanting continued:

"How glorious you are! What fine Children you would have made! Your skills are extraordinary, though your efforts are doomed, for my time has come!" And here the Prophet looked upon them, his eyes burning like suns, his voice deafening as he spoke out loud: "The Great Work . . . is finished at last!"

All around them, the light faded; they turned to see the sun *dim* as the voices of the faithful below cried out in sudden agony. The outlaws stumbled to the edge of the peak and stared down at an ocean of robed, writhing bodies.

"The fek is this?" Wilhelm said.

The supplicants screamed, ripping at their clothing, doubling over, some arching back, others convulsing.

"Bastard's killin' 'em," Torin said, as the cultists collapsed in droves, flailing in violent death throes before falling still. The party watched as nebulous, luminescent forms lifted from the motionless corpses, spiraling upward, ascending to the rooftop and beyond, high over the outlaws' heads.

Tikanen held his head to the sky. "I take no pleasure in your sacrifice, my Children," he declared. "Know that you are all part of something greater now . . . you *are* the Light!"

The ephemeral essences roiled and coalesced into a maelstrom of soul-energy. In the center of the gyre, a spark flared; flames ignited the colossal storm until it seemed as though a second sun burned above them. The outlaws shielded their eyes while the conflagration took the shape of a creature curled in a fetal position.

The goliath form began to unfurl, and the party glimpsed through outstretched hands recognizable features in the morphing flame: a snakelike head, fangs, a serpentine body and long tail. As the creature expanded to its full size, magnificent, blazing wings spread wide. Oldavei's mouth hung open, and his body trembled all over. He looked at Darylonde, saying, "It's my vision . . ." then turned back to view the spectacle above. "Death by fire." The Wildkeeper, with features of hardened stone, gripped Oldavei's shoulder tightly.

The entity vented a scream of triumph that drove the outlaws to their knees as Tikanen's voice continued:

"My will is made manifest! The wrath of the Sun incarnate! Through it, my power is absolute. It will burn nonbelievers to ash, and whomsoever among my Children is touched by its light shall never die. Behold!"

Far to the opposite side of the temple, the fallen bodyguards began to slowly stand.

Oldavei felt the world begin to swim as blood flowed from his wound. Nevertheless, he stumbled to the edge and saw there the fallen bodies of the zealots beginning to move and stir.

Tikanen continued: "All hearts will be ignited by the serpent's flame! The flame of truth, of purity!"

Torin, in frustration, again imagined a tether on the Axe of Dominion as he flung it out in attempt to behead the Prophet; the blade bounced harmlessly from the barrier and flew back to the dwarf's hand as Oldavei returned.

"For it is belief . . ." Tikanen said, his eyes burning more brightly than ever. "Belief sets hearts aflame! You *will* believe . . . whether by choice or not."

"Attacking him . . . won't work," Xamus said. "We need to attack that." His eyes flicked to the fire-serpent expanding in size, engulfing the sky, threatening to set the very air on fire. "And we need to do it now. This is it."

The five instinctively drew together, grasping necks and shoulders. They looked from one to the other, nodding, affirming, their shared experience written on their crimson faces—laughter, tears, heartache, all leading to this moment, to peace in the unshakeable certainty of what they must now do.

"Shit," Wilhelm said, blood flowing freely from his nose as he gripped his friends tighter. "We really are gonna die." His chest heaved. "Fek."

Torin coughed and whispered hoarsely, "*Hamro* . . . ya fekkin' lowlifes!" The dwarf cast one final steely-eyed gaze to his friends.

The very last words they heard were spoken by Wilhelm. The phrase, like the bard himself, was unorthodox, and yet somehow perfect: "Us. Are. Auroboros."

Xamus raised his arm high, the Serpent Mark standing out in stark contrast against his skin. Torin added his hand to the elf's. Oldavei was next, the world beginning to slip away from him. Darylonde followed, face set in grim resolve. Wilhelm, smiling, was last. As one, they closed their eyes and surrendered their bodies to the Auroboros.

The bodyguards collected their weapons and advanced, moving in an unnatural fashion, reminiscent of puppets on strings, their eyes burning much like Tikanen's.

Each of the outlaws' Serpent tattoos began to shine brightly. The Prophet spied the Marks and frowned, struck with a full understanding of the power they betokened.

The outlaws cried out, their bodies consumed in ethereal, varicolored flames. The soul-fire tore free and ascended, leaving the five to collapse lifelessly as their radiant spirit-forms spiraled, coalesced, and formed a sharp-tipped bolt that shot straight into the heart of the Fire-Serpent. Tikanen and the Serpent bellowed in unison; the entirety of the ziggurat shook with seismic force. The flames of the entity expanded, its brightness intensifying . . .

A hush fell on the scene as the Serpent hung suspended for a breathless instant before tilting down, its wings folding limply as it plunged, a star ripped from the heavens, striking the ziggurat like a hammer blow from an angry god.

The world turned white as the structure, tent cities, and surrounding farmlands were all obliterated in an instant amid the unimaginable firestorm.

The infernos raged across the Tanaroch for miles around. The earth buckled. Scattered across the sands, ma'ii and desert dwarves who witnessed the event would later tell their children that it seemed as though the sky itself cracked open. Light flared brilliantly, and then . . . a silence fell. No sound carried, and no wind blew over the desolation that remained.

PART FIVE: UNTO THE ENDING OF THE WORLD

EPILOGUE
ONE YEAR LATER

The last light of day was fading as Lara stepped into the Grove of Lights.

Boughs had woven once again over the stone stage of the Woodsong amphitheater to form a canopy. Argent liquid shone from the Silver Spring. Birdcalls rang through the forest, and wisps once more flitted through the trees.

Lara stepped down to the edge of the spring and stared at her silhouette reflection.

"What is it you're thinking about?" a deep voice asked. The druid turned to see a tree-folk, one that looked remarkably like Goshaedas, though this one was not as tall. The moss-and-leaf beard was only just coming in, and the supple legs hardly creaked at all when the new Caretaker walked.

"I was thinking of Darylonde," Lara said. "And the others." She turned back to the pool, and she could hear the Caretaker descending the earthen steps of the pit. "I was thinking what a shame it is that Lawbrand will never know what they did, what they sacrificed . . . to save a world that cared so very little for them."

"I get the sense that they're not so forgotten as you might think," the tree-folk answered, bending his trunk-legs to plunk down on the lowest seat. "Come," he said, tapping the empty space next to him with a branch-hand. "And tell me . . . tell me more stories about these 'outlaw' friends of yours."

Many miles away in Skarborough, raucous crowds gathered inside the World Famous Stripmine for Open Lute Night, banging flagons on tables in anticipation of the first act. A dark-haired young woman carrying a mandolin strode confidently to the center of the stage. "What's up, you piss-drunk fekkers!" the bard yelled to an uproarious response.

She began plucking a few strings, running her eyes over the crowd. "I don't know who it was that first sang this . . . I just know from someone who knows from someone that it was sung at the Siege of Tidesfar. It's about courage. And overcoming struggle and hardship and impossible odds and kickin' some fekkin' ass with your friends by your side, so let's do this!"

The bard's fingers raced over the strings at a feverish pace, blasting out a frenetic approximation of the chords played by Wilhelm outside the Tidesfar Gates. The woman's voice rang out, loud and clear:

When all that's left is dust and fire, when all else burns away
We rise and face the bastards down, charging back into the fray
We've been kicked and chained and beaten down, lost good friends along the way
But we spit into the bastards' eyes, though it be our final day
We have no creed, we heed no laws, nothin' holds us in its sway
We stand for one another, though it be our final day!

THE END